JOLTED BY DESIRE

She could not resist one single touch. Slowly she rose on tiptoe, and touched her lips to his. If Royce had been jolted by desire before, it was nothing compared with the force that unleashed itself now. He moved back from Lynette just a fraction, but enough to break the contact.

"You must be careful, Cherie. Or you will make me think you are more anxious for this wedding than you have led me to believe."

Lynette was startled by his sarcasm. She saw now in his eyes that his shields were in place. She felt heat rush to her cheeks, and a sense of shame filled her. Was she begging for his touch? She could not deny the truth of it, any more than she could deny that she would have gone into his arms, if he had given one sign that he wanted her there.

VELVET & STEEL

SYLVIE SOMMERFIELD

LEISURE BOOKS NEW YORK CITY

*To Eileen and Guy Shoaf,
two wonderful friends.*

A LEISURE BOOK®

September 1999

Published by

Dorchester Publishing Co., Inc.
276 Fifth Avenue
New York, NY 10001

ISBN 0-8439-4576-1

The name "Leisure Books" and the stylized "L" with design are trademarks of Dorchester Publishing Co., Inc.

Printed in the United States of America.

Prologue

London 1067

Two men sat together in a room lit only by a low-burning fire that cast the room in shadow. The furnishings could be seen vaguely, enough to show that the place was sparsely furnished . . . a warrior's dwelling.

These men were not often alone where unwelcome ears could not overhear their conversation. They were taking advantage of this rare opportunity to discuss a weighty problem.

They had been drinking together through most of the long night, although both held their ale well and showed no sign of its use. They were companions. Men who had lived, fought, and survived together. They had spoken of the battles they had won and the few they had lost. But past memories had been put aside; now they spoke of the purpose that had drawn them together.

Although these two resembled each other in many ways, there was a subtle difference that went beyond hair color or features. It would take an experienced eye very little time to discern that the larger, older man displayed deference toward the younger. It was clear in the way he spoke . . . and in the respect displayed as he listened.

Robert Debayeaux was a man of massive proportions, wide shoulders, and strong muscles. His face was a contradiction . . . old, yet vital. The eyes registered many experiences, not all good or kind. Yet they could smile and soften . . . they just hadn't recently. His hair was a deep brown, with streaks of gray at the temples, and his eyes, a shade of gray that would match a stormy sky.

The younger man had an aura of restrained energy. His blue eyes were piercing, and could be cold enough to freeze the heartiest soul. He was handsome, but not with the handsomeness of a courtier. His was a beauty of strength and grim determination. His clothes gave evidence of his position, for he dressed, not like a soldier as the older man did, but like one of royal blood who wore rich clothing with an ease the older man could never achieve. He was a commanding man, tall and broad of chest and shoulder. His arms were all taut muscle. Muscle acquired by the expert and regular use of a sword and lance.

William the First was a conqueror, and his posture and aura of confidence gave evidence of it. The Battle of Hastings had been over for nearly a year and he was the victor. That pleased him. What didn't please him was a new and serious problem that had just been brought to his attention by one of the few people he trusted completely, Robert Debayeaux. He turned to face his friend.

"What think you, sire?" Debayeaux said. " 'Tis a place that needs protection. We cannot let the wrong hands take control. It is a typical Saxon manor, hard to defend and in need of work, but the location makes it an excellent place for you to build something more substantial. The manor sits on a rise, overlooking a harbor that could prove of great benefit to you, and might cause no end of difficulties for you should an enemy decide to land a force."

"There is no doubt we must do something, but what? The man, this Eldwyn of Creganwald, has not fought our possession, and I think he would like to live out his old age in peace," William replied.

"That is so, but neither will he fight to protect what is no longer his. The manor's strategic position could prove a liability if you are not completely sure of the man who holds it."

"We can't let that happen. We need a warden, one who can build something defensible, and hold it."

"Was there not a young daughter?"

William paused, then turned to look at his friend, and smiled. "By God, you are right. And of marriagcable age if I'm not mistaken."

"Yes. Her name escapes me at the moment."

"What do we care of her name? She's of marriageable age, and that is the answer to my dilemma!"

"No, sire. That is only half the answer. Who do you have in mind? Who do you trust enough to take her and eventually, at her father's death, her holdings in marriage?"

"Ah, must one problem always create another?"

"It usually does," Robert chuckled.

"There are not many who do not suffer from greed. I must choose someone who does not seek to enrich himself at my expense."

"I wish you good fortune finding one . . . unless . . . "

"Unless? Come man, if you have an idea, share it with me."

"I was giving thought to Royce."

"I know his loyalty, and his ability to fight well, but . . . "

Robert looked at William closely, then considered his words for a moment before he spoke. "I know. It has been only a few years since he lost his wife. He adored the woman, and I do not wonder at it. She was not only beautiful, but completely devoted to him. He has been my . . . our friend for a long while. I know he has never put her memory away, nor has he looked at another."

"Then why do you bring up his name?" William asked.

"Because those who care for him wish to help him past this grief he refuses to let go of. It is as if he had followed her into the grave."

"And yet he fights like a madman."

"Perhaps," Robert spoke softly, "in the hope that an enemy will do for him what the church will not allow him to do for himself."

"He thinks to die in battle?" William asked with surprise.

"That is my belief. He is at the forefront of every attack, he is the first over the walls, and he wields a sword without care for his own safety. He has not gained death, but he has gained a reputation that creates fear in your enemies."

"And he is too valuable a man for us to lose."

"Aye, my lord, much too valuable."

"Then I shall discuss the matter with him at once."

"My lord?" Robert laughed.

"Another problem?" William chuckled helplessly.

"If you form this as a request, he will refuse."

"And if I command him?"

"He cannot refuse." Robert smiled and nodded.

"He shall certainly think me the most ungrateful lord he has ever served."

"Better to think that than to go on trying to destroy himself. He will not be able to refuse a command from the king to whom he has sworn his sword and his honor, too, no matter how unwelcome it might be. He will be furious . . . but he will be a good warden, a good husband, and the most loyal servant you have ever had."

"Will he be a good husband . . . forced to the altar?"

"Perhaps not, but he will not dishonor you or the lady. That will do well enough."

"And what of the lady?" William said, considering his own wife, Matilda, who had married him despite his bastardy, and whom he loved with a devotion and loyalty that surprised many.

"My lord, we can only put her in the safest hands we know. At least we will not have to worry about her loyalty. He will see to it. She could do much worse than that."

"Aye, she could marry a brute who would murder her for her lands. Is her father in good health?"

"Reasonably, sire. He was very ill last winter. He is also of an age when he knows his lands are unsafe. Perhaps he will agree to the marriage and make your task easier. She will not disobey her father . . . or her king."

"You are a wise old fox. You guard my holdings, protect a man whom I believe you have come to respect. You mend the problems of a comrade in arms . . . and supply a husband for, I imagine, a very beautiful lady. Is there no end to your good works?"

"I only serve you, my lord."

"I know, Robert, I know," William said softly. "You are truly the most valuable friend I have. A man I can trust. Send word to Royce. I would see him as soon as he can come."

"Aye, my lord."

"Robert, I hope Royce will understand, and not place the blame on you. I would tell him this is my choice alone."

"Sire . . . ?"

"Speak."

"I would go with him. He has become like a son to me. Even if he chooses to place blame . . . I would be with him."

"If I remember right, there is some question of Royce's parentage?"

"Aye. His parents are unknown. But that has not stopped him from great accomplishments, and bringing great honor to his name. He has used his abilities with honor, instead of selling his sword to any bidder as most bastards do."

"You sound very proud."

"I am, my lord. I am. I have known him all his

life. He is a man any man would be proud to call son."

"Even you, old warhorse?"

"Even me, sire . . . even me."

"Know you who his father is, Robert?

"Yes, sire."

"But you choose not to tell him . . . or me?"

"Aye, my lord."

"If I commanded it?"

"It is a name I shall take to my grave, sire . . . no matter what causes my death," Robert replied. He knew quite well that William, a bastard himself, would understand and not press the matter.

"I am glad I have you at my back, Robert," William said quietly.

"Thank you, sire."

"Let us drink a toast then." Both men raised their horns of ale.

"To the marriage and to the settling of at least one problem in this world of problems."

Both men drank, but Robert was not too sure any problems had been settled. He was giving great thought to the wording of the king's order to Royce, and wishing he did not have to be the one to carry the message. He already knew how it was going to be received. He alone knew the depth of Royce's agony. He had suffered with him, watching his silence and his loneliness grow.

He thought of the secret he kept, even from Royce, and the reasons for it. He was proud that Royce had risen above his birth, just as William had done. He also knew that Royce's father was just as proud, and just as crushed that he could not claim Royce as his son.

Robert's dearest wish was that one day the secret might be brought to light. In time, maybe, but for now he would be Royce's friend and mentor for as long as he was needed. He prayed he wasn't making a great mistake with the idea of this wedding. Maybe it was Lady Lynette who would need his prayers, for Royce's heart had been frozen for too long. For now, he must go to Royce, and be with him when he received the request . . . no, the command that would change his life.

Chapter One

Robert stood in his stirrups to rest his cramped legs. He and his squire had paused just outside London, and he was still trying to plan the words he would say to Royce. How does one tell a knight who has fought for his king that he is being rewarded by a forced marriage for that same king's benefit? And how does one mention marriage to a man who finds the very word repugnant?

"Ah, Sybella," he murmured. "How I wish the two of you had never met and wed. How much easier this would be, and how much more welcome. Now it grieves me   and yet . . . " He remembered well the fragile woman who had first awakened Royce's heart.

He remembered how she had taught him to laugh and to love, how she had slowly filled the emptiness of his life with a new kind of happiness. Happiness was something Royce knew little of. She had been so pretty, with her mink-colored hair and her always smiling violet eyes.

He remembered how she had wooed Royce from the path of violence, and led him to see that there could be beauty and love in what he had always considered a barren and joyless world. . . . And he remembered grief after her death. He remembered how Royce had gone for days with no interest in food, how he had not seen or heard what was going on about him, and how near death he himself had been before Robert interfered. But he had saved Royce from lethargy, only to watch him plunge into battle and violence and self-destruction.

"My lord?"

He gave his attention to the young squire who rode beside him. " 'Tis nothing. I'm getting old. I have reverted to conversations with myself," Robert said disgustedly. "Come, let's ride on, lest my courage forsake me completely."

The squire was truly astonished at this. The courage and bravery of his lord were well known. There was none alive who would question it. Those who did had been dispatched long ago. He shook his head in puzzlement as they rode on.

Even though it was just after five in the morning and the mantle of darkness still lay over the streets, London was astir. Shadows could be seen gliding out of back streets and into the main thoroughfare. The horses' hooves made a sharp sound on the cobblestones as the two made their way to a house near the center of the city.

It was lighted and astir as well, Robert observed as he dismounted. Soren took the horses to the stable, while Robert made his presence known and was welcomed inside.

"Is His Lordship still abed?" he asked a servant, but the answer came from the top of the steps before the servant could answer.

"Nay, Robert." The voice was full of amusement. "Did you not stir me awake with a boot at sunrise when I was a lad? I have learned that lesson well, and do not lie abed even now." When Royce reached the bottom of the steps, he embraced Robert, clapping his back heartily.

"I bring greetings from William. He asks how you fare."

"Very well." The reply was accompanied by a close look and an inquisitive rise of an arched brow. "But I do not think you have come all this distance to bring that simple question."

"Nay . . . I have some words from William . . . for your ears alone."

"Is something amiss?"

Robert studied the man he had thought of for nearly twenty-eight years as a son. The hard living, first as an unwanted and unnamed bastard and then as a warrior who had used his sword to make his way in life, could be seen only in the piercing gold of his eyes. Like a lion, Robert thought. Royce's strange golden eyes always gave him the look of a lion.

His hair was thick and somewhat unruly, which enhanced that leonine air. His face was a strong one and could be eased only by a smile, which he used seldom. But a smile could wipe away years, and it could melt a cold heart at the same time.

Robert had trained Royce, fathered him as if he were his own, and they had become companions during the years of turmoil as William sought his throne. Robert knew Royce looked to him for counsel, guidance, and friendship.

They had stood shoulder to shoulder in battle, but nothing in their time together had prepared Robert to bring this news. How proud he was of the tall, strongly muscled man before him, and how he prayed that what he was doing was right.

"Nay. Except I have not yet broken my fast, and am hungry enough to eat my horse, saddle and all."

Royce sensed at once that the news Robert brought was not good, but he knew Robert well. The news would not be given until Robert was ready to give it.

"I have not eaten yet either. Join me. Ferragus, Giles, and the others should be joining us soon."

"After we have eaten, will you ride with me?"

"Of course. Do we have a destination, or do we ride for pleasure?"

"We ride," Robert muttered, "so there will not be an audience for our words, especially those devoted guards of yours, who would slay the bearer of ill tidings."

"Is that what you are, Robert," Royce said quietly, "the bearer of ill tidings? And is the word you bring so bad that my comrades in arms cannot share it?"

"Who knows better than you that William has many problems? We are like an island, surrounded by a hostile force that outnumbers us greatly."

"Is danger afoot? Another uprising?"

"Nay. There are some problems that must be solved without the use of a sword."

"Robert, you test my patience and stir my curiosity. Can we not dispense with food and get to the heart of it? If William needs my help in any matter, you know my willingness."

"Aye, sometimes your too fervent willingness. At the last battle, you nearly got yourself killed. William cannot afford to lose a knight of your capabilities. He tells me to caution you to take better care."

"What tales have you been bringing him? You are ever my watchdog. A man lives or dies in battle at the will of God."

"A man should not tempt fate so often, or so rashly. William is not the only one who worries that you put too little value on your life." Robert held Royce's gaze with his.

" 'Tis my life," Royce said pointedly. "And there are very few who would put any worth upon it."

"Aye, it is your life. But it would grieve many more than you know if it were to be lost. William now has other plans for it. He needs your loyalty, and has asked . . . no, commanded that you comply at once with the message he has entrusted to me."

"What message?"

"It can wait until you have fed me and we can ride out."

"Robert, when you retreat from duty, it can only mean one thing. You do not relish this command."

"I believe it is the best plan under the circumstances."

"But you do not relish it?"

"Nay," Robert agreed reluctantly.

"Why?"

"Because it might bring you to anger . . . even to disobedience."

19

At this Royce was not only shocked, he was disbelieving. He had never considered disobeying the sovereign he was pledged to, and whom he respected and loved.

"Think you I would disobey the king even if he asked for my life?"

"Nay, not if he asked for your life. But what if it were a command that you found impossible to obey?"

"Robert, do you insult me? Do you believe I would break my oath to my sovereign, no matter what the cost?"

"Then I remind you of your oath . . . and tell you that it is William's will . . . his command . . . and his dire need . . . " Robert took a deep breath, then continued, "that you wed the Lady Lynette of Creganwald before the end of the month."

Royce's face grew still and pale. He looked at Robert as if he had just blasphemed. "Wed?"

"Aye, wed."

"You cannot be serious."

"I am sure William has never been more serious. He would show his trust in you, for this Creganwald is vital to him."

"I cannot, and I will not consider such a thing." Royce's voice grew deeper. "You, of all people, know this is an impossibility."

"I know only that this is the king's . . . command. Do you intend to ignore it? Do you intend to tell him you will not comply?"

"Nay!" Royce turned and walked into the next room. Robert followed, relentlessly forcing Royce to face him and give him a direct answer.

"You have already decided your oath is worthless?" Robert asked ruthlessly.

Royce spun to face him, his face stark and his eyes full of fury. But was it really fury, Robert thought, or a look of almost unbearable pain? He felt the hurt like a palpable force, and if he had not been of stout heart, he would have quaked and retreated before it. But he could not afford what Royce might think of as mercy now, because in the long run his strength now might prove Royce's saving.

"You are aware of my reasons."

"I am. But I am also aware that no matter what you do and what you suffer, you cannot bring Sybella back. William needs Creganwald to be held by a man to whom he can give his complete trust. There are few of them around. Also he wants . . . You must produce an heir of this union to insure that Creganwald's future will be secure."

"God! What more do you ask of me? I am not a fit husband for any woman, nor do I choose to be. Robert, for God's sake, bring another name before William."

"Royce, I would speak the truth. It was I who suggested you."

For a startling moment Robert thought Royce was about to strike him. His face was congested with rage, and a kind of despair.

"You, my trusted friend."

"Aye, a trusted friend, and one who loves you well. I, too, could not abide your loss."

"I cannot do this thing, Robert. Go to William, plead my cause. Suggest any other name than mine. If not for my sake, then for the luckless maid who

21

would be a victim in this marriage, for it would be hell for her." This was as close to pleading as a man like Royce would go. Robert understood his plea, but he could not do what was requested. If he did, he was sure that Royce's life would end on a battlefield, and the death would be a waste. He made one last try.

"What of Cerise, if you were to die?" he asked.

"She would forget me. I . . . I have not seen her for over six months."

"How old is she now?"

"She will soon be six."

"Royce, in the name of heaven, what have you done with her?"

Royce had guilt enough to flush and turn away. He spoke in a harsh rasp. "I cannot look at her. She . . . she looks . . . "

"Exactly like her mother. I should think this would be a comfort."

"Perhaps there is something wrong with me, Robert. Each time I looked at her I saw Sybella. I could bear it no longer."

"The poor child," Robert whispered in disbelief.

"Aye," Royce said bitterly. "The poor child. And you would wish another woman . . . and maybe another child to suffer the same fate. Have pity on them, Robert, if not on me."

"You do not need pity. You are not to blame for something that was in the hands of God."

"Don't be foolish, my friend. Had it not been for me, she would still be alive, and you know it."

"I know nothing of the sort. She chose to do what she did. She was happy with you, Royce. It is time to put the past away." Robert inhaled deeply. "I will not ask William to change this command. The marriage must be made, and you are one of the few he can trust to govern the lands well, once her father is gone."

"Her father is alive?"

"Aye."

"Then if he is loyal to William, why is a marriage necessary?"

"Because the lands lie in a strategically vulnerable place, and . . . " Robert shrugged expressively. "There are few William can trust, as he does you, not to squander the wealth or mishandle the lands . . . or make the harbor and lands accessible to his enemies. You see, your loyalty has made you valuable. William cannot do otherwise."

"Robert . . . I have never questioned any command from William. I have served him well. But can you not see what a tragic thing this would be? I . . . I cannot. Ah, Robert." Royce turned his back to Robert, for his voice broke. "Sleep eludes me . . . dreams fill my mind until I fear for my sanity, and still I cannot wash one moment's memory away. I see her everywhere, search for her in my lonely bed at night. I cannot even bear to look into the face of my own daughter because her mother's eyes look back at me. I am a man haunted and I cannot escape . . . I don't want to escape. I have vowed never to marry again."

"And what of your pledge to William, who made of you all that you are? You have given an oath. Do you break it now?"

"You strike at the heart, old friend."

"Royce, you go to the king. If you can deny your pledge, if your honor will see you released from this vow, then I will say no more."

23

Royce gazed at him for the first time since his arrival with the bleak look of one defeated. He knew William well. William would not release him from his pledge, and to preserve his name, his honor, his pride, and all he had fought for in his lifetime, he could not break it either.

"I will need time to send for the child. When is this wedding to be?"

"You are to go to Creganwald before the end of the month."

Chapter Two

The coast of England boasted no place more beautiful then Creganwald. The manor itself sat well back from the sea, but it commanded a perfect natural harbor. Eldwyn of Creganwald had held this manor and its lands all of his life, and ruled it with a strong but firm hand.

He had prayed one of his sons would inherit it when his life ended. But fate had taken his sons from him and left him with only his daughter. He lived in fear that a stranger would gain control over his holdings once he was gone. But his greatest fear was for his daughter.

Summer was losing its hold on the land, and the crisp breeze of early fall whipped the sea waves as they lapped against the shore, breaking into white froth when they reached it.

The same breeze swirled across a nearby meadow and brushed against the soft golden skin of the girl who walked there. The bright sun glistened on hair the color of ripe wheat, and reflected in eyes the color of the cloudless blue sky. She was slender of form, like a long-stemmed flower, and she walked with the graceful ease of one used to the outdoors.

She walked slowly, a heavy basket in her hand; it was laden with roots she had dug from the nearby woods. Some for the cook, and some for her. She had been taking instruction in healing from Maida, an old woman who had been her servant and companion ever since she could remember. As lady of the manor she had no reason to go gathering the roots herself, except that she loved being out and she often liked just being alone.

She had insisted on learning more medicine than she already knew, especially since her father had become so ill the winter before. She had hated the horrible feeling of helplessness. She wanted to learn how to care for her father should he ever become ill again.

How she loved the gauzy English sunshine, the long, slow days, the quiet winters, the fires of home, and English voices. The way spring came, when white daisies made a carpet on the dark, wet earth and when cattle lowed contentedly under a sun caught in a tangle of golden mist. The call of the cuckoo and the smell of hawthorn and the low green hills with the sheep grazing on them and sending out plaintive calls under an evening sky.

Though England was a conquered land, she considered this small corner of it hers—from the still, small blue ponds and lazy streams, to the thatched roofs of the serfs' huts, to the rutted roads and the huge oaks on their knolls.

She was as contented as a woman of a conquered

people could be. She knew her safety depended on the strategic value of her home, and on the reputation her father held as an honorable and trustworthy man. He would be left to govern his own lands using the same justice he had always governed with. Gratitude filled her prayers always, for she had heard terrible stories of the treatment of others who had resisted the conquering army of the Duke of Normandy.

William the Conqueror was building castles in the most strategic places along the vulnerable Channel coast. She had heard he was building them in gaps in the hills and at river crossings, and in and about towns and villages whose inhabitants must be dissuaded from the folly of rebellion.

She supposed that he must feel he needed the huge stone walls of those castles to protect his tentative hold on the land. He piqued her curiosity, this Norman king. But she was not curious enough to leave Creganwald, or to welcome him or any other Norman within its walls.

Her attention was finally drawn to a young girl who was racing toward her. One of the young maids . . . Bridget . . . what could be amiss? The girl was breathless when she reached Lynette's side.

"Mistress . . . Mistress," she panted.

"Bridget, stop and rest, get your breath. I'm sure it's not as important as that."

"Oh, yes, ma'am. It be important. Yer father wants ye to come to him real quick. Come straight away, without stoppin' for nothin'."

"What is the hurry?"

"There was a man at the manor, ma'am, come straight from the king, he did."

"What has that to do with me?" Lynette questioned. But a shiver of apprehension raced through her.

"I don't know, ma'am. True to God, I don't know. You know I don't listen—"

"Bridget, I know that you do. Now what have you heard?"

"This time I didn't hear nuthin'. Klavin caught me. Cuffed me real good, he did, then sent me back to the kitchen. I didn't hear nuthin'. But he was from the king . . . and him and your father been talkin' for a long time. I heard your father roarin', I did. He was mad for a while, then he got quiet. After a while the man left, and your father sent me for you."

Lynette tried to make sense of it, but she could not help the terrible feeling that something was really wrong.

"I'd best go to Father right away," she said as she increased her speed to a half run.

When she reached the manor she entered through a back entrance. There, in a shadowed hallway, she stopped to catch her breath, and to gather her courage. Her father might need her strength, and her courage. He did not need tears, or panic.

Lynette gathered herself together, then went to face her father and to offer whatever help she could. When she stepped inside the door of his chamber, she looked across the room. Her father was standing with his back to her, gazing out the window. Last winter's illness had taken its toll on him. His face was not the ruddy, healthy one it had always been, and his eyes had lost the laughter and challenge Lynette remembered from childhood years.

He had always been a vigorous man, and even in his later years he was still strongly built. He had sired four children before his beloved wife died and the light went from his life. Her death was followed by two of Lynette's older brothers' when a plague struck. He had been left with Lynette and a younger brother, who had died only the year before. Eldwyn's only joy after the death of his wife and sons, was Lynette.

"Papa? Bridget said you had sent for me." His silence was alarming in itself, but when he turned to look at her, his pale face and clenched jaw alarmed her. "Papa?"

"Lynette . . . child, sit down. I have something to tell you."

Lynette's legs grew weak, and she was grateful for the stool she dropped onto. She clenched her hands in her lap, and said a small prayer in her mind, yet she tried to smile at her father and erase the worried look from his face. However bad the news was, they would face it together.

"I have had a messenger from William."

"The king sent someone here? For what? You have given him your loyalty. You have tried to maintain the peace, and—"

"Lynette, it was not about me, it was concerning you."

"Me, Papa? Of what interest am I to the king? He has never set eyes upon me."

"I am sure his interest is in Creganwald. Should anything happen to me . . . "

"I see," she said weakly. No one needed to tell her the message. King William was protecting what now belonged to him. Lynette knew that a woman was only a pawn in the schemes of kings, just as she knew there was no way to fight the inevitable. One day she would have to marry; it was only a dream to believe it would be a man of her choosing and one who would love not only her, but Creganwald as well. Love it as she did. She looked up to find her father's gaze upon her, and his eyes suspiciously moist.

"Lynette, I would not have chosen to thrust you into—"

"I know, Papa. But I would have married one day. Perhaps we are judging the king's choice harshly. Perhaps he is a man who will be fair and kind. When . . . ?"

"He will arrive here within the month."

"And his name?"

"Royce. Known as the Sword of William."

At the name, Lynette's face paled. Stories of the mighty warrior came flooding into her mind. He fought like a madman; indeed, there were those who said he was mad, for he laughed in the midst of battle and killed with a fury. How could a man such as this be expected to show mercy or kindness to a maid . . . an enemy maid?

For her father's sake, she tried to gather her wits, but the thought of marriage to such a man as this Sword of William frightened her to death. But Lynette was, if nothing else, a realist. She knew it would crush her father if she resorted to wails of anguish and tears. She could already see he suffered greatly. She knew the futility of tears against the will of the new king.

Her father had always been her protector, her guide, and her strong arm. She refused to make this any harder on him than it already was. In a time when men bargained away their daughters for position and wealth, her father had always kept her away from view, had never considered her to be chattel he could use. He had loved her, taught her, and held her dear to him. Now she could plainly see that this command from the king brought him frustration and pain. She rose to her feet and went to her father. Putting her arms about his waist, she rested her head on his broad chest.

"Do not grieve over this, Papa. We are judging too hastily. The man cannot be a monster. We cannot say nay to the king, if it is his command that I marry, but maybe we can tame this wolf of a Norman, and find some peace."

Eldwyn of Creganwald embraced his daughter, enfolding her in his arms and crushing her to him. "You know I would have let you choose for yourself."

"Yes, Papa, I know. You have always been kind. But we must face the truth, as you have always taught me. We cannot run and hide from what must be. I will do what needs to be done, and I will make him a good wife. He will govern our lands in the name of the king. But, mayhap, there are things that he will learn as well . . . and mercy may be one."

"I would like to spit him on the point of my sword."

"Aye, and have the king's wrath descend on all of Creganwald without any hope for mercy. Nay, we must submit. I would not see you hanged . . . or worse. And afterward, I would still have to go into this marriage, but without your love and support."

Lynette knew it was her father's inability to rescue her that made him so frustrated and angry. She had to swallow her misgivings and make this as easy for him as she could. He had been so ill the winter before, filling her with the fear of losing him. Even now she could see the pallor of illness upon him. Now she would need him more than she ever had.

"I must go and speak to Maida, and begin to make preparations. When he arrives, he will see the best Creganwald has to offer. He will see that we are not languishing at his feet, and begging. He is the conqueror . . . but in our own way, we can be victors too."

She rose on tiptoe and kissed his cheek. Then she turned and left him looking after her with great pride.

But when she had closed the huge oak door between them, Lynette sagged against the wall as if her strength had drained from her. Marriage to . . . to a madman. A man who fought like a beast in war. How could she bear it if he were equally violent in the bedchamber? She put her arms about her body, feeling as if she were about to disintegrate. She had to agree to the marriage, all there was left to do was to pray.

Lynette went first to her chamber, where she went to her knees beside a huge wooden chest. This she opened and withdrew from it several bolts of fabric. A fine gold-colored wool, a cream linen, and three others of royal blue, soft green, and rich rust. This was to be the fabric for her wedding clothes, but the need for their use had come long before she had planned. Carrying them to her bed, she laid them carefully down. Then she went below in search of

Edmee, who had the finest hand for stitching. It was time to begin the making of her wedding garments.

She found Edmee, with Bridget and several other women, clustered together and sharing the gossip that was spreading like wildfire. She gathered them to help her, and as they sewed they continued the conversation.

"Ye'll be the prettiest bride in England," Edmee said confidently.

"Are ye frightened, mistress?" Bridget inquired.

"Hush, girl," Edmee scolded. "She's nothing to be afraid of."

"But . . . Royce . . . they say . . . "

"Don't listen to rumors, Bridget," Lynette said. She tried her best to hide what fears she had. She'd heard the same tales. "You can't judge a man by what people say. You have to meet him and judge for yourself."

"I don't care," Bridget said obstinately. "I'd be afraid to wed a man like that. Where there's smoke, there's fire."

Edmee cast her a withering look and Lynette had to hide her smile. She wasn't afraid . . . yet.

For over two weeks she and her women worked on the fine material, and Lynette replaced in her trunk the finished garments, which were fine enough to make any young bride proud.

She made plans for the finest feast their limited supplies would provide, taking care not to omit anything that might bring satisfaction and comfort to the new lord of Creganwald.

She meant to show this invader that the pride of Creganwald had not been broken, and never would be. She meant also to prove to him that she did not come to him on her knees, but by royal order of the king.

She intended to see to it that his time here at Creganwald was the most uneventful and tiresome time in his life. He would soon realize that none of the gaiety of court life existed here, that he was buried in the least exciting place in England. She would trust in his desire for power and a place at William's side at court. Before long, they would draw him away and leave her and Creganwald in peace.

She laughed softly to herself. She would give orders to servants who had known and loved her since childhood. Royce, the famed Sword of William, invader of her life and her home, would soon be so inundated with pretty problems, arguments, and annoyances that he would be grateful to run back to William and his court.

There was nothing left for her to do but think of him and what was about to happen. She had not given thought to sharing his bed. In fact, she had done everything in her power to keep that thought at bay. But now she was caught with too much time on her hands, and too many frightening things to think about.

She would belong to him, as his horse and his mail belonged to him. Not even her father could intervene between them even if he chose to beat her. The idea of this marriage kept her nights sleepless, and her days restless. She tried to imagine what he looked like, but the descriptions that had come to Creganwald were always of brutality, battles, bloodshed, until he took on the characteristics of a monster in her mind, and she trembled in fear. She, who had never known fear in her life, dreaded the coming of a man who would put an end to her maiden ways and make her a wife, forever in his hold.

Gradually her fear became resistance. He might possess her, own her, but he would never have the satisfaction of it, for she would never submit anything but the cold shell of her body. This man would never touch her spirit, never find a place in her heart. This she vowed with all the strength of her soul.

Day after day she expected him, and day after day passed without a sign or a word, until the days turned slowly to weeks. Her trepidation grew into annoyance, and then to anger. Conquered they were, but any decent man would have had enough consideration to come when he was expected. Was he deliberately ignoring her, putting her in her place as slave, someone he would get to when convenience allowed? The thought infuriated her. It was the first time she had really felt conquered, and the thought did not suit her at all. She . . . being forced to wed, being less than an afterthought to the man who would wed, bed, and forget her when she was with child.

Grimly she watched for him as the days passed, and her anger turned cold. Her father, along with every servant and every peasant, watched and waited. Their pride, too, was shaken; they hated to think that their beloved mistress could be treated this way.

September's cool nights and warm days gave way to the chill of October and then to the frosts and soft snows of November. Then December made the days short and cold.

Still there was no sign of Royce. Lynette had tried to force him from her mind, but she had little success. The insult was infuriating. She began to imagine reasons . . . he had been wounded in battle, mayhap he had even died. He was on a mission for his king and had not returned. He was ill . . . but none of the reasons could explain why a message had not been sent. Obviously, in his eyes she was not worth such consideration.

She arose one morning to see a blanket of white covering the land. The first substantial snow. It was stimulating, and she decided to go for an early morning ride. In the stable she waited impatiently while her mare was saddled.

Cynric saddled the horse as quickly as he could while keeping an eye on his mistress. "It be very cold, Mistress."

"Aye, but the mare likes the run, and the cold suits me today," Lynette replied as she patted her horse.

"I could ride with ye, if—"

"No, Cynric, I really want to ride alone."

"Are ye angry, Mistress?"

"Aye, Cynric, but not with you." She smiled at his relieved look.

"If there be unwanted visitors, we will—"

"No, you will welcome them as visitors to Creganwald should be welcomed," She commanded, then added softly, "I shall take care of the 'visitors' when . . . or if, they choose to come."

Then she mounted and rode away from Creganwald. Cynric watched her ride off and was glad he wasn't the one in the unwelcome visitor's shoes.

The crisp air was invigorating, and her enjoyment

seemed to be communicated to her horse, for the mare seemed anxious to run, and Lynette did not try to hold her back. They were some distance from Creganwald before she drew the mare to a walk.

They had crested a hill, and the road to the town lay below her. She sat her horse and gazed about her, pleased with all her eyes fell upon. But after some time she thought she saw movement in the distance. She sat very still until the truth of her observation was proven. She was wise enough to know exactly who was coming toward Creganwald. It had to be her arrogant and inconsiderate lord.

A new anger rose in her. The party came slowly, a procession of relaxed and carefree knights. Lynette's fury grew. It had been nearly four months since word of her marriage had been brought to her, and now he came as casually as if he had just finally decided that she was worth the effort.

Well, let him arrive at Creganwald, let him cool his heels at Creganwald. Let him wait for her, as she had waited for him. Let there be no mistress to see to his comfort. Let him see how it felt to wait on someone else's pleasure.

Determined to stay away from Creganwald for as long as she possibly could, Lynette decided there were necessary things to be seen to among her father's serfs. To the surprise and wonderment of the peasants, she visited every hut and every serf her father's lands held.

It was nearing dark when she reluctantly turned her horse toward home. She would not have chosen to go even then, but she knew her father would be worried, and she did not want servants roused and sent out into the cold night to find her.

The sun was a red rim on the horizon when she arrived at the stable.

"Yer father was just about to send out search parties, mistress," said the wide-eyed stableboy.

"Is he angry, Cynric?"

"Nay, mistress, just worried. There be guests in the house. Knights of King William they be."

"I believe they have been expected for some weeks, Cynric," Lynette said dryly. She had just caught the gleam of laughter in his eyes, and knew that every servant must know she had deliberately absented herself. "I shall go in at once to relieve my father's mind . . . and see to our guests."

"Yes, mistress," Cynric replied, but his admiring gaze followed her slim form as she left the stable. This knight who had ridden so arrogantly within the walls of Creganwald had more of a surprise in store than he could have imagined. Cynric turned back to his duties with a smile on his face, wagering with himself that the Sword of William had met his match.

Lynette went inside, and from the hallway she could hear deep masculine voices. They were still at table. She stepped into the light of the room to see a fairly large group of men seated with her father. Suddenly her eyes fell on one, the only one that could be her betrothed. Slowly silence descended on the room, and the tall knight seated beside her father rose to his feet.

Lynette caught her breath. Her eyes widened at the sight of him. He was so . . . so immense! His shoulders were unbelievably broad. Her eyes met his across the room, and again she felt another shock. They were gold . . . the gold of a coin, and they seemed to pierce her. His dark hair was thick and the color of night. He was . . . handsome beyond belief, and Lynette could feel his power even at this distance. For the first time she wondered if she hadn't made a drastic mistake angering this knight. She started across the room.

Chapter Three

Lynette stood only a few feet from Royce, and felt as if he were looking down on her from a great height. He stood relaxed, as if this table were already his own. It brought a flush of annoyance to her face.

She knew that to this man she was less than nothing, a minor problem that would cost him time from his normal pursuits. As she studied him she again took notice of how handsome he was. Then another thought came to her. This was a forced marriage; surely he had another woman . . . or several women, who held his interest. Maybe he would just go through the motions of the ceremony, then leave her and carry on with his lustier pursuits. This was the best she could hope for.

She soon became aware that, as she was studying him, he was studying her. But his thoughts might have surprised her.

Royce had watched her approach, her head

proudly raised and her eyes meeting his. Did he see rebellion there? This was no docile maid who would submit to his attentions, breed a son or two, and leave him in peace with his memories. She was a threat, both to his peace of mind and to his conscience.

It was when Eldwyn rose to stand beside Royce that Lynette realized how truly large Royce was. She had always thought her father the largest man she had ever seen, but Royce stood over half a head taller, and his young, vigorous body seemed to exude an aura of frightening power. She could show no weakness before this man.

Lynette dropped a deep curtsy before him and gave her sweetest smile. All present could plainly see that the smile did not extend to her eyes.

"My lord, welcome to Creganwald. I am sorry I was absent and not here to see to your comfort, but since you did not arrive on the day or even within the month you were expected, I had no reason to believe you would actually honor us with your company."

"Lynette," Eldwyn said sternly.

"Do not condemn her for her anger." Royce smiled. "You are right, demoiselle. It was wrong of me not to send word of our arrival. Had I known your impatience and anxiousness to see to this wedding, I should have arrived with more speed." He watched her cheeks flush with color as a muffled chuckle came from behind her. "But I will rectify my behavior, and assure you the wedding will take place within the next few weeks. I hope you can curb your impatience until then. At least until we can become acquainted."

Now her eyes lit with fury. How dare he imply

she was so eager for his bed! This Norman had a complete lack of manners to smile at the laughter of his men!

"You need not hurry yourself on my account, my lord. Were it my choice, you would have chosen your mate among the willing Norman women, who are not so particular with whom they lie."

Her father's mouth gaped in shock, and a roar of laughter from several knights made even Royce grin. No, this was no docile maid. He could pique her anger, and thereby keep her at a distance. It would serve him well that she found him distasteful; it was the safest way for both of them. But her dislike of the marriage would mean nothing to William; it was her lands he was determined to hold.

It was Robert who rose from his seat to come around the table and offer her his arm. He was somewhat shocked that Royce had not done so himself. Royce was not an inconsiderate man, but Robert knew the reasons for his desire to alienate the girl.

When Lynette was seated between Eldwyn and Robert, she favored Robert with her sunniest smile.

"Thank you, sir knight. It is clear to see that all Normans do not lack fine manners."

"I am Sir Robert Debayeaux, my lady," he said, casually ignoring Royce's dark scowl.

"And where have you wandered this day, demoiselle?" Royce questioned.

"Since my father was so ill last winter, I found it necessary to see to the accounts, and to other work about the manor. I have been visiting the surrounding farms to judge the extent of winter stores."

"You read?"

"And write a fair hand. I can also do sums, and speak both your language and some Latin."

Royce was surprised, but struggled successfully not to show it. He had thought his promised wife would be content with her sewing and household duties. Her learning piqued his interest. It was rare to find a maid who could take an interest in things other than husband and babes.

"It is still to be seen if your accounts are accurate," he replied casually. "William will want a fair accounting in the spring."

"My daughter has been trained, first by her mother and then by my own hand," Eldwyn said stiffly. "She has not made idle claims of her accomplishments."

Royce nodded. "Then tell me"—he looked at Lynette—"how are the preparations for the wedding feast proceeding? I would not want any more wasted time."

"You must have many duties, perhaps many liaisons that will draw you away from here," Lynette said. "If it will hasten your departure, I can arrange for the priest to say the words tomorrow. Then you can be on your way."

At this Royce threw back his head and laughed. "Take what time you need, demoiselle. I have no intention of leaving here until all of William's orders have been carried out." He knew he had to make her position clear or he would have a battle on his hands later. It was better to do it at the start, and give her time to adjust to her fate. "There must be a Norman heir to hold Creganwald in the future."

Royce watched Lynette's face go pale, but to give her credit, she gave no outward sign of her helpless rage. She became quiet, and Royce began to believe she would be easier tamed than he thought. But Eldwyn watched his daughter closely and knew the battle had just been joined.

The meal went on for what to Lynette seemed like hours. Her head had begun to pound, and she fervently desired to be free of this horde of Normans so she could think, form a plan. She would not play the whore for this arrogant beast, or bear his brats. Finally she was free to excuse herself, leaving the men alone to talk and to enjoy their ale.

Royce watched her cross the room and start up the stairs. He had bested her for the time being, but he had been in too many battles not to know this one had just begun.

Lynette climbed the steps slowly, without making any sound. That was why both she and the child that sat huddled on the top step were surprised. The child gave a gasp of shock, fairly leapt to her feet, and raced down the darkened hall into a room.

Lynette followed slowly. No one had told her there would be any children in the group of invaders, and she was curious as to which knight the child belonged. She entered the room and found the child huddled in the center of the bed, her eyes wide and brimming with tears. That there was no maid or serving woman was another shock.

"Who are you, child?" she asked gently. "Is there no one here to care for you?"

"Oriel has gone to get her supper," the child said hesitantly. "Please . . . please, don't tell her I was on the stairs. She will be angry."

"Where is your mother, and who is Oriel?"

"My mother is dead, and Oriel takes care of me."

"Then . . . who brought you here?"

"My papa."

"And who is your father?"

The child was beginning to realize that the beautiful lady meant her no harm. Besides, she liked her kind eyes, and the gentleness of her voice. Oriel never spoke gently unless her father was present, and she was often cruel. Her father never noticed . . . of course, her father never noticed her at all. Her head came up, and her tiny chin jutted in pride.

"My father is Royce. He is the greatest knight the king has. He has fought a lot of battles, and he is the strongest knight of all."

Lynette sat on the edge of the bed because her legs had gone weak. Shock held her silent for a minute. This beautiful little girl was Royce's daughter. But she looked very little like him. Her hair was thick and long, and the color of a sleek mink. Her eyes were large and as purple as summer violets. She was already displaying a promise of real beauty. And yet, the Norman had never even mentioned her.

"Are you hungry?" Lynette whispered conspiratorially. The child nodded vigorously. "Have you not supped?"

"Oriel said I was to stay here, and she would see if there were any scraps left in the kitchen for me."

If Lynette had been angry before, she was furious now. This knight had dragged his child with him and never seen to her comfort. He had allowed her to eat leftover scraps from the table. What kind of monster was he?

"Would you like me to bring you something?"

"Oh, no, Oriel would be angry."

"She will not be angry with me," Lynette stated firmly. The child's eyes grew round. "What is your name?"

"Cerise. Are you truly not afraid of Oriel?"

"No, I am not. Now, you come with me. We will go down the back stairs and see what there is for you to eat."

Still not quite believing there was someone in the world not afraid of Oriel, Cerise slid from the bed and put her trembling little hand in Lynette's. Together they went to the kitchen. Cerise was more than awed by the buxom woman who fawned over her and brought out the food.

"Bless ye, child. Are ye hungry? Well, there's a fine piece or two of the bird from supper and a bit of cheese. I'm sure I can find a sweet to help bring ye good dreams. A child can't find sleep on an empty stomach."

"A piece of bread and some milk, too," Lynette said.

"Of course, of course," the cook replied. A tray was quickly filled, and Cerise carried her mug of milk while Lynette carried the tray. An hour later they were seated in the center of Lynette's bed, nibbling on the cheese and chicken and some crusty bread. Lynette wondered just when the child had last eaten. The thought filled her with new anger. She would face Royce tomorrow and call him the name he so richly deserved.

"How old are you, Cerise?"

"Nearly six."

"When will you be six?"

Cerise paused to think, and Lynette found this

aggravating too. Had the child never had any kind of celebration for her birthday?

"I will be six when the first roses bloom," Cerise said brightly. She didn't know the date, but the roses were her way of marking time.

"We shall have to have a celebration."

"Why?"

"Because you are going to be a year older and you are a very special person. Your father will be lord here, and his daughter—you—will one day be Lady Cerise of Creganwald."

Cerise blinked as if this were something of a shock; then she half smiled as if she thought Lynette might be teasing.

"*You* will be Lady of Creganwald," Cerise replied.

"Yes, but when your father and I have wed, we will both be the guardians of this manor. We must help each other to learn all we must learn to be just and kind and to rule well. You will one day be lady here, so you must learn too."

"I will not be lady here. Papa will have Oriel take me somewhere else. We are always going somewhere else."

Lynette could hear the longing in Cerise's voice for the security of home and family. It only made her angrier with the child's careless father.

"No . . . this time you will stay." She bent toward Cerise conspiratorially. "Perhaps we will see if Lady Oriel won't be going someplace else alone. I've found the lady not to my taste, so we will just have to be friends, you and I, and keep our secrets."

This pleased Cerise, and by the time Lynette tucked her into bed she drifted into sleep quickly.

But Lynette could not find sleep so easily. She didn't know all the truth, but she meant to find it. There was, it seemed, a lot more to this new force in her life than she had bargained for.

Below, men were finding their beds, and the main hall was empty except for Eldwyn and Royce.

"I was informed that you had agreed to this wedding, but your daughter seems to feel differently."

"Lynette has been without her mother for a number of years. It has made her a bit headstrong. But she is a good, obedient daughter."

"I will try not to make this any harder for her than it is already, but this manor must be secured. She must understand her position."

"My lord, no one understands her position better than Lynette. She is a woman of tender sensibilities. She is also a woman of honor, and would not see that honor dragged in the dust. I plead that you but give her time. You will soon discover that she will abide by her vows, once she takes them."

It was not her abiding but his own that Royce was worried about. He did not want a loyal and honorable wife, but a woman who would be content to breed the heir and allow him his freedom. An heir . . . the thought of putting another woman through childbirth set his teeth on edge.

Eldwyn rose to his feet. "I must find my bed, Royce. This old body is not as strong as it used to be. Last winter's illness weakened me, and this winter proves overly long. Good night."

"Good night. I will sit here by the fire for a while yet."

Royce sat brooding for some minutes before he

realized he was not alone. He turned in his chair and looked across the room at the woman who stood in the doorway watching him. It was Oriel, the woman who had been brought along to care for his daughter. She was young, and the sister of one of his favorite knights. Actually, she was quite pretty, and Royce had been tempted to ease his loins with her once or twice. But his fear of a permanent attachment had forestalled him. Better to use the whores he found along the way; then there was no chance of attachment.

But Oriel did not share his feelings. For months she had subtly tried to get Royce into her bed. She had sensed the few times he had looked at her with desire. She had only agreed to care for his brat so she could be near him. It was worth it just to be near on that one night of weakness when he would turn to her. His own honor would take care of the rest. Then she could find someone else to keep his child out from underfoot, while she shared his time.

It was common knowledge that he couldn't bear to be around the child. She didn't know why, nor did she care. The child was the least of her worries. She watched Royce rise to his feet and walk toward her. He was enough to take away a woman's breath, and a wave of hot desire washed through her.

"The child is well?" he asked.

"Aye. I've seen to her supper, and have tucked her warm and safe in her bed. She is sleeping like a baby. I will be by her side till morning . . . unless"— her voice lowered and became seductive—"there is something you request of me."

He did not miss her invitation, and he found his reluctance a surprise. "No, there is nothing more.

Get some rest. I'm sure the child has kept you busy. Good night."

She sighed, but turned away. There was time. She had heard his insult to the Lady Lynette, and was sure his marriage vows would mean nothing if he desired another. She certainly didn't intend for Lynette or his unwanted child to get in her way.

Royce poured another horn of wine, and again eased himself down in the chair before the dying fire. This was the time of the night he hated most. These quiet hours, when memories could not be held at bay and he saw her violet eyes and deep brown hair in the glowing coals.

He felt the same old undefeated agony wash over him, a longing that crushed his breath and squeezed his heart until he felt the pain would never cease.

"Sybella." He whispered her name, and the ache of longing filled him for the nights they had shared in the brilliant ecstasy of love.

He could feel the heat of tears in his eyes, and could not fight the memory of her touch, her kiss, or the unselfish way she had given herself to him without reservation, with a fire that had left him filled . . . and now left him empty. Empty, with nothing to fill the emptiness but longing and a loneliness that was devastating.

He poured wine, the only defense he had, and thought of the child they had created; self-hatred filled him again. But the agony that filled him when he looked at Cerise was too much to bear.

He would see to her care, but he could not bring himself to look into those purple eyes, so like her mother's. No, she was safe, and well cared for. He could not admit to himself that after Sybella's death, he had looked into his daughter's eyes and seen his own guilt.

Because he had wanted a son, Sybella, who should never have considered giving birth, had accepted his seed, and had died trying to give him what he had desired more than anything else. He had helplessly watched her life bleed away. . . . He had wept, and staggered from the room. Later they had brought his daughter to him, and in his agony he could not take her, hold her, or even look at her. All he could see was his beloved Sybella's life bleeding away. It was his fault, and the child he could not release or hold was the proof of his guilt. He had looked into her eyes once, and the bitter anguish had never left his soul since that night. Every time he had seen her from that day forward, the black shadow of guilt and self-hatred had eaten at him until he thought he would go mad.

It was then the devil of self-destruction had filled him. But God seemed to laugh at his attempts. He had lived and had fought again and again with reckless abandon, until he put fear into his enemies that he was a devil who could not be killed. In fact, he had often wondered himself.

Now he was caught in a difficulty not of his choosing, bound by an oath his honor would not let him break. He would go through with this farce of a wedding. But when a child was conceived he would leave . . . and he was certain the Lady Lynette would be glad to see him go. He raised the horn to drink again.

Chapter Four

Lynette was always an early riser, often leaving her bed just before dawn. The hall was still quiet as she left her chamber and started toward the stairs. That was why the muffled cry of pain was heard so clearly as she passed the child's chamber.

Thinking there might be something wrong, she pushed the door open. The sight that met her eyes brought a gasp of outrage.

Oriel was holding the child brutally by the arms and shaking her. The little girl was crying softly, and her tangled hair was flung wildly about her. She stood with her bare feet on the cold stone floor, dressed in nothing but a thin piece of linen.

"Quiet, you little brat, or I will give you something to cry about. I warned you you were not to get out of bed before I told you to. How often must I punish you before you learn to obey?"

That someone should treat a child like this was

abhorrent to Lynette, but that it was the child of the lord of the manor was beyond belief.

"What is amiss here?"

Two pairs of very surprised eyes turned toward Lynette. One pair was filled with cold disdain, and the other with tears of misery.

Oriel was quick to display her arrogance. After all, it was obvious Royce did not respect his betrothed, and she was just a Saxon slave anyway.

"It is not any of your affair. The child was put in my charge. She is in need of discipline."

"What has she done? She is cold and most likely hungry, since you did not see to her supper last night."

Oriel had the grace to flush.

"She is willful, and sometimes needs a strong hand. Besides"—Oriel's eyes glittered with smug and vengeful laughter—"it is not your place to change the rules given by her father. I will take care of her."

Lynette might have let it go at that, but the child's eyes lifted to her with such a look of quiet despair that she could not leave her in the hands of this woman.

"Within two weeks, I will be Royce's wife. This child will then become mine. I will take over her care now. Come here, Cerise," Lynette ordered the child, who looked from Lynette to Oriel with a gaze suddenly filled with hope.

This woman, this kind woman, who had given her food and laughed with her last night was to be her new mother.

She pulled free of Oriel's hand and went to

Lynette, who smiled down at her and brushed her tangled hair from her face.

"Go and dress, and then bring your hairbrush. Find something warm. Then we will go to the kitchen and see what we can find to break our fast."

"Her father will not approve of this. His command was to keep her away from him, his men, and everyone else. She is to be kept out of sight."

The cruelty of such words spoken in front of the child only succeeded in making Lynette angrier than she already was.

"Go to your lord," Lynette said furiously. "Tell him his cruelty will not be permitted under this roof while I am alive. If he cares to take out his petty cruelties on me, I can be easily found."

"You will regret this. He does not want the child in his sight."

"Be gone from here, before I forget myself and do you more harm than you have bargained upon," Lynette hissed.

Oriel was quick to see the wisdom of a hasty departure, but she was not going to let this Saxon wench get the final word. She would make it clear to Royce that Lynette meant to bring the child into his company. That would put an end to Lynette's interference. Royce would see that she was put in her proper place before the wench got too full of the idea that being Royce's wife was going to make her important. She would enjoy seeing Lynette face Royce's wrath.

When the door closed behind Oriel, Lynette turned to Cerise and smiled, and watched a tentative smile appear in return.

"Are you really going to be my mother?"

"It appears I am."

"And I will not have to stay with Oriel anymore?"

"I will speak to your father about that," Lynette said thoughtfully. She was only now realizing that, if the child was forced back into Oriel's company, even for the short time before the wedding, she would pay the price for Lynette's interference. She knew Oriel had left her in a vindictive mood, and heaven only knew what she was telling Royce at this moment. "For now we must get you dressed and fed." Lynette helped Cerise choose something warm to wear, and was secretly appalled at the condition of her clothes. It seemed her father did not even worry about how she was dressed.

When they got to the kitchen, it was already bustling as preparations for the morning meal were under way. Lynette gave orders for the child to be fed, then kept in the kitchen until Lynette returned for her.

"Under no circumstances are you to place her in the hands of that vicious creature, Oriel. If she appears, send for me at once."

"Where will we find you, mistress? The new lord will not take it well should we cause difficulties."

"You needn't worry," Lynette said with grim determination. "I am going to see the new lord now."

The servants watched her leave the kitchen with hidden smiles. The mistress was more than angry, she was overflowing with fury. It was going to prove interesting when those two clashed. Even the old lord often gave way to her anger when she thought she was fighting for something worthy. This time there was a child involved.

Lynette walked with purposeful strides toward the main room, where the sound of men's voices could already be heard. But Royce was not among them, and it was Robert who spotted Lynette first and came to meet her. He knew fury when he saw it and wanted to abate whatever storm was brewing before she and Royce could make the situation between them any worse than it was.

"Good morning, my lady."

"Good morning, Sir Robert," Lynette replied, but her eyes were scanning the group.

"If you are looking for Royce, he is not here."

"Does he lie abed to be served like a king?" Lynette said sneeringly.

"No, my lady. He has been up and gone for two hours. He looks over . . . "

"His property. It is too bad, Sir Robert, that he does not give as much thought to the humans in his care as to the lands and animals."

Robert knew at once what Lynette was referring to, and he sought a way to prevent a more serious problem. "My lady, could I speak with you in private?"

"So that you can make excuses for his actions, for his brutality?"

"Brutality, my lady? There is not a brutal bone in Royce's body."

"Your loyalty is commendable, Sir Robert. But this time I think it is misplaced. How can a man treat his own child like a . . . a . . . " Her voice broke.

"Where is the Lady Oriel?"

"Chained with the dogs, I hope, but most likely carrying tales to Royce of my interference."

"Aye," Robert said softly. "But I beg a moment

56

to talk with you before you loose this anger on Royce."

"Very well," Lynette said reluctantly. She would rather have faced Royce and settled the matter. She was going to fight to keep the child away from Oriel if it was the last thing she ever did.

Robert offered her his arm, and she laid her hand upon it. The two walked out of the main hall and found a quiet place to talk.

"It is against all I know to break a confidence, or to betray a trust," he began. "But this problem has been festering for a long time, and I would see an end to it."

"How can he allow that woman to care for one as small and helpless as Cerise?"

"You know her name?"

"Aye, we shared a very late meal last evening."

"She is to take her meals in her chambers with Lady Oriel."

"It seems," Lynette said scathingly, "that the lady had other more pressing matters to attend. She neglected to see to the child's supper."

"Aye," Robert repeated, "and I can surmise what those pressing matters were. It seems I am the only one who can see the lady has more in mind than caring for the child."

"She is his mistress?" Lynette questioned. The idea was shockingly upsetting. If Oriel was Royce's mistress, Lynette would be able to do little to protect Cerise.

"Nay, not yet. But I do not think she will let go of the idea easily. It seems Royce is the only one who has not seen her intent."

"Sir Robert, can you not tell me why the child is

not allowed in his presence? What could that shy little thing have done to be treated so?"

"All she has done, my lady, is to look like—"

"Robert." The voice that came from behind Lynette was cold and uncompromising. Lynette spun around and looked up into gold eyes alight with an emotion she could not read.

"Royce," Robert replied. Lynette sensed some communication pass between the two men. But the golden gaze held hers, until she felt her cheeks grow warm and a stirring of something unfathomable within her.

She wondered where the vicious Oriel was, and why she was not with him.

Oriel had indeed waited near the stable to have the first opportunity to reach Royce's ear. She had watched his destrier approach, a huge beast that could strike terror in the heart of an enemy. But Royce rode relaxed and at ease, as if his mind was elsewhere. And indeed it was. He had seen, from his early morning ride, that Creganwald was well cared for. He had stopped to speak with every peasant, and heard in their voices the truth about their lord and his daughter.

Well loved . . . honest . . . trustworthy, with the welfare of their people always in mind. Why, did not the Lady Lynette nurse their ills when they were sick? Did not the lord mete out justice with fairness? Yes, the lord and his daughter were well loved . . . . Why did it annoy him so much?

He had almost been upon Oriel before he saw her, and was hard put to control the mighty horse. When he finally calmed the animal, he gave the reins to

Selwyn, one of Eldwyn's stableboys, and turned on Oriel.

"You could have been killed!"

"Oh, my lord." Oriel shed practiced tears, and for a moment Royce felt his heart lurch.

"The child, is she all right?"

"Aye, my lord. I . . . I think so."

"What do you mean, you think so? She is in your care."

"Nay, my lord, no longer."

"Woman! What has happened?"

Just the harsh grate of his voice made Oriel's tears become more real. She shook with fear. What if he didn't believe her?

"The Saxon wench, she took her from our chamber this morning. She would not even let me see that she had eaten. She said that no Norman brat would be treated like the lady of the manor while she ruled here. She said I was not to see her again. Oh, the poor child. What kind of care will she get from a Saxon who hates you and all Normans?" Royce clenched his teeth as Oriel continued. "I tried to explain to her that you wanted her cared for in her own chambers, but she said she would not get any special treatment, but would be cared for in the main hall, and sit next to you and her."

"Hold!" Royce said. "I will see to this."

Oriel had watched him stride toward the manor, and a smile played across her lips. Soon the child would be back in her care, and the arrogant lady would find that the Normans were masters here.

When Royce had come upon Robert and Lynette in conversation, he was at first surprised to find them together. How clever she was. Did she mean to gain support from Robert in her plans to remain mistress of this manor? Did she question Robert on things that were not her affair?

When he spoke Robert's name, he watched Lynette turn to meet his gaze, and he felt more than saw the animosity there.

"I would speak with you, demoiselle," he said firmly. "Alone."

"Royce," Robert began, "I—"

"I am not going to devour her, Robert," Royce said with amusement at Robert's protective attitude. He was a bit surprised that Robert looked as if he suspected he might do just that. Already the wench was undermining him, seeking his own friends and knights for protection.

The sooner he made her position clear, the better for them all. Even the child. It had never occurred to Royce that he never referred to Cerise by name. In every way, he tried to distance himself from his daughter. Reluctantly Robert walked away, and Royce and Lynette stood looking at each other for a silent moment.

"You seem to have run across some difficulties with Lady Oriel this morning."

"I have no difficulties with the creature," Lynette said sweetly. "Let her keep her distance from me, or I shall find a pigsty in which to deposit her."

"Lady Oriel is the sister of Sir Giles. They are of a very fine family."

"Does that justify her vicious behavior? Silk and jewels do not make a lady."

"Lady Oriel has gone to some extent to care for—"

"For your little 'problem'?"

Now it was Royce's turn to flush. Even he had never referred to his child as a problem. In fact, he knew he hardly ever referred to her as all.

"The little 'problem,' as you put it, is my concern, not yours."

"Then where were you last evening when she was crying on the stairs because she was cold and hungry—wallowing like a pig with that 'lady'?"

Royce jerked erect, and his face portrayed his anger. "Lying about the Lady Oriel is hardly just."

"Lying!" Lynette sputtered. "You great oaf! I need not lie about something your own knights are afraid to bring to your attention! Only a man with no conscience at all would subject an innocent child to what Cerise has had to bear. You would wed me, my lord," she added scathingly, "by the order of your king. But let me warn you, Norman, you will rue the day you try to bed me. Before I would breed a child by you, I would place a dagger in my own heart. You are a man with no honor, and even this conquered Saxon would be dishonored by your touch!"

Lynette spun on her heel and was gone before Royce could reply.

Angrily, he walked back into the silent main hall, where every man at table was trying his best to avoid his fierce gaze. Clearly every ear had heard the last words and was waiting for his explosion.

Robert sat, completely engrossed in his food. He had to keep his head bowed. It would do little good for Royce to see his satisfied smile. He had begun to like the stormy little Saxon, and meant to tell her so the first chance he got . . . if she did not take his head off before he could.

Chapter Five

Lynette went straight to her chambers, all thought of hunger forgotten. She was certain she would find a furious Royce at her door soon, and she would pay for what she had said.

Why had she thought he would take her word, or even try to see if the child was well cared for? Hadn't Lady Oriel made it clear that the infamous Sword of William abhorred having the child in his presence? But . . . if he hated Cerise so much, why not have her cared for elsewhere? Why make the effort to bring her with him wherever he went? And . . . what had Sir Robert been about to say to her to ease her thoughts?

Lynette could not face Royce now. She dressed hastily, donning warm boots and a fur-lined cloak, then went to the stables and had her mare saddled. Perhaps if she rode for a while, she would be able to face his wrath.

* * *

Royce finished his breakfast and rose from the table. He had watched the faces surrounding him closely, and noticed that his men conversed among each other and kept their voices subdued. Even Robert was abnormally quiet.

"Robert, attend me for a while. I have something to talk to you about." He strode from the room certain that Robert would follow.

When they had gone, Sir Giles, a younger knight, rose as well and left the room hurriedly. He was young and boyishly handsome, with pale gold hair. He was tall, but would never reach the height of Royce, and his eyes were a guileless blue. He climbed the stairs to the chamber Oriel shared with the child. His knock was answered by Oriel, who smiled and motioned him inside. But once he was inside, he turned and faced her with undisguised annoyance.

"Oriel, what mischief are you about now? Is it true that you are mistreating the child?"

"Mistreating? No, I am not. I care for her, just as Royce has asked me to do. I have not shared my meals or my time with anyone, sacrificing it all for his wishes. He is the one who told me to keep the child out of his sight. I will never understand why he does not just rid himself of her once and for all."

"How stupid can you be? Whether he can look on her face or not, she is still Sybella's daughter. Do you think he could let injury come to her and not take revenge on the person who caused her harm? Oriel, be careful. Do not earn his wrath."

"Nay, brother, it is not his wrath I will get. It is something of much greater value. He does not want

63

this Saxon bitch, he wants a woman of his own breeding. He will never bed her, and she will never breed for him. He will see the way of it, and go to the king and ask to be released from this distasteful duty. Then he will see that it is I who has been by his side."

"You are a fool. Do you think he will go against William, with whom he has fought shoulder to shoulder for years? The king to whom he has sworn allegiance! He will not discard his honor so lightly."

"Honor! What of *my* honor? I have given him much, brother. I deserve better."

"I warn you, Oriel, do not cause mischief here. Royce is not a man to play with, and disloyalty is a great offense in his mind. You had better not have harmed the child in any way."

"I have done her no harm, I tell you. She is favored too much, and feels she can be disobedient with no punishment to follow. I would only discipline her occasionally. But if you see her, you will see she is in good health."

"You think because he entrusted the child to your hands, that he will also find a way to your bed? You have never understood honor, Oriel. Even when our parents were alive, you gave them grief. I will not let you cause harm here."

"You will tell me that you, too, prefer a Saxon wench to me?"

"I do not know her well, but I am not deaf to what is said. She is loved in this hall. Be warned, Oriel, Royce will wed the girl, and he will hold to his vows." He turned from her, but not before she astutely saw the look of doubt in his eyes.

"Something has happened to make you doubt those words."

"Nay, nothing. I have simply come to warn you. I am your brother, and I would not see you come to harm." But he had heard Lynette's words, and knew if Oriel got wind of them she would believe her thinking was right. "Oriel, go to Royce and tell him you are sorry for any misunderstanding. Tell him you will look after the child more carefully. Even though he cannot bear the child now, the day will come when she will mean much to him."

"I find that hard to believe. Do you think I do not know that he still grieves for his wife? I think he would have been better served if the child had died with her."

"Oriel! For God's sake, watch your tongue. This is but a babe of which you speak."

"Well, no matter. Soon you will see whom he favors. I think he is displeased with the wench already. Let her arrogant ways bring her to grief. In time, I will be mistress here, and we will be well served."

"Speak for your own self, I am content being his friend and serving him. If nothing else, consider me when you are about your plans. I will not be party to deception."

"Have no fear, brother. I will go to Royce now. He will put the child back into my hands, and prove to the Saxon maid that she is little here but his slave."

Giles shook his head in exasperation but left the room without another word. Oriel went to her mirror to see that her hair was in order; then she went in search of Royce.

65

* * *

Robert and Royce walked for some distance, and though he was quiet, Robert knew quite well that Royce had a weighty problem on his mind . . . and he sensed what it was. He waited for Royce to speak first.

"Is it true, Robert?"

"That the child is unhappy? Yes, it is true. Does that worry you?"

"You are hard this day, old friend."

"I am tired of trying to prove to you the worth of life."

"We are not speaking of the worth of my life, but of the child."

"Why can you not think of her as Cerise? Does it make it easier for you if she is nameless as well as faceless?"

"I want to hear the truth of this."

"I do not know the truth for certain. I am not much in Cerise's company. Like you, I know of her from a distance."

"Robert—"

"Royce, listen to me. You hold a beast by the tail and you cannot let it go for you are afraid of the claws. I know how hard your having no father, no mother, has been on you. I know you blame yourself and the child for your loss. But still you will not leave her behind. Why? Because you cannot bear for Sybella's daughter to suffer. And yet she does suffer, for she knows her father. And knows he cannot look at her . . . doesn't want her. That must be worse than anything you have ever suffered."

"Robert"—Royce's voice was firm—"I will know the truth of this matter. If Lady Oriel is guilty, I must replace her."

66

"Then replace her with the Lady Lynette. She will one day be your wife, and I can already see she is kind of heart. I believe she will take the child to her and treat her fairly . . . Or are you afraid of just such a thing?"

"I have agreed to the king's demand, and I will do as I have pledged. Will nothing satisfy you?"

"Perhaps I would see you happy also," Robert said quietly.

"You are becoming like an old woman. Mayhap we need a little battle to put you back in good humor."

"I think," Robert laughed, "there is already a battle under way, and I am not too sure of the outcome."

Royce's gaze followed Robert's gesture, and they watched the horse and rider as they raced away from Creganwald.

"She rides well," Royce said, half to himself. Robert smiled. "I think it past time the Lady Lynette and I settled things between us," Royce added firmly.

"Aye." Again Robert smiled. He watched Royce walk to the stable. *Now, let us hope they don't kill each other before we can get them married. There are some things that might just be best settled in the bedchamber.*

Royce's destrier ate the distance Lynette had put between herself and Creganwald. He could follow her easily, for the little mare left a print that was easily distinguished. Soon she left the road and entered the forest surrounding Creganwald. It was a brisk winter day. A fresh snow had blanketed the land the night before, and had created a beautiful scene. It was not hard to spot her ahead of him through the leafless trees. He saw her stop and dismount to lead her horse for a while.

He knew the moment she heard his approach, for she turned toward him. She stood very still, but he was aware of her stiff posture and rigid control as he rode up to her.

"It is not safe for you to be riding the countryside alone, Lady Lynette."

"There is no one on this land who would do me harm. They are all mine."

"You speak easily, but what of intruders?"

"The only intruders here are Norman. Would they would go, and leave our land to us."

"It will never be so. It is time you understood that. There is something of great importance I would discuss with you."

"Ask what you will. I am but a slave who must obey."

"You are not a slave, Lady Lynette. You will be my wife. I am here to guard this land, and we must see to it together. But that is not the subject I wanted to discuss."

"How can I be of help to you?"

At first he looked at her with a guarded look that spoke of his distrust, but there was no guile in her eyes.

"Robert seems to set great store in you. He believes that you speak the truth."

"I need no one to say I speak the truth! Whether you choose to believe me or not is no concern of mine." She turned her back to him, and he drew in a deep breath. He had gotten off on the wrong foot again.

"Lady Lynette, the child—"

"Your daughter," Lynette said as she turned back to face him, her eyes filled with a puzzled look. "I have never known a father who would not even name his own."

"Have you known many knights who cannot name their fathers?" he asked angrily.

So, Lynette thought, that is the crux of the matter. His own bastardy is part of the problem . . . but there is more. . . . What?

She looked closely at him, and for the first time saw the shadows in his eyes. "Do you hate the child so, or is it the mother that you hated?"

"No," he said shortly. "I do not hate the child. I would protect her from harm."

"Protect her, but not give her what her heart seems to long for."

"You have known her but a few hours. How can you claim to know what her heart desires?"

"Her heart desires what every child's heart desires, a loving mother and father. She spoke of you with great pride. In fact, she told me you were the greatest and strongest knight the king had."

Royce had very seldom been silenced because of emotion, but he was now. This woman had a way of going to the heart of a matter and crushing all resistance in her way.

"She knows me little, lady. I have come to you to ask once again the truth of the matter."

"The truth, my lord, is this." Lynette went on to explain how she had found Cerise the night past, and this morning. "I took her to the kitchen, where she will be fed, and I gave orders that she is not to be handed over to your . . . to the Lady Oriel until I

69

return. She is but a babe," Lynette said softly. "Can she not have the run of the manor?"

"Is it not seemly that she be guarded?"

"Aye," Lynette said carefully. "And if you can bring yourself to trust me, I will see to her care."

"I had not thought you would want to be charged with the care of another Norman," he chided.

"She is but a babe," Lynette reminded him again, "and she knows not the hatred between Norman and Saxon. She is innocent, and should not bear punishment." Lynette looked up into his golden gaze. "Not for any cause."

"She is my child," he said softly.

"That is a matter to be debated. Surely it takes more than a single act to make a man a father."

"You have sharp claws, demoiselle. But I must see them sheathed. Whether you will it or not, there will be a wedding . . . and a babe. This is the king's will."

And what of your will, Norman? she wondered. She remembered her threat to harm herself rather than bear his child. She looked at him in defiance.

"I will not carry my threat out. But now that I have seen how you treat the child you have, I can only wish that I will prove barren."

With this she walked to her horse. She felt him come up behind her and thought he meant to help her mount. Instead he spun her about so fast she only had time to gasp before she was crushed against a chest that felt like iron. She was enclosed in two hard arms from which it would have been futile to try to escape.

Her eyes lifted to his and saw his intent. She had

only time to cry "no" once before his mouth took hers in a kiss that spun her world out of control. She was lifted against him while his lips played havoc with her thoughts. Slowly, leisurely, he savored her lips, until she felt that if he let her go she would collapse. Still he continued his assault until she moaned in surrender, and her arms went about him. She surrendered to the uncoiling heat that was filling her. She could not resist the heady taste of him and the strength that took away her breath and her thoughts.

As suddenly as he had taken her, he released her. He put his hands about her slender waist to lift her into the saddle.

For a moment she could only look down into his eyes, eyes filled with silent laughter. So he thought one kiss would undo her. His utter conceit filled her with such a wave of hot rage that she lashed out with the end of her reins. The leather caught him across the cheek and drew a fine line of blood. He did not raise a hand to touch his face. Instead he smiled a smile that turned her heart to ice and sent a shiver of fear through her

"I will be master here. Creganwald will be William's, and you will come to my bed, willing or no. When the rule of Creganwald is secure, I will leave you in peace, demoiselle, for I have no hunger to be wed any more than you do. But understand this. What is mine, I hold. There is no need for your interference in my affairs."

She felt anger at her own helplessness. He did not want her, nor the child of his loins. Would he want a child of her body? She thought not. When William was satisfied, Royce would leave Creganwald. At that moment she hated William with every sense she had.

Lynette urged her horse into motion, and Royce stood immobile, watching her until she disappeared from sight.

Chapter Six

On her return from her ride, Lynette went directly to the kitchen, where she found Cerise the center of attraction. She had been warmed, not only by the fire but by the attention she had received. She had responded to it like a flower to water.

Lynette worried how the little girl would react if she were forced to go back to Oriel. With her jaw clenched in determination, she decided to take Cerise to her chamber with her. If Oriel wanted the girl, she would have to come and get her, and Lynette would make it as difficult for her as possible.

She was distressed that she no longer ruled in this hall, and that her orders could be countermanded by someone as cruel as Oriel.

Once settled in her chamber, Lynette set about putting Cerise in order. She brushed her long mink-colored hair until it gleamed, then braided it carefully in two long braids. While she did, she listened to the child's chatter.

As the time for the midday meal approached, there was still no sign of Oriel.

"Cerise, would you like to go outside for a while? I could show you where we slide down the hill, and where the ice is on the stream."

"Oh, yes!" Cerise's face lit, and her eyes turned worshipfully toward Lynette.

"Then you must dress very warm, and find your warmest boots. Run back to your chamber and get them."

Cerise sat immobile for a moment, the smile disappearing from her face.

"Cerise, do hurry or we will be called to the midday meal before we get a chance to have any fun."

But still Cerise didn't move. Then she looked up at Lynette again. "If . . . if I go back to my chamber, will she be there? She won't let me go."

Lynette stood up resolutely. "Come, I'll go with you. There will be no problem."

But there was no sign of Oriel, and Lynette waited while Cerise put on her warm clothes. The two slipped from the hall like a pair of conspirators. Soon Cerise's laughter filled the air as Lynette displayed how she would take a short run, then slide across the frozen ice of the stream. With flushed face and happy laughter, Cerise played like a child for the first time in her memory.

Within the hall, Royce and Lynette's father were discussing the condition of the manor itself, and the serfs outside it. Eldwyn was relieved that Royce seemed to understand everything and was supplying new ideas for the improvement of the manor.

Eldwyn looked on Royce with new eyes. He

began to believe that this man could hold his land and care for it as well as he could. Finally Royce brought up a subject he had been skirting: Lynette.

"You have educated your daughter beyond what is usual, Lord Eldwyn."

"Aye," Eldwyn laughed. "But Lynette is a stubborn lass, with a mind quicker than most men's. She was a shadow to her older brothers, following them from their play to their teachers. She was hungry to learn, and neither I nor they saw the harm in it. I am grateful now, for she has been the heart of this place."

"You had three older sons?"

"Aye, but the plague took them from me. Now I have the consolation of Lynette."

"I am William's man. Since you have no sons, if . . . when this wedding is over, I will most likely be away much of the time. I will see that you are left well armed, and with men to protect you."

Eldwyn gazed at the younger man thoughtfully. He knew quite well that all here were subject to this man, but he also knew that Royce was as reluctant to go through with this wedding as Lynette.

"Lynette is a woman of great pride. She is not one to be tossed aside when she has served her purpose. Look very closely, and you will see a woman who would make this place a refuge and comfort for you. When I am gone, Lynette will be bereft of family. She is of sensitive nature, Royce. It would go hard with her to be used like a slave."

"Sometimes there are things in life that must be suffered. We all have our duties. Lynette's is to marry and produce a son to rule here. This child will be half Norman, and will one day be master here in William's name."

"And you will steal Lynette's birthright?" Eldwyn said quietly.

"As far as that is concerned, her birthright is already gone. Lynette will be my wife, and you will have to be content to live here under Norman rule."

"I beg you, sir, leave Lynette her pride. You would not want her to consider herself chattel, to be used and discarded like a —"

"As my wife, Lynette will be given all that the lady of this hall is due."

"And she will have to be content with a husband who is more away than present." Eldwyn was angry. "Tell me, Lord, will you come back often enough to keep Lynette with child, or is one heir enough for your king?"

"Hold your tongue," Royce said coldly. "I seek one heir. From that moment on, Lynette will be free to spend her days in contentment here."

"Do you mean"—Eldwyn's face was crimson—"that you think her free to choose a lover?"

"No, I meant no such thing. Lynette will be my wife. She will keep her reputation unsullied."

"Then it is a life of loneliness you condemn her to, not one with a husband to comfort her older years. She will be a shadow of your authority."

Royce felt he was getting himself deeply involved in a subject he had not wanted to discuss in the first place. He was about to put a firm end to the conversation, when Oriel came into the room. Both men looked at her with a sigh of relief.

"Lady Oriel," Royce said as he rose to his feet. It was then he noticed Oriel's flushed face and angry eyes.

"Royce, I warned you the wench was a sneak. She has taken the child and gone."

"Gone?" Royce said blankly. "Gone where?"

"I know not. I only know she came and took the child's warmest clothes, so I believe she intends to travel as far as she can."

Royce cast a quick, angry look at a dumbfounded Eldwyn, and started from the hall.

"Lord?" Oriel spoke as he passed her.

"Yes?"

"I have done the child no harm. I fear you have thought me hard on her, but I have only tried to teach her her place."

"I will find them, Oriel," Royce said grimly.

"And entrust the child to me again?"

Royce looked down into her eyes. "I will do what is best . . . and my daughter's name is Cerise." He strode away, and Oriel turned a satisfied look on a scowling Eldwyn.

"You may create more of a problem than you are prepared to handle, Lady Oriel. Tread carefully. Those in this hall are not as weak and full of fear as you may believe. Lynette would never steal away from the manor like a thief in the night," Eldwyn said. "Nor would she drag the child away. More likely she has found some entertainment for the little one."

"She is not yet wed to Royce, and it is not her place to entertain his daughter. The child was left in my care."

"Then," Eldwyn said mildly, "it seems your care is inadequate if the child prefers the company of another she hardly knows."

Sylvie Sommerfield

Eldwyn's voice was taunting, and Oriel's face flushed as she turned from him and walked from the room.

When Royce reached the stable, his fear was confirmed. Lynette's mare was gone. He had his horse saddled at once. Did she think it would be a simple thing to take the child and run to . . . where? Where did she really believe would be safe from his vengeance? If she thought to hold his child as hostage, she would find he did not react mildly to the theft of what was his.

He rode away from the hall, again following the prints of the mare. He held his anger in control. This time he would have to teach her a lesson, and the thought was unsettling.

He crossed the open expanse of ground and entered the woods, and the tracks continued. Before he reached the far edge of the woods, he heard the sound of laughter. It was still at some distance so he continued on.

When he broke from the trees, he drew his destrier to a halt and gazed in both surprise and amusement at the scene that unfolded before him.

Like two children, Lynette and Cerise were taking turns sliding across the ice. They were playing. The thought brought an unwelcome twinge of pain.

He watched them for several minutes, not wanting to disturb their pleasure. He could not turn and leave, and he could not continue on. He was in an emotional dilemma.

Then Cerise saw him. She stopped immediately, drawing Lynette's attention. She, too, stopped and stood still. It was then that it came to her that his searching them out was the best thing that could happen. He spent no time with his daughter, and had put her in the care of a dreadful woman. Now it was time he looked into his daughter's eyes and faced his reluctance to be with her. A reluctance whose cause was still a mystery to Lynette.

"It's Papa." Cerise breathed the words with a kind of awe. This man was only a shadow in her life, and Lynette realized Cerise looked at him as if he were a god who could not be approached.

"Yes," Lynette replied. "Shall we ask him to join us?"

Cerise's gasp of shock only made Lynette more determined. She waved to Royce, knowing he could not ignore them now. She was pleased when the huge horse started slowly in their direction.

When Royce drew his destrier to a stop, he studiously kept his gaze from Cerise, who was watching him with wide eyes and the look of a doe about to flee.

"Lady Lynette, it would be wise to inform us when you decide to leave the hall. You have everyone in a state of confusion. It was thought that you were trying to escape."

"Escape, my lord? To where? Where is there a place of sanctuary that the Sword of William cannot reach? Nay, my lord, I only took *the child* to play. It seems play has not been part of her life." Lynette turned to Cerise and smiled. She meant to force this tall, formidable man to look his daughter in the eye. "Ask her yourself, my lord. Hear the truth of it from her own lips."

Royce had little choice but to look down into the violet pools of his daughter's eyes. The experience jolted him with a memory of other violet eyes that had looked at him in trust. The jolt was painful, but Lynette's gaze would not let him retreat.

"You are enjoying your play?" he asked Cerise stiffly.

"A-aye . . . P-papa."

The soft sound of her hesitant voice calling him Papa hurt like the cut of a broadsword. He was frightening her, and he found that painful as well. "You are not cold?"

"N-n-no, Papa. It is so much fun. Must . . . must I go back?"

"Do you want to?"

"No."

"Then stay." He knew his words were abrupt and cold, but the glow of Cerise's eyes made it appear as if he had been the best of all fathers.

Lynette saw that he was about to leave, and she could not allow it. Cerise's future was at stake . . . and his.

"I am afraid it is colder than she believes. It is time to go back and find her something warm to eat." She saw the disappointment in Cerise's eyes, and regretted the necessity of ending their play. "I am afraid it is very difficult for me to manage the child and ride. The ride out was too dangerous. Would you take her in front of you for the ride back?"

He would have crushed the child by his refusal, and Lynette knew he would not do that. "Yes, lift her up to me."

Lynette was so pleased she could have sung, and Cerise was sure her little heart was going to burst with the pleasures this day had brought. Lynette lifted the child; and Royce nestled her comfortably before him, tucking his warm cloak about her. She felt as if she were so high above the ground she could fly, and the strong arm that supported her was . . . her father's!

Lynette mounted, and the three rode back to the manor in silence. When they arrived, Royce dismounted, bringing Cerise with him with an easy move. He stood her on her feet, and looked at Lynette.

"Take Cerise in and see she is warmed. See to yourself as well, demoiselle. See that the child has a warm meal, then join us for your meal."

They were back to "the child" again, Lynette thought furiously. Royce was not unaware of her fury, either: it was vividly displayed in her smoldering eyes and pink cheeks.

Lynette took care of Cerise's needs, then walked down the stairs to join the group of hungry men at the table. She was dismayed to see Oriel there, too. Would Royce make it clear to all that Oriel was his daughter's guardian?

Oriel gazed at Lynette with a feral gleam of satisfaction in her eyes. Her look promised as much punishment as was in her power to mete out. Lynette was frightened that Cerise would suffer most of her ire.

"I have made several decisions today," Royce announced. "One concerns you, Lady Oriel."

Lynette clenched her hands in her lap. She was not going to let this pass without a battle. Cerise was beginning to trust her, and Lynette felt her trust was not easily gained anymore. She glanced at Oriel only once; she could not bear the look of satisfaction in her eyes.

"Within two weeks, the Lady Lynette and I will be wed. I think it is time the lady began to consider her duties to me, and eventually to this hall." Lynette's cheeks grew pinker. Did he think she would shirk her duties? Was he subtly insulting her? "I think that it is also time she begin her duties as mother to Cerise . . . my daughter. From this time hence, the child will be in your care, Lady Lynette. Lady Oriel, do not think this is a slight to you. You have done what has been demanded of you with no hesitation. But I believe, if the child is to make this place her home and Lady Lynette her mother, they should spend their days in each other's company."

Lynette smiled at Royce with gratitude in her eyes. She would thank him at the first opportunity, and continue to bring as much happiness to Cerise as she could.

But her euphoria was short-lived, for when they were leaving the table, Royce put out a hand to stop her.

"It is clear the child is developing some fondness for you. I am pleased that it is so. Your father tells me that you are well educated. I would be grateful if you were to educate her to the best of your ability."

"You need not have asked me to do that. I had intended to do my best by the child. Thank you, Royce."

"For what?"

"For believing me," Lynette said softly.

"Do not thank me too soon, demoiselle. It is still my wish that you keep her from under my feet . . . in your chambers if possible. Do you understand?"

"Yes." Lynette held his gaze with hers. "But there is another thing you must take into consideration."

"Oh?"

"We will wed. I know that is an established fact. But what will you do when we are man and wife? Cerise is going to be part of my life, and so she will become part of yours with your will or not. I will not teach her to care for me and then shut her from my life as if she were less than human. It appears she will be under your feet much more than you had planned. Perhaps you should give this wedding more consideration. I am not averse to being the child's companion, but it would grieve me to bear a child and have it treated thus."

Lynette walked away from him, and felt his eyes following her as she did.

Chapter Seven

For the next two weeks, Lynette did exactly as Royce had ordered. She skillfully kept out of his way, and made a point of sharing her meals with Cerise in her own chambers.

At first Royce was satisfied. But he soon discovered he was looking at each open doorway as if he expected her to fill it at any moment. He could not banish the memory of that day at the creek when he had first heard her unrestrained laughter. He remembered also a pair of childish violet eyes, and with annoyance he remembered the fear in them.

The day's business went on smoothly, which annoyed him even more. A problem or two might have diverted his thoughts from Lynette and Cerise. He thought of his daughter's name, and realized he had not given it to her, that her mother must have named her before . . .

His thoughts were just as confused about Lynette. She had never denied him, and she would come to their marriage without force. The old fear struck. Would he have to watch another woman sacrifice her life to give birth to his babe? The very thought brought a trembling to his hands, and a sheen of sweat to his brow.

He had argued with himself a million times over. It was a woman's place to give birth, and she knew the chances she took and must trust God and fate to see her through. No, it was his own guilt that shook him. He had taken Sybella's life, for he had known, as she had known, that the danger for her was greater than for another woman of more robust health.

He thought of Lynette, who seemed to glow with vitality and life. He was so engrossed in his dilemma that he did not hear anyone approach.

"There is a messenger with word from William." Robert carried the packet in his hand, and handed it to Royce, closely scrutinizing his face. "You are well, Royce?"

"Aye, Robert, I am well. It is this enforced inactivity that sets me on edge."

"Of course," Robert agreed so readily that Royce gave him a sharp look.

"All goes well with the men?"

"They are content," Robert replied. "Your lady has seen to every problem and to every comfort. Why, Sir Alaine is smitten with her, and even that old fox Sir Ferragus dotes on her every move and would go off to do her bidding if she but said the word."

"All this has transpired, and I have seen no sign of the maid in the past days?"

"She but reminds us that it is your wish that the

child not be seen, and since she is loath to leave the girl, she takes her meals in her chambers. But they are about every day, just . . . "

"Just not within my sight," Royce said in a strained voice.

"Aye. It is your command . . . not hers," Robert said smugly.

"Then if my every command is to be obeyed," Royce said sarcastically, "let the maid know that I wish her to be present at supper this night."

"Ah . . . Royce I do not believe she will come."

"Oh?"

"You know that the child—"

"Cerise," Royce said with a frown.

"Cerise," Robert repeated. He could hardly keep his face in control. He wanted to smile. This was the first time Royce had said his daughter's name within his hearing. "Lady Lynette is careful of her feelings. She will not have the . . . Cerise . . . slighted."

"Slighted! She has never been slighted! I have seen that she has all the care any child should have. She is dressed well, fed well. . . . Robert, tell the wench to bring the child to supper too. This is her home as much as ours. Or will she not obey that order either?"

"It would be best if the order came from you. She knows well that we would have enjoyed her company long before this. I don't know if she will think it our will, and something that might anger you."

Royce cast Robert an exasperated look and turned from him. "Well enough, I will inform her."

"Aye."

"Robert, you are really an old fox."

"Aye." Robert smiled broadly.

Royce opened the message from William and read. His face gave no sign of the contents. He didn't seem too happy about the news, and Robert wasn't too sure whether he should ask about it or not. But Royce put an end to his doubts.

"For the wedding William bids me bring Lynette with me to London. It will be put off for another month."

"This should prove of interest to the lady."

"You will not mention it to her, or to anyone."

"Royce?"

"Leave be, Robert, I have my reasons. Word of this message is to remain between us for now."

"As you will," Robert replied, but he was puzzled.

"I have a task to perform. See to the armory. It has been brought to my attention that the arms are not in good enough condition, or in sufficient quantities to protect this manor in case of a revolt."

"I will see to it at once."

Robert watched Royce walk away from him with a frown.

Royce climbed the steps to his chamber, and when he closed the door behind him, he was again struck by the emptiness and loneliness of it. He longed for activity to draw him away from the shadows.

He leaned against the door for a few minutes, then turned abruptly and left. He had no idea whether he would find Lynette in her own chamber or in Cerise's, so he checked the child's room first. It was empty. Leaving it, he walked resolutely toward Lynette's.

The door stood a little ajar, and soft voices floated

through. He did not mean to listen, but Cerise's words brought him to a stop before he could push open the door.

"It does not matter if he does not like me. I know I am not pretty . . . and I'm not a boy. I know everybody likes boys better than girls anyway."

"Cerise, who ever told you you were not pretty?"

"Lady Oriel told me that I was ugly and my papa would never want to see me. She said my mother wanted a boy, and so did my papa. They did not want an ugly little girl. That is why I had to stay in her chamber when Papa was at home. She said my mother was pretty. I wish . . . "

"What, Cerise? What do you wish?"

"I wish that Papa would like me . . . just a little bit," the little girl said wistfully.

"You must not listen to Lady Oriel. You are very pretty, and when you grow up, you are going to be as beautiful as a princess. And didn't your papa bring you home the day we went sliding? And he held you before him on his horse, and he did speak to you. You must remember that your papa is a very important man to King William, and he has many weighty things on his mind."

"You asked him to carry me back," Cerise said promptly, "but it was fun, and his horse is so big. I'll bet only Papa can ride him. He is the strongest and most wonderful knight anywhere."

Royce felt the same deep twisting in his chest, and the breath caught in his throat. Ugly! Oriel had told Cerise she was ugly, and that he did not like to look at her. Self-hatred filled him, and did battle with his guilt. He could not find the courage to look into his daughter's eyes, for he was afraid he would see unselfish love there, and that would undo him.

How could she love him when he had done his best to ignore her?

Slowly he pushed the door wider so he could view the occupants without their being aware of him. Lynette sat on a small stool in front of the low-burning fire, and Cerise sat on the floor with her back to Lynette, who was brushing her hair. The sight of her lovely mink-colored hair tore at him.

Then his attention was drawn to Lynette, who was framed by the light of the fire. Her hair was like a golden halo, and the fire kissed her skin to a warm flush. Her slender body was a curved silhouette that stirred an unwelcome warmth within him. In a little more time she would be his wife. He had to resist a sudden flood of desire that struck him unexpectedly. He fought it into submission. Desire was something he would not take to the marriage bed.

It was then Lynette sensed a presence. She stopped the brush in midstroke, and this caused Cerise to turn to see what had distracted her. When she saw her father in the doorway, Lynette could feel her stiffen. She put a calming hand on Cerise's shoulder. "My lord?"

"It is my wish that you and . . . Cerise join us for supper this evening," he said, trying to make the request sound less cold and stiff than it did.

"Aye, my lord, if that is your wish." She spoke with a calmness that only annoyed him.

Royce had never been indecisive before in his life, and he could not believe that he felt a strong desire to join them on the floor and be part of their conversation . . . at least long enough to convince Cerise that Oriel had lied to her.

"It is. There is word from the king I will share with you then."

"I will be prompt."

Royce was annoyed with her calm and detached attitude. It was as if she could not wait for him to leave. Worse, his daughter's eyes were on him, wide and still filled with shadowy fear. It was a look he could not bear.

"Good," he replied, then left, closing the door behind him.

Lynette gave a satisfied smile. After a few minutes she continued her brushing. Tonight she intended to make Cerise as pretty as it was possible for the child to be.

It was midafternoon, and Lynette had insisted that Cerise sleep for a while so that she would not be tired later. She meant for the child to be at her best.

She had left Cerise's chamber and started for her own when the sound of her name being called made her turn to see Robert walking toward her.

"Lady Lynette, can we finish that conversation we began?"

"Of course, Sir Robert."

"Can we go somewhere more. . . . private?"

"Are we by any chance conspiring?" She smiled as she spoke, and he smiled in return.

"I would not be a bit surprised, Lady, not a bit surprised at all."

Lynette led him to her chamber, where she closed the door, then turned to face him.

"And now about your conspiracy, Sir Robert?"

"Not exactly that, my lady. Rather, say I speak for the benefit of a man I would gladly call son."

"Royce?"

"Aye."

"Why? Why do you come to me? Our union has been decided by his king. Who am I do deny what William has decreed? I must marry and produce an heir. After that I'm sure Royce's interest in me shall wane, and he will find other places that need his attention."

"Do not be so angry with him, my lady." Robert's gray eyes softened. "He did not choose this. William and I are responsible. If he had his way, Royce would choose never to marry again."

"Sir Robert, was his wife disloyal to him? Is that the reason he does not trust or care for any woman?"

"No. Let me tell you the truth of it. A truth he cannot exorcise from his soul. It is killing him . . . or rather leading him to do the deed himself."

Lynette's face went pale. "That is against the very heart of the church."

"Aye, and so he would wield his sword and let another do it for him."

"That is wrong!"

"Lady Lynette, will you listen?"

"Aye," Lynette said softly. She sagged onto a stool, and waited.

"I would tell you of a boy who never knew a father or mother, in fact, knew little of the gentleness of love. He was raised by a lord who felt a strong hand could train, and love was not necessary. He learned the ways of men, but not the gentle ways of women. Even the woman who was responsible for his care, the old lord's wife, was cold and ungiving.

Into this barren and hard existence came a lady . . . Sybella. She was sweet and sensitive and she loved him so completely, even he could not believe it. She was as delicate as a butterfly, and he gave her his heart and his soul.

"But she was as fragile as that same butterfly, and both of them were warned that she was not strong enough to bear a child. Though he longed for a son, he would not allow it. He knew that doctors or midwives could help her prevent conception, and he pleaded with her for caution. But, you see, her love for him was as complete as his for her. He wanted a son and she wanted to give one to him. And she knew his desire for a son was an unselfish one. He wanted a child on which to shower all the love he had locked inside during his own childhood."

Robert inhaled a deep breath. He was not used to having a loose tongue or revealing another's secrets. He prayed that if Royce found out, he would be able to forgive him one day.

He looked down into Lynette's sky blue eyes and saw compassion and deep interest. He continued slowly as he walked toward the window.

"She didn't tell him of her condition until he guessed it for himself. He was frightened, and this in itself was tragic for a man who had never tasted fear in his life. He would watch her, spend every possible hour with her, and even go to the chapel with her. I know he prayed more fervently for her life than for the babe she carried. Then she was brought to childbed. They tried to make him leave, but he refused. He suffered with her, and wept when the truth came. She died giving birth to Cerise, and he has been dying every day since. He gave her a part of himself he cannot seem to find again, and he is afraid to love . . . it is too painful an emotion for him. As for the child . . . it seems he blames himself—and the child for taking the light of his life and creating a darkness in which he has lived ever since."

There was a poignant silence when Robert's voice died away. He looked at Lynette, who was unashamedly weeping.

"How terrible for him and for Cerise," she said softly. "What a price love has exacted from him."

"So you see, Lady Lynette, why it was Royce's name I put before William? I have forced him into a situation he does not relish, because I know that not just his, but Cerise's future too is at stake."

"But I am not the one who can save him. He must accept his daughter's love, and see that her need for him far surpasses his need for forgiveness."

"You have much wisdom for one so young. I had hoped you could find a common ground between them, for they need each other."

"I will do everything in my power, Sir Robert. I wonder if Royce knows what a friend he has in you?"

"To speak truthfully, Lady Lynette, there are many days and nights that I have wished heartily that he had never known Sybella's love, for he may never find his way back from his loss."

"He is a strong man. Did you know he came to my chamber?"

"No."

"To ask both Cerise and me to join him for supper. I have never heard him speak to her, except a word or two the day he found us by the creek, but today he did. It was not all we would have wished, but it is a beginning."

"It is no less than a miracle, Lady."

"Sir Robert, I still cannot understand. Why did he not turn to the child to help him fill the void? Surely she loves him still?"

Robert sighed. "Because Cerise is a mirror image of her mother. When he looks at her, he sees Sybella."

"Poor Cerise. She believes he cannot, or will not, look at her because she is ugly, and a girl."

"She told you this?"

"Aye," Lynette said angrily, "but the thought came from the Lady Oriel."

"Lady Oriel," Robert said in disgust. "I have never taken to her. She is too much like the old lord's wife." Robert did not look directly at Lynette, and that brought a question to her lips.

"Does the Lady Oriel . . . look to him for more than the guardianship of his daughter?"

"That is more truth than that she likes to care for the child."

"And Royce, does he . . . ?"

"If he takes a vow with you, Lady Lynette, trust this. He will not break it. He will not dishonor you . . . or take a mistress."

"It would be less my dishonor than his own, Sir Robert. For myself, any vows said before God will be binding."

"Aye, Lady. That I believe, and that is what he needs."

"We are, then, conspirators."

"Lady, I would conspire to bring him a peace he has not known since Sybella. If that is your wish, then we are indeed conspirators. I ask you this, Lady. Take the time to know him and to judge for yourself. Take the time to know and love the child, for she is truly innocent in this, and she needs him as much as he needs her."

"Aye, and she loves him so unconditionally that she has taken the blame on her shoulders that he does not love her."

"You bring the child to supper tonight then?"

"Without doubt, and looking her prettiest. I suspect the Lady Oriel will be present?"

"No doubt," Robert replied with venom. "She thinks the way is open now since the care of the child falls to you. She would wind her way into his bed, and through his own sense of honor force herself into his life."

"Well . . . we shall see."

Chapter Eight

Robert left Lynette's chamber, drawing the door closed behind him. He had a satisfied feeling that was abruptly dispelled by a soft and venomous voice.

"So, Sir Robert. Already the lady plays her games. Have you spent a pleasant afternoon? Tell me, do Royce's other knights have the same . . . advantages?"

"Lady Oriel," Robert said quietly as he turned to face her. He wondered if she had been listening at the door. "You should not judge others by your own motives, Lady," he said coldly. "The lady is above reproach, and there is no question of *her* honor." He watched with great satisfaction as Oriel's face grew livid.

"The Saxon is no more than a slave, forced down his throat by William. I have little doubt that you had a hand in it as well. All that is important here are her lands. All know that her father has been ill. I have seen his kind of illness before. He has difficulty getting his breath and grimaces from the pain in his chest. If she does not recognize his imminent death, I do. The lands are valuable to William. Royce can hold her lands and still take a wife of his own kind instead of that woman, who will most likely slide a knife between his ribs one night. He will be bound only by his oath to William. He'll search out his comfort where it is welcome, and realize his mistake."

"Ah, Lady," Robert replied with amusement, "being bound by his oath is something you will never understand, since you have never been bound by aught but your own whims and desires. His oath, madam, is binding enough to satisfy me . . . for he will break his oath to no man . . . or woman. Remember, she will bear his title."

"Yes, his title." She smiled. "But I wager she will bear nothing more. He will not have it, and we both know why. She will be little more than his wife in name, and the keeper of a child he cannot bear to see. He loathes the child, and if the maid becomes attached to the brat, he will loathe her as well."

"Are you frightened, Lady Oriel?" Robert asked softly. "Can you see, as I do, that the day will come when he can put away his grief? When that day does come, it is this very maid he will turn to, for she will be his wife. The day will come when he will look at Cerise with love, and bring his daughter to him. That day will also be the end of your presence here. Are you afraid, Lady Oriel?" he repeated.

"Do not be so certain, Sir Robert," Oriel said

coldly. "Another day may come before you can bring your plans to fruition. Maybe . . . sooner than you think."

Oriel brushed past him, and only after she was gone did the smile fade from Robert's eyes. He knew this lady too well to take any threat she made lightly. But what harm could she cause? The thought worried him.

Lynette found the prettiest clothes that Cerise possessed, and carefully braided her hair. She could tell that Cerise was very nervous. The child followed every move Lynette made as she, too, dressed in her finest. She followed her with an anxious and wary look, as if she expected Lynette to desert her and leave her to the mercy of the great group of huge, imposing men who would be seated at her father's table.

Lynette finally smiled down at her when it was time to leave their chamber. "You are very pretty, Cerise. I'm sure your papa will be proud of you. You remember everything I have told you?"

"Aye," Cerise said hesitantly. "I am to mind my manners and to speak only when I am spoken to."

Lynette had cautioned her to this for the simple reason that she wanted it to be Royce who acknowledged Cerise by addressing her first.

As they walked down the stairs, the strong voices and laughter of men rose to meet them. Cerise paused, and Lynette could feel her tremble

"Cerise," she said softly, "there will be many times in your life when you will have to face problems with nothing more than your own courage. Remember, you will be the daughter of the Lord of

Creganwald. As such you are expected to have courage and faith. I believe your father will not deny your courage if you display it."

"What if he does not speak to me?"

"Then you will eat your meal, smile, and be as pleasant and sweet as you can be. There are others among his men who would be your friend. Speak to them and see the result. Remember to be proud of what and who you are. Others will know by your actions that your papa has a good and gracious daughter."

Cerise nodded and tried to gather her courage, but Lynette could see how difficult it was. She was a grown woman, and Royce could have a drastic effect on her; she could well imagine how the child felt. But she could see the forming of determination and this pleased her. Cerise was no coward.

When the two entered the room, a hush fell over it. Lynette could have laughed in exultation when she saw Cerise's chin lift and her shoulders straighten as she walked toward the table with all the pride of a princess.

The tables were formed like an open-ended box. At the center table, Royce sat, with Eldwyn next to him and Sir Giles next to her father. The two seats on his other side were empty, and Robert sat where he would be next to either Lynette or Cerise. The seat next to Robert was occupied by Oriel, whose face struggled to contain her wrath.

She had come to the hall a few minutes earlier and tried to occupy the chair next to Cerise. Robert knew her viper tongue would soon reduce the child to tears, so he had taken the chair that would put him between Cerise and her.

Lynette was wise enough not to put Cerise next to Royce. For now she would sit between them, a buffer.

But Royce paid little attention to their arrival . . . or so it seemed, as he engaged Eldwyn in conversation. But he was acutely aware of their arrival. He had watched their progress across the room, and for a long moment his eyes had dwelt upon his daughter.

A weary pain seemed to slowly fill him, and he dragged his eyes away. She was beautiful, and he had meant to tell her so, to ease her lonely child's heart and give her some assurance. But another pair of violet eyes filled his mind, and the soft, moaning cry of a woman as her life slipped away.

"Lady Lynette," he said, "does the child have a mount of her own?"

"Nay, my lord, I believe not."

"Then we will see to it tomorrow. I would have you teach her to ride, since I am well aware you ride exceedingly well."

"I shall do my best," Lynette replied, but her heart ached for the little girl who would have given her soul for one glance or word. The meal continued, and soon the murmur of conversation began to flow about them.

Robert knew Royce better than anyone else. He knew Royce was struggling to keep his gaze from wandering toward Lynette and the small creature beside her.

Unaccustomed to meals at the main table, and in such a large group, Cerise was too nervous not to make a mistake. Her goblet was larger than her small hand could manage, and though she struggled to follow Lynette's lead and put it down gently, it tipped and fell. Cerise's eyes grew wide and she clenched her hands in her lap.

"Such disgraceful manners," Oriel exclaimed. "It would be best if you are kept to your chambers until you have learned how to conduct yourself."

Cerise's eyes filled with tears. But Lynette was enraged.

"At least the child has her youth to blame for not having perfected her manners. They will be corrected with care. It is the lack of manners in one of your . . . advanced years that is unforgivable. Surely you have been taught better than to insult the daughter of your lord. Or mayhap your education has been neglected. If so . . . I shall be glad to inform you."

Robert wanted desperately to shout his laughter; Sir Alaine choked on his wine, while broad smiles were hidden behind hands and with bowed heads.

Oriel's face reddened, and she looked at Royce, who was regarding her with a dark frown.

"The child has not shared our table before, Lady Oriel, and mayhap she is a little nervous. Her manners are quite suitable. It is unnecessary to call any lack to her attention. It is not her fault that her training is not as it should have been. I trust Lady Lynette is doing her best to rectify the matter. She will be at table with us for all meals from now on."

"Of course," Oriel said with feigned deference. "I was but trying to counsel her, my lord."

"It is best to counsel with gentleness and in private, Lady Oriel, or the learning is only made more difficult."

"Until this moment my tutoring has been adequate," Oriel said coldly.

"Aye, but tutoring falls to a child's . . . mother. Since that is impossible and Lady Lynette will soon become my wife, the situation will be hers to deal with. You will be relieved of duties that have restricted you. You will have time to yourself to follow pursuits of your choosing. I am grateful for your time and devotion. You will always have my thanks."

Oriel knew that she was momentarily beaten. She could see it in Lynette's eyes, and in the nearly worshipful look with which Cerise was regarding Royce. She could do little but smile and accept what he said with good grace, but Robert did not like the look in her eyes. He began to wonder if Lynette would be the target of her vengeance. He meant to keep a close eye on both her and Cerise.

It was then that Cerise could restrain herself no longer.

"Can I truly have a mount of my own and ride with Lady Lynette, Papa?"

Robert held his breath. Lynette closed her eyes and silently prayed. *Don't crush her now . . . please . . . please.* Royce turned to look at Cerise, and again the violet eyes played havoc with his mind. But he struggled to fight the vision, and the misery it brought.

"Yes . . . Cerise . . . you shall have a mount of your own, and if the Lady Lynette is willing, she can give you instructions in riding. It . . . it would please me if you will learn all that she is willing to teach."

"I shall learn, Papa. Anything you want me to learn . . . anything." Cerise's voice held a longing that even Royce could not miss.

A wave of fierce guilt washed over him, but it was a redeeming guilt. He had loved Sybella, and had caused her pain and suffering and ultimately her death. Now he was causing as much pain in their child . . . her child. The delicate and pretty creature who looked at him from Sybella's eyes saw only the father she needed. She did not condemn, but regarded him with such a look of love that he flinched before it.

"Cerise, it is enough that you learn what Lady Lynette thinks adequate for a child of your years." He turned his gaze on Lynette. "You will agree to this, demoiselle?"

"Aye, my lord. Cerise is a very intelligent young girl. It will be a pleasure to instruct her."

Royce seemed content with this and returned his attention to his food. The meal was, to Cerise, the highlight of her life, and she began to brighten when, as the table was cleared, others came to speak to Lynette and occasionally spoke to her.

When the meal was over, Lynette decided Cerise had had all she could manage for one night. She excused herself and Cerise from the small group that surrounded them and started for the stairs. But before they could go up, Lynette's name was called. They both turned to see Royce walking toward them.

"I should like you to join me in the morning. I ride out to survey the extent of the land and its condition. Since, as your father tells me, you have seen to the manor for the past two years, you are best informed to aid me."

"Aye, my lord. At what hour would you like to ride?"

"As early as possible."

Royce was caught by a mischievous smile that twitched the corners of her mouth. "I have been known to ride even before the sun rises."

"Well enough," he agreed. "I will break my fast with you at sunrise. Sleep well, Lady Lynette." Lynette paused, then took Cerise's hand and started up again. "Cerise?" His voice was gentle, and both Cerise and Lynette turned again. "Good night."

Cerise was sure her heart would burst. He had given her care to Lynette, he had promised her a mount of her own with instructions in riding, and he had come to her rescue at Oriel's attack. Now he was wishing her a pleasant good night. It was all her little heart could bear. Standing two steps above him, she came eye to eye with him. Impulsively, she bent forward and placed a shy and delicate kiss on his cheek.

"Good night, Papa." Then she was gone, and Royce stood stunned. His gaze returned to Lynette, who had just realized that Cerise had done the perfect thing at the perfect time.

"Good night, my lord."

Royce remained silent, but he watched the gentle sway of her hips as she climbed the stairs, and fought the confusion that filled him. He called her name before she reached the top, and she again turned to look down at him.

"William has sent word. The wedding is to be postponed another month. When he goes to London, he requires our presence there. He means to stand at our wedding."

"Does he fear that he will not see the deed done?"

"Nay." Royce smiled for the first time. "There is

no fear of that, demoiselle. You, and Creganwald, will belong to me."

If he meant to cause her annoyance, she would do likewise. "I trust your word, Royce, and will put no barriers in the way. If you seek resistance, my lord, seek elsewhere. The sooner the wedding is accomplished, the sooner I can return home and go about my duties. I have been lady here for all my years, and take no pleasure in leaving my duties longer than necessary. Unless, of course, this duty is not to your liking either, and you would lengthen the time before it is done."

"Nay, Lady," he said grimly. "We will return as soon as the words are spoken."

Lynette paused for a moment, then walked back down the stairs to stand just above him. "I am sorry for my shrewishness. This night you have made Cerise very happy. I know it must have been difficult for you, and I thank you for your kindness to her. I do not believe, Royce, that you are as formidable as your reputation would make us believe. To speak true, perhaps you will make a good lord here. A manor must be ruled not only with justice, but with love. Until this night, I had doubted that love still existed in your heart. Mayhap . . . I was wrong."

Royce stared after her with a look of surprise on his handsome face.

Chapter Nine

For some reason, sleep eluded Royce that night. He sat before the huge fireplace alone, his long legs stretched before him and a glass of wine in his hand which he kept filled from a bottle next to his chair.

His gaze was fixed on the glowing embers, and he heard no one approach until a voice came from just behind him.

"You cannot find rest tonight, Lord?"

Royce turned to look up into Oriel's face and observed that she was dressed for bed. Her garb left little to the imagination. He also had to admit that Oriel was an attractive woman. He wanted to condemn her for her obvious cruelty to Cerise, but he, too, had been cruel in his own way.

"I find it easier to think when I am not abed," Royce replied. He rose and offered her a stool nearby. Deliberately Oriel put herself between him and the fire, in the hope that she could stir his senses.

"You have weighty things to consider, my lord. It will not be easy to control the Saxon swine hereabout. Of course, William has chosen well. Your reputation must have assured him that you knew what force it would take to put these heathens in their proper place, and make them understand that resistance would only lead to their deaths."

"You think it wise to rule with force?"

"It is the only thing they understand. They are defeated, and William rules. If they do not learn obedience, then it is their own destruction they will understand."

"Lady Oriel, I have found it is easier to rule living and productive people. Their deaths will only make fewer hands to serve this manor. It is easier to rule justly, and show what mercy you can."

"If you show justice, they will take advantage. Lady Lynette is an example. Already she has taken over your child's care without showing any consideration for your thoughts. She would raise herself above her station."

"Her station?" Royce questioned. But Oriel missed entirely the gleam of annoyance in his eyes.

"Aye, Lord. She is but a slave here. You must use an iron hand or she will believe she rules here, not you." Oriel smiled as if they were sharing a confidence. "If you give her freedom, she will take more and more. Then she will turn loyal men and women against you. One day she will bring revolt. She pretends submission, but she will begin with those you trust most. Only this morning I met Sir Robert coming from her chamber."

Royce laughed softly. "You think Robert would turn traitor?"

"Who is to say what men will do . . . given the right incentive?"

"Lady Lynette's reputation has preceded her. She is not free with her favors, nor has she been accused of that by any lips."

"There are none but her own surrounding her . . . until now. Other knights at your table look upon her with favor."

"They may look, Lady Oriel. What lusty man does not? But there are none who would betray me . . . and Lady Lynette is a woman who is wise enough to know the consequences should she have such ideas."

"And . . . what would be the consequences to her should she do so?"

"That," he said thoughtfully, "would be in William's hands."

"Yes"—Oriel smiled—"I thought it might." She rose, and Royce rose at the same time. They stood inches from each other, and the delicate scent of her came to him. But he was as surprised at his lack of reaction as she was.

"It is very late, Lady Oriel, and I would not want to bring your brother's anger to the point of challenge. Sleep well."

Oriel was sorely disappointed, but she smiled and left him there. He wondered if he could have taken her . . . and if he would have found any satisfaction if he had. He doubted it.

Annoyed with himself, he tossed the last of his wine into the fireplace and heard it sizzle as he strode toward the stairs.

He dreamed that night, strange dreams he could not understand. In them, the vision of Sybella he had clung to faded into childlike eyes of lavender blue . . . and then silken strands of hair the color of ripe wheat.

He woke in the morning far from rested, and tried to push the unwanted dreams from his mind. When he reached the bottom of the stairs, he wasn't surprised to find Lynette already waiting for him.

"And I thought you were an early riser, my lord. I have been waiting this past hour for you," she teased. "I am about to perish from hunger. We were to break our fast together, but I was about to eat alone."

"I am sorry, my lady," he replied with a smile, "but I shall make up for my tardiness. I am interested in seeing if your abilities live up to the praise your father has given. I can judge firsthand the loyalty you have acquired."

"You will find the people willing and able, my lord. And you will find them loyal to my father and to me."

"And to William soon, through me. Lady Lynette, you would be wise to urge your people to give their loyalty to those who rule these lands now."

"Do you believe I would jeopardize one life to thwart William, when I know he has the power to destroy everyone living here? Do you think me a fool, my lord?"

"Nay," Royce laughed. "I would never be so unobservant as to think you a fool. In fact, I am in your debt."

"If you mean Cerise, you owe me no debt. She is a pleasure to care for."

They started into the main room as they spoke, and

Royce paused to look closely at Lynette again, as if he was considering whether she spoke the truth or not.

She smiled. "It is true. She is a very sweet child."

"Come, let us break our fast. There is much to be done. I should like to see the accounts today also."

The meal was hasty, a crust of bread and cheese washed down with ale, and soon they were in the saddle.

They rode for some time, and Lynette was well aware that he was watching her closely.

"I do not understand you," he finally said. "You are . . . different from what I expected you to be."

"And what did you expect? A fierce woman waiting at the gates of Creganwald with a sword in her hand? It is an amusing thought, but in combat I hardly think I could stand against you."

"And so you believe there are other ways to do battle?"

"Mayhap you seek battle where none exists. This land has been in my family for long years. I value it, and the people who live and work upon it. I would not see them suffer needlessly. Not if—"

"Not if you sacrifice yourself in marriage, and bring peace here," he finished.

"Sacrifice? Did I suggest such a thing?" Her look was one of such innocence that Royce laughed. It had been a long time since he had laughed so freely. It was a surprise to him.

Again they rode in silence, and she knew he was lost in thoughts that did not especially please him. Was he thinking of the woman he had loved so fiercely that her loss would make him want to lay down his life?

Royce's thoughts were confused. He wanted this girl's resistance, and instead she gave him smiles to fight against. How could he make her understand that a true marriage between them was impossible? He lived with a ghost that would not free him, and he did not welcome any other woman's presence in his life.

What made matters worse was that though she rode beside him, her horse was just a stride or two ahead, and he could not keep his eyes off her. She rode well, as he had noticed before. She was also quite beautiful. She had been angry at Oriel's treatment of Cerise, and had stormed at him that she would bear no child of his. He hoped that refusal was still in her mind. He preferred her anger and resistance to her docile submission.

William had given him a month's reprieve before the marriage, and had told him to bring her to London. But he intended to take her to London before that. There were many knights in William's service, knights who would willingly take his place as Lynette's husband. If Lynette were to find another, one who was acceptable to William . . . The king might be willing to replace Royce.

He would show her to the court, and the court to her. Like any young woman, she would be excited. Once she had won another heart or so, he would broach the subject to William. Time was what he needed . . . time.

Lynette's thoughts were more on him than he would ever know. She had been prepared to hate him, to do battle in every way possible. The taking of Creganwald by the Norman horde had created resistance. But Lynette's realistic assessment of her home, her father, and her responsibilities made her strong and quite capable of doing what was necessary to protect them. A woman had never had choices about marriage, and she knew she could have fared much worse than being promised to Royce.

She was also surprised at how aware of him she was. It was not the fact that he was the handsomest man she had ever seen. A handsome face could cover a great deal of evil. No, it was the shadows in his eyes, and the bitter hurt she had seen when he looked at Cerise. He was wounded and carried a scar that could not be seen, but that bled with every beat of his heart.

She looked at the hands that held his reins, and saw the power of them. They were large, his fingers long and shapely. She could feel again the strength with which he had held her. Those hands could wield a sword with ease, but she sensed they could be gentle and warm. The thought was surprisingly unsettling.

This brought another memory. That firm mouth upon hers, creating a sensation she had never experienced before, and that hard frame molded to hers, causing a confusing emotion that she found very hard to put from her mind.

One day he would be her husband, the man she would live with, sleep with, and whose children she would bear. She was again shocked that the idea caused no fear in her. Was she falling in love with this hard and seemingly ungiving man?

Another thought came unbidden . . . it would not

prove a difficult thing to do. She already knew he was not the fierce and vengeful man that rumor portrayed, and she wondered if he did not use that reputation as a shield for his own protection.

The lands around Creganwald that would be in his control ran for miles along the shore, and if one turned inland, the miles were just as many. It was much too large a holding to cover in one day's ride, and Royce knew it. But he meant to see the shore defenses, to speak to some of the serfs, and to understand Lynette better by observing the care she had given to those who served her.

At every stop, she was shown a deference that came not from force but from true devotion. He was well aware of the regard in which she was held. Many times she was approached unreservedly by those who served her, and was asked questions to which she gave honest answers.

He listened as she asked after the health of this child or that man. She advised remedies and offered help to those who were ill. He kept his silence, but missed little. And his regard for her grew with every mile they covered.

It was nearing time for the sun to set when they found themselves at the edge of a small cliff that overlooked the calm harbor. From here they would return to the hall. But for a few minutes they had stopped to rest the horses, and to enjoy the view. He lifted her from her horse, and they walked together to the cliff edge.

They stood for a few minutes simply enjoying the breathtaking view. The sun was a red glow on the horizon, and the sky seemed to be painted by the brush of a master painter in hues of purple, gold, crimson, and shades of blue.

He turned to face her and was instantly held by the picture she made. Strands of her hair, loosened by the breeze, blew across her cheeks, and the mist of the water made a dewy softness on her creamy skin. Her eyes were full of a kind of pride. This land might be owned by William now, but her heart lay here forever.

As he gazed at her, another face formed like a shadow over hers. He had known a maid as fair, and he had taken her life. He would not do so again.

"It is always beautiful," she half whispered.

"Even when the cold is upon it as now?" he asked with a smile.

"Aye, even then."

"Lynette . . . I would leave for London within the next five days."

She turned to look up at him, surprise in her eyes. "I had thought William expected us just before the marriage."

"Aye, he does. I had thought to go early. The court is an interesting place. Perhaps you would enjoy some time there before you are wed and your duties keep you here."

Lynette had the feeling that he had left a great deal unsaid, and it puzzled her. Yet his eyes held no sign of duplicity.

"You are anxious to return to court?"

"A bit," he lied without a sign.

"Perhaps to see if there is another more promising reward for your devotion to William than the meager lands of Creganwald?"

That she had struck to the heart of the matter so

quickly shook him a bit, but he returned her question with a smile. "Perhaps."

"Perhaps I can be of help to you." She returned his smile with the same honesty.

"I had thought you might."

"You would see me choose a maid to warm your bed in place of me? Would you then, if I found such a maid, release me from our promise?"

"That is not for me to decide," he retorted. "William wants this manor held in his name. I am certain there are many who would covet these lands. If you find one to your liking, maybe William will listen, and grant you a choice."

"But you must have a . . . better reward before you release your hold on Creganwald."

"Aye, you have struck to the heart of it. I am not a wealthy knight, like some who have a banner to fight under. I have given my sword to William in the promise of reward. If you can find another . . . of better circumstances . . ." He shrugged.

Lynette could happily have run him through with his own sword if she could have lifted its weight.

"I will look forward to our trip to London, my lord. Trust that I will study each maid very carefully. It is my fervent prayer that I may find the foolish girl, and guide you to her as rapidly as possible."

"You are angry, my lady? I but thought to give you choice as to who is to rule here." He needed her anger, and meant to push it beyond the area of reason . . . before she considered the possibility that he might be using her for his own purposes.

Royce did not know that Robert had told Lynette more of the story than he himself would ever have revealed. He was sure that she believed he was looking for another with more wealth than she held.

"Of course, I would have made you a more than adequate husband. I have had no complaints of my . . . ah . . . attentions."

Her anger was already at the boiling point, and his arrogance pushed her over.

"Perhaps your . . . ah . . . attentions," she mimicked, "have been judged by those who know nothing better than the mating of beasts."

"Perhaps not," he replied mildly.

"I do not choose to judge for myself."

"But how can you choose fairly," he laughed, "if you do not know what is offered?"

Lynette could see the deepening glow in his gold eyes and the intent buried there, and she backed a step away from him. But he had expected her retreat, and a hard, muscled arm snaked about her waist before she could consider turning and fleeing to her horse.

She was suddenly pressed against the breadth of a chest as hard as the stones of the manor. His mouth slanted across hers, catching her parted lips in mid protest, and feasting hungrily on their softness.

A sharp gust of wind caught the cloak he wore and wrapped it about both of them. Suddenly she was caught in a cocoon of blazing heat that smothered her from toe to head. His mouth demanded, and hers responded without her will. She tried to pull away, but he held her relentlessly.

A strange warmth began to grow in the depths of her body, and her pulse quickened until the thunder of her heart matched the beat of his. Suddenly, without her knowing, her arms went about him, and she moved against him, pressing her body even tighter to the warmth that was drawing every nerve taut, and shaking the foundation of her world.

When the kiss ended, it was hard to discern who was the more shaken or surprised, Royce or Lynette. Neither could believe the heated emotion that had whipped about them.

But it was Royce who recovered first, and he smiled an aggravating smile, meant to arouse an emotion he could deal with better.

Lynette cast him a murderous look. "Any knight in the realm will be preferable to you. Do you think another man's kiss cannot compare to yours?"

"That"—he grinned—"is up to you to decide."

Chapter Ten

"It is best we return to Creganwald," Lynette said, a little surprised at the huskiness in her voice. She was finding it difficult to control her erratic breathing. What made it even worse was that Royce seemed not to be affected at all. He simply smiled and let her go.

But Royce was fighting his own battle. He agreed with the wisdom of returning to Creganwald. He didn't like what was happening to his self-control. Some subtle voice deep within had urged him on, suggesting he might not like it if she did choose some able knight to share both her bed and Creganwald in his place.

Still, it was the wisest thing for her to do, because he was not the right man for a sensual and very feminine woman such as Lynette. He could offer her nothing except being married to a husband who could never fully love her, who had ghosts that would always walk between them. No, alienating her was best.

He released her with a taunting laugh. "See, cherie, now you will have something to measure the others by."

"Then I imagine I shall have to look for him in the king's stables."

"Ah, let me give you one warning, cherie. Try to sheathe your claws. No man wants to be ripped apart in bed. Better you smile and pretend to be docile."

"You needn't worry, my lord," she said much too sweetly. "I will turn into the most complacent woman . . . for the right man. He will not have to do battle with my claws. He will be too busy sharing my embraces."

She watched him scowl at her words, then turned to walk back to her horse. She refused his aid to mount, and he surrendered to her fierce look with a shrug, and mounted his own horse. They rode back in silence.

Searching out Cerise to share her evening meal, Lynette found her playing in the center of her bed. It was obvious that when Lynette was gone, Cerise preferred her own company to facing Oriel. Lynette worried about how Cerise would take her going to London. Quite possibly she would be left to the mercy of Oriel again.

Lynette sent a maid for food for Cerise, and began to talk to her about her day. Soon Cerise was relaxed and chattering.

Lynette didn't know that Cerise had become an expert at gleaning information and had already heard talk of the proposed trip. She had been sure Lynette would not leave without her, since she was going to be her mother one day.

She would be with both her father and Lynette, which pleased her a great deal. It really didn't matter to her if they were in London or here at Creganwald, as long as they were together.

She was beginning to think that once Lynette and Royce were married, all would be well in the world.

But that night Cerise was wakened by a nightmare that sent her flying to Lynette. Wakened from a sound sleep, Lynette gathered the child to her and drew the furs over them both.

"What were you dreaming?" Lynette asked when Cerise's trembling abated.

"We were lost."

"We?"

"You and me, and Papa was looking for us but he couldn't find us. He was mad . . . and he was sad . . ." As she considered this, she faced the question that was always in the back of her mind. Would her father really be sad if she were gone? The thought brought new tears, for she wasn't too certain he would be.

"Why were we lost, Cerise? And where were we lost?"

"I don't know. Somewhere where there were lots of big rocks, and . . . it was dark . . . and . . . "

"Don't worry," Lynette calmed her, "we won't get lost. I'm sure your father will not let that happen. And we will be clever enough not to go near any piles of big rocks."

"Are there big rocks in London?"

"What do you know about London?" Lynette asked in surprise.

"That you and Papa are going. He will take me, won't he, Lynette? He won't leave me with . . . her?"

"I don't think so," Lynette replied hopefully. She meant to talk with Royce at the first opportunity. She would beg to take Cerise along if she had to. "Hush now, and try to sleep. It will be fun to see London. Maybe we will have time to see the shops, and perhaps buy you some pretty ribbons for your hair. Would you like that?"

"Oh, yes." Her mind taken from her dream, Cerise soon found sleep, but now it was Lynette who lay awake. Would Royce really care if she and Cerise were taken from him in some way? The thought was surprisingly painful. In the quietness of her chamber, she could allow herself to examine, with her usual realism, her feelings toward Royce. He would be an easy man to love, if his heart were not so cold. His wife had died . . . and taken him with her. It was some time before she found sleep.

Robert and Royce stood in the early morning air and discussed the preparations for the trip to London. Royce meant to leave a number of his men for the protection of Creganwald. He had just toured the armory and could see that Robert's work was progressing rapidly, and well. Few knew arms better than Robert, and under his direction the manor would soon be well protected.

Eldwyn, who stood with them, was somewhat awed by the progress, and the amount of arms Royce thought necessary.

"Our thick English oak doors and this hall have been adequate protection before."

"Aye, Eldwyn, that is why your hall is in Norman possession now. If the Saxons had known as much about building castles and garrisoning them, Duke William might never have conquered and been crowned last Christmas. If the Saxons had possessed anything more than earthen mounds within wooden or dry stone walls such as these, they could have offered more resistance."

Eldwyn was little pleased with the truth of this, but it could not be denied. "You will have this hall well protected if you have time. William calls you to London. Perhaps he means another lord to rule here."

Robert cast him a sour look. "You do not know him. He has never broken his word, and he will not now. This hall has been spared because you have proved you want to live peacefully under his rule. Many were destroyed to prove who is king."

"I did not mean to anger you, Sir Robert." Eldwyn smiled. "I only meant to compliment Royce on his fortifications."

"They will do for now," Royce answered. "But I have other plans to build a stronger and more defensible building in time. One of stone. This hall will stand, but it will be added to and improved." He turned to Eldwyn. "As for London, will you not change your mind and come with us? I think Lynette worries about your health, and would have you closer at hand."

"Nay, my lord. I will admit I do not feel as well as I should. I fear the trip would weaken me further. I heartily wish this winter would end. The cold seems to bite to the marrow of my bones."

"All the more reason to go. I would hate to have Lynette unable to enjoy the court and London for worry about you."

"To speak of Lynette, I paused by her chamber to say good morning, and found Cerise asleep in her bed. When I questioned Lynette, she said the child had a terrible nightmare and came to her bed. It is strange, is it not," Eldwyn said softly, "that a troubled child would not seek the comfort of her father, but would go to someone she has known for so short a time."

Eldwyn's point did not miss its mark. Robert was much more aware of Royce's controlled reaction than Eldwyn was.

"All children have nightmares upon occasion. Perhaps something has disturbed her. She will recover from it, I warrant." But Royce was thinking of Oriel, and the treatment Cerise had received at her hands. He hoped there had been no more confrontations.

Robert smiled to himself, and thanked Eldwyn silently for the disruption of Royce's peace of mind. "Aye," he agreed amiably. "Why should the business of knights be disturbed by the upset of one child? She will recover . . . in time."

Royce cast him a fulminating look. He chose not to answer, continuing instead with the discussion of his future plans, which he well knew might be carried out by someone else.

For the balance of the day, he held a surprising battle with himself. He did not need to go to Lynette over something as petty as a child's dream. She was a woman, and she could deal with it much more easily than he. He kept himself active, and tried to push all thoughts of Cerise and Lynette from his mind.

But full night put an end to any duties he could tend, and as he ate a quick meal of bread, meat, and ale, Lynette slipped back into his mind . . . and lingered until annoyance prodded him to his feet and carried him to her chamber.

He chose not to knock but merely pushed the door open and stepped inside. His gaze flew across the room to a sight that left him a bit breathless. He was conscious of a stir of emotion he had thought long since defeated: desire.

Lynette was in the midst of giving Cerise a bath, and the two had been laughing over something. That was not the difficulty. It was obvious to him that Lynette had just quit the tub of water herself, for she was wrapped in only a thin sheath of linen, and the moisture on her body made the linen cling in a most seductive way. It revealed more than it concealed. Her slim, rounded form captured his gaze. Her hair had been carelessly caught up on her head in a mass of ringlets that were already escaping to cling to her cheeks and throat. Her face was flushed, and her eyes were dancing with humor.

Neither was aware of his presence yet. Lynette drew Cerise from the water and vigorously dried her and wrapped her in a fur.

Beside the tub knelt another of the young maids that had been part of Eldwyn's household, and it was she who noticed Royce's presence. She sucked in a deep breath, for the huge, dark lord scared her speechless. The sound of her indrawn breath drew Lynette's attention and she turned.

Lynette sat back on her heels in surprise, and Cerise watched him with wide eyes, her hand still resting on Lynette's shoulder. Royce absorbed the picture, without realizing it would never leave his mind.

He smiled at the young maid, only because he thought she might be about to faint from fright. "Take the child to her bed." He might have tried to speak gently, but to the maid his voice was a command that sounded like the roll of thunder. With no hesitation she rose. Lynette knew there was no use arguing, and she didn't want Cerise upset.

"Go to bed like a good girl. I promise I'll come say good night and tell you a story that will chase away all the bad dreams."

"You promise?"

"I promise." Lynette kissed her cheek, and watched as the maid led her from the room. Then she turned to face Royce. Without thought, she stood erect, and that put her between Royce's view and the fire. The flames were burning brightly, and the light shone through the damp linen as if it were no longer there.

Royce's gaze raked over her, and his body reacted whether he willed it or not. She was a vision who made a man's thoughts go to his bed, and the image of her in it. He struggled to bring his thoughts back under control.

"I was told Cerise was having bad dreams." Even as he spoke them, he knew his words sounded vague and more like an excuse.

"Aye, my lord," she replied. "She came to me last night. It is a thing that will pass, I'm sure. In time, as she feels more secure, she will not be troubled."

He tried to concentrate on what she said, but his mind and body were having a war with each other, and he could not keep his eyes and his thoughts from wandering.

"My lady"—he smiled wickedly, more for his own benefit than hers—"I suggest you find something less . . . revealing to wear."

Lynette had forgotten her undressed state, and now she looked down at herself, and her cheeks reddened. She fairly ran to her bed and drew forth a fur. She swung it around her, displaying silken limbs and delicious curves that made him sigh in disappointment when they disappeared beneath the material.

"Have you eaten?" Lynette asked to distract him.

"Aye," he said shortly.

"Then it is Cerise's dreams that brought you here, and nothing else?"

"That and to tell you to pack her things as well. I would not leave her here while you are gone."

"Lady Oriel goes with us?" she asked, but kept her head averted so he would not read her eyes. She was still certain Oriel was his mistress.

"Since her brother is close to me, it is necessary that she be in our party." He crossed the room to stand beside her, which was disturbing enough.

When she had hastily put on the fur, her hair had come loose, and now it tumbled about her in golden profusion, its gleam touched by the light of the fire.

Gently he lifted one shimmering curl from her shoulder and rubbed its silkiness between his fingers absently. "Does it distress you that Lady Oriel travels with us? Would you leave her behind, cherie?"

The implication that she was jealous was aggravating, and she backed away from him, her chin tilting stubbornly.

"Where any of your mistresses travel is none of my concern. I am not your wife yet, and would put no barriers in the way of your rutting pleasures."

"Rutting pleasures." He laughed in surprise. "I have not taken my pleasure with the lady."

"Mayhap," she replied, angry at revealing her feelings, "it is because her brother is near, and not because the lady would fight you should you choose to do so. Or is it because you still see greater wealth elsewhere? I am told Sir Giles has little more than the shield he carries and his weapons. Still . . . would he really be angry if you bedded his sister? Mayhap they both hope you are her future?"

"You think it is only the wealth my sword has acquired for me that is my attraction for a lady?" he asked softly. Lynette totally missed the sparkle of challenge in his eyes.

"Your sword has won you much, why not the Lady Oriel? She is Norman, and one who would appreciate your conquests."

"And how do you know you would not appreciate my . . . conquest?" His finger traced across her collarbone with a light touch. He meant to taunt her, make her angry so she would deny him. But he never meant to find her skin so smooth and soft, nor to see awareness leap into her eyes. "I have never left a dissatisfied maid in my wake."

Lynette slapped his hand away, and could have screamed at his teasing laugh. All her fury rose. This arrogant Norman needed a lesson. She knew he had no place for love in his life, and she knew he fought the idea of marriage. Did he think he could sample her whenever the mood struck? Did he think to find her a husband who would look the other way when the king's right arm decided to have his wife?

She knew he didn't see *her*, but a woman and situation that had been forced upon him. What annoyed her even more was that he was trying to drive her away from him by making her afraid. Well, she was not afraid of him. Not now . . . not ever.

She looked up at him and smiled. "Am I to understand, my lord, that you have had second thoughts, and now desire to wed me? I am disappointed. I had thought to find a knight of my own choosing to make the bedding more . . . pleasurable."

His eyes narrowed. The lass did not frighten easily. He felt a swift touch of admiration.

"I said, I cannot change William's mind. But as for a desire to wed . . . I have no real desire to wed anyone. This marriage will be for profit, and to keep your lands safe. It will be to my benefit if you do choose another, and find me a wench who carries a fat purse. Then I will not have to lift my sword to guard yours."

"And what of Cerise?" she said softly. "Once I find a wench to your liking and a lusty knight to mine, what of Cerise?"

If his look was one of pain, it was gone too fast for her to capture. "The . . . Cerise takes well to you. I . . . I would be grateful if you would keep her here. I would reward you well."

"Have you always had to pay for all you've gotten? Has no one rewarded you for just the pleasure of it . . . or for love?"

"Aye, Lady. I have been rewarded with love. But

what becomes of it? In a breath it is gone, or destroyed. Nay, I shall take more visible rewards."

"How do you measure your rewards, my lord? By the wealth you acquire . . . by the conquests you make, or maybe by those who have learned loyalty and love for you despite little in return?"

"Little in return?"

She shrugged. "Know you of the love Cerise holds for you?"

"She does not know me," he said gruffly.

"I believe the child knows more of you than you of her."

"That is not possible."

"No? Until we leave for London, would you consider doing something for me?"

"Ask."

"Actually not for me—"

"What is it you ask?"

"Give Cerise some moments of your time . . . perhaps at meals. You must eat, and she would find a great deal of pleasure in your company."

"What kind of game do you play, demoiselle?"

"Game? Must it be a game to introduce a father to his own child? Unless, of course, she has given you so much trouble that you cannot abide her."

Royce looked down into her eyes, and fought a battle to keep from tasting those soft curved lips, inches below his. "Perhaps it is better that she does not know me. I have been absent from her life since birth. It would be better to keep it so."

"Better for her . . . or for you?"

"Has Robert developed a loose tongue after all?"

"Sir Robert is your friend. Aye, he has told me of your loss."

"Then you can understand—"

"No, I cannot understand. If you had died, do you think her mother would have abandoned the child you conceived together? I think not. So much for the courage of warriors." Lynette's voice grew gentle. "She is part of both of you, and she should be a comfort, for as long as Cerise is with you, you hold part of Sybella in your heart."

"And if you are forced to be my wife, would that not prey on your mind?"

"Nay. She must have loved you with her whole heart, and that was before you ever knew me. Why should I be jealous of a beautiful memory? Can you not see what you could do for Cerise? She never knew her mother. You have the key to all the memories. Share them with her, and you may find they rest gentler on your heart. You may even find that you can have peace, and share the future with another . . . no matter who she may be. Does your daughter not deserve at least that much?"

Royce looked down at Lynette in fascination. She was unique. "Ask me to lift my sword in uneven conflict, ask me to lay down my life in battle. All this is easier than to look into Cerise's eyes and know that but for me, Sybella would still breathe. Of all things asked of me, that is the hardest to bear."

"But you are wrong," Lynette said softly. "We are not the commanders of our fate; it is in the hands of God. It was His will, and would have been His will had you not even married."

He had drawn away from her and the logic of her words, and she felt the withdrawal. His eyes had become bleak, and his body tense.

"I would you prepare the ch . . . Cerise . . . for travel. We will leave within the week."

"Aye, my lord," Lynette replied. But she was not resigned to his coldness. There had to be a way to release him from this pain, and she felt, with Cerise's help . . . she would find it. She refused to question her reasons.

Chapter Eleven

Somber clouds covered the moon, and lightning sent spears of brilliance through the darkness. The sea grew in fury, and waves crashed against the shore with fierce violence.

Royce was the first wakened by the storm, and he rose from his bed to rekindle the fire. The room had grown very cold. Instead of returning to his bed, he sat in a large chair by the fire and extended his legs to brace his feet on the stone hearth. Gradually, the warmth of the fire lulled him into a shallow sleep.

It was not the same for Cerise, who lay frightened in her large bed. Every corner of her room had shadows that became monsters in her mind.

She thought of the safety and comfort of Lynette's bed, and gathered her courage to flee her room. She slid from the bed and dashed to her door. But when she started down the darkened hallway, a glow of light came from under her father's door.

Hesitantly she pushed the door open and tiptoed

in a few steps. She could see him before the fire, and curiosity took hold. She went to his side and found him asleep. The fire was warm, and the chair in which he sat was large.

Cerise climbed up beside him as carefully as she could, and curled against his warmth. He was so big, and so wonderful, this father of hers. Her heart longed to be lifted onto his lap and held in safety. Slowly the fire warmed her, and she rested her head against his chest and put one arm across his waist. It hardly reached across him, but she could feel the steady, solid beat of his heart, and for now that was enough. Her heavy eyes closed in the security of slumber.

Lynette, too, had been wakened by the storm, and she had thought at once of Cerise, who must be frightened. She rose and went to Cerise's room, only to find her bed empty. The door to Royce's room stood part way open, and the firelight drew her attention. She pushed the door open a little further and stepped inside.

The scene that met her eyes brought tears. Royce was asleep in a chair, and curled against him was a sleeping and obviously contented Cerise.

She tiptoed further into the room and paused by his chair. It was then that Royce became aware that he was not alone. He opened his eyes, and the first thing he was aware of was Lynette . . . only he was certain she had just stepped from his imagination. Then he became aware of the slight form curled against him.

He looked down on Cerise, and for a moment could not understand the situation. He raised one hand to touch lightly the small hand that rested on his chest, and suddenly his heart swelled with a warmth he was unprepared for. There was a constriction in his throat that threatened to cut off his breath. Wondering why Cerise had come to his room, he looked up at Lynette, and her smile was soft.

"She but seeks safety from the storm, Royce. Shall I carry her back to my bed?"

"No. . . . I will put her back in hers." He rose with such care that Cerise never wakened when she was lifted in strong arms. But Royce didn't move. He was totally unprepared for the emotion that filled him when he cradled his daughter in his arms. She was so little . . . so defenseless.

Lynette watched emotion fill him, and a new and amazing one filled her. Again she thought how easy it would be to love this man. To make the three of them a family. To share . . . No! She would not think this way. He did not want a wife, he wanted wealth.

"My lord?"

"Perhaps, if she is frightened . . . I should put her with you. If she wakens again I would not want her afraid."

"Aye, come, we'll put her in my bed." Lynette turned from him, and he followed. In her room, he laid Cerise gently on her bed, and Lynette covered her. Then she turned to him.

"I will rekindle your fire. It's very cold in here," he said.

"Thank you."

Once the fire was blazing again, he rose and Lynette walked to the door with him. He paused there, and looked back at the bed. This time she could not read the emotions in his eyes.

"Lynette . . ."

"Aye?"

He looked down into her eyes, and their gazes blended for a moment. "I don't know how . . . I mean . . . she is so . . . "

"As I said, she but sought safety. Who better to run to in a storm than the man she believes can do almost anything?"

"She believes that?"

"Aye, and most likely more. Does that make you uncomfortable?"

"No . . . Yes. I'm unsure. It is not good to have someone depend upon you to that extent."

With the firelight behind her, Lynette was a shadow; the light of the fire haloed her hair until it looked like a silvered mist flowing about her. They stood close enough now that her scent came to him like the scent of spring. It jolted his senses and stirred something deep inside him that he had guarded for a long, long time.

From where Lynette stood, his face could be clearly seen. In the glow of the fire his eyes seemed deeper gold, and she could see why Cerise had gravitated to him, for an aura of power and strength flowed from him to envelop her.

Royce raised one hand to gently touch her hair.

"You have been very good to Cerise; I'm grateful. Perhaps . . . perhaps if I . . . " He struggled for the words to match his thoughts. She felt a wave of intense emotion, first of sympathy and then of something much stronger. She wanted to draw him to her, hold him and wash away the terrible misery he had suffered.

Lynette lifted both hands and cupped his face

between them. "Royce, all you have to do is reach out to her. She has stored up so much love for you, you cannot imagine. Heal your own pain by healing hers. Look at her and know that love has never left you. It is here in your child."

Royce looked into the depths of her eyes, and knew the truth of her words. He had felt it when he cradled Cerise in his arms. He laid a hand over one of hers, and became aware of what a soft and feminine creature she was.

Lynette faced the truth with her usual practicality. She wanted to touch and be touched by this man, and if given half a chance, she would go to him as a willing wife. She felt warmth fill her, release a kind of joy within her that she knew she would have to control. He did not want her. He had yet to put his ghosts to rest.

But she could not resist one single touch. Slowly she rose on tiptoe, and touched her lips to his. If Royce had been jolted by desire before, it was nothing to the force that unleashed itself now. But the wave of desire was followed by one of guilt. Sybella's face came into his mind, and the horror of what he had caused. He could not reach for happiness again when it could only cause more grief. He did not know if he could ever rid himself of the guilt that ate at his soul. He moved back from Lynette just a fraction, but enough to break the contact.

"You must be careful, cherie. Or you will make me think you are more anxious for this wedding than you have led me to believe."

Lynette was startled by his sarcasm. She saw now in his eyes that his shields were in place. She felt heat rush to her cheeks, and a sense of shame filled her. Was she begging for his touch? She could not deny the truth of it, any more than she could deny that she would have gone into his arms if he had given one sign that he wanted her there.

But of course he did not want her there, and she vowed silently there would be no more mistakes such as this. There was room in his heart for only one woman, and she was not that woman. That woman was as alive now as she had ever been, and he had no intention of letting her go.

"I meant the kiss as a way to thank you," she said defensively.

"Feel free to thank me at any time," he chuckled.

"You needn't expect gratitude from me any time soon, my lord. Unless, of course, you help me choose a knight to wed who has more regard for affection truly given."

She watched his smile fade and felt a sense of satisfaction. She had no idea that the thought of her in someone else's arms had formed before him like a portrait, and he did not like the scene.

"Good night, Lynette. Sleep well."

"Oh, do not worry yourself, sir knight. I will sleep well. Let me wish the same for you." She backed up a step and began to close the door between them. Royce waited for the door to shut, then placed one hand against it and closed his eyes to gather control.

He'd wanted to take her in his arms and test the softness of those lips. He had wanted more, and he hated himself for the desire that could not be leashed.

He turned and walked back to his chamber. He lay for a long time before sleep came, and in that time he decided that they would leave for London as soon as possible. The sooner he found . . . or she found the man who would please her, the better.

Lynette climbed into her bed, careful not to disturb Cerise, who slept peacefully. Lynette, too, found sleep difficult to attain. She lay staring into the fire Royce had rekindled, and thought of him.

She felt more for him than she wanted to feel, and in the darkness she did not deny it. Her whole body was alive with the desire to feel his arms about her, and she would have accepted his kiss with pleasure, had he simply reached for her.

Now they would go to London, and each would search out another to fill the days and nights to come. It was a situation that was nearly impossible. She refused to lie to herself. There were few knights who would compare to him . . . few she would not find lacking. She began to wonder what William would say if both of them came to him with choices of their own. Surely it didn't matter to him who ruled the lands of Creganwald, as long as they were ruled in his name.

Royce stirred uncomfortably in his bed, for every time he moved to find a more comfortable spot, he imagined the scent of springtime swirling about him. His imagination played havoc with his thoughts until he cursed under the strain. For he could see Lynette as she had looked fresh from the bath, her body warm and still damp, her hair loose about her. He could still feel the softness of her skin, and taste the sweet taste of her mouth.

It was pure lust, he argued, and lust could be cured with any willing wench. He refused to answer the question of why he did not go in search of a willing maid to slake his lust. He fought his body for control, and after a long while he slept.

The next morning he gave the order that they would leave for London the following day. Packing what they would need kept Lynette busy most of the day. It was midafternoon before she realized she had seen very little of Cerise since they had broken their fast just after sunrise.

She went in search of her, and soon received the surprising word that she had not been seen since the morning meal.

Lynette felt a bit alarmed, and went at once in search of Oriel. But there was no satisfaction to be found there. Oriel was busy preparing her own things for travel, and made it clear Lynette was an interference.

"I'm sure the child would not have been so free had she still been in my care," Oriel said coldly.

"No," Lynette answered, "I suppose not. But then she would have been imprisoned in her room and left to her own devices."

"Better that than trying to explain to Royce why you cannot find her. I surmise there are many places she could run into grief."

The words brought a picture to Lynette's mind that frightened her. She knew Cerise had been fascinated with Royce's destrier, ever since the day he had brought her back from the stream. She also knew the huge horses were dangerous. Only a man with a great deal of strength and courage could handle one. Had the child gone to the stables and been tramped under the hooves of one of the beasts?

Panic filled her, and she raced to the stables. They were empty . . . or so she thought at first. But then she heard a soft giggle, and the muffled sound of whispered voices.

She followed the sound to a shadowed corner, and when she approached she saw a sight she had never believed she would see.

Royce was kneeling with his back to Lynette, and Cerise was there beside him. They were examining something in the hay-filled corner that Lynette could not see. She walked toward them, but both were so engrossed that they did not hear her coming.

As she grew closer, she could see a litter of kittens that had recently been born.

"No, Cerise, you cannot take any one of them to London with you. They are too young to leave their mother. You wouldn't want it to die, would you?" Royce was saying, and his voice was gentle and warm. Lynette swallowed the constriction in her throat, and fought tears of pleasure.

"No," Cerise answered hesitantly. "Papa . . . can I hold one?"

Royce reached out and lifted a tiny bundle of calico fur in his hand, then settled it in Cerise's two hands. "Be very careful, don't hold it too tight," he cautioned.

"Oh, I won't," Cerise breathed. She had never felt so happy in her entire life. She only remembered climbing on his chair last night and falling asleep. Early in the morning she had wakened in Lynette's bed with the idea that her father had had her taken away.

This morning she had eaten with Lynette, and had been asked to go to her chamber to make certain there was nothing else she wanted to carry to London with her. She had been busy going through ribbons and such when she had turned to find her father standing in the doorway.

At first she tried to think what she had done wrong. Then she decided that he had come to tell her to stay out of his room. She had known it was wrong. She had been told many times to stay out of her father's vicinity . . . but last night . . . last night was a pleasure she would not have forgone even if she was to be punished.

Then she realized what that punishment might be, and her heart almost broke. She might be given into Oriel's care again, and that would be the worst punishment of all.

"Papa?" she said hesitantly, for she could not understand his intent look. Was he angry?

Royce crossed the room to stand beside her and she looked up what seemed like an immense distance. He knelt before her, bringing them eye to eye.

"Cerise." His voice was gentle. "Was it a bad dream that wakened you last night?"

"No, Papa. It was just the wind. I . . . I was frightened. I'm sorry. I won't come in your room again. You won't give me back to Oriel, will you? I'll be good, Papa, I promise. I won't come in your room again. I'll—"

"Hush, child," Royce said. He felt a tenderness sweep over him, combined with self-loathing. He had made her as she was . . . frightened and lonely. "It was all right. You may come to me if you are ever afraid of anything."

"Really?" She looked at him as if this were too much to believe.

"Yes, really. Cerise . . . I'm sorry to have hurt you as I did. One day, when you are older, I will tell you why—"

"Uncle Robert already told me. It's because you miss Mama. And Oriel said you never wanted me because I'm an ugly girl. It's all right, Papa." She moved to stand closer, and reached a hand to pat his shoulder consolingly. "It's all right."

Her last words undid him. He gathered her into his arms, and felt her slender arms come about his neck and return his embrace.

"Oriel was wrong, Cerise. You will remain in Lynette's care." He held her a little away from him. "And you are the prettiest girl in all of England."

Cerise looked at him with a half smile of doubt on her face. This was too much to believe. He was just trying to make her feel better. Royce saw her doubt and smiled.

"Have you ever heard of me telling a lie?"

"No."

"Then why would I lie to you?"

"Just to make me feel better," she said with conviction. "But I really don't mind. If . . . if you like me . . . just a little bit . . . I really don't mind."

"Ah, Cerise. I would like to learn to love again. Perhaps we can teach each other. We will start . . . as you say . . . with just a little bit. All right?"

"Yes," she whispered. Royce took her in his arms again, and ignored the tears that burned his eyes. He had a long way to go with Cerise, but maybe he could find his way back to her trust.

"Would you like to come with me to the stable? I have something to show you."

Cerise nodded and the two of them left her chamber. As they went down the stairs, face after face gaped in surprise, but all remained silent. Near the stable they saw Robert, whose smile grew broader as they grew near.

"Good morning," he greeted them. But his eyes were on Royce. "And a good one it is, I think."

"You are right, old friend. One of the best," Royce agreed.

"And you, little one," Robert said to Cerise. "Where are you off to?"

"Papa is going to show me a secret, Uncle Robert."

"Hmm, maybe there are some secrets Papa will tell me later. I am surely interested."

"I don't doubt that you are, Robert. But I don't think it's much of a secret. I have a feeling it is what you have planned from the start. What other little plans do you have?"

"I?" Robert said innocently. "What other plans could I have, other than to journey to London with you and see you married?"

"Come, Cerise," Royce said. "Robert . . . we'll talk later."

Now Lynette stood and watched them together and was warmed by the rightness of it. His barriers had been beaten down with the embrace of a child. How she wished . . .

"What is so interesting?" she inquired. Both Royce and Cerise turned to look at her.

"Oh, look, Lynette! Papa found some kittens."

"So I see. How pretty they are." Lynette spoke to Cerise, but she was aware of Royce's gaze upon her.

"Papa says I must leave them here while we go to

London. Do you think they will run away before I get back?"

Lynette didn't want to say that she thought Cerise might not be coming back. "No, they will stay here. Their mother has been here for a long time, and they won't leave her for a while."

"Papa, may I show Uncle Robert?"

"Aye, take one to him," Royce laughed. "I'm sure he is most anxious to see a new batch of kittens."

Cerise was off at a run almost before Royce stopped speaking. There was a long silence after she left.

Chapter Twelve

"You were right," he said softly.

"My lord?""

"Lynette, I have a name. Is it distasteful to you?"

"No . . . Royce. It is not distasteful," she replied. She looked up at him as he took the few steps that separated them, and the longing of the night before came alive. She tried to study him with detached interest, but such detachment was nearly impossible when his presence was enough to take a woman's breath away. "About what was I right?"

"She is full of love. But she is just as full of distrust."

"Do you not think she has a right to her distrust?"

"Aye, I suppose she does. I have been unfair to her. To try to ease her life and perhaps my own, I have sentenced her to the same childhood I lived. Last night was a revelation, and I am grateful for it. Perhaps I can make up for my neglect in time. I shall have to teach her to trust me." He changed the subject. "Is all ready for us to leave tomorrow?"

"Aye. I foresee no problems, unless a new snow falls."

"Good, I would be on our way as soon as the sun is up."

"Are you so anxious to get to court, Royce?" she asked without looking at him. Both knew that the other sought only a way out of the dilemma in which they found themselves.

"It is William's command that we marry there. Besides, there is no way out of this situation without the king's permission. Once I have brought you to court and you have had time to make some decisions, there will still be time to prove the wisdom of your choice to the king."

"And then you will be free of this unwelcome duty."

It came to Royce quite suddenly that he was not as anxious for this release as he had been but a few weeks before.

"You have made it clear that it is just as unwelcome to you. Why should we do battle, when the answer is before us?" he asked.

"You speak true. Freedom of choice is the answer for us both. But do you believe the king will release us as easily as that?"

"William considers only the need to hold the land. If the . . . the knight is one he respects and trusts, then I see no obstacle."

All the while they were talking, Lynette's discomfort with the situation was growing. How could she say to him that the choice William had already made was not as distasteful as she had first thought?

How could she tell him that she would reconsider their bargain when she knew he wanted to be free?

"Then it should be a simple matter?"

"Aye . . . simple."

"Royce . . . " She had to tell him.

"Royce," Oriel's voice repeated from the doorway, and both Royce and Lynette turned to look at her. "It seems there are some difficulties, and Sir Ferragus has been searching for you to settle a problem." She smiled a most pleasant smile at Lynette. "And your father is ill."

Lynette's alarm rose. "My father! What is the matter?"

"I'm afraid I have no idea. It might be best if you were to go to him as soon as you can."

"Yes . . . of course," Lynette said distractedly. She remembered too well how sick her father had been the winter before. She left without another word.

Royce was watching Oriel. He could hear Cerise's voice saying that Oriel had told her she was an ugly little girl and that was why he did not want her near. Looking at Oriel now only made him feel worse about what he had put the child through.

Oriel had watched Lynette's departure, and now as she turned to look at Royce her smile warmed. "Will you be glad to return to court, Royce?"

"It is of little importance, Oriel. If Lynette's father is too ill for her to leave him, there is little reason for us to leave."

"But what of the king?"

"I am sure he can continue to rule without our presence."

"Then . . . your marriage is of little importance as well?"

"I did not say that. I believe this marriage is of great importance to William, and I would not consider going against his will."

"To ask you to wed a Saxon just to possess her lands is much. Why can he not just take the land and let you wed one of your own? You can still rule here. William need only give it to you."

"Then he would have to oust Lynette, her father, and all those loyal to them. It would cause much grief for nothing. This manor can be ruled peacefully. William seeks peace and a chance to build and rule without any more problems."

"What are a few more Saxons? And of what value are that sick old man and his daughter?" She came close and laid her hand gently on his arm. "There are those who would stand beside you and rule here with but a word."

"There is the matter of my own benefit as well. I am not the wealthiest of William's knights, but he has given me the honor of holding this manor in his name. My honor is in the bargain, and I hold it too dear to destroy."

"You would let a Saxon do it for you?"

"There is no reason to believe she would do so. Oriel, put your hatred of everything Saxon from you, and your hatred of Lynette. She has done you no harm. You have been generous with your time and patience, I know. But I want no more animosity to linger in this company from now on."

Oriel's face revealed her struggle for control. "You will regret the day you set eyes on her," she said quietly. "And the day you ignored my warning. I would have given you more than she ever will, and you turn from me to one who would see you in the dust. Yes, Royce, you will regret this day."

Oriel waked away, with her shoulders stiff and her teeth clenched. Lynette had won for now, she thought, but once they were back at court they would see who the final winner was. One way or another she would have Royce and Creganwald . . . and she would find a way to rid herself of the woman who had come between her and her wishes . . . yes, one way or another.

Lynette flew to her father's chamber, where she found him seated before his fire in deep contemplation. She went to his side at once and knelt by his chair.

"Papa, Oriel told me you were ill."

"Nay, daughter, it was but a passing thing. A small pain that took my breath for a minute, but it is long gone. Do not worry so, I am fine. It was not the strange malady that attacked me last winter. Then my breath was short, and the pain in my chest and arm was severe. This was a little thing. Most likely something I have eaten."

"You would not say that just to stop me from worrying?"

"I would not. Did I not moan like a child last year?" He laughed. "You know I bellow like a bull when I feel you are needed. You leave for London tomorrow, and I do not want you to worry. I am well, and when this cursed winter has passed, I will be completely better."

Lynette relaxed with a sigh. She dragged a stool near her father's chair, and sat down beside him.

"Papa . . . I must talk to you."

"What worries your mind, daughter?"

"With all honesty, what think you of Royce?"

"Royce," Eldwyn said thoughtfully. "I have watched him these past days, and I have begun to believe he has the best intentions for Creganwald. He has plans that will see this land improve, and he would build here a stronger castle and make Creganwald a fortress that will protect its people against anything."

"That is his plan for Creganwald, Papa, but . . . what of him?"

"He is a strong man, Lynette. I have listened to his men, and heard the talk of the servants. I know he is respected . . . respected, not feared. There is a great deal of difference." Eldwyn looked at her closely. "What troubles you? Do you find him wanting?"

"I am afraid that is the problem," Lynette said miserably.

"How can that be a problem?"

"Papa . . . he does not want me."

"Impossible."

"Not so impossible." She smiled. "You have love for me, he does not. He . . . he is still in love with his wife." Lynette went on to explain, and to tell her father of the unspoken bargain she and Royce had made. "So, you see. It is wealth he wants, and for me to choose another and present my petition to William. He will not argue the matter . . . if he finds a woman wealthy enough to take my place."

"That is the most unbelievable thing I have ever heard of!" Eldwyn exploded. "To choose a woman for him, while he chooses another husband for you.

He cannot insult you this way! William shall hear of it!"

"No! Papa, please, say nothing. There is worse I want to tell you."

"What could possibly be worse?"

"That I have come . . . I think . . . to love him," Lynette said softly. Eldwyn was silenced for a minute, before a look of understanding crossed his face.

"You love him and you believe he still loves his wife, and you have made a bargain that will break your heart if it comes to pass. That is truly a dilemma."

"Yes," Lynette said miserably. "He is willing to marry any woman with enough wealth, and prefers one who will not demand his time or presence. That is not marriage, it is a . . . a . . . I have my pride as well."

"Then win him, daughter," Eldwyn said quietly.

"What?"

"Win him. Warrior he might be, knight he might be, and bitter he might be. But beneath all that he is a man. Whether you believe it or no, a man needs the warmth and the strength that home offers. For a long while . . . I would say since the death of his wife, he has wandered without that comfort, until he believes it came only with Sybella. Show him it is not so."

"Oh, Papa, I'm . . . I'm afraid."

"You?" Eldwyn chided tenderly. "You have been afraid of nothing since you could stand on your own two feet."

"But I am."

"Perhaps you have made him believe that it is

you who would prefer any other but him. Perhaps," Eldwyn said quietly, "it is his own pride that speaks. If his desire is not to marry . . . and you claim that another would please you more . . ."

Lynette considered this in a new light. She had told Royce more than once that she preferred to choose another.

"Oh, Papa, this is such a muddled affair. I wish I really knew his mind."

"I wish I really knew her mind, Robert. She is a puzzle," Royce said.

"What woman is not? You will wed the girl," Robert laughed. "And that will give you a number of years to understand the puzzle. That is, if a woman's ways can ever be understood."

"There will be no wedding."

"What? Do you choose to go against the king's will? I thought your honor was above breaking your pledge." Robert scowled, his brows drawing together and his mouth growing tight.

"We have struck a bargain, she and I."

"A bargain?" Robert said suspiciously. "I see your hand here."

"Nay, it is her choice I would honor. She wants the right to see if there is another way."

Robert knew quite well that Royce was skirting the issue. "She has no choice."

"She has the right to petition William for a choice. Should she find a knight William trusts and who will care for the land as William's man, why should she not wed him?" His gaze met Robert's directly, and for a second Robert was without words. Then another thought came to him.

"This sounds more like your thoughts than hers. What does she know of court or William's wishes . . . unless you have set her to thinking on this line?"

"Robert—"

"There is more to this than you are saying. What have you forced upon this girl?"

Royce could almost have laughed at Robert's anger, had he not hit so close to the truth. He had never lied to his mentor, and he didn't intend to start now. Of course, *all* the truth was not necessary.

"She was reluctant about the marriage, and you know it was not to my liking. I simply informed her that she had choices. So . . . we made a bargain."

"So you have said." Robert's look got darker and darker. "You had best explain to me just what you had to bargain with. It is the king's wish that you marry this girl."

"We both know that William is well content with Matilda. He loves the woman completely. Do you not think," Royce reasoned softly, "that his ear will be open when this girl . . . this beautiful and innocent girl, pleads for him to give her a man she could wed with pleasure? Especially if she has another that the king would look favorably upon. He will see the right of it and give her her choice, and Creganwald will be held in his name as he desires."

"And what will you do, you foolish whelp, if William decides you will wed whether you like it or not!"

"Do not be angry, old friend." Royce's face grew somber. "It is her welfare that is uppermost in my mind. She is too gentle and sweet to be condemned to a life with my nightmares . . . and . . . I would not see her in Sybella's place."

"So far you have described her as beautiful, gentle, and sweet. Are these not then good reasons for a marriage? Many have been wed with less. As far as what happened in the past, you must learn one day to put it where it belongs . . . in the past. Lynette is a different woman, and she is strong and healthy. There is no reason for such a thing to happen again."

"I would not put her in Sybella's place," Royce reiterated quietly.

Robert studied his face intently for a long and very uncomfortable moment. Then his brow cleared. He considered his next words carefully.

"What does it matter to you the outcome, if she bears the heir William wants?" He shrugged.

The look Royce turned to him was filled with rage. The same old fear held him.

"I will hear no more about the subject. The bargain has been made, and I am sure of the outcome. She is a woman who will attract many, and surely one of them will meet her demands. William is not a fool. He would have a happy subject bending to his will, rather than one who will only learn to hate him more every moment she spends in a loveless marriage."

"And you?"

"I will be free to go on with my life and . . . "

"And?"

"I have much to make up for with Cerise. I have been unjust, and I would try to mend our relationship. She does not trust me."

"But she loves you."

"She is in love with the stories she had heard of me, and the man she has built in her dreams. That is not me. But I will have to replace that dream with something more lasting."

"It is good, Royce. I am happy that you have finally accepted her for the loving child she is. But—"

"Nay, Robert, leave it at that. The matter is settled. We have only to contend with William, and I am certain I can get him to listen to reason. He desires peace among his people. This is the best way to keep peace at Creganwald."

Royce left Robert with a thoughtful gleam in his eye.

The company left early the next morning, a much larger company than Lynette had expected. She had kissed her father a rather fearful good-bye, for no matter how much he professed that he felt fine, to Lynette his face seemed pale.

"Papa, you will send word if you need me?"

"You send word of the marriage and I will come to you."

"Please take care. Take your medicine and don't overdo yourself. I love you, Papa."

"And I you, child. Now, kiss me once more and go. Your man awaits you."

Lynette did kiss him again, and even as they rode away she looked back to wave again and again.

Royce followed her movements and had no intention of rushing her departure.

A small caravan of wagons carried clothes and valuables and refreshments for when they would stop along the road. Royce's men accompanied them to make sure of their safety. Royce, Robert, Oriel, and Lynette rode at the front of the column.

To Cerise's surprise, Royce had taken her before him. He had discovered what good company she could be, and how intelligent she was. And to add to that, he had lost too many years, and wanted to try to build a bridge of understanding between them.

Almost every time Cerise opened her mouth, it was to speak of Lynette, until it was as if Lynette rode beside them. Lynette had put some distance between herself and Royce, and rode beside Robert, who kept her occupied with conversation about William so she would have no difficulty when she arrived at court.

It was a slow progress, but their arrival in London two days later came in the midafternoon. The air was cold, and slightly damp against the skin. They came first to a broad thoroughfare, where the city dwellers had set up their stalls and shelters to sell their wares. Lynette was as fascinated as Cerise. Both would have stopped to make purchases had not Royce made it clear they would go on.

When they arrived at their destination, Lynette was surprised to find a large, three-story domain. The bottom floor would be for Royce's men and the main hall in which they would all share their meals.

The second floor was reserved for Oriel, Cerise, and Lynette. The top floor was Royce's alone. It took less time to get settled than Lynette could have imagined, and she realized that Royce's household was run with efficiency.

The chamber to which she was led was not really large, and had only one window that looked out on the city. A large bed and two chests made up what furniture there was.

Lynette was just putting away the last of her

things when Cerise peered around the corner of her door.

"Papa says to come below when you are ready, food is being prepared."

"Thank goodness. I'm starving."

"Lynette?"

"Yes?"

"Papa says we are going to meet the king while we are here."

Lynette sat slowly on the bed. It was unsettling to be reminded that she would soon be meeting William, the man who held her future in his hands.

"Are you afraid?" Cerise could not believe that the look on Lynette's face was fear.

"Yes, I guess I am."

"You don't need to be."

"And why don't I need to be?" Lynette smiled at Cerise's attempt to reassure her.

"Because Papa said he would be there, and the king likes him. If Papa says he likes you, then the king will be nice to you." Cerise spoke with such conviction that Lynette had no intention of telling her the king might be the one who separated them forever. She had grown fond of the child, and parting was going to be difficult.

"I'm sure he will be," Lynette replied. But she was thinking how much happier she would be if Royce had chosen to stay at Creganwald, and had been content to wed her. She would have given almost anything for him to turn to her, and let go of the memories that haunted him. At this moment she came close to hating Sybella. She remembered Robert's words, that there were many times when he wished Royce had never met and married her.

Now she would have to keep her part of the bargain, and look among the knights that gathered around William for one who could take Royce's place.

This brought to mind the other half of the bargain. Unhappily, she imagined the women who would fall eagerly into Royce's arms, all of them wealthy, and all of them willing. She began to hate them too.

"Please hurry, Lynette," Cerise begged. "I won't get to stay up late if you aren't there. I will have to eat and go to bed, for all the knights are gathered."

"I'm hurrying." Lynette laughed and finished by hastily brushing and braiding her hair, then splashing some water on her face to remove the signs of travel. Within minutes they joined the others for the meal.

Chapter Thirteen

The dinner that night was a relaxed and easy one, for the king would not arrive this first night, although many of Royce's friends did. When Lynette and Cerise were brought into the main hall, a number of curious eyes watched and wondered who this beauty was and what the chances were that she was wealthy and available.

Royce was soon surrounded by ambitious knights, hungry knights, and worse, knights with wealth and honorable intentions. He made introduction after introduction, smiling through clenched teeth. It was the honorable ones and the ones who had been his friends that bothered him most. Among these was Brendwyn, an old friend and frequent battle companion.

"Ah, Royce, it is good to see you again. I have been hearing any number of stories about where you had gone off to. I even heard you are planning marriage again. Of a certainty, I knew that wasn't true."

"Brendwyn, you know better than to listen to rumor," Royce replied, but he kept his gaze from Lynette.

"And this lovely creature." Brendwyn smiled at Lynette. "I have never seen you at court before. Has your husband been keeping you under a watchful eye? I should not wonder."

He was outrageously charming, and Lynette liked his open smile and the hint of laughter in his eyes.

"I'm afraid I have no husband, sir, and this is the first time I have been to London. I am Lynette of Creganwald."

Lynette responded to Brendwyn with gay, light-hearted banter, and soon a crowd of young knights had gathered around her. She was ready of wit, and she quipped and told stories that brought laughter and admiring looks from the knights surrounding her. Royce could do little more than watch; after all, he had given her the chance to choose. Still, he studied them all closely, and found some fault or other with each one. None of them were acceptable as husbands for Lynette. This one was too conceited, the next too much a womanizer, another too sly . . . and on and on.

Standing next to him, Lynette would often look up at him with a smile of innocence that set his teeth on edge.

When they all gathered at the table, he made certain his chair was beside Lynette's, just as Brendwyn made sure he sat on the other side of her. Cerise sat next to Robert, who seemed to her to be in exceptionally good spirits tonight. In fact, he chuckled under his breath as if he had a secret he could not share with anyone.

After the meal was finished, Cerise was reluctantly taken to bed by a maid of Lynette's choosing. She would have loved to remain in a corner where she could watch the dancing that would take place.

The hall dissolved in merriment as the dancing began, and Lynette was taken often from Royce's side. When he danced with her he voiced his displeasure at what he called a group of mindless knights in heat. He heard the tinkle of her laughter and had to smile in response.

"How can a woman make a choice if she does not study each knight by himself?"

"There is plenty of time to make a decision once the king arrives. You need not fall into every set of arms that open for you."

"Oh, I have found that there will be plenty of opportunities." Lynette laughed as she danced away from him, then returned. "I have had so many offers to ride and to hunt, and to join one or the other, that I fear I will have my days full, and most likely a knight chosen before William arrives."

"How simply you go about your choices. Do you not question their motives?"

"What should I question?" Lynette asked as the dance ended and they stood close together. "Their motives are the same as any others'. To find a maid with lands and a good name, and with the king's help gain possession of both. My only problem is quite a different one."

"Oh, what is that?"

"Since I cannot dance with any of the ladies, I must rely on what is said to me about each one. It is going to make it difficult to choose the right one for you. I have seen any number of ladies that are read-

161

ily available. For instance, Lady Clotith. She has a delightful sense of humor. Perhaps," Lynette said mischievously, "she could even teach you to laugh. And Lady Anne, consider how pretty she is, and Lady Meggie—"

"Enough! You take this bargain too fast. It will take more than one night of dancing to make such a decision."

"Oh, aye." Lynette looked up at him. "But I am going to be so occupied in the next few days that I fear I will see little of you, and how can I make suggestions if you do not consider them seriously? We must come to some agreement before William arrives . . . mustn't we?" The question was spoken gently, and before he could answer, Lynette was swept away by another enamored swain.

Royce considered the three ladies Lynette had mentioned. Lady Clotith. She was of a wealthy family with a good name. She was pretty, with sable brown hair and soft, doe-like brown eyes . . . but her eyes were not the sky blue he had come to enjoy . . . and her skin was not nearly as soft and silky looking . . . even her smile was not as . . . He shrugged that thought away. She would not do for a number of reasons.

He looked at the others and found fault with each one. This one's hair was not nearly so thick and golden, and that one's form was not nearly so softly rounded and yet slender. Another was not nearly so . . . and Cerise! Of course, Cerise. He had to consider her. She loved Lynette, and it would have to be someone Cerise would respond to. It would take some time to discover that. He smiled at his own cleverness.

Lynette saw the smile, and her heart felt as if it would stop. He had chosen! There was a satisfied look on his face, and she felt the pleasure of the evening flow from her body. How simple it was for him. He felt no love for her, and so he had casually chosen from her own suggestions.

Grimly she fought to keep her thoughts to herself. He might have chosen, but the game was not over yet.

For the next few days she was almost overwhelmed by the invitations she received from one young knight or the other. She rode with one, ate with another, and when she could bear no more, she escaped to Cerise's room, where she could laugh and play and relax her vigilance and keep thoughts of Royce at bay.

She and Cerise grew even closer, and as Cerise bloomed under the new attention she received from her father, she opened her heart to everyone around her.

Lynette kept as far away from Royce as she could. If he had made his choice, she did not want to hear the name, for she would hate the woman.

Royce was annoyed at Lynette's absence, yet he understood it. If she was to choose another, it was best he did not interfere until that choice was made. Only when William arrived would they join forces and approach the king.

There had been no sign of Oriel either, and when Royce questioned her brother, he simply said she had gone to visit relatives. Royce had no way of knowing that Giles wished heartily she would stay away from court. He did not like the way she had looked at Lynette, and he knew her too well not to believe there was some form of vengeance deep in her heart.

It was two nights before the king was expected when Oriel returned. She arrived late in the evening, with a large group of knights, among whom was the one she had traveled to find.

The entire group was tired from travel and had their horses seen to while each found his bed. Oriel, her face calm with contained satisfaction, went to her brother's chamber to let him know she was back. When he opened his door, he found it difficult to keep from revealing his displeasure. He felt guilty; after all, this was his sister, and she had been on her best behavior since they had left Creganwald.

"Oriel."

"It is late, brother, but I thought you would be concerned for my safety."

"Of course. Did you have a good journey?"

"Aye, it was pleasant."

"Oriel, you look quite satisfied with yourself. You have finally decided to lay aside your ambitions and forget Royce?"

"I have decided to let fate take its course. Sometimes there are things out of our control."

Giles knew he should feel relief at her words, but something felt wrong. Oriel seemed calmer and even friendlier than before she'd left. Maybe she finally understood that she could do nothing about Royce and the Lady Lynette.

"When does William arrive, Giles?" Oriel asked.

"Sometime within the next three days, I'm told. Why?"

"I am anxious to see him."

"Why?"

"Why such a suspicious question?"

"Oriel, why?"

"Because I choose to speak to him about my future."

"You have a request of the king?" he asked in disbelief. "Oriel, we are on the king's sufferance now. It is not our place to make requests. All that we have, we owe to Royce, who took me into his service when few others would. I have little but my sword and shield, and my arm. That was enough for him. Surely you do not believe we can ask more?"

"You think too shallowly, brother. If one does not ask, one will achieve nothing. Besides, have we not a friend in Royce? Will he not speak for us should we make a small request? We are the conquerors here, and yet you and I live like the lowest. Look at that Saxon bitch, she lives as if she were the conqueror. There are those who would show her her place." Oriel ceased to speak, as if she had said more than she had planned.

"Who? What have you been up to since you left us?"

"Oh, really, Giles, I have been up to nothing. Why can you not welcome me home, and cease your questions? You are my brother, my only protector." Her voice gentled. "Is there not enough love in your heart that you can only think the worst of me?"

Giles felt guilty, for he always did think the worst of Oriel, and even now he was just as suspicious as she claimed.

"I'm sorry, Oriel. Sometimes you make me worry that you do not judge consequences before you act."

"Will there be any festivities tonight?"

"Aye, are there not always? This court does not stint on its feasting and celebrating."

"Good, it has been long since I have had any pleasure. You know how it is at Wallham."

"There are a great number of knights and their ladies here awaiting the king. I'm sure you will enjoy yourself."

"I'm sure I will," Oriel replied with a half smile. She left her brother and went to her own chamber. As she walked her smile grew broader. "Yes, brother . . . I'm sure I will."

The court was too crowded for Royce's taste, and he was glad he had a separate dwelling for himself, Cerise, Lynette, and his men. When they returned home that night, he felt a sense of relief. He liked the peace of his own dwelling, and the absence of the clamoring crowd at court. He had always avoided the court as much as he could, and these past few days assured him he had been right.

He could hear the men below, slowly settling for the night, and felt a comfort such as he had not felt in a long time. This was his home, the only real one he had known, and all who were close to him were under one roof and in his care . . . at least for now. That brought a stab of annoyance. If he retained Creganwald, he would have a place he could build into something permanent, and Cerise would have the kind of life Lynette had had. She would be in a place where she could put down roots, and learn the kind of pleasures and freedoms that had been denied him. But that meant marriage and . . .

He forced the thought from his mind. He was not

going to open that door again; it was better left closed.

He felt the urge to see Cerise. He knew she must have been asleep for hours. But he was moving toward his door before the thought was finished. He paused outside her door, surprised to find light revealed through the crack at the bottom. Cerise must still be up. He pushed the door open and stepped inside.

The fire in the hearth was burning brightly, indicating that it had been rekindled. Seated before the hearth were Cerise and Lynette. They had been whispering together and laughing softly, as if sharing confidences. Furs had been brought from the bed, and both were nestled in them comfortably. This time the urge to join them was not ignored, and he was halfway across the room before they saw him. Cerise was quick to smile, but Lynette wondered if she had not made a mistake in coming here.

She half expected Royce to order Cerise to bed, or her to her own chamber. She did not expect him to join them, seat himself comfortably, and invite a more than willing Cerise to crawl up on his lap. He drew her closer to him; over her head he watched Lynette. The fire glow was creating a miracle with her hair, and her skin was a melding of ivory and cream. He did not miss the look of discomfort in her eyes, and yet he would not have left for any reason.

"It seems that too much excitement has prevented sleep from finding you."

"Aye." Lynette smiled. "There has been much excitement of late. But . . . I am told the king comes soon, and there are things that I know you want decided by then. So I must take time from the celebrating to think on what must be considered."

"And . . . and you have come to a decision?" He held his breath, hoping a name would not be said to settle a matter he could not settle in his own mind.

"No, not yet. There are so many to choose from."

Cerise was not following the conversation at all. It was as if there was some dark secret between the two people she loved, and she wasn't too sure she liked it. She squirmed around in Royce's lap and looked up at him.

"Papa, when can we go home?"

"Home?"

"Back to Creganwald. That's home now, isn't it?"

"I . . . I'm not sure yet, Cerise."

"But you said—"

"We must wait for the king to make the final decision. Can you not be happy if we must live somewhere else?"

"No, Papa." Her alarm was rising. "Lynette won't be somewhere else, and I don't want to live with . . . " Her eyes rose to him in horror. "With Lady Oriel." She said it as if it were the worst punishment in her imagination.

"Cerise, I promise you, you will never live with Oriel . . . ever." He smiled down at her, but saw her uncertainty remained. "Now, what were you two talking about?"

"Lynette was telling me a story."

"Oh, about what?"

"Just a tale of princes and princesses and their adventures," Lynette answered.

"Go on with it."

"I . . . no . . . I think it's time Cerise went to sleep.

It's late, Cerise. I'll finish the story tomorrow night."

"All right," Cerise said, disappointed. But she knew Lynette had already told her several stories, and that it was time to sleep. Royce watched as Lynette took Cerise to the bed and covered her carefully.

They walked to the door together and continued to Lynette's room without speaking. Royce was not sure what his feelings were; he only knew he needed to talk to her and he didn't want to say good night. They paused before her door.

"May I come in? I wish to talk to you."

"Do you think that wise? It is late."

"It is important," he said firmly.

Lynette didn't want to hear his decision, didn't want to hear the name of the lady who would take her place . . . and worse, she didn't want to tell him that it was impossible for her to choose a knight to replace him, that there was not a man walking who could match him. She did not want to weaken and beg him to stay with her, and if she let him into her room now, she had a feeling she might do just that.

She looked up at him, and he was startled by the vulnerability in her eyes; it unsettled him.

"Please . . . no. I . . . I'll speak to you tomorrow. I am sure you can tell me what . . . anything . . . then. Good night."

She stepped inside her room and closed the door before he could find an excuse to stay. He paused for several minutes, considering the look in her eyes. Had she found someone to please her and was waiting only for the king to arrive? He walked slowly to his chamber, his mind on a bargain that was getting more uncomfortable by the minute.

Once in his bed, he folded his hands behind his head and considered his alternatives.

Lynette, too, considered the situation, and wished she could cast her pride aside and tell him that he was the only one she would choose. She thought of all Robert had told her, and wondered if there really was a way to reach Royce's frozen heart.

She longed again to feel the strength of his arms about her. Tonight she would have surrendered to that desire and begged him to stay, whether he married someone else or not. That was how shameless she had become. She would go to him right now if she had not known that he had no room in his heart for any other than Sybella.

"Oh, Papa, how can I win him when his every thought is of her? When he doesn't want me? How can I . . . " She paused. Was her pride more important than anything? Was it so important that she should let him go? Was she a coward that she could not go to him with the truth and learn what his answer would be? No. She would not let pride stand in her way. Tomorrow she would go to him and reveal her feelings. If he denied her, then what did it matter whom she chose?

Tomorrow . . . tomorrow . . .

. . . *Tomorrow,* Royce was repeating to himself; tomorrow he would force her to face him and hear what was in his heart. Tomorrow he would tell her he wanted to return to Creganwald with her and Cerise. Would she refuse him? If she did, would he fall back on the king's command? The answer was an unqualified yes. He meant to keep her, one way or the other.

Both made a decision, and both looked to tomorrow to put an end to their difficulties. Both decided to take their lives in their hands. And fate made a decision too.

Chapter Fourteen

Royce woke very early and was breaking his fast in front of a newly rekindled fire long before most of the men were stirring. Neither Lynette nor Cerise was awake either. Royce had just finished eating when Robert, sleepy-eyed and quiet, joined him.

Robert found a comfortable place close to the fire and with ale and food in hand turned to Royce.

"You rise early."

"Aye, I found sleep difficult."

"Something preys on your mind?"

Royce considered his words before he spoke, and this drew Robert's closer attention.

"It is my thought, Robert, to see an end to this bargain between Lynette and me."

Robert took a deep drink of ale, and tried to control his relief and pleasure at these words.

"Lynette has already chosen another?"

Royce looked on Robert with a dark scowl. "Nay, she has said no word to me. But it is not because there have not been enough rutting idiots stumbling around her. You would think her a pot of honey and they a swarm of bees."

Now Robert could have shouted his joy to the rooftops. Royce was jealous of the attention Lynette was attracting.

"Then why rid yourself of the bargain?" he said slyly. "Let her choose, and you can be gone and forget this . . . swarm. You cannot fault them. Lynette has beauty enough to draw them even without the land and the king's favor." He shrugged. "You can hardly blame them. She is a tempting morsel for any red-blooded man."

"That is not the plan I have in mind. Robert, I would see the king's will done," Royce said stiffly.

Robert could not help a bit of tormenting. "How very generous of you. Surely the king will be well pleased, but what of the maid? Mayhap she does not want to see the end of the bargain. Mayhap," he added quietly, "she would rather choose?"

"A bargain made can be a bargain broken, if both agree. I do not intend to take nay as an answer. If need be—"

"You will force her to comply," Robert said. He leaned forward and said in a different tone, "Why can you not just find out where her heart leads her . . . and tell her that you tread the same path? A few soft words and a touch of love will stand you in good stead."

"I don't think she would believe me. I have said too many harsh words to smooth them with soft ones now."

"You truly think she will hold to the bargain?"

"Aye."

"Then you should find the truth of it. Speak to her first, and if you find the bargain settled in her mind . . . then the king's command will be your weapon."

"Mayhap you are right. I will speak to her today. Since the king does not arrive until tomorrow, there will be time to make sure her will and mine are the same."

"Take her from this hall," Robert laughed, "or you will be fighting off lovesick swains while you try to convince her."

"Aye." Royce smiled. "We will ride out this morning as soon as she wakens."

"Royce, make no mistake. The lady is held in esteem by all your knights, and all she comes in contact with."

"Even you, old friend?" Royce was amused, for he knew Robert spoke the truth.

"Aye," Robert chuckled. "Especially me. I have given thought to how pleasant it would be to see her each day. My old age would be greatly brightened."

Before Royce could speak again, there was a knock on the door. A message was brought to Royce, who read it with first a look of shock and then dismay. He turned to Robert.

"The king has arrived a day early. He commands our presence . . . now."

"Now?"

"The message says *immediately*. I surmise that means now."

"Aye, the king does not twist his words."

"Robert, you know the confusion around him. This may take hours. You and I may not get back here before nightfall, if then."

"There is little you can do about it."

"I know."

"What if you were to ask Giles or Ferragus to take Lynette to the yuletide fair? There is much to show a maid, as you well know."

Royce brightened at Robert's suggestion, and he went to kick Giles and Ferragus awake. Into their foggy minds he finally forced the mission he required of them. The task was an easy one, for both were fond of Lynette and enjoyed her company.

"Take Cerise with you or Lynette will worry over her care and want to return too soon. See that your day is well spent and that there is little time left, other than to prepare herself to meet the king when she returns."

Royce and Robert left soon after, and rode quickly to answer the summons. They were welcomed by a host of old companions, and finally found their way to William, who added his welcome to theirs.

"You have come a day before you were expected, sire," Royce said. "Otherwise I would have been here to greet you."

"I know, Royce. The roads were clear and the travel was easy. I wanted to meet the maid, Lady Lynette. Have you not brought her with you?"

"Nay, sire, she will see to Cerise and join us later."

At the mention of Cerise's name, William was a bit surprised, for he had not heard Royce say her name in his presence before. He exchanged a quick look with Robert, and knew the tale would be given in full later.

"Come, join me for a meal. We have much to talk about."

Royce could have groaned. This would indeed take hours and there would be no chance to talk to Lynette before she joined them later that evening.

The activity around them grew with each passing minute, as knight after knight appeared. It was some time before Robert was able to speak with William.

"And so, Robert, how do your plans work? I heard his child's name for the first time. 'Tis a good sign."

"Aye, but there are other signs that bode better. The lass has unlocked doors with a gentle touch, and has brought Cerise to him. I believe he has opened his eyes, and once we have them wed, the problem will be well resolved. You will have a loyal subject happily ruling your lands with care, and with the help of a lady I have come to see was the best thing to have happened to him."

"Excellent . . . excellent. I am glad there is an end to his grief."

"I see that as a good possibility." Robert smiled. "The lady is most interesting. She has been, as Royce put it, surrounded like a pot of honey by a swarm of bees."

"And that pleases you?"

"Aye, a great deal. Tell me, have you ever seen anyone take from Royce what he considers his?"

"And he considers her his." William chuckled.

"Aye. He is chafing under the idea that he might lose her, should you change your command."

"I am the one who wanted this wedding; why should I change my command?"

"It seems," Robert said calmly, "that Royce and the lady made a bargain."

"A bargain?"

Robert explained the bargain quickly. "Now, I think his heart is not in it, nor do I think hers is. But each thinks the other is set upon it. She will come to you."

"He does not want to be free?"

"I think not, and I am almost certain that the lady would go most willingly to him should she really believe he has changed his mind."

"Robert, I will not change my command."

"Thank you," Robert replied simply.

"Do not thank me. I care deeply for Royce. He has been loyal to me from the beginning, and I understand his grief. Had I lost Matilda, I believe I would have cared little for going on. We will see this to the end. What else can prevent it, if both are in agreement?"

"Aye, what else?"

Lynette was surprised to find both Robert and Royce gone when she arose; she was even more surprised when she was told of the king's early arrival and the need for Royce's hasty departure. She was assured that they expected her to come later. Then Giles and Ferragus informed Cerise of the yuletide fair and said they would take both her and Lynette, if Lynette agreed.

Cerise pleaded, and Lynette surrendered with a laugh. She enjoyed the ride and the fair and, most of all, Cerise's enthusiasm, but she wondered what Royce might be saying to the king. Her hopes to win him would come to naught if he asked William for release. She wished she had had time to speak to him before he left. She was prepared to toss her pride out the window and tell him that there was no other man she would want as husband and future lord of Creganwald.

When the shadows grew long, she was eager to head for home. A message from Royce was already there: she was to dress and accompany his men to meet the king.

She made her way to her room, unsure of what to expect from the upcoming interview. She was no more to the king than a means to an end. What did it matter to him if another were chosen? But her heart would break if she lost Royce.

Lynette sank slowly down on a chair. Tonight she would meet William. She summoned up everything she had ever heard said about the king.

He was loyal to those who were loyal to him. . . . He adored his wife and was surprisingly loyal to her. . . . He was reasonably just. But what did all this avail her if Royce wanted freedom? He was a loyal knight of William and would most likely be given his way.

It was an impossible situation! How could she cold-bloodedly stand in a gathering of William's knights and their ladies, and casually pick a lady to suit Royce? And just as casually pick out a knight to suit her, as if she were in the marketplace choosing a cabbage for the evening meal? The more she thought of it, the more impossible it became.

But evening came whether she willed it or not, and she found herself more richly attired than she had ever been, on the way to meet the man who held her future. . . . and her heart . . . in his hands.

She was surprised to find Royce waiting for her close to the door, so that he could be the first at her side. He was pleased to see his knights surrounding her protectively and meant to thank them heartily the first chance he got.

"Lynette, you look very beautiful."

She looked up at him in surprise. This was the first compliment he had given her. But his look was warm, and she returned his smile. "Thank you."

"I must have some time to speak to you about something important. I would like to talk to you before you make any requests of the king."

"Do you think he is going to consider your petition?"

"I hope so," he said, testing her.

"So . . . so do I . . . if that is what you wish." She wondered if her heart would break when William freed them from their pledge.

Lynette had not known what to anticipate when she entered the room, but she had not expected to be inundated with admiring knights almost from the moment she and Royce entered the throne room. Lynette was quick to notice that Royce received just as many looks from the ladies of the court.

The announcement of the king's entrance put an end to Lynette's thoughts and to the stabs of jealousy she felt. She wanted to meet the king, look into his eyes, and try to see for herself if he was the kind of man who would bend because of a pleading request from a conquered lady. Her doubts shivered through her, and Royce bent closer.

"Are you all right?"

"Aye," she said, looking up at him in surprise. Obviously he was somehow aware of her thoughts and feelings. Royce gazed down upon her and was about to say more when a buzz of excitement pervaded the hall and William entered.

Dressed in brilliant robes of state, he made a fine appearance, but Lynette unconsciously compared him to Royce and found even the king wanting. He was a massive man, commanding and well made, yet he stood half a head shorter than Royce. William's face revealed nothing of his thoughts, and Lynette could read nothing but mild interest as each knight greeted him.

Yet she saw a subtle change when he paused by Royce. And then he was looking at her. He was magnetic, and she found herself smiling up at him.

"You are Lady Lynette of Creganwald," he stated as he searched her face with interest.

"Aye, Your Grace." She sank into a curtsy and rose to stand before him proudly. William kept his thoughts to himself, but he felt pleased that a man he respected and admired would hold Creganwald and this lively maid.

"I would be more interested in you than in your lands, were I the one chosen to govern them. Have you any complaints of your warden, Lady Lynette?"

"Nay, sire, but . . . there are matters of which Royce and I would speak to you in private." William saw a flicker of doubt and pain touch her eyes fleetingly, and gave a puzzled frown at Royce.

"It is nothing of great importance, sire," Royce said. "A small matter we can speak of in private." He did not want the words said in the presence of the entire court.

Lynette was shaken and struggled to retain her smile. He did not even consider her important enough to discuss until the festivities were enjoyed.

Royce saw the puzzlement in her eyes and had no answer she would accept.

"Lynette . . . I must talk to you before we discuss our . . . situation with the king," he whispered, bending close. But Lynette was in no mood for his games.

"Discuss? I believe we have been of the same mind. What has changed?"

William had been listening to someone else, but only with half an ear. He tried to hear what Royce whispered, but he couldn't.

"Much has changed. Will you hear me out, or must you be obstinate?"

"Obstinate?" she hissed. " 'Tis as much your will as mine. You are as changeable as the weather. I do not understand you at all."

Chapter Fifteen

Royce took Lynette's arm, intending to drag her to some place out of earshot where he could convince her of his intentions and plead with her to put aside their bargain. Her resistance was small compared to his strength, and he might have succeeded in his intent had not a bustle of activity near the door drawn their attention.

Lynette was spellbound by the two who had just entered the room, but what she felt was small compared to Royce's reaction. His muscles tightened, and when she looked up into his face, it was drained of color and looked as fierce as if he were facing a mortal enemy.

She returned her gaze to the two people who stood framed in the doorway. The two men were standing side by side and both were gazing around the crowded room as if they were looking for someone. One took a step forward, and it was then that his gaze fell on Royce. Lynette knew these were no strangers, but they were certainly not welcome guests either, at least not by Royce. She could hardly take her eyes from them. One was considerably younger than the other, and Lynette wondered if they were father and son.

The younger man was . . . magnificent! It was the only word that came to Lynette's mind. He was as tall as Royce, and his shoulders as broad. His face was strong, with a gold tanned skin that was a perfect foil for the amazing and vivid green of his eyes.

Behind him stood the second man, and he, too, was enough to take a woman's breath away. His hair was a thick silver mass, as was his beard. But his years sat well upon him, for he looked strong and vigorous. He was brawny and heavy of chest and arm. His amber eyes surveyed the crowded room as if he were well used to the gathering of nobility.

Lynette would not have been alarmed except for the look on Royce's face, and the fact that beside the older man stood Oriel, with a look of satisfaction on her face.

"Who are they?" Lynette whispered to Royce. For a moment she thought either he hadn't heard her or chose not to answer.

"That is Sir Tearlach, and the knight is his nephew, Sir Beltane. They are distant relatives of William," Royce answered between clenched teeth. "Strange, I did not know Lady Oriel was acquainted with them."

"You know them well?"

"Aye, too well," he replied. He said no more, and Lynette was certain he did not mean to say more.

He also made no motion to meet them and in fact

turned his back to speak to Robert, who had just joined them.

Royce knew he would have to put off the discussion with Lynette, but he would have her safely in his home tonight and would force her to listen if necessary.

"I see the Lady Oriel has returned," Royce said to Robert.

"Aye, and, in good company," Robert replied. "I did not realize she knew those two."

"Nor did I," Royce said. He was regaining control. Lynette could feel him struggle to relax his body. It aroused her curiosity about the two and their connection to him.

"Aye," Robert said uncomfortably. "William is much in Tearlach's debt."

Lynette did not miss the look that passed between Robert and Royce, and she knew there were old and unresolved problems here.

"Robert . . . " Royce began, but he was interrupted by the older man, who laid a hand on his arm and smiled.

"Hold your words. They come this way."

When Royce turned to face the approaching group, it was as if he were about to speak to old and welcome guests.

"Ah, Royce, it has been some time since we have crossed paths." Beltane smiled. His gaze moved quickly from Royce to Lynette. "And I see you still have the most exquisite taste in women."

"Lynette, may I present Sir Beltane. Lynette will soon be my wife," Royce added, almost as if it were a warning to Beltane.

"How fortunate you are," he murmured. "I had

not thought you would ever marry again. But of course, time, the appearance of a pretty face, and some wealth are enough to draw any hotblooded man from his grief." He turned to Lynette and smiled. She returned his smile hesitantly, for she could sense that this man meant trouble for Royce. "How lovely you are, Lady Lynette. We have not seen you at court before."

"Thank you, sir." Lynette could not help the fascination she felt. He was a man of charisma, and she flushed when his eyes moved over her. "I am a simple girl of the country, Sir Beltane, and I have never been to court before."

"When is this wedding to take place?" he asked.

"Within the month," Lynette answered.

Beltane laughed softly. "That is a long time to keep a lovely creature like yourself safe. You had best be very careful, Royce, or someone will steal her from under your nose." He turned his smile on Lynette, and again she was struck by the almost perfect handsomeness of this man and the devastating power of his personality. "Lady Lynette, may I present my uncle, Sir Tearlach. He and William are distantly related."

Lynette got the feeling she was supposed to be impressed by this. Did he think she would suddenly decide Royce was lacking royal blood and turn to him instead?

"I did not expect to see you at this gathering, Sir Beltane," Royce said. "When I saw you last, you were engaged in a turn at arms . . . over the favor of a lady, I understand. Tell me, did you win? Is the lady yours now?"

Beltane smiled more broadly. "You are mistaken

as to the cause of the battle, and of course I won. But there has never been a woman I have raised my sword over . . . nor would . . . until now."

Lynette felt Royce stiffen, and she too felt a tingle of fear run through her. Royce and Beltane were looking at each other like predators about to fight over prey.

"Lady Lynette," Beltane said with a smile meant to charm. "You are mistress of Creganwald, are you not?"

"Aye."

" 'Tis rare for a Norman lord to be forced to marry a Saxon to retain her lands. I should think you would rather choose among your own kind. Unless . . . you put a very high price on your favors."

"I had little choice in the matter, Sir Beltane, but I believe it would have been impossible to have chosen better. Royce is a valued knight of William's. I would give my favors to no man, but I would honor the marriage William has set for me, and the man as well."

Beltane's smile froze. Robert contained his laughter with a great deal of effort, and Royce would have liked nothing better than to take Lynette in his arms and kiss her until she was breathless. But Lynette was aware only of two things, Royce's pleasure and the deepening interest that warmed Beltane's eyes.

Before anyone else could speak, William approached. His face wore a troubled look. While he introduced Lynette to several other knights, he avoided both her gaze and Royce's.

"So, Royce, we have not seen you for a number

of years," Tearlach said and none could miss the viciousness in his voice. "It seems you were right to sell your sword to the highest bidder. William is now king. And this Saxon wench will be your wife. There are rich and favored lands that go with her. William has made many hasty decisions. This one must be examined."

"There is little to examine," Royce said. "The lands and the lady have already been promised to me. I keep what I have earned by the strength of my arm . . . with the strength of my arm."

Tearlach laughed a boisterous laugh. "Still the wild one, are you? Mayhap you are right, and mayhap not. Time will tell the tale. There is many a slip 'twixt cup and lip. Do not drink too hastily for fear you may choke."

"Enough, Tearlach," William said, and there was a flush of anger on his face. "Let us join the others and put away trouble for tonight."

"Of course," Tearlach said softly. He bowed slightly to Lynette and moved away to greet others.

But Beltane lingered. He had been watching both Royce and Lynette throughout the confrontation, and the glimmer of avarice and lust lingered in his eyes. If he knew his uncle, there was a way to stop Royce, and he now had his eye not only on Lynette's lands . . . but on Lynette as well.

He did not often see a beauty who caught his attention as this one did. She was rare; a lady of exquisite beauty, yes, but he knew there was much more. She was a woman of strength, who would turn to fire in a man's arms, he warranted. He meant to be the one to catch the flame. He also needed a way to strike Royce. His hatred of him went back a number of years, and he never forgot someone he hated as much as he hated him.

Robert was silent. He promised himself to take the first opportunity to get William alone and put a few pertinent questions to him.

"Lady Lynette," Beltane said, "William is to honor my uncle with a visit tomorrow afternoon. It would please him, I know, and it would please me, if you were to join us."

"I am afraid that is impossible, Sir Beltane."

"You disappoint me, dear lady, and I know William will be disappointed as well. If you should change your mind . . ."

"I do not believe I will. I have a great number of things still to do, and so little time to do them. Mayhap, after the wedding you will honor Royce and me at Creganwald."

"Of course. I intend to renew my friendship with your future husband as soon as possible. We have a great deal in common." He smiled at Lynette and bowed slightly to Royce, then left them.

Royce had been watching Lynette in fascination. Either she was the most accomplished liar he'd ever known, or she was going to go through with the wedding. He felt excited by the thought, but he intended to have his question answered as soon as possible.

Lynette wondered if he was angry at her announcement that she intended to go through with the wedding. He was looking at her strangely, as if she were responsible for difficulties in his plans.

"Lynette, would it distress you if we left now?"

"Now? But the king—"

"I shall tell him you have become ill. He will not mind. It's important for us to be alone for a while."

"No, of course not, if that is your wish."

"It is my wish," he said firmly. He took her arm and literally dragged her toward the king, to whom he made hasty excuses. He took her away before he could see William's smile fade to a dark scowl.

Robert joined William, and waited for a moment to talk. He did not like the presence of Beltane; still less Tearlach.

He knew quite well that Oriel was behind their appearance, and that this was only the beginning of whatever problems she had stirred up.

"Tearlach has not changed these past years," Robert said quietly.

"His kind of man does not change," William said coldly. "He is the kind to demand a tooth for a tooth."

"And a life for a life?"

"Robert, think you I would give any life to him?"

"Who knows better than you and I that kings are often forced to do what is good for the many, instead of what is good for the few?"

"This king does not forget those who show loyalty. There are many ways to cage a mad dog."

"Cage him," Robert said, "or he might have to be put out of his misery."

"I do not think it is Tearlach who will cause problems. I think Beltane is the greater threat. He has seen what he wants, and he has a way of getting it."

"Not this time. The last time should have made him wiser . . . this time, I think . . . Royce will kill him."

"Tell Royce," William said thoughtfully, "that it

would be wise for him to keep the lady close until the words are said that make them man and wife."

"Aye."

"And ever after," William said softly, without looking at Robert. "Tell him to hold both Creganwald and the lady close, and to trust no one. There is something afoot, Robert, and I do not know what it is yet. But what he holds dear, he must protect. He knows these people well, and knows that they do not respect the possessions of others, nor are they afraid to take what they desire."

"He will be warned. And you may trust that Royce has many friends who will watch his back for him."

"Good," William replied. Others joined them, and there was little chance for Robert to ask any more questions. He sought out Oriel, and waited until he could approach her in private.

"You have played your game well, Oriel," he said quietly from behind her back.

She spun around in surprise. But Robert had to admit she was not shaken easily. She smiled.

"Robert, you startled me. I do not know what you are talking about. What 'game' do you have in mind?"

"Play the innocent with someone else. I see your fine hand in this. Leave be, Oriel, or I will put a stop to it."

"Really, Robert, I do not know what you mean. I have done nothing. I was a guest in Sir Tearlach's home, and he was kind enough to escort me here. I have no one but my brother, and we live on Royce's sufferance. My worth was taken by that Saxon. Can

I be blamed if Sir Tearlach was kind enough to escort me back to my brother?"

"You are one to hold your hatred close to your heart, and seek revenge for a grievance that was not of her making. Lynette will be Royce's wife and there is little you can do about it."

"But he does not want the marriage. Mayhap he needs only a way to relieve himself of this duty."

"And find his way to your bed. Think you he would wed you instead?"

"He would have turned to me if that slut had not been forced down his throat!" She said rashly.

"No, Oriel, you are wrong. He would not have turned to anyone. It was Lynette who released him from his grief, and it is only she who holds the key now."

"We shall see, Robert, we shall see."

"I warn you . . . "

"And I warn you. Stand away, before you find you face an enemy who is not so easy to destroy."

She spun away from him, and Robert watched her retreat with misgivings. One enemy was easy to face, but three were a threat to be taken seriously.

He watched William from across the room. What did the king mean when he said there was more than one way to cage a dog? There were a great many things in William's mind that Robert could never fathom.

The secret he carried himself was now a weight he would gladly rid himself of. But he couldn't. He had to keep it, and make sure it was not used to destroy Royce and all he had acquired.

Chapter Sixteen

The ride back to Royce's home was a silent one. Wrapped in her cloak against the cold, Lynette failed to notice that Royce watched her closely. She did not care if he was angry. She herself was upset and more than a little afraid of Beltane.

She had been wondering if she could have seen him before, and now it came to her. In her mind she had always had a vivid picture of the favored angel of God, Lucifer. He was beautiful, the fathers had told her, and in his conceit had been expelled from heaven. Well, Beltane had that look of wicked beauty that could lead anyone astray.

She had felt his eyes on her, and could still feel the heat of them. She wondered if this had angered Royce. It was not her fault that Beltane looked at her as he did. She was glad she had made it clear she would wed Royce, even if it had made him angry.

If he wanted to ask William for freedom from his pledge, so be it, but she would have to tell him tonight to find his own reasons, for she could not say the lie that she wanted to be free. She could only tell him of her love and make him understand that she would choose no other.

Royce was as deep in his thoughts as she, but his were far different. He had heard her words and hoped they were true. He had made her a bargain, but he did not mean to hold to it. Whether she cried deception or not, he meant to make her his wife.

When they arrived, their horses were taken and they went inside. Lynette started up the stairs and Royce followed behind her. But when she walked to her door, he took her arm and she was forced along with him to climb the second set of stairs to his chamber. Once inside, he closed and bolted the door behind them, and they turned to face each other.

The fire had been fueled against his arrival home and it lit the room with a mellow glow. The room was warm and Royce went to her and took the cloak from her, leaving her standing there while he walked to the opposite side of the room to lay it aside.

He turned to face her again. Lynette watched him approach, and spoke before he could say the words she didn't want to hear.

"I am sorry if I have set your plans awry, but I could not speak words I know to be a lie."

"And what is the lie, Lynette?"

"Royce, when you came to Creganwald, I was angered that I should be given away by a king who was not even mine. But you came, and you were not as I expected. I wanted to hate you . . . but I cannot. I have come to care for you more than I had thought it possible to care for any man. Royce, I . . . I would put our bargain aside, I would wed you, and I would tell you that . . . I . . . I have come to love you."

Royce wasn't sure he had heard right, for her voice had grown soft, and he could see her hands clenched at her sides. He strode toward her and took her by the shoulders in a grip so tight, it drew her up almost on her toes. She gave a soft cry of fright.

"Lynette, have I heard you right? Did you say . . . "

"I know this does not please you, and if you wish your freedom, I will go to the king and plead for it."

"Freedom!" He laughed. "Freedom from you is the last thing I will ever want. Lynette, I have tried to adhere to our little plan, but in my heart I have wanted to hear you say it is no longer your wish."

"You . . . you have . . . "

"I have come to love you, little Saxon," he said gently. "And I have ached with the wanting of you. I was certain it was you who wanted your freedom."

"No! Oh no, I do not." She half laughed and half cried. "I do not."

"Then you shall never have it," he said as he gathered her to him. Their lips met in a flaming union, his seeking the fullness of the truth and hers answering with all that she had stored in her heart.

Her arms slid about him to hold him even closer, while she sent his senses soaring with the heat of her passion. It grew within him like a force, draining him of all the old, familiar pain while it replaced sorrow with a joyous overflowing of love. He filled himself with the taste and the feel of her, forcing the light of her love into every dark corner and brightening the shadows until they were no more.

When he released her lips, it was only to frame

her face between his two hands and gaze into her eyes. They were warm with newly ignited passion, and he saw there all he would need to sustain him.

"Lynette." He sighed her name as one speaks a prayer. "I had thought it impossible to know love again. I was closed in the darkest of hells. 'Tis you who bring the light."

"Royce, I would give you all that I am if it would bring you the full knowledge of peace and the love I have for you. I would speak my vows before God, and feel the full joy of knowing we are one."

Royce was filled with so many emotions that he could hardly find his breath.

When his mouth took hers this time it was in a gentle tasting, meant to stoke the passion already simmering. She responded completely, her hands caressing and her body coming fully against his. The kiss grew deeper and deeper until she felt as if she were melting, her body reforming itself to mold more perfectly to his.

Only when she felt as if she were adrift on a sea of white-hot need did he snatch her up in his arms and carry her to the bed. Beside it he stood her on her feet, and was pleased when she began to remove his clothes. With fingers that trembled, he helped her to remove her clothes. Then they stood, her slim, golden form pressed to his hard, muscled one. He let his hands roam for one moment to caress soft shoulders, slim curved back and hips, then to the warmth of her breasts, where his hands lingered to feel the sweet swells.

Her hands were just as busy, for she did not fight the urge to know him as he would know her, all and completely. She explored the breadth of his shoulders and the hard muscles of chest and arm, then put her arms about his waist and pressed herself against him, her lips touching randomly and with building heat.

They found the softness of the bed together, responding fully to each other, as if each knew what the other desired and what would heighten the pleasure more.

He heard her whispered murmurs of pleasure and delighted in them, more than he had ever known. She gave so completely that hot blood surged through his veins and crashed against his spirit like waves upon a welcoming shore.

As he entered her body, her lips were hot and moist beneath his, and her body arched to meet him, giving as fiercely as he, demanding as fiercely as he. The rapidly building passion ran like a river of molten lava through their veins. They were left with no other thought than the pulsing need for appeasement.

His kiss and the hungry heat of his body drove her beyond the brink of sanity to the burst of fulfillment. It left them both gasping and clinging to each other while they rode the crest, then tumbled from the heights to a quiet peace that filled their spirits with a warmth neither had known before.

When he looked down into her eyes again, he saw the warmth of her love and the promise in her eyes. He smiled.

"Our bargain is well met, my love."

"Aye," she whispered softly. "And the next bargain we make will be vows before God. I would wed you, Royce, and return home to Creganwald. I need not the conflicts of the court nor the conspirators here." She smiled up at him. "Especially those who conspire to win you."

"Is this jealousy I hear?"

"Aye, my lord. 'Tis jealousy. You are mine and I would share you with no old lovers. That is a day past, and I would snatch you from temptation."

"Ah, Lynette, the only woman who tempts me is here in my arms. There is no other I would seek." He bent to kiss her lightly. "But I would return to Creganwald as well, for there are, as you say, forces here that would entangle us. There is contentment at Creganwald, and I have found a promise of peace there."

"Must we wait for the king's word to seal our vows?"

"Aye, we must. But I will speak to him tomorrow and urge him to all speed."

Lynette did not know why she suddenly felt a cold breath pass over her, and she clung to Royce in a fierce embrace.

"What is it, my love?"

" 'Tis nothing. A moment's fright."

"Fright? Of what?"

"I do not know. I . . . I only wish we were back at Creganwald now, and the vows already taken."

"As do I. There is nothing to worry you. William has already promised Creganwald to me, and he does not reward loyalty with betrayal."

"Our marriage is not a fact yet, and he need only give Creganwald to another and provide your reward with something else."

"Then I must urge the marriage, to ease your mind and to assure you that I will not surrender you or Creganwald to another." He could still sense her unrest. "Lynette, is it William's or my intentions you question?"

"Nay! Royce, it is . . . those three at the king's dinner. It is the hatred I could feel, and their parting words. It was as if Tearlach knew something more than we, and Beltane . . . " She shivered.

"Beltane is to be considered, for I have bested him more than once, and he is not one to forget such things."

"And Oriel?" she questioned softly.

"I have only recently discovered that Oriel can be cruel, but she wields no power." He took her chin in two fingers and lifted her head to look deeper into her eyes. "I will tell you true that I thought to seek her out once, but my spirit fell against the cold walls of hers, and when I found the truth of her cruelty to Cerise . . . Lynette, this treasure I have found here is not a moment's, nor a year's, but the joy of a lifetime. I would willingly make my promise to you that I lay before you my life and my love for as long as there is breath in my body."

Lynette was overcome with a flowing warmth, and she reached up to put her hand at the back of his head and draw his mouth down to hers. Their lips met and the kiss was a seal that each knew would never be broken.

The kiss slowly grew into a rare and deep passion that had more than just the heat of desire, but a calm and perfect blending. It moved slowly, like the flow of a tranquil and deep river, and they surrendered to the perfection of it.

They savored the feel and the taste of each other with hands and lips. They sought to give as much pleasure as they received, and as it steadily grew it blazed into a passion that was met with joy and complete surrender.

Later Lynette gave in to contented sleep, and Royce lay holding her and trying to control the nagging feeling of worry. He looked down at her sleeping face and felt again that possessive hunger. He knew in his heart that a day would never come when he would not need the sweet and healing woman who lay so relaxed in his arms. Slowly he put the past behind him, and for the first time felt the peace that had eluded him for so long. He reached for the memory of Sybella and knew that from this point on, he would be able to think of her without pain and to remember only the happiness they had shared.

Lynette's head rested on his shoulder, and he could feel her soft breath against his skin. One of her legs was lying across his and one hand rested upon his chest.

He lifted her hand gently so as not to waken her and held it to his lips. Her hand was delicate, and he wondered that the touch of it could set him on fire and restore all that had been stolen from his life.

Again he thought of Sybella. He allowed the memory for a moment, then put it away, for Lynette was his saving grace and she deserved all of his heart . . . without shadows.

His arm tightened around her and she stirred. She sensed his thoughts and looked up at him.

"Are there ghosts in your heart, my lord?" she whispered.

"Nay, Lynette, only happiness and gratitude. I have held on to my ghosts too long. I had lived . . . no, I had died, and you were the breath of life that reanimated me. There will be no more shadows, for I have found the fullness of love in you and I would put the memories away. I would share a happy life with you."

Lynette felt tears sting her eyes, and her heart swelled with the love she felt for Royce. Words were not necessary, for he brushed away the tears with gentle kisses and soon they turned to more. They spent the coin of their love freely and with the deepest of pleasure.

Others could not find the night so full of pleasure. William stood looking out over the city, his mind deep in the problems that tormented him.

A man of his word, he cursed the day he had made a promise he now did not want to fulfill. He could not betray a man who had given so much, not only to his cause but to him as well.

But there were those of lesser honor who would insist on the fulfillment of a vow made long ago, despite the agony and difficulties it would cause.

He found it hard to understand the need for vengeance. Nor could he understand the man who would take vengeance by using another. He understood the enemy who met him with armor and sword, but not the one who contrived in secret.

He had wrestled with his thoughts for hours, and no solution presented itself. A test of honor he could understand . . . a test of honor . . . for the first time in hours, a smile curved his lips.

* * *

In a distant part of the city others thought the same thoughts, only with more satisfaction.

Tearlach sat with a drink in his hand and chuckled over his cleverness. Near him Beltane, too, smiled the smile of one who nears success in an endeavor. Oriel sat nearby, caught in her own private dreams.

"Find your bed," Tearlach said to Oriel. "It is not necessary for you to bother your mind about the outcome of this. Creganwald is as good as Beltane's, as is the maid Royce covets so. He will find his sword has won him naught but broken promises and lost dreams."

"All is done?" Oriel asked quietly.

"Before the two are wed, he will find all that he thought his is gone. We will see the pride of this knight in the dust yet."

"I would have us wed before his eyes," Beltane said with a serpent's smile. "And I will display my ardor while he watches and curses his king." Beltane looked closely at his uncle. "You have never told me why your hatred of him is so strong. What has he done to gain it?"

"That is not your concern," Tearlach said harshly. "It is enough that you know I seek your gain as well as mine."

Oriel said nothing. She simply rose to her feet and went from the room to her chamber. Although Giles had argued against it, she had decided to remain a guest in Tearlach's home.

Beltane was amused at Oriel's gullibility. Did this creature think they were working toward her ends as well? She had been useful, and soon her usefulness would be done. To Beltane all things were valued only until their usefulness was fulfilled. There would be time soon to awaken the stupid wench to the fact that neither Royce nor Creganwald would ever be hers.

Chapter Seventeen

Royce woke before the first light of dawn touched the horizon. He wasn't too sure what had wakened him, until the knock on his door was repeated, this time very urgently. He rose from the bed slowly so he would not waken Lynette, grabbed up his trews and drew them on, then made his way to the door well prepared to rid himself quickly of the nuisance.

When he flung the door open, it was to face Robert and Giles, whose worried faces and grim lips told him something was amiss.

"Robert, what has happened?"

"Royce —" Robert's voice was filled with anger. "I could hold the news no longer. Every servant has searched every place possible. Lynette cannot be found. I have roused your men, and we are set to search the whole of the city. I fear there are those who meant her harm last evening."

"Ah . . . Robert, Giles"—Royce smiled—"set your minds at rest."

"How can you greet this news so calmly? Do you not know what may have happened?"

"Robert . . . please . . . do as I say. Call off the search. Lynette is safe."

Robert looked as if he did not understand the words for a minute and Giles looked even more puzzled; then understanding came to both almost at the same time. Two pairs of eyes widened, and two rather sheepish faces broke into broad smiles.

"I shall tell the men to cease the search," Giles said and made his escape before he broke into very pleased laughter. Every man and woman in the household would be delighted to hear this news.

Robert stood his ground. He studied Royce's face, and felt a surge of pleasure. It seemed the ghosts had been laid to rest and all by one slight girl. He was as happy as if these were his children, and his smile was evidence enough.

"Robert, stop Giles before he announces to the world that Lynette is here."

"Aye"—Robert grinned—"but I will have to tell Cerise. She is the one who raised the alarm. She went to Lynette's room and found her gone. The child is beside herself."

"Send her to us." Robert turned to leave. "Robert," Royce said dryly, "I didn't mean at this moment. Keep her with you for a while. Lynette still sleeps."

"Aye," Robert repeated. He would do just that. There were many ways to keep a child busy, and he intended to find them all. He was wise enough to know that passion needed to be followed by time to talk . . . and time to renew the night's pleasures. Royce closed the door on the sound of Robert's pleased chuckle. He turned to walk back to the bed, only to see Lynette sitting up in the middle of it, her eyes full of laughter and her cheeks flushed.

He paused to absorb the picture she made: all that shielded her from his gaze was the brilliant hair tangled about her.

Lynette, too, was just as fascinated. Royce walked slowly toward her, and she could feel her pulse begin to pick up a stronger beat. She could actually feel his caress like a physical thing long before he reached her side.

He stopped beside the bed and held her gaze with his. Slowly a smile lifted the corners of his mouth, and the gold of his eyes warmed. He reached to gather the mass of her hair in two hands, one on each side of her face, and drew her slowly up to him. Their lips touched, caressed, and grew hungry. Royce knew without doubt that she would be able to raise this hunger in him with her slightest touch or the quickest glance.

"It seems the place is in an uproar."

"Why? Has something gone wrong? Cerise, is she . . . " She paused before the laughter she saw in his eyes, and looked at him in puzzlement.

"There has been a search going on . . . for you."

"For me? But . . . oh . . . " Her cheeks grew even pinker, and she sat back upon her heels. "They . . . "

"They think aright, that you have spent the night with me, as you will from this day onward for the rest of our lives. Does it distress you, Lynette?"

"Nay," she finally laughed. "It is not our secret. But then"—she ran her hand up his arm to rest on his chest—"I would shout my love for all the world to know. We will be wed! We will be wed!" She was beautiful in her enthusiasm, and he snatched her from the bed to clasp her to him, filled with the amazing joy her full acceptance brought. She looped her arms about his neck and threw back her head, laughing in sheer ecstasy.

As he slowly slid her to her feet, she rested against him. His lips began to explore.

"We should go down."

"Aye," he murmured, while he pressed a light stream of kisses against her throat.

"We should not dally longer."

"Nay, we should not," he responded, but the assault on her senses did not cease.

"Royce, your food awaits."

"Nay, my better meal is here." He swung her up in his arms and returned to the bed.

When they finally did come down to break their fast, there seemed to be an air of jubilation in the hall. They were met with warm greetings, quick laughter, and looks of definite approval for the lady their lord had chosen. Be she conquered or no, she was the lady that had brought peace to the man they would have followed into hell.

For the knights that shared his fortune, she was to be loved and protected as if she belonged to each of them. Lynette's heart swelled with the pleasure of it.

When she asked after Cerise, it was to find she had been taken into the city by Giles, who had orders from Robert to see to her every whim . . . and to keep her occupied until well after the midday meal. Robert had joked that even Royce would not keep Lynette abed after that. But the others had laughingly responded they had their doubts.

After they had eaten, Royce took Lynette out to explore the city. She found treasures: ribbons for Cerise's hair, and a comb and brush of silver. Royce watched her, warmed by her unrestrained love for his daughter. He knew quite well that a stepmother was not always kind, and he was grateful for the concern she displayed.

The thought of the three of them returning to Creganwald was a welcome one. He would gladly leave behind the intrigues of court. His thoughts turned to Tearlach again, and he felt uneasy. Worse was the memory of the way Beltane had looked at Lynette, as if she were his possession.

His thoughts, wandering now, came to rest on Oriel. He knew Giles was not happy about his sister's choice of companions, but he sensed relief that she had chosen to stay away from Lynette and the household.

More than ever, he regretted the way he had entrusted Cerise to Oriel. When they reached Creganwald, he would wipe that memory from his daughter's mind.

"What causes you to scowl so, my lord?" Lynette questioned.

" 'Tis naught. I but think of the hours between dawn and night as wasted ones now." He grinned at her flushed cheeks.

"I did not think you had access to my thoughts," she said. "It seems they linger along the same path. But you must curb your appetites, my lord," Lynette laughed. "For there are long hours before you, and your daughter will demand her share."

"Children should be abed early," he responded, enjoying their easy banter.

"Would you have her and the whole household abed before the sun sets?"

"Aye, if it were in my power. But since it is not, I shall seek the earliest moment."

He enjoyed her laughter and joined in it, and the ride home seemed more joyous. But as they approached the dwelling, they found Ferragus riding toward them.

"Something is amiss?" Royce asked.

"Only that there are guests in the house, and I would find my pleasure elsewhere."

"Who has come?"

"Beltane has escorted Oriel back to her brother's care. My lord, it is an excuse."

"An excuse for what?"

"Why, to see Lady Lynette, for a question as to her whereabouts were the first words to pass his lips."

"He is foolhardy," Royce said softly.

"He is nothing, my lord," Lynette said quickly. "But he may have some influence at court and could stir up trouble. Let us not anger him if possible, for I believe he means you as much trouble as he can provide."

"He most likely does, and should he look your way, he will find all his heart desires."

"You have known Beltane a long time, haven't you?"

"Aye, I have."

"Why is his heart set on bringing you grief?"

"Because he is a coward, and has no honor . . . though I can prove neither. We have crossed swords before, and I did not complete what I should have completed."

Royce became silent, and Lynette knew she was

not going to get any more from him. She promised herself to find Robert alone and question him about the enmity between Royce and Beltane.

When they arrived it was to find that the hall had lost most of its festive air. Lynette knew the presence of Beltane was much to blame.

They had hardly stepped inside the main room before Beltane rose from a seat near the fire and turned to face them. His smile was white and guileless, which Royce knew as a sign that he was at his most dangerous.

"Beltane," Royce said quietly, "had I known you were coming, I would not have wandered far from my dwelling. It is good to protect one's domain when you arc near."

"Always the sharp and ready tongue, eh, Royce? I but come to return the Lady Oriel to her brother."

"You could have sent word. I'm sure Giles could have come for her. I did not know that she was desirous of returning here, when the hospitality of your family had been offered."

Beltane smiled and shrugged expressively. Oriel was to be his eyes and ears here in this hall. He knew she was blinded by her ambition, and by her foolish belief that Royce would turn to her when Lynette was eliminated.

"I also bring word from my uncle. William honors us with his presence for the celebration of the coming yule season. He joins my uncle in bidding you attend."

There was no way that Royce could refuse, and Beltane knew it. Royce wondered how this had come about, for William knew well the feelings between him, Beltane, and Tearlach.

"Of course, we shall attend."

"William will be spending some time with us. He and my uncle have some"—he gestured with a wave of his hand—"old warrior stories and past times to talk over."

"I had forgotten that William and your uncle fought together for some time before I knew him," Royce said thoughtfully.

"Let me offer you some wine, sir," Lynette said to Beltane, to erase the dark and suspicious look from Royce's face.

"I am afraid I cannot stay, Lady Lynette, but thank you for your gracious offer. I look forward to seeing you soon. The celebration will be the day after tomorrow."

Beltane crossed the room and stood near Lynette. She was well aware of Royce's dark look, and the dangerous quiet that filled the room.

At that moment the door opened and Giles and Cerise entered. He was laughing at something, but the laughter froze when he saw Beltane.

"Giles. I have had the honor of escorting your sister back to you. She and I have had some enjoyable and enlightening conversations during her stay with us. But she was most anxious to return here."

"Thank you for your trouble," Giles said. "But I would have come for her if you had sent word."

"So Royce has said, but I really wanted an opportunity to invite Royce and the lovely Lynette to a celebration."

Cerise stood very still, her eyes on Beltane and her hand grasping Giles's. The child's silence drew Lynette's attention. Lynette had a feeling Cerise knew a great deal about Beltane. It had not occurred to her until now that Royce's daughter had been an observer all the silent years of their estrangement. Yes, perhaps Cerise had more answers than she knew.

Lynette was relieved when Beltane left. She immediately took Cerise to her room. Royce watched her go before he turned to Giles, who pressed his lips into a thin line and breathed a ragged sigh.

"You are a danger to him in William's court," Giles warned. "Watch your back. He would think nothing of putting a knife between your ribs."

"I know," Royce replied. "But there is no way I could refuse his invitation. I am worried about William's sudden closeness to Tearlach."

"And well you should be." Robert's voice came from the stairs. He continued to speak as he entered the room. "Tearlach is clever and deadly, and I believe he will remind William of any debts owed."

"What kind of debt, for what?" Royce was quick to ask.

"Would that I knew. I have heard word that William frets under the obligation, and would find a way to repay."

"Robert, think you William will hold back the day of the wedding because of Tearlach?"

"I do not know, but if it were I, I would press the king to make the day sooner. Beltane has his eye on anything that will bring you down."

"I can understand Beltane's feelings toward me, but it is Tearlach's motive that worries me most."

"Tearlach needs nothing but his greed and jealously to spur him on," Robert said shortly. "He knows you have found favor with William, and he covets that favor. He would see you stripped, if it was in his power. And you intend to walk into his home like a lamb to slaughter."

Royce laughed. "Knowing one's enemy is half the battle. It is better to face him than to turn my back and let him work his plots behind it."

"Royce," Robert said softly, "I have looked into Beltane's eyes . . . he covets too."

"Aye," Royce answered with the same note of caution. "But Lynette belongs to me, and for her he would have to fight to the death."

"He does not fight in the open. I only caution you to beware."

"I will. Robert, Oriel has grown close to Beltane. Perhaps you could question her. Maybe she has some answers that will prepare me."

"I will do my best to find out." But Robert had his doubts as well, for Royce did not understand Oriel as he did. He was more ready to believe that Oriel would add to the problem rather than help him find a solution to it. Yes, he would question her . . . and would choke the truth from her if he had to.

Chapter Eighteen

Royce took the steps two at a time in long, purposeful strides. He made his way to their chamber, and was pleased to find both Lynette and Cerise there. He knew Lynette was afraid of what Beltane's invitation meant.

He answered Lynette's question before she voiced it, and saw the relief in her eyes. " 'Tis naught for you to worry over, an invitation only, and it will provide me a chance to press the king on our marriage."

He turned his attention to Cerise, admiring the bright ribbons Lynette had woven into her braids. He calmed Cerise's fears, then turned his full attention to Lynette.

He could see she had been watching him closely.

"Robert and I both think Beltane wishes to settle the score between us, with you."

"Royce!"

He went to her and caught her to him, holding her

tight and smiling down into her eyes. Lynette smiled and put her arms about him. He was not going to allow her to worry unduly.

"He can do us no harm, Lynette, as long as we do not forget that he is not to be trusted."

"And so we honor this invitation?"

"Aye, I would know what kind of game he plays, and . . . I would show the king your impatience to be my wife." He laughed softly. "And my impatience to have you," he added, his voice a caress.

"I wish we could eliminate the days and hours until we can return to Creganwald and begin our life together."

"I wish the same. I cannot be gone from here soon enough. I am weary of court and battles. I would find peace at Creganwald and forget my roaming."

Her eyes grew moist with happy tears, and she drew her arms tighter about him. He would not have denied her invitation had not a fascinated Cerise reminded them of her presence.

"Papa?"

Royce released Lynette reluctantly and went to his daughter, kneeling beside her. "You have a question, Cerise?"

"Can I go to this 'invitation' with you?"

"I am afraid you cannot, but you will be richly entertained. Maida tells me she has any number of new games to teach you, and she also has several new stories. Besides, the hour of our return will be late, and you could not stay awake."

She seemed satisfied with this, and Royce did not look in Lynette's direction, for he did not want her to know his real reason for the refusal. Royce sent

Cerise to her own chamber and turned again to Lynette.

But Lynette had not been taken in for a minute by his excuses. "You see more threat in Beltane's invitation than you have admitted," she stated rather than asked. "Why did you refuse Cerise?"

"The truth of it," he said seriously, "is that I do not much like the idea of the three of us being in the same place at the same time. I put little past Beltane, and even less past Tearlach."

"And you advise me not to worry."

"Lynette, we must find what is in their minds, and we cannot let them have access to the king without our being there to prevent his hearing untruths. It is for our own good that we go." He came to her again and took her in his arms. "I would have a day chosen, and this wedding over. Once we are safely at Creganwald, they can offer no threat."

"Then"—she smiled up at him— "I must charm the king, and lay my dearest wish before him."

"Your dearest wish?" he repeated, but already his gaze was warming her.

"Aye, that you will soon be my husband."

He bound her tighter to him and savored a long kiss that brought a sound of contentment from her. He would have carried it to the completion he wanted, but a knock on the door interrupted. He cursed under his breath, and heard her muffled laugh as he reluctantly let her go. Lynette realized her own desire was as hot and intense as his.

They were called to a meal, which turned into a happy and laughing affair. Only Giles seemed withdrawn and thoughtful. Both Lynette and Royce knew he had his sister's schemes in mind, yet neither knew what had transpired between them after Beltane's leaving.

Giles had gone directly to Oriel's room and had entered quietly, without knocking. She was seated before the hearth, brushing her hair and humming lightly to herself. She looked completely satisfied.

He thought of their childhood days, and the number of times he had gotten her out of trouble, not to count the number of times he had taken the blame for things that were her fault.

She had always been unruly and a bit wild, and yet she was his sister, and he could do no less than see to her care since the untimely deaths of their parents.

He had been overjoyed when Royce asked her to care for Cerise. Giles knew that Oriel would have had an honored place in Royce's life if she had seen to her duties, and not sought what was not hers.

Giles loved her, and that was why she could arouse his anger so easily. He did not want her to reach for trouble, and eventually heartbreak, with both hands as she always did.

"Oriel." He spoke her name quietly. She spun about in her chair, surprise on her face.

"Giles, you frightened me. I did not hear you knock."

"I did not knock." He came to stand close to her. "Oriel, the truth of it. Why did you go to Tearlach's?"

"Why do you question a short visit with friends? Or are you more distressed to see me return?"

"Why do you speak thus? It is my concern for you that brings me to you now. I have tried to warn you."

"Your only concern is for Royce and that bitch he beds."

"Stop it, Oriel!" His voice cracked with anger. "She is to be his wife, and she is a lady of gentle nature and kind heart. You know well that I care for you, sometimes more deeply than I should. I cannot see you hurt, even if it is by your own hand. I owe Royce more than my life, and you owe him yours as well. Who was there to take care of us when we were left with nothing? It was not Tearlach, that is for certain. He would have left us destitute and begging on the streets."

"I do not know why you choose to remind me of this now. We are comfortable because your arm is strong, and your abilities make you of value. If they did not, you would find yourself on the street soon enough."

"If you believe that, then you have no understanding of Royce's heart. He would never turn his back on us, and neither would his lady."

"His lady . . . his lady. Why should she be his lady? It was I who cared for the child when he would not receive it in his presence! It was I who would have made a proper lady for his home! It is I who am of the same blood! Why choose a Saxon slut over a lady of finer ways?"

"You are blind! And you will be led to your own destruction if you listen to Royce's enemies. Oriel, listen to me. For the first time in your life, listen to someone who has your good at heart, and not someone who would use you to cause hurt."

"Giles, I do love you, brother, but this time you are wrong. I have done nothing to warrant your anger, and I plan nothing. Why must we quarrel over things that exist only in your mind? Do you see me as evil?"

"Of course not. But I know well you will play with fire, and that it is you who will be burned."

"I will not be the one to cause Royce trouble. I will remember my place, and yours. Will that suffice?"

"You speak the truth?"

"Aye, the truth."

"You will accompany me to Tearlach's tomorrow night?"

"Yes, I am looking forward to it. I want the Saxon witch to see the way Norman ladies conduct themselves. It will teach her well. Mayhap she will scuttle back to her hole and forget her ambitions."

"Oriel, let it be. For now let us agree. You will not hear the suggestions of those who mean Royce and Lynette harm."

"No. I will whisper any words of hostility I hear in your ear." She laughed softly, and was suddenly the younger sister he had known in childhood. She came to him and embraced him, kissing his cheek and taking his hand in hers. "Leave off, brother. Let us enjoy the festivities to come."

"Well enough, I take it upon your word." He smiled, for this was the sister he knew. At times like this he saw the child's face superimposed on the woman's.

They talked for a while, and laughed together over times past, until he was assured, and left her. Only then did her smile fade, and for a minute tears glistened in her eyes. Then she brushed them away and returned to her chair to continue brushing her hair.

* * *

The evening grew long for Royce, and he chafed under the continued pretense of laughing conversation, when he wanted only for everyone to find their beds.

He might have thought he had himself in complete control, but there was no one present who did not see and understand his impatience: indeed, Robert and several others had a silent wager that he was not going to last much longer.

Royce maintained his self-control until Lynette bent near him and laid her hand on his thigh. He could feel her touch burn through him, and her husky voice pressed him to the limit.

"My lord," she whispered, "the hour grows late, and it is long past the time for Cerise to find her bed. I will go and see to her."

Cerise had found a comfortable place on Robert's lap, and had enjoyed hearing the talk swirl around her. She had never been so cosseted or felt so wanted. She liked to watch her father talk, liked the low rumble of his strong voice, and the warmth of his laughter. She wished this night could go on forever.

Royce watched Lynette take Cerise and climb the stairs. The seductive sway of her hips held his attention until he realized that Robert had spoken to him twice.

"It will be a good day when we put this city behind us and find our way to Creganwald. My days of fighting are over. I would find other comforts now."

"Aye," Royce said. He did not miss the smiles that surrounded him this time, and he had to laugh in return. "I will admit that the days before this wedding are long. I would be off for Creganwald tomorrow, had the king set the day."

"We shall force an answer tomorrow night." Robert laughed. "Or the king will risk forcing you to abduct the lady."

"You have hit on it, my friend. One or the other will take place soon, I can promise you that. Good night. And let us have no search parties in the morning . . . in case anyone is lost." Their laughter and a few pointed remarks followed him up the stairs.

Royce went first to Cerise's room, where he found her sound asleep. He stood over her bed for a minute and looked down at her. The thought of their lost years stirred a poignant feeling of regret. He had lost them but he would fill the rest of her years, and hope she filled his. Suddenly his life seemed so full and promising that he found it hard to believe how short a time it had been since he had wanted to end it. Now he had everything in the world to live for. He bent to kiss her lightly, and drew the covers closer about her.

Lynette's room lay directly across the hall from Cerise's, and he crossed to her door to push it open. But the room was dark. Then he smiled and pulled the door shut.

He mounted the stairs to his chamber with winged feet, and paused only a moment before he pushed the door open, stepped inside, and closed it behind him.

Lynette was a vision. She sat in the middle of his bed, with nothing but her smile and the golden mass of her hair between them. He crossed the room and stood by the bed. He could have spent a long time just drinking in her beauty, but Lynette would have none of that.

She smiled and lifted her arms to him, instantly winning the reaction she wanted. He laughed with her as he tossed aside his clothes and joined her on the bed.

Her parted lips met his with a fire that shot through him like lightning. Her hands moved over him as if she were memorizing every taut muscle under the warmth of his flesh.

Her feverish kisses left him gasping in pleasure. Her slim body was molded to his, and she was doing marvelous things with her hands, spiraling his senses upward.

But he could not lie there passively when his body and senses were so alive that each breath was a whisper of her name. He bound her in his arms and rolled until she was beneath him. Now his hands began to work the same magic on her. They caressed, searching out the most sensitive places and tormenting her until he sensed her urgency. But he did not want this to end quickly; he slowed his caresses to allow his lips to follow the path of his hands. The curves and valleys of her body felt the heat of his searching mouth, and she arched against him.

When she felt she could bear it no more, he came into her and she met him with welcoming passion. They moved as one. With a knowledge given woman from the beginning of time, she knew he was completely hers. The fiery culmination came like an explosion, and they rode it to its fullest completion.

Chapter Nineteen

Lynette woke slowly. She lay quiet, for there was no light but the rays of the slowly descending moon, which seemed to leave the room in a gray white mist. She felt the delicious warmth of Royce's body pressed close to her, and heard his soft, relaxed breathing. One of his arms lay across her, as if he must hold her near even in sleep.

She lay recalling the hours just past and the exquisite passion they had shared. Wrapped in a cocoon of warmth, she rested against him and thought of the day he had come to Creganwald, and how resistant she had been.

She thought of all she knew of him now, and how each new piece of knowledge seemed to draw her closer to him. Gently she let her fingers stray over the flesh of his ribs, and linger against his chest. She felt the stir of love deep within her, and considered the days and nights to come at Creganwald, and the moments they would have to share.

With a sigh she turned more fully into the length of his body and nestled against him. Only then, when his arm gently tightened, did she know he must have been awake for some time.

"Where were your thoughts?" he whispered against her hair.

"With my wishes."

"And your wishes?"

"That word had not come from the king to delay our wedding, or that we had been wed before it arrived. Then we would be home now."

"It is my wish also, but our wedding will come to pass quickly now."

"It cannot be too soon. I do not like the thought of remaining here in London overlong."

"We have the day ahead of us. Would you like to see more of the city?"

"Nay, I would close myself here with you if you have no duties to attend. Cerise needs our attention as well. I would join with you to give her all."

Royce turned to face her, and the breaking dawn cast its light so that he could see her face clearly. He smiled down into her eyes, and she was warmed by the regard she saw in their golden depths.

"You have opened doors in my heart and in my spirit that I had thought closed for all time. I have erred, and you have led me to a new path. Cerise and I have much to thank you for."

"Then I must rise and see to the day's work." She stirred, but his arms would not release her.

"There is time for that. For now let us remain away from others and have this moment for ourselves."

"You would make me a lazy wife." She smiled up into his glimmering eyes.

"Nay"—he grinned—"I would show you where your duties lie, and help you meet them."

"It is nearly daylight." She tried to wiggle free, her cheeks flushed. But he held her to him.

"All the better. I want to see your face, and look into your eyes when you are deep in passion. Do you know they darken like stormy skies? And you make a sweet small sound when the fullness of it is upon you."

"Royce." Her voice was pleading, for her body had long since begun to grow heated. She was surprised at herself. But his hands and mouth had begun to waken her, and she responded. His touch ignited that fire whenever he reached for her.

Soon she was lost in the feel and touch of him. His mouth claimed hers, and set her head spinning.

Time sped by, but they did not care, for the moments were preciously spent. It was late in the morning before they went down the stairs to break their fast.

The entire place seemed wrapped in their happiness. Knight greeted knight with smiles, and laughter flowed like a river. All were caught up in the lingering looks and gentle touches shared by Lynette and Royce. It was clear to see their entrancement with each other.

In fact, the day seemed to have wings now, and the time to leave closed upon them. Reluctantly, Lynette finally retired to their chamber to prepare for the evening.

Royce joined her, and when the tub was brought and filled for her bath, he sent the maids from the room so he could enjoy watching her. He remembered the day he had come upon her and Cerise and the clinging wet linen she had wrapped about herself then. It was added to all the sweet memories he was storing away.

He could smell the springtime scent of the soap she used, and remembered it well from the times he had inhaled its heady fragrance. He meant to see that there was no end to her supply of it.

Too soon the bath ended, and she began to dress. The gunna she wore was of a shade of blue that matched the color of her eyes, and her hair was combed into a more gentle style; still, he liked it loose and free about her better.

His bath was quick, and soon he, too, was dressed in finery, and receiving her warm and approving look.

Robert and Giles would attend also, and when Royce and Lynette went down the stairs, they were already waiting. She smiled brightly at their compliments and glowing approval.

The ride to Tearlach's dwelling was no short distance, yet they arrived some time before the king. All the festivities would await William's arrival, but they were offered no end of tasty foods and drinks.

Tearlach seemed in a jovial mood, which set alarms ringing in Royce's mind. Tearlach smiled at Robert, acknowledged Giles with a warm welcome, then turned his attention to Royce and Lynette.

But Lynette was watching Beltane, who had just seen their arrival and was walking toward them. She could feel again the heat of his gaze, and actually felt unclothed. This man's beauty of face and form was more perfect than Royce's, who bore the scars of his hard life and the battles he had fought. Still,

Lynette thought Royce the more handsome and powerful looking.

"Lynette." Beltane breathed her name, and smiled the smile that had captivated more than one unsuspecting heart. Lynette smiled, but moved just a step closer to Royce and was grateful for the comfort of his hand at her waist. "Welcome."

They had hardly had time to move about the huge room when the king was announced. Lynette welcomed the sight of him, hoping he would put an end to the feeling that happiness could still be snatched from her grasp at the lift of his finger.

William greeted Robert, Lynette, and Royce warmly, yet Lynette felt a reserve in him. She soon realized that William wore a mask, for he greeted all the other knights and their ladies with the same enthusiasm. Combined with Tearlach's air of joviality and Beltane's look of satisfaction, the king's manner awoke real fear in Lynette.

It was late in the evening before either Robert or Royce could get the king's ear. Robert was the first to broach the subject. He was one of the closest to the king, and he knew William had never broken his word before. His trust in William was solid, but he wanted the king to confirm his commitment.

"Your Grace?"

"So formal, Robert? There was a time when you shouted '*William*' above the heads of my swarming enemies."

That he referred to old times and old memories boded well, Robert thought. Royce, who stood close by and was just as heartened, spoke to the man to whom he owed his worth, and to whom he had pledged his loyalty.

"I would speak to you of a pressing matter, sire."

"Can this not wait, Royce?"

"Nay, sir. Were it of less import, perhaps. But this matter is urgent, and I would go on with my plans if the word can be given."

"You speak of the beautiful Saxon and Creganwald."

"Aye, sire. The day of the wedding is still not named. I would return to Creganwald and see to the lands, and the building of the castle you want situated there."

"I am afraid the day cannot be named just now," William replied.

"Sire?"

"I have another duty to perform before I will be able to return to London to see your marriage performed. Thus, you will have to curb your impatience for the lady until I return."

Royce was stunned, as was Robert. And yet the king had not said the wedding would not take place. Royce was not going to let the word go without a battle.

"It is early in the year, sire. Though the snow is heavy now, it will begin to melt soon. If the castle is to be started in the spring, work must be begun on the plans for it."

"There is still time. I will send one of my best builders to aid you. For now, the wedding must wait. I am bound in a problem I must see to." He turned to Robert. "My friend, on my return there is something of grave importance I wish to discuss with you. I need your help in a matter that will require some thought."

"I am always ready, Your Grace."

"Aye, Robert, I know. But this time I may be requiring more of you than ever before." He turned back to face Royce. "And, Royce, have heart. All things will be accomplished in time. See to your welfare, and do not hear words meant to shake you. In the near future, you will need your strength and courage as well. For now . . . matters must lie where they are."

He seemed to expect no argument from either man, and in truth both were stunned to silence. Royce felt his heart sink, and knew there was little he could do about it.

To openly fight the king was unthinkable. It would only lead to his being stripped of everything he had ever won . . . and Lynette. He could not afford to lose her because of words that would avail him nothing.

When the king moved away, both men were silent. Robert was struggling to control both his rage and a feeling of helplessness. Royce felt the same rage but it was tempered by thought.

"There is something foul afoot here," Robert growled.

"Aye, and that smirking piece of waste, Beltane, has a hand in it. I could see his happy state all evening. What power does he wield?"

"None that I know of. He has not fought with William, and he has no support at court. Yet . . . "

"Yet something has happened. It appears the king is caught in something that is not to his liking either. Mayhap he searches for a way out of it."

"Aye, that is possible. But why not confide in us?"

"If his hands were tied somehow . . . "

"And Lynette?"

"I must take her back to Creganwald, where I can defend her. It will prove difficult to tell her." Royce looked about him, and for the first time in the past hour realized he had not seen Lynette. He was not given to panic, but this time he had to struggle for control.

Lynette had seen Robert and Royce in conversation with William, and felt a sense of relief. Surely on the morrow, they would be preparing for the wedding. She smiled to herself. The bustle about her became pressing, and she sought a small alcove near the end of the hall to wait for Royce.

Caught up in pleasant thoughts, she was unaware of another presence until the shadow fell across her. She looked up to see Beltane standing between her and the crowd in the hall, effectively shielding her from the sight of anyone else in it.

For a moment she was shaken, but she regained her thoughts. They were near a crowd of people, and he could do her little real harm. No, he meant to intimidate her.

She had to admit that if she were of lesser heart, his ploy would have been very effective. She rose to her feet as if to move around him, but his hand caught her arm and she was drawn to him.

She would have fought in earnest then, but they were near the hall and Royce. She knew blood would be let if Royce learned what was happening, and she would not give her enemies any excuse to set her wedding aside. She glared up at him, and he laughed softly.

"Your eyes seek him. Has the bloom of the rose already been plucked? Aye, it has. Well, he has tasted his last. You were not meant for a man such as he, who has no blood royal, nor anything that is not the king's gift."

"What he has was won by his own strength. And he has my regard as well."

She could see the brilliant glow of lust in Beltane's eyes, matched by a raging anger that she could not be frightened.

"Nay, little rose, there will be no marriage. You will never be his. Soon I will be the teacher to lead you into passion."

"Not while there is breath in my body. The king is a man of honor, and he has promised Royce already."

"I want you to keep in mind, sweet Lynette, that although the king is an honorable man, he is also very devout, and what he must do, he will. You will soon see that it takes more than a sword to hold you and Creganwald."

"It will take no more than Royce's sword to separate your head from your body, should he see us thus. Leave me be, Beltane, for I have all now that I will ever want, and I seek no more than to return to Creganwald and be Royce's wife."

"You need seek nothing, for nothing is what you will find."

"Why? What is in your mind that you speak so foolishly?"

"Foolishly? Nay. Let us see what time brings to light. Ask your lover if the wedding date is set. Ask him if he really thinks he can take you if the king decrees otherwise. Yes, ask him, for his answer will bring you to me."

"Nay," she said quietly, her chin lifting in pride,

"for before it would bring me to you it would see me dead and Creganwald in ashes about me." She tore her arm from his and moved around him. His gaze was filled with the hunger of a ravenous wolf. His eyes followed Lynette boldly, even when Royce finally found her.

When she stopped beside him, Royce could read the anger in her eyes, and in the flaming color of her skin.

"You are well, Lynette?" he questioned softly. At her nod, he spoke again. "What passed between you?"

" 'Twas naught, Royce. He crows like a rooster, it is of little matter. He knows where my loyalties lie. He will bother me no more."

Royce was not satisfied by her answer, and looked across the room at Beltane. He was eager to leave the gathering, but there was no way they could depart before the king did.

Royce dreaded explaining to Lynette that they must wait even longer to set the wedding date.

The hour was late when they finally did return home. He watched her prepare for bed, and she felt his eyes upon her. In her heart, she knew the words he was going to say.

"Beltane claims there will be no wedding at all," she blurted out.

"Then he misjudges William."

"He spoke as if he knew a secret. He said the king would always keep his word . . . but that he was devout as well, and we should not forget that. He . . . he spoke with such certainty."

"William's devoutness has always been well known. If anything, it should assure his word."

231

"I . . . I'm frightened."

Royce came to her and took her in his arms. "Do not think on it now, Lynette. There is time to find our answers. Trust this . . . Beltane will not have you. That I vow."

His vow frightened her even more. If Beltane wished to force Royce to fight, she would be the cause. She couldn't bear the thought of his death. Her whole body trembled. He took her to their bed, and spent careful and long hours erasing all the terrifying thoughts in her head. Tomorrow . . . he thought. Tomorrow he would find the answers for himself, and tomorrow Beltane would be finally and irrevocably warned.

Chapter Twenty

Royce slept little, and he slipped from the bed long before Lynette awakened. But even then he was too late to find William. The king had left the night before, and was many miles away by morning.

Royce then sought out Tearlach and Beltane. When he entered the hall, it was as if Beltane were waiting for him, and in fact, he had been. He knew Royce would come, for he knew Royce well.

"You took longer than I expected," Beltane chuckled. "I had wagered you would be here at the crack of dawn."

"If you wagered I would be here, then you must have wagered as well on the outcome of my visit."

"The outcome? Of a certainty. You will threaten, and grow angry, and eventually you will know that you are going to lose what you now consider your prize possession."

"You are a fool, Beltane, if you lust after Creganwald, and more a fool if you desire Lynette."

"And you are a fool to think I would not. She is a delightful creature, is she not? Tell me, Royce, have you bedded the wench yet?" He smiled his satisfaction at the reaction Royce struggled to control. "But of course you have. I had thought you beyond the taking of a virginal little slave . . . ever since you laid your last one in her grave."

This time he did not get the reaction he expected, and he pretended wondering shock. "Tell me not that you have found love again?" His tone was derisive and malicious. "How unique, and how wonderful. When she warms my bed, I will remind her of you."

"I will warn you this one time, keep your distance from Lynette or my sword will taste more of you than it did the last time." Royce's voice was frigid.

"I will look forward to it." Beltane's voice was as deadly cold as Royce's. "I have waited long to challenge you."

"You don't cease to amaze me," Royce chuckled. He meant to push Beltane's temper, for he was a man who showed little control when anger took over. "I had thought you nursed your wounds for a long time after the last time we met. I imagine it will take another lesson to make you understand who is the better."

With satisfaction he saw Beltane's eyes flare and his face grow mottled. He was certain that if Beltane had had his sword near, he would have attacked. Perhaps with another push . . .

But before he could speak again, another firm and strong voice came from the the entranceway to the hall.

"Have you come here for battle, Royce?" Royce

and Beltane turned to see Tearlach coming toward them. He had a smile on his face and a look of confidence that Royce knew could not be shaken as easily as Beltane's.

"Nay, not to battle, just to bring a warning."

"A warning?" he said with feigned wonder. "Now, why bring a warning to us? We are but knights of William, like you. We only abide by his commands."

It was his sureness, the look of satisfaction in his eyes, that worried Royce. This man held a secret that he meant to use against him. But what? What secret would turn an honorable man like William against him, and cause him to break his word?

"Tell me, Royce, would you raise your sword against the king's command? I think not. When the king returns we will have this out, and you will see that, bastard though he might be, he still recognizes that his crown can be better served by those of nobler blood."

Royce felt the threat to the marrow of his bones, yet he could not believe that William would resort to such deception. He had fought for him for years, and had known that William's own circumstance made him understanding. Why had he given him Creganwald if he meant to place it in another's hands?

" 'Tis the maid." Beltane smiled maliciously. " 'Tis the maid he cannot bear to lose."

"Ah." Tearlach breathed the word softly. "So. Another lass . . . another Sybella?"

"Is that what drives you, Tearlach?" Royce asked softly. "Does it still plague you that I won what you thought to hold? Did Sybella's coming to me deny you the wealth and lands your son wanted? Or did it sit heavy on you that she chose a bastard with only his sword instead of Perrin?"

"Don't speak his name! He was a knight honored. He was of purer blood. He was the one who should have been chosen!"

"He was a man who knew as little about honor as Beltane . . . or you. He was a man who cared little for the woman, and more for her possessions and her closeness to the king. Sybella knew him well . . . and chose for herself. She thanked God that the king let her choose. Creganwald has been given to me to hold . . . and so has Lynette."

Tearlach glared at him for a minute, then fought for control. He smiled. "There is many a slip 'twixt the cup and the lip. Kings have been known to change their plans when it is expedient for them."

"Not William," Royce said firmly.

"You have such faith," Tearlach chuckled. "Shall we just await William's return and trust to him to do what he wills?"

"I will, just as I will watch my back, and protect Lynette." Royce turned to Beltane. "But listen to this and listen well. Keep your distance from Lynette, Beltane, or God will not be able to protect you from me. I will see you dead if one hair of her head is touched."

"I need not fight for what will be freely given me in good time. Go, and teach her well to please a man, for soon a true man will be riding between her thighs. I shall be grateful for your instruction."

Royce felt a surge of rage such as he had never

felt before, and it took every bit of will not to play into their hands and attack Beltane. He felt a driving need to see him lying in his own blood.

But he knew that was what they wanted . . . to tell the king that Royce had deliberately provoked them. No, he would await William's return to London, and force them to see William as the king Royce knew him to be.

"Remember what I have said, Beltane," Royce said quietly. 'Your life hangs in the balance, for if you reach to take what is mine, I will take both your hands . . . before I kill you. Remember that." There was a cold silence. Beltane's smile faltered, and then Royce turned to leave.

"That bastard!" Beltane gritted. But Tearlach turned a cold eye on him.

"That bastard is a very clever man, and would provoke you to fight before the king has played out my game. And you would fall into his trap. You would let your anger control you until you found yourself face to face with death. Then all our plans would have been for naught. Hold that ugly temper of yours, or it will defeat us."

"It should arouse your anger as well. Perrin died at Royce's hand, and over Sybella, who should have belonged to Perrin from the beginning. Do you stand by and let him insult us, while Perrin lies in his grave?"

"Think you," Tearlach said through clenched teeth, "that I forget . . . that I will ever forget? But I will not play to his hand. No, I will succeed through his own faith in his king. I would leave him powerless to do anything but relinquish what he holds dear. Do you not think it will pain him more to have it taken when he cannot battle? If he chooses to fight"—his voice lowered—"who does he fight . . . his king? Would he be guilty of treason?"

"I would see him dead," Beltane ground out harshly.

"Aye, see him dead . . . but not until you have made him suffer. There are ways to finish him . . . but not until he pays in full."

Beltane made a frustrated and angry gesture and strode from the room. Tearlach watched him go and scowled darkly. Beltane's temper would be their undoing yet. He would have to keep a close eye on him.

Royce rode as if the furies of hell followed, rode until his anger was temporarily exhausted. Only then did he return home. When he walked into the hall, it was as if a pall had fallen over it. He strode across the floor to face Robert, who had risen to meet him.

"What has gone wrong? Where is Lynette?"

"She awaits you in your chamber."

"What has happened, Robert?"

"Word has come from Creganwald. Lynette's father is deathly ill. They plead for her to return."

"Damn! This is the worst time. How can we leave when the king has commanded us to stay until his return? We must have his decision, Robert, for there are forces at work whose methods I do not understand yet."

"Lynette will want to go to her father as fast as she can. I do not see how you can hold her here. At this moment she weeps."

Royce looked toward the stairs, then clapped Robert on the shoulder and went to mount the stairs.

He paused by her door for a moment before he pushed it open and stepped inside. Lynette was seated by the window, and when she turned at his entrance he could see the tears on her cheeks. He went to her and took her in his arms.

Lynette rested her head against his chest and felt the comfort of his arms. When she drew back and looked up into his eyes, he saw her need and knew what she would say before she said it.

"Royce, I would go to my father."

"Lynette . . . "

"He is near to dying."

"We cannot leave before the king returns."

"You cannot leave. But, Royce, I am just a slave. The king does not need me here to give his command, and you can send word of the day he has selected. I will return at once, I swear."

"You don't understand the dangers."

"I only understand that . . . if my father . . . I must see to his care, and that he is given proper treatment."

"I know how you feel, and yet I fear for you. I would not have you at Creganwald without me there to see to your safety."

"What do you fear, Royce? It seems all our enemies are here. What harm could they want to do me? I am the prize they seek, and they would only anger the king should they do me harm."

"Lynette, would you stay near Creganwald and not venture outside its walls unguarded? I will send Robert with you and more of my men, so that the gates of Creganwald are safely guarded."

"Should Robert not stay with you?"

"Robert is to be trusted, and I would have him guard what is closest to me, should anything go wrong."

"Royce, what is happening?"

"I don't know."

"You have been to see Beltane."

"Aye."

"Why? Surely all can see he hates you. What has happened between you that he hates you so?"

"It is an ancient hatred, Lynette, and goes back to Tearlach's son . . . Perrin."

"His son?"

"Aye. It was long ago, but Tearlach remains vengeful. He is not the kind of man to face me with sword or lance, but the kind who would like me alive and suffering as much as possible."

"Why suffering? What is the wrong he feels you dealt him?"

"Perrin and I . . . were once foster brothers. He was the son of a knight of some bearing, while I was no one's son. Yet Robert saw to my placement in the castle of a knight for fostering. Tearlach did likewise for Perrin, and we were of the same age. Still, we were not of the same position, and there was no one who did not call it to my mind as often as possible. Perrin and I . . . we grew to hate each other."

He walked away from her to stand at the window, but Lynette knew he was seeing the past and not the view that lay before him.

"I was not exactly the most pleasant of young men. Every day, I felt the differences between us. I was jealous at times, and more than once I wished it possible to face him with sword in hand and put an end to it. Truthfully, I was a miserable and wretched boy, and it looked as if I would grow into the same kind of man. My foster father taught me well what it means to be different. He was a cold man who felt I must stand alone. I learned to do just that."

Lynette came to stand beside him, and he slid his arm about her and drew her close. He did not want to say words that would hurt her, but he knew it was inevitable.

"It was after I had taken service with William. I had proven myself in battle, and my abilities were evident to all but Perrin, whose hatred for me began to fester because of William's kindness and his rewards for my loyalty." He turned to face her and drew her into his arms.

"I knew little of love, Lynette. I had never tasted it or shared it with anyone. I knew force, and hate, and the rule that I must hold what was mine by might. It was then that Perrin brought Sybella to court. We met, we loved, and we earned Perrin's spite, for he had brought her to court in the hopes she would see how important he was and wed him. When William was receptive to our request to marry, Perrin went wild. He claimed my bastardy made a union between us wrong. But Sybella and I married. We had been married less than a month when Perrin went to Sybella in my absence. He . . . he truly believed that Sybella . . . anyway, I forgot all, and I took up my sword . . . I fought and killed him."

"And Tearlach has waited all this time for a chance at revenge."

"It is the first time anything or anyone has been dear enough to me for him to use."

"What do you think he plans?"

"I don't know, but it will be what I least expect. That is his way."

"Then . . . then I must not go?" she whispered, and he could see her distress.

"No, you must be with your father now, my love. It would be cruel to keep you from him. But Robert must go with you, and you must swear that you will give Tearlach no chance to harm you. You must not ride out alone . . . ever, nor must you allow strangers within the gates. Promise me this."

"I will do whatever puts your heart at rest."

"Would that I could go with you, but if William returns and Tearlach gets his ear first, it is impossible to know what evil he will call up."

"I will be cautious."

Royce cupped her face in his hands and looked deep into her eyes. "I have found you, Lynette, and I cannot lose you. I have been half a man, and empty for so long. Guard yourself well."

She could see the fear that lingered in his shadowed gaze, and would have given anything to erase all the terrible memories he still carried. She slid her arms around him and lifted her mouth for his kiss.

Chapter Twenty-one

Royce's lips lingered against hers, tasting the sweetness and slowly savoring it as if there were nothing and no one in their world but them.

"Ah, Lynette, how I will miss you. Just the thought has made me lonely."

His eyes captured her gaze, and she could feel her breath become short and fast; her heart's steady beat began a new and rapid rhythm. Again she met his kiss eagerly, her soft lips warm and moist against his. The blood surged through his veins, as wild and turbulent as the ocean's waves in a storm.

Then he lifted her in his arms and carried her to the bed, heated by her warm and willing response. He kissed her long and passionately, and the building passion exploded through him like flame. The same throbbing need tore through her with such force that she could only breathe his name.

They fell to the bed together, and soft laughter followed as they untangled themselves from clothes that seemed to number more than they had donned in the morning.

Soon they lay flesh to flesh, and he caressed the smooth coolness of her body until she could hardly think. Almost of their own volition, her hands returned his heated seeking and brushed the breadth of his chest and lean ribs. They sought more and more of each other's touch, holding at bay the end to this magnificent torment.

But the passion spiraled upward, ever upward until neither could bear it. When he joined their bodies she trembled with the joy of it, and moved with him to a shattering climax.

Later they lay together, savoring these few stolen moments for as long as they could.

"Royce?" Lynette said quietly.

"Mmm?"

"What of Cerise?"

Royce considered this for a long time. "I would like nothing better than for her to stay here with me. But I will be at court most of the time, and she would be allowed no freedom, for I could not guard her as I should. It would be better for her to go with you."

"Maybe we should go to her now and tell her so that she has time to prepare, for I think she will resist just a bit. She has found you, and will not let go so easily."

"That is heartening news, but we must look to her welfare."

"I will leave tomorrow?"

"In the morning. I would like as much distance between you and London as possible before you

244

make camp. I will tell Robert to make the journey as fast as you can safely travel."

"Then I must be up and about the packing," she said, but Royce was not ready to release her so quickly.

"A few minutes more," he murmured as he pressed a soft kiss to the curve of her shoulder. "I would hold you for a while."

But the minutes passed, and still he could not release her. There was an urgency in his grip that could have made Lynette weep, for she knew he clung to happiness as if he might never hold it again.

When they went to Cerise, she was both excited and dismayed at the same time.

"Why can I not stay with you, Papa?"

"Because I will be away from here and I do not want you to be lonesome. If you go with Lynette, I will not have to worry. I will come for you as soon as I can . . . or I will send for you as soon as possible."

Lynette knew what he meant. He would come for them . . . if the wedding presented some problem, and he would send for them if all was well. She closed her eyes in a silent prayer.

Cerise and Lynette spent the next hour packing their things, while Royce spent the time making sure Robert knew just how careful he had to be.

That night when they all gathered for the evening meal, the entire company was doing its best to remain cheerful. Royce watched as each of his men, trying to be as subtle as possible, took the time to speak to Lynette and tell her how missed she would be, while they also tried not to show that they were overly concerned.

Royce would have been amused if he was not already missing Lynette and Cerise. Cerise was so excited that it was hard for Lynette to get her to bed. While she took over this task, Royce and the men were talking.

"Tearlach sounds overly sure of himself," Robert grumbled. "Mayhap his posturing was just for your benefit, and he has no plan."

"No," Royce disagreed. "Beltane is the one to bluster and to grow angry. But Tearlach is dangerously sure of himself. He is certain that William will change his plans, yet I cannot believe that is so."

"Nor can I," Giles said. "I know one thing. If Lynette's father dies and the king does change his mind, neither Lynette nor Cerise will be safe at Creganwald. Tearlach would like nothing better than to have Beltane master there, and himself in residence as . . . " he shrugged. "You know what would happen to Lynette."

"Aye," Robert agreed. "How better to get back at you than to hold the two you value? You"—he looked closely at Royce— "would do whatever he demanded, and that would mean surrendering all."

"He will never have that pleasure," Royce said. "I will see Beltane dead before I will let him touch Lynette."

"We have gathered a small force, Royce," Giles said, "but how would we hold Creganwald with it if he has the king's word? It will mean disobedience."

"Then . . . I will disobey," Royce said quietly. This silenced the group, for Royce's loyalty to William was well established.

None of them knew what to say, and one at a time they drifted from the group to consider private thoughts. Only Robert and Royce were near the fire when Lynette came down. She found a stool and sat near Royce.

"Lynette, we will leave very early in the morning. It would be best to travel as fast as we can. I do not want word to reach Tearlach until we are well gone." Robert spoke quietly, but Lynette already knew the danger if Tearlach chose to take them along the way.

"I will be ready, Robert. And do not worry about me. I have ridden hard over Creganwald many times. I, too, would be gone early, and hope to find my father's health improved. I would not find . . ." She paused, and could not finish the thought. Royce took her hand, rose from his chair, and walked with her to the stairs.

Robert watched them go, and the old pain struck him. If Royce were to lose her, too . . . The thought was not one he wanted to face. He, too, sought his bed. After a while the hall grew quiet.

No one saw the young man who slipped from the hall and went to the stable. He led his horse out and rode into the night. He rode hard through the quiet streets of London in the wee hours of the morning. The man to whom he was to deliver the message was waiting, and he was well rewarded.

Tearlach crumpled the hastily scrawled note in his hand and smiled in satisfaction. "The lady and his brat leave for Creganwald in the morning," he said quietly, as if his thoughts dwelt on something pleasurable.

Beltane stood near, and his eyes reflected the same interest. "I shall follow."

"Nay, not yet. Let them arrive in safety."

"If I come to Creganwald after they are safely behind its walls, I will never be allowed inside."

"Royce will see that they are well protected on the road. Nay, in the morning you will ride to the court. There you will request that Giles and his sister, the Lady Oriel, accompany you to Creganwald."

"But it is well known that Giles is a friend of Royce's."

"Of course it is. How else will the doors of Creganwald open to you? The man is trusted, both by Robert and by all the men who follow Royce. If he rides with you and asks to enter, none will deny him. Even if you are there. They will suspect naught."

"Aye, there would be no reason not to open the doors, for there will be no fear of me."

"There will be no fear . . . and you will cause no concern. You will be charming, and attentive to the lady and the child. We will let word be known that she has welcomed you at Creganwald, and that you find her . . . enchanting."

"What can we gain from that? Let us take what we want."

"Can you not see the forest because of the trees? William will be the first to hear the rumors about the 'lady' of Creganwald. He will wonder that she has invited you within, and perhaps feel he has chosen the wrong man to hold Creganwald. That will make it easier for me to force him to make his decision."

"I have felt it is more than a 'decision.' "

"Aye, William will do as I have asked, because he is the man he is. But I will make it easier for him to make the decision."

"How will you bring the king to our way of thinking?"

"That is a secret I intend to share with no one . . . not even you." *Especially not you*, he thought. "It is enough that I give you Creganwald, and the wench. William thinks upon it at this moment, but he will find no way around it. It is now only a matter of time before I have what has taken me long years to get. Be content with that."

Beltane asked no more questions, but he considered how he would rid himself of the hold Tearlach had on him as well. He would rule Creganwald without any help from anyone . . . and he would enjoy Lynette for a long, long time.

Royce found it painful to let Lynette and Cerise go the next morning, but finally, in the first gray light of dawn, he watched them ride away.

When he re-entered his home, it suddenly felt very hollow and empty. He stood for a moment, realizing that he had lived a life of loneliness for years, until Lynette had opened the doors and shed light, casting out the shadows. He also realized what the empty years would be like if Lynette and Cerise were not part of his life. The thought would have overwhelmed him if the memory of Lynette's last kiss had not built a shield.

He had to be busy or his problems would seem insurmountable. He had his horse saddled and rode from the city, spending the balance of the day considering his plans for Creganwald . . . and his future.

Giles was surprised when Oriel asked to accompany him to Creganwald a few days later. He knew there was no love for Lynette in it, and he had thought she meant to stay near Royce.

"Nay, brother, it is best I keep some distance between us. I would make peace with Lynette, and bury what has passed."

He was pleased, and agreed quickly. He hoped Oriel would find pleasure at Creganwald, and perhaps some peace for her troubled nature.

Robert was vastly relieved when Creganwald came into view. Lynette rushed to her father's chamber, to find that he was very ill indeed. He was abed, which was a rare thing for him. His breathing came in shallow gasps, and his color alarmed her. She could see the faint bluish color of his skin, and there was glistening perspiration on his brow. Lynette swallowed her fear and knelt beside him.

"Papa?"

"Lynette . . . my child . . . you have returned. Is . . . is the wedding done with, then? Does Royce come . . . with you?"

"Nay, Papa, do not talk. You must get well."

"You are not wed?"

"The king had affairs to attend to, and the wedding will take place upon his return. Papa, why did you not send for me sooner?"

"Do not weep, child. I will be all right, now that you are here." He seemed to drift off into a shallow sleep, and Lynette took that time to see to the household, and to give orders for her father's care.

For the next three days, Lynette hovered over him, and there seemed to be no improvement. She was not the only one who worried about her father's condition; Robert was just as concerned. So concerned that when word came to him that Giles and Oriel had arrived with a body of men and sought entrance, he welcomed the addition of a friend.

Giles had not realized that Beltane rode with the company until they were well on their way. By then he was helpless to do anything about it, for Beltane was a knight of good standing with William and he could not challenge him. He decided to let Robert give him the advice he needed. He flinched inwardly when he considered Robert's reaction.

It was only after Robert had given orders to greet the guests and make them comfortable that the name Beltane was mentioned as one of the guests. He was stricken and raced down the stairs to find Giles, Oriel, and Beltane in the great hall. With them were a number of Beltane's trusted men. Robert had unwittingly let the enemy within.

Robert's glare at an ashen-faced Giles promised mayhem when he had the opportunity to get him alone. He sucked in a harsh breath and even harsher words and held it until reason took over. Giles was most likely a pawn and helpless to prevent Beltane from traveling where he would. He knew Giles's loyalty.

Robert walked into the room, and both men turned from their conversation to greet him. One in innocent friendship and the other with a satisfied and frighteningly open smile.

"Beltane, what do you do here at Creganwald?"

"I but seek friendly hospitality."

"The king . . . ?"

"The king has not returned to London yet, Robert. We have traveled hard, and a horn of ale would quench a dry throat."

"Of course," Robert replied, and gave the order for ale to be brought. "Why do you travel so far from London now? I had thought your mind would be on the king's return."

"It is, but I feel safe in his decision and would determine for myself the condition of Creganwald."

At that moment Beltane's eye caught Lynette coming down the stairs. He watched her approach, and Robert watched him. He cursed himself again and again for the mistake he had just made. Yet he was not outnumbered, and he meant to put his men on their guard. They would keep a close eye on Beltane. One misstep, and Robert swore to himself that he would lock Beltane away, even if the king hanged him for it.

Robert did not miss the hungry look in Beltane's eyes, or the heat of his gaze as he watched Lynette approach.

Lynette came to an abrupt stop when she saw Beltane. Her look of fear was soon masked. She approached the men and tried to keep her uncertainty and discomfort from them.

"Lynette, had I known you were traveling home, I would have offered our services as an escort," Beltane said. "You left London rather suddenly. Nothing is amiss, I hope?"

His solicitude was much too sweet to suit Robert, and Lynette viewed it with suspicion as well. She would order the household to see to the comfort of her unwelcome guest, but she herself would stay out of his way caring for her father.

"I am afraid my father is very ill and I must see to his care. Please feel free to request anything you need. I am sure Robert will see that you are well taken care of."

"How distressing. I will stay to make my services available . . . in case you should need any assistance. Creganwald is not safely guarded. I could see that right away. Why, if I were set on taking it . . . I don't believe I could have been stopped. We must see to your safekeeping, else Royce might find you flown when he returns."

"I will send servants to you and leave you in Robert's capable hands," Lynette said coldly. "Rest assured, Sir Beltane, that Creganwald is adequately guarded. Any intruder will find strong swords raised in its defense. . . . Please excuse me."

Lynette left them, before her fear showed in her eyes.

Surprisingly, as the days wore on, Beltane showed no sign of creating any problem, which puzzled Robert, who set guards to watch his every move.

Lynette confined herself to Cerise's room and her father's, and received reports from Robert. The next week passed, and there was no untoward movement from Beltane.

Eldwyn grew worse, and Lynette remained by his bed much of the day, and often at night. She was leaving his room late one afternoon when she came face to face with Beltane.

Chapter Twenty-two

Lynette was so surprised that for a moment she could not react. But Beltane was gazing at her with a sympathetic and comforting look, and that alone raised her suspicions.

"My love, you look as if you need some rest. Come for a ride with me. You have been locked in this sickroom for days. Surely there is someone who can give you some relief."

"My father is too ill, and I must be by his side." She tried to move around Beltane, but he took hold of her arm and drew her close to him.

Beltane inhaled the scent of her and felt his body react. He wanted her. His smile was meant to charm, but to Lynette it looked feral and darkly suggestive.

"Lynette, why do you go on with this? You know the king's will is law, and his will shall make Creganwald mine. It would be better for you if you forget Royce. He will not go against whatever the king decrees. He will not jeopardize all he has won for one maid."

Lynette could hear the murmur of voices from the hall below, but essentially she was alone. She looked coldly at Beltane, and spoke in a voice calmer than he expected.

"I am not a possession with no more feelings than the walls of Creganwald, and I will not be used by you to wreak revenge on Royce. I am going to be his wife, not because the king has ordered it, but because it is my wish as well."

"You are making a large mistake. Royce has no power at court, but I do. It would serve you well to heed me, and prepare to understand what Royce already does . . . that you and Creganwald are out of his reach. He has long deserved to be put in his proper place."

"But," Lynette said with a smile, "I thought, when he came here, that the king had put him in his proper place. We have all taken him to heart . . . especially me, and I eagerly await the moment we are wed. Then Royce will have the right to do with you as I would like to do—toss you from the walls of Creganwald."

"You are foolish, Lynette. Already Royce is being told of your . . . disloyalty and your welcoming me here."

"Royce will not believe your rumors. He knows well that I await him, and would go to no other man. He knows, because I have given him cause to know, that there is no other man in my heart . . . nor will there ever be."

Lynette had time only for a shocked gasp before

she was caught in his arms, and his mouth took hers in a wild, impassioned kiss. She struggled, but for nothing. Her strength was no match for his. Worse, she knew if she cried out, there might be bloodshed, and Royce would pay a dear price if Beltane was killed here.

Still, she continued to do battle. He forced her back remorselessly against the door, and his hands began to fondle her with no regard for her muffled protests.

Then as suddenly as he had attacked, he was letting her go, and she realized that Robert had grasped him by the shoulders and thrown him against the wall.

Beltane pushed himself away from the wall to confront an equally angry Robert, who stood toe to toe with him and regarded him with a sneer of contempt.

"Rape has always been your way, Beltane, but this time you have laid hands on the wrong maid. Until the king's word says different, this maid and Creganwald belong to Royce, and I will hold each from harm. It seems you need reminding."

"You interfere, Robert," Beltane snarled. "The maid offered me an invitation."

"You lie!" Lynette cried, frightened that Robert might believe it.

"Aye, lady," Robert replied with scorn in his voice. "He lies. Lies and treachery have always been his way. Keep your distance from the maid, or I might forget what a coward you are and separate your head from your shoulders."

Lynette could not believe that a knight as handsome and as honored in the court of William could be so deceptive and brutal. To look upon him was to see his beauty . . . but to know him was to realize the ugliness of his spirit.

"This you will regret." Beltane's gaze burned into Robert as if he would see him dead, but Lynette noticed that he did not reach for a weapon; he truly was a coward. "And you will regret as well." He turned his fury on her. "When you are mine, we will see who is the master."

"You will be master of the pig stalls should I find you handling the lady again. Mark my words well, Beltane."

Beltane straightened, and cast one last smoldering look at Lynette before he left them.

"You are not hurt, lass?"

"Nay, Robert. I was unprepared. I shall be more careful in the future."

"I would show him the gate, but I do not want to anger the king."

"Robert . . . he spoke as if he knew there would be no marriage. Can the king have changed his mind?"

"Nay, he has not . . . but there is something weighing on his mind that puzzles me. I have tried to find word of things past concerning Tearlach and William, but none here know anything of it. But there is a secret, I know."

"I wish Royce would come."

"Aye, as do I. But by now William has returned to London, and has decided what must be done. I would not be surprised if Royce sent for you soon." Her eyes brightened with hope. "Rest assured that Beltane will not bother you again. I will warn the others. Alaine is impatient to challenge him, and the others wait only for a word from me to test him."

"I would have you do naught to cause any change in the king's mind."

"That is how I feel. But when Royce comes"—Robert grinned—"I will not stay anyone's hand, least of all my own. If I can get to him before Royce."

They continued down the stairs to join the others.

The balance of the night passed with no further sign of Beltane, who had ridden out after his confrontation with Robert.

But late that night, Eldwyn grew steadily worse, and Lynette rushed to his side. She remained there as the hours passed, bathing his face and washing away the sweat of his brow. Deep in her heart she knew this day might see him gone from her, and the thought of it broke her heart.

Robert came in again and again to see if there was a change, and she could only say the change was for the worse. Robert knew the end was near as well. He went down to his men and gave orders for word to be sent to Royce that Eldwyn was near death.

"Tell him the hour nears, and his lady is in need of him."

"Shall I tell him of Beltane's presence?"

"I would be little surprised if he did not already know of it. Tearlach would be the first to begin the rumors."

"Rumors?" Alaine questioned.

"Beltane and Tearlach no doubt hope it will be said that the lady welcomes Beltane with open arms. It will give the king cause to consider what Tearlach has planned."

"What think you he has planned?"

"Would that I knew. But he wants Creganwald

in Beltane's hands, and will do what he can to poison the king's mind against Royce being lord here."

Alaine's face had reddened and his eyes blazed in indignation. "He would darken the lady's name for his own benefit?"

"Do you put it past Beltane?"

"Nay, I do not. I will ride with all haste. Royce would slice him from breast to groin if he knew of his intent."

"It is the one thing we do not want before the king's decision is given. After that"—Robert shrugged—"it will be an interesting thing to see. Go, Alaine, and get the word to Royce. He will not want his lady alone in this dark hour."

Alaine left at once. Again and again over the next two days, Robert returned to Eldwyn's room and found Lynette there.

The third night when Robert returned the dawn light revealed the exhaustion on Lynette's face, as it revealed the death on Eldwyn's. She had done all it was in the power of anyone to do, and she knew her beloved father was slipping from her life.

Unrestrained tears stained her cheeks, and her face was pale and sorrowful. Robert knelt beside her as she prayed. Then he slowly rose and, against her will, drew her to her feet with him.

"Oh, Robert."

"I know, lady, it is hard. But you have done all you can. He is in the hands of God. I think Royce will come soon."

"You have sent word?"

"Aye."

"But he was not to leave until the king returned."

"He will leave," Robert said positively. "He will be at your side as fast as he can."

"Robert, does he know . . . ?"

"Have no doubt of it, lady, he knows. There is no love between him and Beltane, but he will not endanger you or Creganwald with hasty action. He would just be with you."

"I would have him here," she said softly, her exhaustion evident in her voice.

"I am going to bring you some food. You have not eaten and you will grow ill."

"Thank you. I cannot leave him."

Robert left the room quietly, and returned some time later with food. He watched to make sure she ate, and sat with her while the hours dragged Eldwyn's life away.

Lynette sat near the bed, and when her head dropped back in exhausted slumber, Robert kept watch over both.

The bright sun woke Lynette, and she found herself stiff and weary from her uncomfortable position. She went to her father's side and found little change. Robert sat nearby, and came to stand beside her.

"I didn't mean to sleep."

"You needed to rest, and I kept watch. If there had been any change, I would have wakened you."

"Go and find some food, Robert. Send Selwyn to me. I want to bathe and change him so he will not suffer any discomfort."

"Lynette, for a small time come away from this room. Just until Selwyn can carry and heat the water, and prepare him. It will do no good if you are too ill to be of any help to him . . . and Royce will be questioning our guardianship should he return to find you in your bed. I will see to your father's care."

"You will call me if there is any change . . . any change at all?"

"I swear."

Reluctantly she agreed, and he watched her as she dragged herself to the door. Robert sat near Eldwyn's bed and wondered what would happen if the lord of the manor was dead and the new lord had not been chosen.

Lynette found that no matter how exhausted she was, she could not sleep. She longed for Royce's strength, and to have him hold her and let her rest in his comfort. She rose from her bed and walked to the window.

A sound drew her attention, and she turned to see the door swing open and a tall form fill it.

"Lynette?" At the sound of her name, she uttered a soft cry and ran to the security of Royce's outstretched arms.

Chapter Twenty-three

Lynette stood by her father's grave, dry-eyed now because she had cried all her tears. Beside her stood Royce and Cerise, who held Lynette's hand. Cerise understood sorrow and the loss of a father, and she had remained quiet even as she clung to Lynette as if to support her.

For the two days before Eldwyn died, Royce had been Lynette's strength, silently holding her when she felt overwhelmed by sorrow, and cradling her in his arms at night when she could not find sleep. Now he stood beside her while the priest spoke the words of solace.

Royce had not mentioned the king, their marriage, or the presence of Beltane. He kept his thoughts to himself, but Beltane knew he was annoyed by his presence, and it pleased him.

When they all walked slowly back to share the food Lynette had ordered laid for them, she excused herself and went to her chamber. Royce followed, and Beltane's cold gaze dogged him.

In his mind he saw them in each other's arms, and the thought tore at him. He felt Robert's eyes on him and returned his look with a smile meant to annoy . . . and it did.

Within her chamber, Lynette went to her bed and lay upon it. Royce came to her and lay beside her and took her in his arms. Few knew more about grief than he, and he knew Lynette needed to heal herself, that there were no words he could say to aid it. He meant just to be beside her and to let her have someone to cling to.

"Must I go back to London with you now?" she asked quietly.

"Not until you are ready to leave Creganwald," he replied.

"You will stay with me?"

"For as long as you want me to stay."

"What of William?"

"Grief is a thing he knows much about. He would not rush you from your father's grave to a marriage."

Lynette turned to face him and saw the gentleness of his gaze, and the protection of his love. "I will take a day or two, then I will go with you, for I fear what Tearlach might do while you are away," she said. "He hates you too much to let any opportunity pass. I know it is why he has sent Beltane here."

"He sent him to darken your name before the king and to make William believe you would have Beltane rule here."

"You have heard . . . "

"The well-placed stories and the vague rumors,

aye, I have heard. But Tearlach does not know the meaning of trust, or he would not have wasted his efforts." Royce smiled at her. "Tearlach has never known love either, or he would not try to place Beltane between you and me."

"You never doubted me?"

"No, Lynette, not for one moment."

"What are you going to do?"

"Make sure he finds no success, and that the king is informed of the truth. I know when William returns I will be there, and if I must remind him of his oath and his honor, then I will do what is necessary." He pulled her closer to him. "I will leave most of my men here to guard Creganwald. You, Cerise, and I will return to court where we will be waiting when William arrives. I must find out what is afoot. Tearlach and Beltane are too . . . confident and too pleased."

"Why would William change his mind?"

"Robert says William owes Tearlach a debt, but I know not what it is."

"Then there might be no way to fight this."

"Aye, Lynette . . . there is always one way."

His voice was so cold that Lynette felt a shiver of fear go through her.

"I could challenge Beltane, and the king would be forced to acknowledge the one who succeeds."

"What if he refuses to fight?"

"You do not know Beltane's temper. He can be forced to fight, and anger is not a good weapon."

Her arms went about him, and she moved closer. He sensed her fear, but he had no words of comfort. He meant to rid himself of the threat to their happiness once and for all, no matter what the king ruled.

* * *

"I want you to follow my orders tomorrow," Beltane told his man as they conversed in a quiet corner of the hall. "See that you carry them out as I have told you. Don't make a mistake."

"I will see that it is done. Will you carry her back to London with you?"

"Aye. Mayhap we will stop and see a priest along the way. Once the deed is done, there is little they can do about it, and I intend to see to the consummation of the marriage. Once Creganwald and the maid are mine, you will be content with your service here and your reward?"

"Aye, you have been very generous."

"Good, then see that the business is done right. If you fail, Royce's sword does not know the meaning of the word mercy."

"So I have heard. He cannot be as good as he claims."

"No?" Beltane laughed. "He does not claim. But he is as good as every enemy he has bested has claimed. Unless your ambitions outweigh your sense, do not challenge him."

"The deed will be done," the man replied, but Beltane could see he had not convinced him about Royce's prowess with a sword. If the man was foolish enough to find out for himself . . . then let him pay the consequences. As long as he had Lynette and Creganwald, he didn't care.

That night Lynette and Royce had their dinner served in their chamber with only Cerise for company. Cerise had clung to Lynette, understanding her grief and sympathizing. She didn't know the words to say to make it easier, but she tried to make Lynette feel loved. She had found her father, and she knew how she would feel if she lost him again.

Lynette would have spent the night comfortably secluded with Royce and Cerise, had not a young maid come to the door to knock timidly.

There was a household problem, and despite Royce's offer to handle it, Lynette felt it better if she went. She was mistress of Creganwald, and her authority had to be maintained now that her father was gone. She followed the girl to the kitchens and within minutes solved the minor dispute.

She left the kitchen and climbed the stairs slowly. It would not be the same for a long time in this hall. She only hoped she could make Cerise's days as happy here as hers had been. Caught in her thoughts, she was not aware of another presence in the shadowed hall until a hand reached out and gripped her arm drawing her into a half-open doorway opposite her room.

"Beltane!" she gasped. "You fool! What do you think you are about? Royce will kill you!"

"Nay, he will not. Not if you are wise enough to understand what will occur. I have come to give you the chance to make this easier on him. The king will soon make it known that Creganwald is mine. He—"

"No! He will not."

"Aye, he will. If you want it to be easier on Royce, all you need do is submit to me. Tell him that you choose the king's will . . . and me."

"You addle-brained ass! You snake! Do you think I would give myself to you? I would rather be dead, as you will be when Royce hears of this."

"But he will not hear of this," Beltane ground out. "For when he finds you, you will be in no position to tell him the truth. If he finds you in my bed . . . naked, will he believe you then? Will he not believe you left him to come to me?"

His intent was obvious, and Lynette began to fight in earnest, but a sharp blow across her face stunned her and she was dragged further into the darkness. She could feel his hands moving over her, and she knew a fury that was like a red flame before her eyes.

She fought valiantly, and for one moment gained her freedom. But Beltane stood between her and the half-open door. In the semidarkness, Beltane could see her clearly, and the sight inflamed him. He would have had the caution to wait until the following day's plans had been carried out if he had not seen her go to the kitchen and followed.

Lynette could see him only as a dark shadow between herself and the light. She meant to scream the house down if he took another step toward her, but the chance for that never came. Behind Beltane, and across the hall, a door was pushed slowly open. Royce stood very still, but the broadsword in his hand rose slowly until the point was directed at Beltane.

"You have tormented me, wench," Beltane was saying to Lynette. "Why not make it easier for the both of us? The time will come when William puts your hand in mine, and there will be nothing Royce can do about it."

"You will not live to see that day." The voice that came from behind Beltane was like shards of ice, and Beltane swung around to meet the cold gaze that matched it.

"Bastard! I will not fight you for what will be given to me!"

"You will not fight me because you are a coward, and I will not kill you in the house of an honorable man who has just been laid in his grave. But leave here, Beltane, before I forget all honor and slice your heart out here and now."

"You have interfered for the last time, Royce. You will regret this when you face the sure defeat that is coming. I will see you pay."

"You have just one hour to ride away from Creganwald." Royce's voice was firm. "After an hour, I will believe that you wish to die and will grant that wish. Gather your men and get you gone."

Beltane knew that not only did Royce mean it, but he might accomplish it as well.

"Mayhap you are right." He smiled a grimace of a smile. "We will let the king decide."

He cast one last look at Lynette, brushed past Royce, and was gone. But Royce turned from the door and followed him down to the hall, where Robert and the others rose to their feet in surprise. Lynette was only a few steps behind Royce.

No one spoke while Beltane announced gruffly to his men that they were leaving. More than one puzzled look was cast at Royce, who stood calmly nearby and said nothing while they gathered their possessions and left.

When Beltane and his men were gone, Lynette and Royce explained some of what had happened.

"To throw Beltane out will magnify Tearlach's wrath," Robert said cautiously, but his lips twitched.

"It will magnify his wrath," Royce admitted. "And we must follow close on his heels, for he will carry a tale that will cause as much harm as he can."

Royce turned to Lynette, but she met his unspoken question with a smile. "I will be ready to travel when you wish."

He was obviously relieved at her reaction, but he only turned to give the order that all were to prepare to travel at the first light of dawn. Then he turned and followed Lynette back up the stairs.

It was only after Cerise had been taken to bed that Lynette questioned him.

"He will go straight to Tearlach?"

"No doubt. Beltane is a handsome face behind which a sluggish mind rests. He needs to be guided, and Tearlach is the guide. Beltane only knows what he wants for the moment; Tearlach has a far-reaching plan, and I wish I knew what it was."

"Royce, do you think William will be back by the time of our arrival?"

"I hope he does not arrive before, but either way, it is time to make an end of this. I would play Tearlach's game and learn what his goal is."

Royce threw himself down in a chair near the fire and sighed in disgust. Lynette came to kneel by the chair and look up at him.

"Royce, if I plead with the king, mayhap it will bring him to our way of thinking."

"He was already thinking our way. It was his order that brought me here and commanded this marriage. But something has changed his mind, something powerful."

"What can we do?"

269

"For now, all we can do is return to court, put the lie to any tales Beltane might carry, and do our best to remind the king he has given his word."

"Royce, I . . . I could not bear to wed a man such as Beltane."

Royce reached for her and drew her onto his lap. Her arms went automatically about his neck. He rested his head against her breast and spoke quietly.

"You will beg no one, not even the king. If a man is not as good as his word, he is of little use. I have served William faithfully for a number of years. That alone should be enough to secure his favor. I have his word, and that should be all that is needed. But if it is broken . . . then I will see that Beltane never finds satisfaction in his gain."

Lynette knew by his voice that he would listen to no arguments about this. He had put his trust in William for many years and had never regretted it; now he would do it again and see what the value of his friendship was.

Lynette held him close to her, and soon the soft touch of his lips against her throat told her his thoughts had turned to other things.

She sighed softly as his lips found hers and she surrendered to the pleasure of his touch.

Chapter Twenty-four

The trip back to London was not as slow, as comfortable, or as happy as the first had been; it took only one full day of hard riding. They arrived late in the day, and by the time the group was settled, it was too late to find any answers to their questions. What they did hear was not too pleasing: the king had returned that morning and was not in the best of moods.

It worried them to find out that Tearlach had been with the king for most of the time he had been back.

Robert found sleep an impossibility and sat in the shadowed hall contemplating a horn of ale, and murderous thoughts against Tearlach.

He dozed as the fire grew lower and lower, and a pounding on the door went unnoticed for a few minutes before it drew his attention. Since no one else was awake, he stumbled to the door himself, promising vengeance on the careless person who chose to call at this hour.

The young man who appeared before him was reasonably sure he was not going to be greeted warmly. He began to speak before Robert could demand the reason for his presence. In the darkness Robert did not see how the visitor was dressed.

"I seek Robert Debayeaux."

"I am Robert Debayeaux. Who seeks me?"

"I am come from the king, sir. He bids you attend him at once."

"Now?"

"Aye, sir, now. He bids you to bring no one and tell no one where you go. Come by the back entrance, and someone will be waiting for you."

Robert wasn't sure it was not some kind of trick, but could think of no one who sought his death. Then the clouds covering the moon drifted past, and he recognized the king's messenger.

"I will be there as fast as I can." The young man nodded, but waited expectantly. "All right, I'm coming now."

By the time Robert found his cloak and returned to the door, he expected the messenger to be gone. But he'd waited. Robert smiled, realizing the man intended to see he didn't dally.

They rode without a word, and the young man took Robert's horse's reins as soon as he dismounted. Robert took the few steps to the back door, and found it opening before he could knock. He was ushered inside and was quickly beckoned up the stairs.

William stood by a nearly dead fire awaiting him. He was completely alone, and this was enough to make Robert understand that he was to share a secret that William would most likely deny should word of it go beyond this room.

"Robert, thank you for your prompt attendance. Come and share a horn of ale with me. There is much of great importance I must discuss with you. Who in your household knows you have come?"

"No one. I was awake and answered the door myself. As far as anyone in the household knows, I am abed like the others."

"Good."

"What can be of such importance?"

"A matter that concerns our mutual friend."

"Royce? I have heard rumors, and Beltane was at Creganwald. It seem he is sure of possession . . . and Eldwyn is dead and buried."

"Aye, I had word. How was Beltane welcomed at Creganwald?"

"Not as you have been led to believe." He went on to tell William the tale of Beltane's ejection from Creganwald. "He had no concern that the girl had just buried her father, and I truly believe he would have taken her on her father's grave if the opportunity had presented itself," Robert finished with a disgusted look.

"Robert . . . would Royce fight for her?"

"What?"

"I said, would Royce fight for her?"

"Aye, he would take on the whole of England for her, I've no doubt of that. But why should he fight for what has been given him freely?"

"Because a petition has been laid before me, adorned with a promise made so long past that I had forgotten."

"Petition? Tearlach?"

"Aye."

"He wants Creganwald for Beltane . . . and to strike Royce."

"Aye."

"Say him nay, my lord. For if he holds Creganwald, there will be no safety for you. Who would know whom he dealt with and opened his harbor to if he ruled there? He would betray you, or Beltane would."

"And yet I cannot say him nay."

"Why?"

"Because I must pay the debt I owe or have him forever about my neck, claiming that my word is without foundation."

"Then you will agree? You cannot. Your word has already been given to Royce."

"Why do you think I question you about his regard for this maid and Creganwald? Will he fight for her, Robert?" William's voice was firm and ungiving.

"Why? When? How do you propose this battle?"

"Royce must challenge Beltane as soon as the word is given, and in front of the entire court, so that none will believe I took part in this."

"Do you think Tearlach will let Beltane fall into that trap? He will caution Beltane to refuse to answer Royce's challenge, and there will be nothing Royce can do about it."

"Unless he forces the matter."

"How?"

"Royce knows Beltane's weaknesses well. He has longed to cross swords with him, but I have put a stop to it. I cannot stop him if he feels the cause is just, and he wants to claim that his honor has been slighted."

"It has been slighted. Royce would feel you had betrayed him. He has stood firm in your honor, trusting in your word."

"There are times, Robert, when a king must do . . . things he would not choose to do. I would choose to have Royce at Creganwald, but Tearlach presses me hard to honor that vow of long ago. I have need of my 'sword,' but I cannot ask Royce directly, or word will reach Tearlach's ears. This challenge must come from Royce, and his anger at me will make it believable."

"Whcn?"

"When the decision is announced."

"Before the whole court?"

"Aye, that is the best place. Then Beltane will have too much pride to back away."

"Has it occurred to you that Royce might lose such a battle?"

William smiled at Robert. "Has it occurred to *you* that he would?"

"Nay." Robert smiled in return.

"Robert . . . if Royce sees this as betrayal, he may be too angry to issue a challenge. It might be better if you were to insert thc idca subtly and allow things to take their course."

"I am not to warn him of what is to happen?"

"His response might be more . . . unrestrained if you were to . . . suggest that he be prepared to defend what he desires. Let him know that I will look favorably upon the winner. If Tearlach were to get wind of this before it happened . . . If word were brought to him that you had prepared Royce for such an event . . . "

"How would such word reach his ears?"

"I cannot name anyone, but I feel there is someone within Royce's household."

"A spy? Within our house!"

"Word cannot have leaked out any other way. Every move you make is known by Tearlach."

"I cannot believe that any of our men . . . " he paused.

"You have a name?"

"Lady Oriel," Robert said angrily. "It could be no one but she. She has had her eye on wedding Royce one day, and your gift of Creganwald did not sit well with her." Robert paused. It had just occurred to him that William needed Royce to rid himself of a threat. But he still didn't know what the threat was, and he didn't think William was going to tell him. "You would use him?" he asked quietly.

"It is a dishonorable thing. But I have no choice. If Royce will not fight . . . then Creganwald will be Beltane's. But if Beltane is defeated, Tearlach will be stalemated."

"Royce will not forgive you for this."

"I do not seek his forgiveness and I can live with his anger. But he will have Creganwald and he will have the maid. Mayhap . . . eventually he will understand that sometimes even a king's hands are tied."

"You would lose his regard to give him his heart's desire. You are right; when his anger is gone, he will see the right of it."

"Move with caution, and make sure this does not

get to your spy. Make sure also that you whisper the right words to Royce, for I want the scene played out with no suspicion of my involvement."

"I will tread carefully." Robert laughed. "I want no part of his anger either."

"I wish him well, Robert, you of all people know that. I do not like it to appear before all my knights that I have betrayed a trust. I will stand before them and claim him undisputed owner for his lifetime and for the lifetimes of his heirs. But he must raise his sword this one last time."

Robert gazed at the king he loved and trusted, and wished heartily that he had the power to reveal more of what he knew. But he could not. He could only do all in his power to realize William's hope for Royce.

"When this is finished, have I your leave to tell him the truth?"

"Only when you are certain that word will not reach Tearlach's ears. If it does . . . Royce will have to guard both Creganwald and Lynette, for there is no end to the revenge Tearlach will seek . . . and no protection I can give him."

"I will be careful. I will also see to it that the Lady Oriel finds a home somewhere else, preferably many miles from Creganwald."

"Excellent plan. You had best go now, before the sun rises. I know how many ears are attached to the doors here. Be cautious, and see that you are not discovered leaving. Tell Royce . . . Nay, if I am ever forgiven, I will tell him all that needs to be said myself. If I am not"—he shrugged—"there are no words that will do. I long for peace, Robert, and that will only come when the holdings of my empire are in the hands of those I know I can trust. I know Royce's loyalty, and can depend upon his honor in holding Creganwald."

"You can depend upon it. You can also depend upon my gratitude that you have found a way around this problem."

"You and I have campaigned too long together for your gratitude to be necessary. When this is finished, we will raise a horn or two in honor of our success. Fare thee well, Robert, and continue in Royce's service as devotedly as you have in mine. Spend your aging years in the companionship and peace you have earned."

"I almost look forward to tomorrow, for Beltane has long deserved what I know Royce will mete out. Once Lady Lynette asked me if she and I were conspirators, when I told her of Royce and his past. I told her, aye, we were. One day I will have to tell her how far that conspiracy has gone, for she will be distressed when Royce challenges Beltane and she will place the blame squarely upon your shoulders."

"And her Saxon blood will cry out at my betrayal."

"I would not be surprised," Robert laughed. "Mayhap I will have to restrain her from picking up a sword herself and seeking her own satisfaction."

"I need no other battles, my friend. Seek the first occasion to tell her the truth. Just make certain none know of it before time."

"I will be cautious."

Robert slipped carefully from the room, and was a bit surprised to find the same messenger waiting for him. "Your horse is ready near the back gate," he informed Robert, then melted into the darkness like a shadow.

Robert rode slowly, considering what words he would use with Royce to prepare him for a battle he had no idea was approaching.

When he arrived home, he was pleased to see that the place was still shrouded in darkness. He was careful when he let himself in, for the men slept in the hall, along the wall, and he did not want to be making up reasons why he was roaming about.

He made his way to his chamber and to his bed. But sleep was not easy. He considered going straight to Royce and telling him all the king had said, but he knew Royce might take Cerise and Lynette back to Creganwald and defy anyone to take it from him.

He would have justice on his side, but that course of action could only lead to tragedy, for William would be forced to see that his word was obeyed.

William was right. He must warn Royce to fight for what he wanted.

His plan laid as carefully as he could manage, Robert sought sleep. The rest of the matter lay in the hands of God. God and the strong arm of Royce. But he had made another decision as well. When Royce was in total possession of Creganwald, and Lynette was wedded to him, he would confide his secret to Royce. It had weighed too heavily on his mind for too long. He even wondered if it would not be better to tell William . . . yet he knew what might follow. William did not yet have a firm grasp on England, and this word, slipping into the right ear, could be disastrous.

He hated the secret he had to hold, but he loved the man he held it for. Now, soon, if fate was fair, he could share it and be free of it once and for all. This thought followed him into sleep.

Chapter Twenty-five

Robert felt as if he had barely closed his eyes when he heard the awakening of the household. He rose hoping to find Royce alone somewhere for a moment. He had to prepare him to issue the challenge.

Dressing hastily, he made his way downstairs to find Royce already there, breaking his fast with Giles and Alaine, who insisted they were going to accompany him to hear the king's word on the marriage. They were prepared to have a lively wedding as soon as the word was spoken.

Royce was laughing at their enthusiasm, and Robert could see his confidence.

"Good morning, Robert. You are showing your years, lying abed like this."

"Lying abed! It is hardly dawn. Your enthusiasm is showing. Where is Lynette, still abed?"

"Nay, Lynette was awake some time ago. She is taking care of a problem."

"Problem?"

"She is explaining to Cerise why she cannot go to court today."

"How clever of you to put that burden on her."

"Aye," Royce chuckled, " 'tis better her than me. I have discovered the little lass has a way of twining me about her finger and having her way."

"The little lass or the other?" Alaine teased.

"I have a strange feeling it is going to be both," Royce said.

"That would not surprise me either," Robert said. "Have you told Lynette *she* cannot come to court this morning?"

Royce looked at Robert in surprise. "Not come? Why should she not come? Do you foresee a problem?"

"Who can say when problems will arise, with men like Beltane and Tearlach present? They are creators of problems. If I were you, I would wear my mail and make sure my sword was handy."

Royce looked at Robert with a frown. His countenance was bland, but was there something elusive in his eyes? Did Robert have misgivings about the gathering today?

"Do you truly believe Beltane will cause a problem today in the presence of the king?"

"I simply said that if I were to go into their presence, I would be prepared . . . unless you have begun to think the reward not worth the battle."

"Not worth the battle?" Royce repeated. Now he was certain there was something in Robert's words that meant more than he understood. "I will fight anyone who tries to separate us. Lynette must come with me this morning. But do not worry, Robert, I will make sure neither Beltane nor Tearlach causes trouble. I do not trust either of them any more than you do."

"I would take great pleasure in spitting Beltane on the point of my sword," Alaine said agreeably.

"As would I," Giles agreed. "He is not a man to trust. At Hastings, he was always a step behind and well protected. And yet he is no mean swordsman; he can wield a powerful and very deadly blade. He simply must be pushed into it. He is no laggard when it comes time for the spoils, either."

"And he is no laggard when it comes time for the ladies," Alaine said. "His handsome face brings them to his bed easily enough."

"Aye," Robert said quietly. "But have you noticed that few of them stay very long? I have a feeling he is none too gentle with a maid. I would not want one of mine in his hands."

The two knights agreed, but Royce's attention was fully on Robert now. He knew him too well not to know there was a message there for him, but what? He had no intention of letting Lynette fall into Beltane's hands.

Before he asked the question, Royce's attention was drawn to the stairs, where Lynette was just descending. There was a quiet moment while the four watched her approach. She brought a smile to each face.

"You have convinced Cerise?"

"Aye, my brave lord," Lynette laughed up at him. "But it has cost you a promise."

"A promise?"

"Aye, I told Cerise that you would take her to choose that pony you promised at Creganwald, and that you would purchase the one of her choice . . . tomorrow."

"There is little I can do if you have spoken in my name. I shall just have to agree."

"Such a fierce fight you offer," Lynette chided. "When she asks for more, will you give it so readily?"

"Most likely," Royce laughed. "And I do not doubt that Robert, or any of the others, will follow on my heels and give her what she cannot wheedle from me."

"You are going to raise a tyrant."

"Nay," Royce said softly, "I have been wise enough to choose a mother who will correct our spoiling."

It seemed to the knights present that there was more warmth in the hall when Lynette was present. These men had fought long and hard behind Royce, and now they looked forward to the promised days of peace and happiness at Creganwald.

Robert said nothing more. He knew Royce had felt his subtle hints, and though he said nothing, Royce was not one to take chances. He would go prepared to fight for what he wanted, and that was all that Robert could do without coming out and telling him the king's plans.

It was decided that five of Royce's best men would accompany him to court, including Robert. Oriel was sorely disappointed when it was not suggested that she could go as well, and she made her dissatisfaction known, to the embarrassment of her brother, who was one of the chosen knights. In the end, Oriel got her way. She would ride with them.

Robert watched her performance with a face

devoid of all emotion, and that alone caught Lynette's attention. At her first opportunity, she questioned Robert.

"You are not pleased that Oriel will accompany us."

"Nay. The lady always has a motive of her own, and she is not to be trusted." He turned to look intently at Lynette. "Do you understand my words? I would take it as a special favor to me if you would keep away from her.

"What has caused this new fear?"

"Lynette . . . I would trust you to keep a confidence."

"Aye, Robert?"

"Even from Royce."

"Nay. I would keep no secrets from him."

"This is for his benefit, and not to cause harm. Oriel has been carrying word of all that passes among us to Tearlach. Do not tell her anything Royce might say to you."

"She is spying on Royce's household!"

"Aye."

"Why? What has Tearlach to gain?"

Lynette's mind was quicker than Robert had thought, and he knew he would have to be more careful or she would have the whole secret from him.

"He hopes to hear something that would harm Royce, or cause him to turn from you."

It did not ring true to Lynette, and yet she would never believe Robert would lie to her. "Do not worry, Robert, I will confide nothing to the lady."

There were more and more people gathering in the hall, and private conversation was soon impossible. Lynette escaped to her chamber when the hour grew near for them to leave. She chose carefully the gunna she would wear. It was a deep rust in color, and the garment she wore beneath was of soft gold. She bound her hair in a gold snood, leaving small fine wisps to frame her face. As she was finishing her preparations, Cerise peered shyly around the door. Seeing her reflection in the mirror, Lynette turned and motioned her in.

"Oh, Lynette, how very pretty you are," Cerise said in an awed voice as she came to Lynette.

"She is beautiful." Royce's voice came from the doorway. He paused there to study the picture they made . . . the two most perfect beauties he had ever seen. One an innocent, with a sweet look of childish trust, and the other . . . his pulse picked up a beat and he could feel his blood warm. He knew she would always be able to reach this well of love inside him and replenish it with a look or a word.

He walked toward them, and Lynette rose to move into his embrace. Cerise beamed up at them as if they were the fulfillment of all her dreams.

"We have to leave now." Royce spoke to Cerise, standing with one arm around Lynette. "I hope we will be back early, but there is no way for us to know. Try to stay out of mischief."

"I will. Papa, will we go home tomorrow?"

"I doubt it. The wedding can't take place that quickly, and the king will want it to be held here. We'll try to make it as soon as we possibly can, believe me, Cerise."

They bade her good-bye and went back downstairs to join the group that would accompany them. Occasionally Royce would glance at Robert with the nagging feeling that something was very wrong, and Robert tried not to look uncomfortable under the scrutiny. He wondered if Royce would forgive him for what was about to happen.

There was an excitement about the court, as if everyone felt that something portentous was about to happen. As William entered the hall, all the women sank into deep curtsies. Royce knew his first sense of alarm when his eyes met the king's and there was no warmth, no smile of greeting, and no look of contented approval.

He turned to look at Robert, who was scowling so darkly that Royce felt his heart stop. Something was amiss. His gaze went around the sea of faces until it found Tearlach and Beltane. There was a look of satisfaction in their eyes, a look that could only mean trouble for Royce.

The men who stood beside Royce were completely unaware of his thoughts, but he had frozen where he stood. Suddenly he knew that his feelings had been right, that somehow Tearlach had managed to change William's mind.

He looked down into Lynette's eyes, and knew something else. If Lynette was not his, Beltane would never live to know it. His thoughts spun until they settled on what he would have to do. Lynette felt him go rigid, and when she looked up at him, she could see that his jaw was set and there was a sudden fierce look in his eyes. Her heart sank, and she knew a fear that shook her.

Both of them looked toward the king, who was preparing to speak to them.

Lynette watched him as he spoke. Again she felt his magnetism. This was not a man who would make a promise and then break it. But she realized that kings did whatever they considered necessary. With sinking heart, she also knew there was no higher authority to which they could appeal. William was speaking when she returned her attention to his words.

" . . . and there has arisen the necessity to reverse my decision. A prior claim has come before me, and I find the cause . . . right and true."

He continued to speak, but Royce's gaze had gone from him to Beltane. The two men looked at each other, the heat of their gazes coalescing into a tangible force. Beltane wore a smile of triumph as the words filled the hall.

" . . . and so the lands of Fallwell will be awarded Royce for the span of his lifetime and that of his heirs. The lands of Creganwald and the Lady Lynette will be the property of Beltane for him and for his heirs."

A silence fell over the hall. Beltane felt the greatest of pleasure; Lynette felt as if her heart would stop; William felt his betrayal most potently; and Royce seemed to have frozen, his face unreadable. Only when the silence became unbearable did he release Lynette's arm and walk toward Beltane.

Chapter Twenty-six

Beltane felt his confidence slip as Royce grew closer. Royce's eyes were no longer calm gold, but looked as molten and hot as the heart of a raging volcano. Beltane felt the heat of them, and something deadly shot through him like the bite of a sword. He would not fight this man . . . he could not. He tasted death and the taste was bitter.

Still, he did not need to fight. Lynette and Creganwald were his. He need only control his temper and there would be nothing Royce could do, unless his own honor meant little to him.

Many glanced at the king, who was watching but seemed not to be disposed to stop the confrontation.

William was, in fact, mentally urging Royce on, as was Robert. But Lynette was imagining Royce fighting . . . perhaps dying. She could see his strong body covered in blood. Had it been in her power then, she would have given herself to Beltane rather than see harm come to Royce.

"You are a thieving and dishonorable snake, Beltane," Royce said loud enough for all to hear. "By some stealth you have tried to take what is not rightfully yours. I find you a coward, and a knight whose honor should be stripped from him to prove to all knights that your breed cannot wear the spurs of knighthood and stain them with dishonor."

Beltane's face was growing colder and more furious by the second, and Tearlach was glaring at him, willing him to control his fury. *Hold that ugly temper*, Tearlach prayed. *Don't be a fool and fall into his trap! Don't let him force you to lose what we have done so much to gain.*

Beltane was trying to do just that, but Royce continued the verbal assault until Beltane knew every knight was looking at him and wondering if he was too much of a coward to defend himself. It seemed as if Royce had some unique power to touch the deepest fury in Beltane.

"You were a coward at Hastings and you are a coward now. You use someone else to force your claims where they are not wanted, and you have not the heart to fight for what you want." Royce continued toward him, but Beltane was trying to remember Tearlach's admonitions. He would hold Creganwald if he did not respond to Royce's pressure.

Royce had drawn off his gauntlet as he walked toward Beltane and now he was close enough to challenge. He struck Beltane across the face with the gauntlet, and the sound exploded in the silent room.

Beltane had reached the end of his tolerance. Fury gripped him; every word of caution Tearlach had uttered was forgotten. He could not tolerate this treatment and keep any kind of pride. He struck back. And when he did, Royce smiled. Tearlach groaned with disgust, and both William and Robert controlled their smiles of satisfaction.

A collective sigh drifted over the entire crowd as the two men faced each other. It was only then that William spoke again.

"It seems there has been a challenge presented. What say you, Beltane?"

"This bastard has no claim to Creganwald!"

"And I say," Royce said quietly, "that Beltane is still a coward, and that he has too much fear to fight for what he wants. Instead he will hide behind thievery and lies to keep it from being known that he is not strong enough or honorable enough to place at risk what he has tried to steal." Royce looked calm and firm, while it was obvious that Beltane seethed. "I claim Creganwald and I claim the right to contest your possession by right of arms. Will you hide, Beltane, or will you face me and see who will be master there?"

"What is mine I can hold, bastard!" Beltane hissed through gritted teeth. "I will see you dead and take greater pleasure in enjoying the spoils. I shall think of you while I enjoy the wench and bring Creganwald under my rule."

William revealed nothing of his feelings, but he, too, could have struck Beltane for his arrogance. William did not relish the way he had been forced into this matter. But he did relish the battle that was to come.

"Then there is little more to be said," William said. "Beltane, as the one challenged, you have the right to choose the weapons."

"I choose the broadsword," Beltane snarled as his hate-filled gaze met Royce's.

"Royce?"

"Aye, I will fight him with any weapon of his choice."

"Then broadswords it will be. The battle will be held on the morning after next."

"Until this is decided," Tearlach said coldly, "it is wrong for the maid to stay beneath Royce's roof. She may become Beltane's, and he would want her unspoiled . . . unless . . . "

Royce turned his dark look on Tearlach, and would have liked to cross swords with him as well for the public insult to Lynette. But he knew how clever Tearlach was, and he didn't want Lynette to face the sharp sword of the man's scorn. Already her cheeks were pink with embarrassment at Tearlach's words.

"You need not worry about the maid," William inserted quickly before Royce could answer. "She will remain with me until this is decided."

But this situation did not make Royce feel any better. He wanted Lynette at his side. He did not want to give her up even to the protection of the king. It took William only a moment to recognize this, and he smiled.

"Do not worry, Royce, she will be in good hands." That Royce was not too pleased with him was just as obvious to William, but he could bear the cold look, until the time came when a full explanation could be made.

It was Robert's hand on Royce's shoulder that kept him from saying the words on his lips. He turned to look at Robert.

"Keep faith in your own self, Royce, and we will find an end to this that will satisfy even Tearlach himself." Robert spoke quietly, and Royce held his gaze for a long moment trying to read the message there. Robert had a great deal of explaining to do.

Royce could not believe that Lynette would not lie beside him this night. He looked at her and his arms felt empty already. Her wide blue eyes watched him closely, for she feared that he was about to lay down his life for her. She wanted to cry out, to run to him, and to hold him close so that he would not make such a sacrifice.

But already the king was dismissing the entire party, and when he held out his hand to her, there was little she could do but to place hers on it, cast Royce a look of worry, and leave with the king.

Royce left with the few who had arrived with him, but Robert was not among them. He had felt it wise to find another place to rest until the night had passed and with it some of Royce's anger.

"You damned fool! Don't you realize you could have had Creganwald and the maid if you had just kept hold of that uncontrollable temper of yours? You played into his hands like a child, and now you must fight him."

"I will fight him and I will kill him. This has been a long time in the making, but I will take his slurs and accusations no more."

"And if he wins?"

"He will not."

"You will have no revenge on him. If you kill him, his life is done and nothing can make him suffer. If he kills you, he wins Creganwald and the wench, and where will your revenge be then?"

"My revenge . . . or yours?"

"Ours, you arrogant idiot. I had found the way to make him suffer for untold years to come. Every night he would have had to think of her in your bed, and every day he would have longed for the wealth that had slid from his hands so easily. Now you have handed him the possibility of having all and neatly turning the tables on us."

"I regret what happened, in the face of what you say now. But how was I to stop him and the things he said? He would blacken my name."

"All you had to do was laugh in his face and accuse him of jealousy and of being unable to lose with honor. No one would have faulted you, and you would not have had to lift your sword. You would live to enjoy, and he would have lived the balance of his life in torment. Fool!"

"Is there no way out of this?"

"When you answered his challenge before the king's eyes?"

"I will have Creganwald and Lynette, and we can find another way to strike back at him."

"Has the woman bewitched you?"

"I would have her." Beltane's voice was more firm and final than Tearlach had ever heard it before, and he knew that Beltane was not going to be his tool in this matter any longer. . . . He wanted the maid.

"I want Creganwald." Tearlach's voice was just as firm. "The manor is strategically located. I want the power to hold it, and to use it for more than you would ever guess. If my plans are ruined because of your heated loins . . . "

"Be damned to Creganwald! There is room there for you and any force you care to rally. I will enjoy its fruits and the fair Lynette. You can make use of its location at your will, I care naught."

"I advise you to win this battle, Beltane. And if you do and you can make him cry mercy, we can still have what we both want. Defeat him . . . but let him live."

"You can trust in that. I know Royce's way of battle. Have I not watched him thousands of times? I know his weaknesses as well as his strengths. I will bring him to his knees for you. Will that satisfy your revenge?"

"Aye," Tearlach said quietly. "Aye, bring him to his knees . . . then leave the rest to me."

Royce knew he was going to miss Lynette beyond anything, but he had forgotten Cerise. He could have groaned with dismay when he saw her waiting at the top of the stairs.

Her face was bright, and she flew down the stairs to throw herself into his arms. When she had kissed him soundly, her next breath was for Lynette.

"Where is Lynette, Papa?"

"I'm afraid she has to stay with the king's party for a day or two."

"Why? Are they getting ready for the wedding?"

"No . . . not just yet."

"But, Papa—"

"Cerise, Lynette is fine. In a few days you will see her again and help with the preparations for the wedding. Does that satisfy you?"

Royce could see at once that it did not satisfy her at all, and that she had begun to worry about Lynette's return. But he had no answers, for he was just as worried. He would defeat Beltane . . . he could not lose her.

Lynette took supper with William and Matilda and a number of the knights and ladies. She was silent most of the meal, and William knew she was not happy with him.

That night Lynette found her bed colder and emptier than it had ever been. She prayed for Royce. As she drifted off to sleep, she recalled a few words spoken to her by Matilda just moments before she climbed the stairs to her chamber.

"Have heart, Lynette," Matilda had said in her soft and gentle voice. "All is not always as dark as it seems. Royce is a strong and able fighter."

"I do not want him to raise his sword and face death for me."

"What cause other than those they love the most brings men to battle? Consider the alternative if Royce did not answer Beltane with a challenge. Do you think he would allow you to go so easily?"

"You do not understand . . . I would give myself if it would keep him from harm."

"And dishonor him more? Would you have him surrender all he has desired just to keep himself from harm?"

"I would have him live and not see bloody wounds upon his body."

"Aye, I would never see William raise a sword again. But if his honor called, and he had to defend this land and all he has won, I would gladly stand

and wave good-bye, and give him my love and my blessings."

"You are of much stronger fabric than I."

"Nay, I am not. Listen to me, child. When the time comes, you will dress in your best. You will tend your hair and make yourself as beautiful as you can. You will take your seat beside William and me, and you will smile, and show the man you choose that you have as much courage as he. Do not let him go into this battle with the sight of tears upon your face, for it will weaken him. Trust me in this . . . you will serve him better with a smile than with a tear . . . and you might be surprised at the outcome."

Matilda had patted her arm and left her standing and watching after her. Lynette considered her words and saw the truth in them. Royce needed her as much as she needed him, and she would not weaken his arm for worry about her. She would do as Matilda had said . . . she would smile . . . and she would pray.

Chapter Twenty-seven

The next morning Lynette woke to the sound of activity below. She rose, aware that she had slept long. But she had not really found sleep until much of the night had passed.

Thoughts of the night past still lingered in her mind, for to her surprise she had felt close to Royce. It was as if she had wandered with Royce to a place of dreamlike quality.

Royce, too, had been caught in something his logical mind could never explain, for he felt Lynette reach for him and opened his mind to the misty apparition that appeared there. She spoke to him.

His eyes closed, he walked with her and touched her hand. He could taste the sweetness of her . . .

She felt him, knew he was beside her, and put her hand in his and felt his strength, and parted her lips for his kiss . . .

He held her close to him and knew the warmth of her giving body . . .

The pale mist swirled about them as they melded together and found the perfection of their united heartbeats, and the will that created the power to cross the barriers of place and time.

It was a dream, he knew . . . she knew . . . but it was so real that neither of them could ever deny that they had found each other in the mist of dreams and had renewed their vows to each other there.

Now day was upon her, and she bathed and prepared herself to face the people in the hall below. This would, she knew, be the longest day of her life.

But as she reached the bottom of the stairs, her eyes scanned the crowd and touched on . . . Royce!

She had thought she would not see him again before . . . but he was here, and she was so glad that he was. She knew the moment he sensed her, for he turned and looked toward the stairs.

She crossed the room to stand near him.

"Lynette." He breathed her name softly, and she could feel his presence enfold her and calm her. "Are you well?"

"Aye, and you?"

"I dreamed—"

"Yes, I know."

"Was it real or a wish?"

"It was the most wonderful of realities. We are bound, you and I, and nothing, no one will change that . . . no matter what the outcome of the duel."

She watched him smile. "There is only one outcome possible. Beltane will lose all he has planned on and more."

"I know."

"You have faith?"

"In you? Always. Do not fear for me, my love."

"By the time another day passes, you will belong to me. Have no fear of that."

She had no time to answer, for another voice sounded nearby.

"Have you come to bid her farewell, Royce? Such a touching scene." Beltane's voice was taunting "You needn't worry, I will show her how to dry her tears, for she will be too well occupied to think of the bastard who tried to reach for what belonged to his betters. Once I have removed you from her thoughts, I will replace you with other . . . warmer ones."

Royce's eyes narrowed, but he did not respond. He had come only under the king's sufferance, and in the hope of seeing Lynette again and confirming his dream of the night before. She had known, he could see it in her eyes, and he did not intend to give any excuse for the king to change his plans again. If William chose to end the challenge and give Lynette to Beltane, that was his right. Royce could not risk that eventuality.

"There is nothing for you and me to say to each other, Beltane. On the morrow, my sword will speak for me. Have you seen a priest? Mayhap your soul needs cleansing before you give it up."

Royce's cool arrogance grated on Beltane's nerves, and he would have attacked him where he stood, but another voice interrupted his flaring fury.

"There is many a wager put on a different ending to your duel." Tearlach's voice was calm, and both Royce and Lynette knew that this was the more fearsome enemy. This man did not lose his control, nor did he allow his anger to govern.

"Tearlach," Royce said calmly, "you have sent

the wrong dog to hunt your victims for you. Why do you not call him off until you can teach him better?"

There was a low growl from Beltane, and a soft and malicious laugh from Tearlach.

"You are overconfident. Beltane is a seasoned swordsman, and his sword has let more Saxon blood than most. He will try to let some Norman as well."

"He will try," Royce said casually, "and he will fail. You should find better to carry out your plans."

"Ah, such arrogance. But pride is often broken when it is too confident."

Lynette was aware of Beltane's heated gaze upon her and did her best to ignore the way his eyes crawled over her. Royce was just as aware, and the stoked fire within him grew hotter.

Just then the king and Matilda arrived, and with them Robert, who came to Royce's side at once. His arrival sent Tearlach and Beltane away to converse in private. Royce would have liked nothing more than to overhear what they were saying, but he turned to Robert.

"You were missed last night," Royce said to him with a touch of amusement. "What kept you away from us?"

"I was unwilling to test your humor," Robert laughed. "And I wanted to hear what was being said among those at court and across the city."

"You knew of the king's plan and did not think it of enough interest to tell me?" Royce looked into Robert's eyes. His favored friend did not drop his gaze.

"I do not deny that I knew, but will you judge me before you know my reasons? Has your trust in me failed now?"

"Nay, Robert, there is nothing that would cause that. I but ask your reasons."

"And I would answer that my reasons must be mine alone for a while longer. In time you will know."

Lynette had been watching Robert closely and now she smiled as his regard turned to her. She could see his contained sense of relief, and she too wondered at the cause.

"Robert, will you remain close to me tomorrow? There are those whose company I would not share."

"Aye, lady, it would be my honor. But have no fear, for I well know the weight of Royce's sword, and I have faith that we will see Beltane on his knees."

"And you think that is enough?" Royce's voice was so cold and unfeeling that alarm coursed through both Lynette and Robert. "You think if he begs for mercy he should be allowed to live and continue his nefarious conspiracies?"

"Killing him will serve no purpose. Shaming him and teaching him that you are powerful enough to hold what is yours is enough."

"No, it is not enough." The few words were said with such a chill that both Lynette and Robert were shaken. This duel was not to prove his rights; it was to kill a man who had reached to touch what Royce considered too beautiful for his merest glance.

"Royce . . . " Lynette began, but the look Royce turned on her was enough to make the words freeze in her throat. He was containing a terrible anger, and she had a small taste of its fury when she looked into his eyes and saw no mercy there. She cast a helpless look at Robert, who began to search for words to calm Royce.

But they remained unspoken, as the press of the crowd began to grow. Royce knew he could not be alone with Lynette. He had come to feast his eyes on her again and to be near her for as long as he could. There was nothing more to be gained here. Motioning to his knights and to Robert, he made his way out of the hall.

Lynette watched him go and could have wept, had she not known there were eyes that watched for this weakness. She would not allow her enemies that pleasure. She meant to find her way to her own chamber, and remain there for the balance of the time until the sun rose tomorrow. Climbing the stairs, she slowly walked toward her chamber. She opened the door and found Beltane there.

She tried to back away, but he was too swift, and she found herself dragged inside and the door pushed shut. Instead of the fearful reaction Beltane had hoped for, Lynette was filled with fury.

"You fool! Do you dare dishonor the king's word like this? He will have your head." She spat the words at him.

"Nay, Lynette, I would only speak with you in private."

"I have left the hall to seek solitude. There is nothing we have to say to each other. Leave! I would hate to take the pleasure of killing you from Royce."

"You are sharp of tongue, but I have come to see whether you value Royce's life."

"More than you could possibly imagine," she said coldly.

"Then tell the king that you agree to my claim, and I will not kill Royce front of your eyes."

"I could not claim a lie before the king and before Royce, for he knows my heart and that I am his."

Beltane took hold of her shoulders and forced her against the stone wall with such speed and force that the breath was nearly knocked from her.

But Lynette knew one thing for certain: she must show no fear. She regarded him coldly and would not let him see the fear that was making her heart pound and her knees weak.

"Beltane," she said with all the regal bearing of a princess, "you would do well to leave me be. William will not tolerate such treatment of a maid in his court."

"I would treat you as a woman should be treated," he whispered as he pressed his lips against the soft flesh of her throat. "I would give you all, Lynette, a life at court Royce could never even dream of." His breath was hot against her skin, and she could feel the heat of his body as it pressed urgently against hers. "You should have been mine."

"I would never have been yours!" Lynette began to struggle in earnest. No one knew of Beltane's presence here, and if he were to claim she had invited him in, maybe he would be believed. "You are making a fatal mistake."

"No mistake." He laughed raggedly and continued to press her against the wall. His hands roamed over her and his large body was too solid for her to move.

"Beltane." The one word was spoken so clearly that it echoed in the room. Both Beltane and Lynette spun about to see the intruder, Beltane with a curse and Lynette with a gasp of relief. Robert stood in the open doorway, and his stony gaze caused Beltane to drop his hands from Lynette and back a step away. Lynette almost sagged to the floor. "Will you never learn what does not belong to you? William will be less than pleased to hear of this."

"What good will it do to run to him?" Beltane blustered. "He will do nothing. The wench beckoned me inside."

"Liar!" Lynette almost shrieked.

"Aye," Robert agreed. "It is the thing he does best. Do not worry, Lady Lynette, none will believe it. I don't intend to tell anyone about finding you here, and not because I think anyone will believe your lies. It is because I don't want anything to interfere with your meeting Royce tomorrow. The duel will settle all."

"Aye, settle all. There will be time for my pleasure with the wench when I have disposed of Royce." Beltane cupped Lynette's chin in his hand and swiftly kissed her. She slapped his hand away and glared at his smiling face. If she had had Royce's sword, she would have struck him down.

When Beltane had left, Lynette turned to Robert. "What brought you here, Robert? I have never seen anyone more welcome in my life."

"I knew when Royce left that Beltane would grasp the first opportunity to corner you. As soon as I missed you in the hall, I came to look for you."

"How I wish this day was over." She paused, for when this day was finished, tomorrow would dawn. Robert could see where her thoughts traveled and he rested his hand on her shoulder.

"Do not worry, Royce will not come to harm."

"Beltane intends to kill him."

"His intentions will count for little when they meet. Royce will be the victor, Lynette."

"He could be injured . . . perhaps . . . "

"Nay, will you take my promise that he will come to you without another scar to mar him?"

"I will try."

"Lynette, if it bothers you to remain under Beltane's eye here for the rest of the day, will you consider going riding with Alaine and me?"

"That would please me very much."

"Good, I will meet you in the stables as soon as you can change your clothing."

He watched her smile and was satisfied that he had taken her mind off Beltane and the situation for a while. He would never let her see that he was not quite as assured of Royce's success as he claimed to be.

The afternoon was pleasant, and both Robert and Alaine believed that Lynette had relaxed.

But Lynette played the same game as they. For she knew that no matter how skilled knights were, when they faced each other with broadswords, and the desire to kill in their hearts, one of them would most likely die. The thought sent a shudder through her. She smiled, and laughed, and chatted with Robert and Alaine, and all three hid their fears from each other behind a gaiety they could not feel. Tomorrow loomed like a specter.

Chapter Twenty-eight

The morning came, lightened by a bright sun and unseasonal warmth. Although warm cloaks had to be worn, there was no sharpness in the slight wind.

Lynette had found it impossible to sleep and had spent the night alternately praying and keeping her thoughts on the hopeful words Robert had said.

She could not help wondering what Royce was doing right now. Would he be awake and thinking of her? Would he try not to think of her to keep his mind free of distractions? She dressed slowly, as if she could resist this unbearable thing.

Royce was not surprised that he slept soundly. He had always grown calm before a battle, a thing that never ceased to amaze not only him, but those surrounding him.

When he came down to break his fast, he found himself surrounded by well-meaning friends full of advice. Finally he laughed and told them to leave him be, that he had to spend some quiet time with his daughter.

He took a confused Cerise aside and they walked together to a spot where he felt they would not be interrupted.

He was again surprised at her quick mind, for she seemed to know that he was going on some mission of great import. She said nothing, asked no questions, yet he felt she knew he wanted her close to him.

But the time had come to go, and he lifted her in his arms and held her. She put her arms about his neck and hugged him fiercely. Then he stood her on her feet, and she watched him mount his huge destrier and ride away.

The field where the duel was to take place was a rough square of land, surrounded now by three-sided tents which had been erected to protect the benches arranged for the spectators. Charcoal-burning braziers warmed the area within, and hot coals were available for the feet of those who felt the cold.

The sun glimmered on helmets and mail-clad arms, and reflected the brilliance of shields and the metal of the horses' harnesses. Color was abundant in bright surcoats and in the banners that adorned each tent. It glowed in the dresses of the ladies present, golds and reds, greens and blues. It was a magnificent display, and the excitement was as brilliant as the colors.

Lynette was to be seated on one side of William, with Matilda on the other. She wished she could have sat beside Matilda, for she desperately needed her support.

She didn't want to watch, but neither could she drag her eyes from the field. This was not the usual joust, where the combatants would face each other with lance and horse. This time there would be nothing but one knight and one sword against the other.

Steeling herself, Lynette tried to retain her control, but her hands felt as cold as ice. What if Royce fell here today? She could not bear the thought, but it refused to go away.

When someone took the seat beside her, she looked around to find a smiling and obviously satisfied Robert.

"Good morning, Lynette. It is a fine day."

Lynette was staggered by his open smile and air of pleasant good humor, as if nothing of great importance was about to happen.

"How can you be so calm?" she said, half in anger. "Royce could die out there."

"Nay, Lynette, he will not die."

"You cannot be that certain. Beltane is so—"

"Aye, he is devious and he is tricky . . . but he cannot fight as Royce does, and he does not fight for the reward Royce does." He laid a hand over hers. "Lynette, you have not seen Royce in battle. I have. Now he fights not just to fight, but for something so dear to his heart that he will not let it go. Have heart, lady. You are to see a side of Royce you have never seen before."

Lynette heard a soft chuckle from the other side of her and turned. William was not looking at her, but she knew it was he who had laughed so softly and she saw the pleased smile on his face. A sudden thought came to her that the king might have arranged this on purpose. Her quick mind grasped the idea, and pursued it until the truth came to her. William had found the only way he could give her to Royce with no objections from any quarter! At that moment William turned his head and met her gaze . . . and he winked.

Tearlach and a company of friends came to find a place close to the king's position, as if to imply that they had William's blessing.

The fight was about to begin, and Lynette had yet to catch sight of Royce. At the end of the two lines of tents were the tents of the combatants. She knew Royce was there and she longed to go to him, to hold him and . . . she inhaled deeply and lifted her chin. He would not expect her to lose faith in him, and she did not intend to.

"Excellent," Robert whispered from close by.

She had been told that they would not fight on horseback this day, but she could see Royce's destrier standing outside his tent. Then the tent flap was pushed aside and Royce strode into the sunlight. Her heart caught in her throat, and she would have stood had not Robert touched her arm lightly. There was a roar of pleasure from the viewers.

On the other side of the field, Beltane was stepping from his tent and looking across the field toward Royce. Both men mounted their destriers and rode to the center of the field and turned the huge horses to face the king.

Both men dismounted and bowed slightly toward the king, but Royce's gaze was locked on Lynette. It was then she realized he was not as heavily armored as Beltane. But the broadsword he bore glittered in the sunlight, and it was easy to see it had been honed and well prepared for this moment. The shield Royce carried bore a lion's head, with teeth bared and claws poised to tear; beneath it was a sword. The shield spoke of his bastardy and his ability at the same moment.

The heavy leather he wore would be no barrier to a sword, and Beltane and everyone present knew it. The sight of Royce's leather caused a rustle of laughter, for it was as if Royce had claimed that Beltane's sword would never touch him.

Beltane fought the rage that filled him, for Tearlach had cautioned him that Royce would try to provoke him.

"I would hold no advantage," Beltane claimed loudly. "Give me time to remove my armor, for I would give the bastard every chance."

Royce was a little surprised, but he merely acquiesced. Robert was very surprised, for he knew Beltane to be just the man to take every advantage he could. He turned to look at Tearlach and saw his smile. Beltane had been well cautioned.

Beltane's armor was removed, and again he met Royce in the center of the field. They faced each other, only a sword's distance apart.

Shields held high, swords at the ready, they awaited only the signal to begin. Lynette could have groaned in her fear, the fear that she would see Royce's blood shed this day . . . and for her.

The signal was given and for one breathless moment the tips of the two swords touched. Then each man backed away from the other and began to circle cautiously.

Beltane attacked first and the crash of his sword against Royce's raised shield echoed across the field. It was followed by another and another, and Royce fell back before the onslaught.

Then suddenly, Royce struck again and again. His sword was met by Beltane's shield. They were getting the feel of each other. These initial parries were mild . . . to everyone's eyes but Lynette's.

If Lynette were not so frightened, she would have seen what Robert saw, that Royce was beginning to enjoy the duel. Beltane brought his shield wide to counter a blow and raised his sword to strike what he thought would be a fierce blow. But Royce was like a shadow; he was not in the position Beltane expected him to be. He jabbed Beltane with the point of his sword hard enough to draw blood, but not hard enough to do any harm other than annoy Beltane and put him off stride.

Lynette was filled with a swelling pride. Despite Royce's size, he was quick and graceful, and it was thrilling to watch him. She was breathless at his daring and his control. There followed a furious exchange, in which Royce received a touch that bled so much that he looked more injured than he really was. Lynette saw nothing but the blood, and felt as if her heart would stop, but a glance at Robert calmed her, for he looked as though nothing unusual had transpired.

But now the battle seemed to change, to take on a note of cold deliberation. Few were aware that the reason was Beltane's growing anger at Royce's jeering taunts. Moments passed while steel clanged upon steel with tremendous force.

The shields became dented and bent, and then

one mighty blow from Royce's sword finished Beltane's shield. With a curse he tossed it aside and took hold of his sword two-handed. Royce's laugh rang across the field, and he tossed his shield aside and took his sword in both hands.

Both men were bathed in sweat and panting. For them time seemed to stand still, but for Lynette it seemed the fight had gone on for hours. Blow after blow was struck, and time after time a raised sword parried the blow.

"You will never see Creganwald," Royce grated. "I shall hold a celebration in your honor, while you nurse your disappointment."

"Damn you, you bastard!" Beltane panted. "I will slice you to pieces here."

"That would make me late for my wedding, and I do not think that wise with one so beautiful as Lynette."

Royce watched Beltane struggle to maintain his control, but he knew that anger had always been his opponent's weakest point. He pressed Beltane back with several hard blows. It only made Beltane's temper shorter.

"All this effort for naught, Beltane," Royce chided derisively. "For Lynette will not have you . . . and I will not let you live to take her."

"You speak as if it were decided."

"But it has been . . . at your birth, when you were refused the gift of honor. From thence it was only a matter of time until that fact was discovered by all."

Beltane no longer fought the red haze that was swirling before his eyes. His hatred of Royce was overcoming his caution.

The two pounded furiously upon each other, and

slowly . . . slowly, Beltane began to bend beneath the brutal rain of powerful blows. After a while he began to realize he was on the defensive, and tried to press an attack. But his weary arm and his lack of ability made it difficult.

Now Beltane could only stand, feet planted, and take the brunt of the powerful two-handed blows Royce was delivering with unbelievable strength. Royce had done exactly as Robert had known he would do. He had closed everything from his mind but Beltane. He fought as he had fought all his battles, with single-minded devotion and complete disregard for himself.

Lynette could not believe that this furious whirlwind of a warrior was the gentle, loving man who had held her and made love to her with the softest of touches. Each blow he delivered would have sliced Beltane in two if his upraised sword had not deflected it. But that sword was wavering . . . weakening . . . lowering.

Beltane knew by now that he was losing, and a white-hot anger wiped away the last of his caution. He struck and struck again, but each effort was less hard. Royce watched for the opening he needed, the moment when Beltane's defenses were lowest. When it came, he struck Beltane's sword a blow that sent it from his numbed fingers. It glimmered in the sunlight as it turned over and over in the air and landed, point deep, in the earth. It vibrated for a moment, then became still, and Beltane faced Royce.

It would have been so easy to kill him where he stood, and Royce found it hard to resist doing just that. But he did not want his wedding marred with blood. Beltane knew he looked death in the face and felt his legs go weak, yet he did not flinch. Royce had to credit him for that.

"If you want me to beg, bastard, then you will wait a long time. Kill me now, or you may regret it."

"I do not murder an unarmed man. Let it go, Beltane. Announce the fact that you relinquish all right to Creganwald, and you and I will be finished here."

Beltane inhaled a deep breath. He would have liked to do anything but what Royce asked, but he had little choice. He was not going to lay his pride in the dust for Tearlach.

With a voice that carried across the field, Beltane announced his defeat. Royce made it as difficult as possible.

"I relinquish . . . " Beltane began, but Royce tapped him smartly with his sword.

"Louder. I would not want any ear to miss your words and their meaning."

Beltane glared at him, but raised his voice so it carried across the field.

"I relinquish any claim I have on the manor and the Lady Lynette of Creganwald."

"Excellent, Beltane." Royce smiled a feral smile. "And I hope you don't forget this, for if we cross swords again, I shall surely kill you."

William and Robert exchanged a glance that did not go unnoticed by Tearlach, who felt his defeat even more potently than Beltane . . . except he had not relinquished anything . . . nor had he admitted any kind of defeat. Lynette wanted to smile, but all she could see was the blood that stained Royce's leather coat.

Beltane walked from the field, and Royce came to stand before the king. Lynette could see the coldness in his eyes as clearly as William could.

"Is the bargain well met, my lord? Or are there others who wish to dispute my claim?"

William knew the justice in Royce's anger and he had no battle with it. "Nay, Royce, the bargain is well met. Tonight we will celebrate. Will tomorrow do for the wedding, or do you need time to recover?"

There was a hint of amusement in William's eyes, but Royce was in no mood to see it. He stabbed his sword into the ground and went to Lynette. With a slight bend of the knees, he grasped her about the hips and lifted her so that her hands rested on his shoulders and she laughed down into his eyes. She bent to kiss him and her hair fell about them. To the cheers and applause of the crowd he spun her about, and she threw back her head and laughed. Then she bent to Royce again and whispered in his ear.

"You are mine now, Royce, all mine."

"Aye, lady," he whispered back, "and you are mine."

Chapter Twenty-nine

Royce wasn't pleased that Lynette would spend the night before their wedding with the king's household, but he did not want to approach William with any request. He still smarted at what to him seemed like betrayal.

William knew it and so did Robert. Lynette was almost certain of it as well, and just as certain that she knew the reasons for William's actions.

When Lynette came down to dinner, she was seated close to William and Matilda. Royce was placed too far away to talk to her in private, but he intended to get her alone as soon as he could.

He watched her and realized just how much he had missed her these past days. Her head was bent close to William and she laughed at something he said. Impatience tore at Royce, for he remembered well the sound of that laughter, softened in the quiet of the night. The scent of her lingered with him as if she rested in his arms. Beneath the light of the torches her skin seemed even softer and her hair more golden.

But it seemed that there was to be no opportunity to see Lynette alone, for when the meal was finished, Matilda motioned to Lynette, and Lynette rose and followed her up the steps and away from Royce's view.

Several of Royce's knights came to sit near him and subject him to some ribald teasing about the marital state. Royce laughed good-naturedly with them and shared a few horns of ale. There was no doubt in his mind that the night was going to be a long and lonely one.

Robert could easily see that Royce was keeping his distance from William, so he went and sat down next to him. They were talking comfortably when Royce's attention was drawn aside and he turned to see Tearlach and Beltane enter the room.

Tearlach's gaze found Royce, and although his face remained impassive, there was a coldness in his eyes that Royce understood quite well . . . the matter between them had not been settled. There was a silent promise that one day it would be.

"He would be wise to bury this now," Robert said.

"He will only bury it with my body," Royce replied. "And that will never happen if he continues to use men like Beltane to carry out his plans."

"Tomorrow you wed Lynette. My advice to you is to quit the court and find your way to Creganwald. There you will be in command, and can watch for any treachery."

"Aye, it is my thought as well. As soon as the wedding is over, Lynette and I will be on our way."

"Royce, you have to go to William."

"Why? I have won the game he set me to. I have taken back what was given me in the first place. Am I to thank him for the chance to die for what he promised and then denied?"

"Do not be a fool, Royce. You know William better than that."

"I thought I did, but it seems he can break a promise whenever the mood is upon him."

"He did not choose to break a promise. He did what had to be done to make sure Creganwald remained in your hands. Otherwise he would have been forced to honor a pledge given before you joined him."

"What pledge?"

"I do not know and I have not asked. I can reveal this to you now. The night before the battle was set, I joined William to talk of what had to be done."

"You mean . . . this conflict with Beltane was planned by you and William?"

"Actually by him, but I agreed to the contest, for I knew as well as he did that you would hold Creganwald. I knew the outcome of the contest would be exactly as it was. But it released the king from a vow, and for that he is grateful."

"Any more gratitude from him might find me dead and buried," Royce replied, but Robert could see the beginnings of a smile in his eyes.

"You have held what is yours, and no one can claim Creganwald."

Royce glanced at Tearlach and found his gaze still on him. "I don't think Tearlach is a man to surrender so easily."

318

"Aye, you have a lifelong enemy, but there is little he can do. You need only watch your back. Neither he nor Beltane are ones to forget easily."

"I will arm both myself and Creganwald."

"And will you go to William now?"

"Robert, how much of my life have you planned?" He laughed at Robert's injured look. "I must watch carefully or you will be planning more."

"I would plan on children soon, so I may play grandfather." Robert chuckled in satisfaction. He did not see the shadows in Royce's eyes.

"Nay, there is no need for children."

Robert was silenced for a moment, then he regarded Royce carefully. "You would have no heir for Creganwald?"

"Cerise will inherit and she will wed."

"And Lynette? Will she not want children of her own . . . of yours? I believe she loves you more than even you can imagine. I saw her face at the battle. She will want her love for you to bring the son you desire."

"And you think I would take such a chance? Do you think I would allow Lynette to take that chance with her life? There are many ways to prevent such a thing, and I would have a careful midwife to instruct Lynette on them. I will not chance losing her, Robert . . . and I will hear no more about it." He added before Robert could protest, "You are right. It is time to go to William . . . and then prepare for our return to Creganwald." He rose and walked toward William. Robert's gaze followed, filled with shock and pity. Royce could not wash Sybella's death from his mind, even now.

William watched Royce approach and felt a lifting of his spirits. He had thought that the truth, when Robert confessed it, might anger Royce.

"Well, Royce," William said when he had found a chair near him. "It seems Matilda has stolen your lady for the balance of the evening."

"It seems so. And I must find my way home."

"We are getting older, my friend. There was a time when we warred all day and drank all night."

"I find my mind set now on quieter pastimes. I would go to Creganwald when the ceremony is over tomorrow. There is much to be done there."

"I will come before the summer is gone and see what you have planned for it. Royce, I am much pleased that Creganwald lies in the right hands. Take care . . . protect it well. It is valuable to me as well as you. Those who fought you have no regard for the possessions of another, and may still go to some lengths to gain what they have lost."

"Creganwald will be easy to defend, when I have done all I plan to it. It will also be productive."

They continued to discuss the strengths and weaknesses of Creganwald for some time. Neither spoke of the duel or its cause. It was enough for both that all was silently understood. Royce took his leave as soon as he could.

Tearlach watched him go, and vented his fury on Beltane.

"I could do no more," Beltane grumbled miserably. "The man is a demon with that sword."

"And he is clever enough to prey on your inability to hold your temper and use your head. It appears, if I am going to rid myself of the bastard, that I must do the deed myself."

"What do you plan?"

"To wait. I have waited all these years, a few added months will make it just that much more pleasurable."

"But—"

"Ask no more. In due time we will see just how well Royce can hold Creganwald for the king. In the meantime, it would serve you well if you were to mend your relationship with Royce."

"Mend! It is unmendable! I would still like to meet him again. This time I would have more caution."

"Nay, you will mend it, and your best means to that end is the Lady Oriel. She makes her home with her brother, does she not?"

"Aye, Giles. But Royce will not welcome me within the walls of Creganwald. Besides, the Lady Oriel is not to my taste. My mind is set on sweeter fare."

Tearlach turned a furious gaze on Beltane. "Then make her to your taste! Teach her to bend to your will. That handsome face of yours has bent the will of more than one unsuspecting lady. This one will bring you Lynette and revenge."

"I do not understand."

"Then come to my chamber tonight when the others are abed. We have much to talk about." Tearlach rose and left a puzzled Beltane looking after him. He could not see what could be done about the matter now. In the morning Lynette would be Royce's wife. What could be done afterwards to change that?

* * *

Oriel had been alternately proud of Royce's power with the sword and furious that Beltane did not succeed in defeating Royce and taking Creganwald and Lynette from him. She had dreamed of comforting Royce in his loss and thereby showing him the depth of her passion for him. He would understand, once and for all, that she was the right one to stand by his side.

In the quiet of her chamber she curled up in her large and lonely bed and longed for Royce. What she would give to feel Royce's hard, strong body beside her and to feel him caress her in her need. She could feel the fiery hunger flood her and groaned her frustration.

How she hated Lynette, yes, and even his daughter. She hated all who took him from her. If there was only a way . . . only a way.

Lynette, too, was sleepless. But it was excitement that kept her awake. Tomorrow the time would finally come. She and Royce would wed and leave this place of intrigue and hatred. They would return to Creganwald and find their promised happiness there.

The bed was both a delight and a torture, for she could feel Royce's presence and remember the nights they had shared.

She thought of the joys of being his wife. Her dreams continued, welcome and fulfilling.

They would have children, she and Royce. Sons, tall and strong. And daughters, as lovely and intelligent as Cerise, who would draw the strongest knights in the kingdom to make Creganwald even more secure.

She thought of her happy years at Creganwald, and the thought of children to roam its fields and hills warmed her. She laid her hand on the flat plane of her belly, and realized she could be carrying Royce's child at this minute.

This reminded her of Sybella and Royce's experience with her, and she wondered if Royce was still haunted by her tragic death. She did not know if her mother had had difficulty with her birth, for she had not wanted to see the grief in her father's eyes when she was spoken of. Now there was no one to ask.

She pushed the thought aside. All women were frightened of giving birth, but she was healthy and strong and she would not see problems where there might not be any. For now there was just tomorrow . . . and the beginning of a new future.

This was enough to bring satisfaction and finally peaceful sleep.

Chapter Thirty

Today is my wedding day, Lynette thought with a surge of pleasure. She snuggled deeper in the furs upon her bed, and considered all that had happened in just a matter of days.

What had appeared as a disaster a few short days ago, was going to turn into the most wonderful day of her life. Before she could consider her good fortune any further, the door opened and a young girl peered around it.

"Everyone is beginning to gather, and the priest has come, lady. Her Majesty asks if you will bathe and dress, and join her to break your fast."

"Aye." Lynette smiled and tossed aside the furs. "Bring me water."

The girl disappeared, and before long buckets of water were heated and being poured in the wooden tub that had been set near the newly revived fire.

Lynette bathed and smoothed sweet-scented oil upon her body, then dressed in the soft green velvet gunna she had brought for this occasion. She brushed her hair until it shone, then pulled it back from her face in a cluster of curls into which she twined the matching green velvet ribbons Royce had bought for her. She had never been more prepared . . . or less prepared . . . in her life.

She looked at herself in the mirror and knew she was a little afraid of Royce's tormented past. Silently she prayed, not to wash the memories from his mind, but to give her the power to make new and better ones that would bring Royce happiness.

Lynette joined Matilda for breakfast and was surprised that Matilda kept the conversation light and filled with amusing stories and laughter. Then she realized Matilda was trying to get her to relax. She was grateful, for the laughter did ease her nerves.

She was also surprised that Matilda had taken Cerise under her wing and found a good place for her to view the ceremony.

When Lynette came down the stairs with Matilda, she was met by admiring stares and murmurs. Her eyes flew across the room to rest on Royce, and she felt her breathing quicken. He wore a deeper green than she, and the color complemented the midnight of his hair and the gold of his eyes. Lynette was aware of no other in the room, even the king.

Near Royce stood the priest, and when Royce smiled, she started toward him . . . alone. She had missed her father terribly, but not as much as she did at this moment. Tears stung her eyes, and she was unaware of the knight who came to stand beside her until she turned and looked into Robert's understanding gaze.

He held his arm for her, and she had her hand upon it. Slowly he led her to Royce's side. The priest smiled at her, and Royce knelt in the clean rushes and gently drew her down beside him.

The words were spoken, and they sang through Lynette's mind. Her awareness of Royce close to her was exquisite. These words they spoke now would unite them forever.

The ceremony seemed to pass quickly and then they were being congratulated, teased, and in general made a great deal of, until her head swam. Cerise was thrilled with the brilliance of court, and the excitement and joy of the occasion. She realized she was being pampered, petted, and made much over. What she did not realize was that she was being so thoroughly entertained that she did not need to cling to Royce and Lynette.

Lynette was aware of Royce's molten gold gaze as he looked down into her eyes, and aware of very little else.

She was surprised that the wedding was so early, and even more surprised when Royce told her they would be leaving for Creganwald after the midday meal.

"But . . . I thought . . . " She blushed and heard his soft chuckle.

"That I would spend the night under this roof? Nay, my own men are problem enough, and God only knows what devilment they might consider. But we might be in for more than just devilment here, and I would have this night perfect."

She smiled up at him with a promising smile that could have, in his mind, melted the strongest armor he owned. She was his now, and nothing short of his death would take her from him.

The day dissolved in merriment, and Royce and Lynette were toasted, while their baggage was packed and loaded in carts. By mid-afternoon they were on their way.

Robert and the balance of Royce's men rode ahead. Robert had been told that Royce and Lynette would continue on to Creganwald at their own pace, until they found a place to make camp for the night. None of this pleased Robert much, for he felt Royce was leaving himself too unguarded.

"At least tell me where you will be, and when to expect you at Creganwald. Thus if you do not appear in time, I can set a search."

"Know you the inn at Wellby?"

"Aye, but it is not the fairest of places."

"It is now. The keeper has been given a round sum of money to see to the cleaning of the place, and that no other travelers find shelter there. We will have the place to ourselves."

"You have been busy."

"Aye." Royce's brows drew together in a frown. "I do not feel safe here, and I would not distress Lynette with the possibility that trouble could come on such a night."

"Think you that Tearlach would choose this place, with the king here, to cause harm?"

"What better place, if he can accomplish it without suspicion falling on him?"

"Aye . . . and if he sends men to follow, we are to make it appear that you still travel with us."

"That is my plan."

* * *

Royce and Lynette traveled slowly, enjoying the ride and being together with no demands upon their time. It was a while before Lynette noticed that Royce was deep in thought.

"Royce, something weighs heavily upon your mind?"

"Aye, I have something of great importance to discuss with you. As soon as we arrive at the inn, we must talk."

"Something is wrong?"

"Nay, nothing is wrong. It is only something we must settle between the two of us."

Lynette breathed a sigh of relief. Nothing they could settle between the two of them was cause for worry. She was willing to agree to just about anything Royce wanted. She continued the journey in silence, while Royce searched for the right words to make her understand what must be.

The inn was clean and the proprietor beside himself with the pleasure of welcoming this knight and his lady, a knight who had paid and paid well for the exclusive use of his inn. The innkeeper and his wife swore they would be at Royce's disposal at any time.

"Has the food been prepared?" Royce asked first.

"Aye, lord. It is ready and prepared as you have asked. I have made the room ready and we will serve you whenever you wish."

"Come, Lynette, let us wash the dust of the road from us and enjoy a good supper."

They were led to a room that was both large and clean. Water was brought, and they both were relieved to wash the evidence of travel from them.

They had gone farther than Lynette had imagined they would, and she was a bit tired. When a knock came upon the door, and Royce swung it wide, a table was carried in, and soon it was laden with food. Lynette suppressed her laughter until the innkeeper left.

"Royce, the two of us could eat for a week on this much food."

"I only asked for generous portions"—Royce shook his head in surprise—"not for all the food left in the inn."

"Let us eat. Then perhaps you can tell me what has been plaguing you all day."

They sat across from each other and ate their meal, while the dying sun bathed the room in a haze of pale gold light. The fire had been lit and was burning low, so Royce rose and renewed it to keep the room warm. He returned to the table, but she could see that he had lost his interest in the food.

"Royce . . . is it Creganwald that causes you to be so thoughtful? Do you feel there will be problems there? I assure you, that is not so. My people will take you as their own. Their loyalty will be yours."

"It is not Creganwald that worries me."

"Then what makes you so quiet and thoughtful?" She rose and came around the table and sat on his lap to loop her arms about his neck. "It is not doubt of me, is it? If that thought is in your head, bid it be gone. I love you, Royce, more than I thought it possible to love anyone."

Finding her warmth in his lap and her soft arms around his neck did not make what he meant to say any easier for Royce. He could feel his body's reaction, and knew that her touch was enough to set him afire. How was he to concentrate when her close proximity was already playing havoc with his senses?

"Lynette . . . listen carefully to what I say." He took her arms from about his neck and held both her hands in his. "You know that I love you, I would give my life for you if it were needed . . . but . . . I cannot take yours. In that way I am as much a coward as the worst of cowards."

"I do not understand. It is no longer a thing to consider."

"But it is. There is something I have decided, and on this one thing I will have my way. You must consult a midwife. You will heed my words and their advice. . . . There will be no children."

Lynette was so shocked that for a minute she could only look at him in stunned silence. "No children? But, Royce . . . "

"Nay, Lynette, don't argue. It is a thing that we must agree on. Don't you see, love?"

"Aye," Lynette said softly, "I can see." And she did see. He would make their marriage an empty shell before they would even have time to make it perfect. "I see that you think only of yourself. That you are afraid. That you would cheat me of children. What kind of wife will I be, Royce? What kind of woman? Half of one, unable to bring you and Creganwald an heir. . . . I am to be denied something I desire with all my heart because you will not let it be?"

Royce released Lynette and rose from the chair, then walked to the window. She followed him, looking at the rigid breadth of his back and considering what she could say to turn his mind from this idea.

"Royce . . . please look at me, talk to me. Let us decide this matter together."

He turned to face her. "On nothing else will I say you nay. Nothing but this. I cannot allow something that might take you from my life. I cannot . . . I will not."

"Did you wed me just to have Creganwald?"

"Nay!"

"Why, then? It was not out of love. If you loved me, you would not ask such a thing."

"Lynette . . . understand."

"Nay, there is no understanding. I will not be cheated and I will not be sacrificed to your fear. Allow me to be a wife . . . or let me go."

Chapter Thirty-one

Royce could not believe his ears. He reached out and took Lynette by the shoulders in a grip of iron. She had to be convinced both that what he thought was for her good, and that his love for her was complete. At that moment it flowed through him as rich and powerful as old wine.

"Don't you know that I do this for you? It is only a matter of drinking a potion that will insure your flux every month. It is nothing to interfere with us."

"Nothing to interfere with us? You would have me barren, the subject of pity, never to know a child's love? Has Cerise's love not come to mean more to you than that?"

"Aye, it has come to mean a great deal, but she has already lost one mother! I would cheat her again . . . and I will lose you?"

"But you cannot be sure of that. I am a different woman. I will not be punished because you choose to punish yourself! If you love me, and if I mean more to you than Creganwald, then you will not ask that of me."

She had to convince him, and the only way to reach him was through his love for her and his honor. She knew he did not want only Creganwald. She could feel the force of his love for her, but it would never bloom, nor would it last if she could not convince him she would not die as Sybella had died.

"You know that you mean all to me, Lynette," he said quietly.

"I only know what your words say. What does your heart say, Royce? Tell me true, do you not want sons of your loins? Have you not looked into Cerise's eyes and seen a love that makes it all worthwhile? I would not be happy if you held this fear always. Can you not put it away now?" Her voice grew gentle. Instead of trying to back away from him and break his hold, she moved into his arms. "Can my love and my certainty that all will be well be enough for you?" He drew her so tightly to him that she could hardly get her breath. "If you were called by William and had to go to battle, do you not think my fear would be the same torment? Would you say nay to William and hold yourself within Creganwald's walls, all because I fear your death?"

"That is a different thing. A man must go to battle."

"Aye, and a woman must fight her battles as well. . . . It is the way the good Lord created us. Each of us must have courage to let the other face what must be faced. It can only draw us closer together . . . bind our love more firmly. You have never shared your fears, so you think you are the only one to hold them. When you fought Beltane, I thought I might die. But I watched, and I was as frightened as it was possible to be. My love gave me faith . . . let your love do the same for me."

"This is how you felt when I fought Beltane?" He inhaled a ragged sigh. "How can it be borne? I am wondering if you do not have more courage than I."

"Nay, I have no more courage than any other. I have as much love as you, and that is what will see us through whatever we have to face." Lynette laid her head against his chest and clung to him, for the next words were going to be hard to say. "I cannot bear a marriage that is cold and ungiving. I know that the king's will is for you to hold Creganwald. But I cannot bear this half marriage and the thought that our love will have no fruit, no children to warm our late years. I must have all of you, Royce . . . or I want none at all."

Royce held her a little from him and looked intently into her eyes. He could see clearly that she meant exactly what she said.

"I love you, Lynette. You know that is the truth."

"Aye, I know. And I love you. I would give you the freedom to be and do whatever makes you complete and strong. I ask the same of you." Her voice was quiet, but the words were firm.

"I am afraid," he whispered. Then he drew her back into his arms, and his mouth found hers in a deep and seeking kiss.

The kiss grew until it seemed to melt her very bones, leaving her weak and at the mercy of the curling heat that Royce could always create with a touch.

Catching her face between his hands, he held her

while he took her kiss deeper and deeper, parting her lips and slipping his tongue between them to find that sweet remembered taste. The sensual penetration brought a moan of combined pleasure and surrender from her, and she began to seek him as fiercely as he was seeking her.

She had only time to utter a gasp as he released her mouth and swung her up into his arms in one smooth movement.

When he carried her to the bed, she was already trying to loosen his shirt, and when he set her down near the bed he began to help. Soon they tumbled to the bed, heated body pressed to heated body.

She wanted him passionately, but he held the passion in check. He went slowly . . . so slowly that she could hardly bear it. He caressed her fevered flesh and sought with gentle hands the moist heat between her thighs. At the stroking of his fingers, she thought she would go mad. She ached to feel him within her, filling that pulsing place and carrying her to delicious completion.

But Royce intended to hold this sweet fire for as long as he could. He slowed his caresses and again assaulted her mouth with tender, soft kisses, letting them drift to her throat and the softer flesh of her breasts.

He loved the way she called his name and met him touch for touch. The thrill of it nearly sent him over the edge, and finally he could cling to reality no longer. He groaned his pleasure as he sheathed himself deep within her, and felt her response as she tightened about him and lifted to meet him.

Now there was nothing but the magic that exploded between them. They fanned the flame of their passion and rose with it to a shuddering fulfillment. It left them without words or the ability to speak. They held each other until the pace of their heartbeats slowed. Then Royce bent his head and kissed her tear-stained eyes, then her cheeks, and finally her soft mouth.

"Ah, Lynette," he whispered, "Lynette, how I love you."

She held him cradled in the soft curves of her body and knew a contentment that warmed her heart, and gave her a vision of tomorrow and all the tomorrows to come.

When Lynette finally slept, Royce lay awake, holding her and fighting his fears. He understood all she'd said, but past visions interfered. His arm tightened about her at the thought that fate could take her from him. She sighed softly in her sleep and nestled closer to him.

He knew that no matter what she said and how right she might be, he could not stand the thought of her bearing a child. He would rather face all his worst enemies unarmed than to have her taken from him.

Still, he knew another thing. She would not stay with him if he forced her to obey his rules . . . and he could not let her go. Feeling her lying close to him filled all the emptiness he had ever known.

He remained awake, and in the small hours of the morning she wakened again, and the night blossomed with their soft, slow, wonderful loving.

When they arrived at Creganwald, both Royce and Lynette were warmly welcomed. Robert fairly beamed upon them, for he could see that something new flourished between them. The entire household seemed to come to life. Lynette and Royce renewed their bonds with Cerise, who seemed to blossom before their eyes. Royce knew quite well that Cerise loved Lynette as a child loved her mother, and that Lynette felt a mother's love for the little girl.

But Lynette could still read the shadow of fear in Royce's eyes. As one month followed another, she learned his heart. Each time her monthly flow came, he seemed to breathe a sigh of relief, and for several days after was reluctant to touch her.

But he would come to her for the simple reason that he felt empty without her, and could not resist the touch of her and the joy of holding her.

Spring came on the land suddenly. Trees blossomed and green shoots came up from the earth. It brought with it a soft breeze from the ocean, and a renewal of Royce's building plans.

Summer found the new walls of Creganwald castle growing. Under Royce's hand the land seemed to yield and prosper. A sense of rightness filled everyone, and slowly . . . slowly, guards were lowered.

Royce and Lynette would ride out to see to the serfs who farmed the land, and to settle disagreements and any other problems. It became common to see them together. All who lived on Creganwald land knew that the lord and lady were of one mind and one goal: the good of Creganwald and all its people.

The castle rose majestically, set on a solid mound which had previously borne a wooden building. The advantages of such construction were mainly military; there were no corners for attackers to pick away at or undermine, and no "blind spots" which defenders could not cover.

It had three spacious floors, a chapel and a number of smaller rooms in the turrets. The castle was set up to guard against the king's enemies from across the water, as well as those within the country.

Royce could be seen daily, working with the laborers, going over his carefully drawn plans, and listening to anyone who had a suggestion that might make the castle more defensible or stronger.

Lynette had been teaching Cerise to ride the pony Royce had gotten for her. She was well aware that Royce, though it did not seem so, kept close watch on her every move, and provided guards when she and Cerise rode out.

Lynette heard Royce's laughter, felt him relax with her, slowly felt him put the past away. Soon, she thought, soon.

Giles was puzzled that Oriel did not return to Creganwald. Since their parents' deaths, he had been her supporter. He hoped that she had put aside her dreams of Royce and would return soon. He missed her, and prayed she would find a knight to her liking and marry. There was more than enough room at Creganwald now that the castle was nearing completion.

He and Robert rode out early one morning to hunt. Work on the castle's exterior was nearing completion, and Lynette was occupied both with the orders for the making of furniture and seeing to Cerise. Royce was overseeing the building, so Giles and Robert were alone.

"I cannot wait for the castle to be finished," Giles said.

"I suspect there will be a large celebration when it is done," Robert agreed. He, too, had relaxed and had begun to enjoy every day.

"Do you think William will come?"

"Nay, he has more to do than to see to one lord and his lands. Besides, he knows Royce will have built something worthwhile, and will have trust in its defenses."

"I could defend this place against an army if need be."

"That is its purpose."

"You think someone will try to take it?"

"Nay, if I had feared anything, it would have been an enemy within. But Beltane has no chance of using treachery here, and Tearlach . . . he will be given no opportunity."

"Treachery from within," Giles mused. "There are none who have not come to love Lynette as they do Royce. I would see heirs for Creganwald and know it safe for the foreseeable future."

"Aye," Robert said thoughtfully. He knew that Royce and Lynette were happy with each other, but he had begun to worry that there would be no heirs forthcoming. It was not unknown for a woman to be barren, and in such circumstances a knight could take another wife . . . Still, he knew this turn of events might just make Royce happy.

"Robert!" Robert looked at Giles in surprise, drawn from his thoughts suddenly. "Creganwald is to have its first guests."

Robert followed Giles's gaze, and saw the line of travelers in the distance.

"What banner do they fly?"

"I cannot tell from here. Do you think it a good idea to ride swiftly to Creganwald and tell Royce to be prepared?"

"Aye, you ride back. I will ride to meet them."

Robert was not easily shaken, but he had a strange feeling that these visitors did not bode well for Royce. He rode toward them.

After traveling some distance he reined in his horse in surprise. Beltane! He would recognize the banners anywhere. What would Beltane want here? There was only one thing he might achieve . . . his death.

Yet he rode with confidence and in the open, as if he feared nothing and no one. There was a mystery here, and Robert intended to get to the bottom of it before it led to something tragic.

Chapter Thirty-two

When Robert drew his horse up beside the column of travelers, he was surprised to find not only Beltane but Oriel as well.

"Lady Oriel," Robert said. "I am surprised to see you here . . . and in this company. What do you here, Beltane?"

"I but bring the lady to her brother," Beltane answered much too quietly and with too much pleasure to suit Robert.

"Robert," Oriel said with a smile, "I would seek my brother to tell him good news."

"Good news? Such as?"

"That is between my brother and me," she replied coolly.

"That is between Royce and you, if you desire entrance to Creganwald. As far as you are concerned, Beltane . . . I do not think you will find welcome here. Mayhap you should consider turning the Lady Oriel's safety over to me, and leave now."

"I think not, Robert. It is best to lay this before Royce."

Robert did not like the confidence with which Beltane spoke. Nothing would bring about Beltane's welcome at Creganwald. He meant to speak again when the sound of approaching horses stopped him. Royce would put an end to it.

When Royce brought his horse to a halt beside Robert, his face was an unreadable mask. He glanced once at Oriel, then his gaze fixed on Beltane.

"Have you come to finish what was begun?" His voice was cold.

"Nay, Royce," Oriel said before Beltane could reply. "I have asked Beltane to escort me here, since there was no one else free to do so. I come to tell my brother news that will, I think, give him reason to be pleased. Am I no longer welcome here?"

"We have crossed swords, Royce," Beltane said, "and there is no cause for us to do so again. I have come in peace."

His voice was oily smooth, and Royce did not trust him for a minute. But he could not call what he said a lie either. He was a knight of William's and had come to make Oriel's travel to her brother safe.

"What is the purpose of your journey?"

"Let Oriel speak with her brother first. If you still choose for us to leave, then I will argue the point no further. We come with William's blessing and to put an end to our . . . difficulties."

Royce could do little other than agree, but he had a feeling Lynette was not going to be pleased. He glanced at Robert, who wore the same puzzled expression.

"It has been a long journey, Royce," Oriel said softly.

"Come, then, and find rest and food," Royce replied. He drew his horse aside, and he and Robert fell in together to start the ride back.

"I would not trust either one of them," Robert grumbled.

"I do not," Royce said beneath his breath. "But mayhap it is better to have an enemy where you can watch him. If he has business here, I would know what it is. I'm sure Giles will be pleased to see Oriel, but even he was full of questions. I bade him stay at Creganwald and see to its safety, just in case this is a trap of sorts and others wait to attack from elsewhere."

"They will find our new walls hard to penetrate."

"Just so," Royce said thoughtfully. "Mayhap they seek a way in . . . or a weakness."

"Aye."

"Ride ahead, Robert. Send two groups out to check the countryside. I won't be taken by surprise, no matter how strong my walls." Robert started away, and Royce called to him again. He rode back to Royce's side. "Tell Lynette of our visitors. Let her be prepared as well."

During the ride back to the castle, Royce tried to consider what motive Beltane could have, but there was no answer.

Lynette was both as surprised and as wary as Robert and Royce had been, but there was little to be done. She welcomed their first guests and sent orders to the kitchen for food to be prepared.

Giles welcomed Oriel with pleasure, but he was

annoyed to see Beltane there. He wanted to question his sister alone, but it was close to the evening meal and there was no opportunity for private conversation. It had not occurred to him yet that Oriel had deliberately kept her distance from him.

The dinner seemed much too pleasant to both Robert and Royce. Beltane paid only as much attention to Lynette as any guest would pay. His attention seemed to be more on Oriel.

The surprise came at the end of the meal when Beltane rose to make a toast. He saluted the king first, and then when all had drunk, he raised his horn again.

"I give you another toast. To the reason that brought me here. To let Lady Oriel talk to her brother . . . and get his consent to our marriage." Oriel smiled as if she had held a wonderful secret and was satisfied at its outcome.

Her brother and the others at the table received this news with different degrees of shock.

Giles looked from Beltane to his sister with a gaping mouth. Robert's hand froze around his horn of ale, and Royce and Lynette sat stunned.

"We have petitioned the king already and he has decided to come here. I'm sure that his visit is primarily to see what you have accomplished, but Oriel would be married with her brother in attendance, and to have William present would be an honor to us all."

His listeners struggled to hide their distress, and Beltane nearly laughed at their attempts. The rest of the evening was highly pleasurable for him. He had gained what he wanted, entry into Creganwald castle. Once his plans were accomplished, he had another surprise for these fools.

Giles was worried, for of everyone present, he was the one who was most uncertain whether Oriel and Beltane really meant to marry. Some mischief was at work here. He was sure that Beltane had drawn his sister into something that even she did not fully understand.

He meant to get his sister alone and renew the warning he had made her. He had worked long and hard for Royce's trust, and he was not going to let her greed and her feelings for Royce ruin all he had won. But questioning Oriel left him even more worried for she seemed docile and calm.

"I know that Royce and Lynette are happy, and now I seek happiness for myself. It is what you claim you always wanted me to do."

"I did not know you looked upon Beltane so. He is Royce's mortal enemy."

"That is over and settled. He regrets it. He paid me court, and we found we had much in common. Do you not wish me to be happy also, Giles?"

"Of course I do. I just don't want you to make a mistake. I don't like or trust Beltane."

"Mayhap once we are wed and all the problems have died, you will see a different man. For my sake, brother, try to let the old enmity die . . . let us find some peace."

Giles agreed with the sentiment . . . but he did not see Oriel's satisfied smile after he left.

Lynette had not planned on visitors at all and certainly not Beltane or Oriel. She had been on edge all day and had planned a special evening alone with Royce. It was time to tell him what she had known for some time, that they were expecting a child.

The presence of enemies in the castle would made it harder to tell him news he did not want to hear in the first place.

Royce did not share her dreams yet, and her pregnancy would make things between them strained for a while. She refused to admit that she was a bit frightened herself and desperately needed Royce's strength to see her through childbirth.

Now she waited in their chamber, after preparing herself very carefully. Royce was still in the great hall, sharing drinks with his men and his unwanted visitors.

If her pregnancy caused a breach between them, then she would have to stand it, until the child was born safely. Only then would Royce accept it.

She was so caught up in her thoughts that she did not hear the door open and Royce enter. He stood by the door for a minute looking at Lynette, studying her thoughtful expression and wondering where her mind lingered.

She sat with her hands limp in her lap, her head bent slightly forward. Her golden hair fell about her, shielding her eyes from him.

He felt something new . . . different and . . . almost lonely about the way she sat so silently. Lonely? He could not think that. They had been happy, he knew he made her happy. There was only one subject they skirted and never spoke of. He crossed the room and knelt before her chair, startling her from her thoughts. He watched her smile and lift her arms to rest her hands on his shoulders. Of course there was nothing to worry about.

He stood, drawing her up with him and into his arms. With pleasure he accepted her kiss, and lost himself in it for a moment.

When he released her, she remained with her arms about his waist. "Royce, are you tired? Would you like me to massage the tiredness from your shoulders? You need only lie across the bed and—"

"Nay," he said softly. "I would lie upon the bed with you and ease more than my tiredness."

"Come then," she replied warmly. "Let us see to your easing."

"Always you are here, and always you know what will make the day's end perfect."

They lay together enjoying the freedom of their pleasure. Sharing long and lingering kisses and sensitive touches.

"Royce, there is something of great importance I must talk to you about."

"You mean the presence of Beltane. He will not make a move that I do not know about. As for Oriel, I believe Giles is going to do his best to keep her from the terrible mistake of wedding such a man. I cannot believe she has chosen to do so."

"Perhaps she has not."

"Then you think she and Beltane plan some deceit?"

"Aye, but what the purpose of it is, I cannot tell."

"They wanted access to Creganwald . . . but why?"

"I wish we could have sent them away."

"This wedding is favorable to William and Oriel

347

as our own is to us; how can we send them away? They came with no one of arms and in peace. I suspect William sees a chance to make peace between his own."

"It is easy for William. He does not have to have the vipers in his own nest."

"We will let it go for a while, but do not worry, there is not a moment when they will not be watched. If they seek to betray us, we will teach them a final lesson they will not forget . . . if he lives through it."

"I would see them gone," Lynette said, and the tone of her voice caught Royce's attention.

"Lynette, you said there was something of importance you wanted to talk to me about. Was it about Beltane? Are you frightened of him?"

"Nay, I am not afraid . . . not of him."

"But you're trembling."

"It is not from fear, Royce, but excitement."

Royce turned and rose on one elbow to look more intently into her eyes, and suddenly he knew. He knew without words. She watched his face pale a bit and sensed his struggle for control.

"You are going to have a child." It was a statement, not a question.

"In the midst of winter, when the yuletide is over. Oh, Royce, don't turn from me! Don't be angry! I could not bear it if you didn't want it or me. I love you, Royce, and this child will be the most beautiful expression of my love."

"I could not turn from you, my love. It would tear the heart from my body to be without you. I am the one who is afraid. Lynette . . . "

She reached out a hand and laid it against his

cheek. "You must not fear. I will be well, and we will have a beautiful son. You must see, Royce, that I am strong and willing. I would give you some peace from your nightmares by showing you that what happened once will not happen again."

He caught her to him and kissed her as if she would disappear. The kiss grew, and her joy grew with it. She did not know that the blackness of the fear was upon him, and that he had to cling to her to keep his sanity. She was happy, and he would not change that no matter how it tore at him. He would hold her now, and as often as he could, for he was afraid their joy might not last. Perfection rarely did.

Assured that making love to her would not hurt her or the baby, he proceeded to make such gentle and tender love to her that it brought tears to her eyes.

Later, when she fell asleep, he lay chilled with the darkest of thoughts. He could not lose her . . . he could not!

He would send out word that he wanted the best of doctors and midwives. He would fill Creganwald with them if he could. Royce realized that all the doctors in the world would assure him nothing, but he would feel better. He meant to have the best care for her, even if it meant searching the whole of England for them. He could not lose Lynette . . . he could not.

Royce felt her body warm and safe in his arms, and gently laid his hand on her belly. Within her still slim form his seed grew. Perhaps she was right; perhaps it was a son.

Chapter Thirty-three

The only person with whom Royce shared the news of Lynette's pregnancy was Robert, who was overjoyed. Robert was as certain as Lynette that Royce would have a beautiful son.

The castle was now crowded with people, and Lynette expected some problems to arise, especially with Beltane present. But nothing did. Beltane kept his distance from her and was polite and easy when they did cross each other's path.

But hardly another week had passed before other visitors began to arrive. Some were from William, and Royce knew that William might come any day.

Royce was pleased and worried at the same time. The king's arrival might mean ridding himself of Beltane sooner. But it also might mean danger to William if what he and Robert thought was true. He wanted desperately to find out what Beltane was planning, but that knight gave no sign of doing anything but preparing for his wedding.

Robert had one of his men keep Beltane in view at all times, and he was a bit disappointed that Beltane gave him no cause to eject him from the castle. As far as Robert was concerned, it was the calm before the storm . . . but he could not figure out where the storm might come from.

Giles was the one who noticed that, for people who planned to marry, Beltane and Oriel spent little time together. He mentioned his observation to Royce and Robert.

" 'Tis entrance to the castle they had in mind, but why . . . why?"

"It is strange, isn't it?" Royce said thoughtfully. "It's as if they were expecting someone."

"The only person expected is William, or so Beltane said."

"I do not trust Beltane. I would lay the blame on Tearlach, but he is many miles distant. I have word he is within his castle walls. Robert, do you think there is a plan afoot to harm William when he arrives?"

"It is a good place for some kind of treachery. Mayhap they intend to find some way to lay the blame on you if they succeed."

"Good Lord, Robert . . . do you think they plan murder?" Giles asked.

"I do not put anything past them. But how? We are well armed, and surely the king will come well escorted."

"Some form of treachery. By damn! I feel as though the answer is under my nose!" Royce slammed his fist in his palm.

"Most likely it is, and we'll feel like fools if it has been staring us in the face all this time and we have never seen it," Robert replied thoughtfully.

"All we would need is for Tearlach to come." Giles's voice was heavy with disgust at the thought.

"Good Lord, don't suggest such an idea. Let the spider remain in his web," Robert replied.

"Well, it would answer questions, wouldn't it?" Giles said. "We could be reasonably sure that both your life and William's were in danger."

"A trap." Royce considered all he knew of Beltane and thought the idea plausible.

"And you to take the consequences should something happen to William here," Robert replied angrily.

"How well they made use of Oriel. I wonder what they promised her," Royce mused with a grin that faded at Robert's next word.

"You," he said bluntly.

Royce turned to look at Robert in shock; then he laughed . . . but his laugh faded before Robert's grim look.

"We have to do something now," Royce said.

"What?" Giles asked.

"We are going to take better precautions with our defenses."

"What better precautions can we take?"

"I'll tell you exactly what we're going to do . . . and what I think could be happening." Royce went on to explain a plan that widened Robert's eyes in surprise.

"I'll see that it is done," Robert said. "I'll be careful that it doesn't slip that any number of our men are to be away."

"Lynette is already fretting under my guard. I shall have to take her riding, and keep her with me as much as possible."

* * *

Lynette was indeed feeling the weight of Royce's concern. She felt him hovering and wished for time to ride out alone. But he had made it clear that she was not to leave the castle unless he or Robert and a few knights were with her . . . to see she came to no harm.

Her body did not yet show any signs of her pregnancy, and Royce had urged her to keep it a secret until Beltane and his men had left Creganwald.

But as the days went on, she felt more and more stifled. When finally Royce suggested that she ride out with him and Cerise the next day, she grasped the idea quickly. She needed even the smallest taste of freedom.

Beside that, she needed time to talk to Royce, for they never seemed to be alone anymore and she was afraid it was her pregnancy that was forcing them apart. He came to bed late at night, and was up very early in the morning. Tomorrow, she vowed to herself, she would find what was in Royce's heart no matter what she had to do.

It was a night designed for stealth. The moon was nearly obliterated by black clouds, and shadows made it easy for anyone who did not want to be seen to lurk within them.

No one, not even the guard Royce had set, saw the lone man who slipped from the manor and clung to the shadows until he was well away. He carried a message from Lady Oriel, who had given him coins to keep his silence.

He had not taken a horse for the simple reason there would be questions he could not answer. A horse had been left for him at an appointed place by those who waited to hear his words.

He found the horse, and two hours' hard ride later found the camp he had been told to look for. He carried his message to the man for whom it was intended, and a few hours later slipped back inside the castle.

The day promised to be beautiful and Lynette rose early, thinking she might need to remind Royce of his promise to take her riding. But he hadn't forgotten, for he and Cerise were waiting for her. Cerise was excited and her excitement was communicated to the two adults.

They rode out with Giles and Ferragus a short distance behind them.

"Do you think we need a guard, Royce?" Lynette asked.

"I would not take the pleasure from them." He smiled. "Giles feels it is Oriel who brought danger here, and he would be the first to protect you from all harm, even if it is imaginary."

"Are we in danger because of Beltane's presence?"

"Beltane is a nuisance, and when the wedding is over we will suggest, firmly, that he go."

"Maybe then we can find some quiet. I swear the castle seems full of noise, and there is always someone underfoot."

Cerise had dropped back a bit, to listen to a story Giles was telling her, and Lynette had the opportunity she'd been waiting for.

"Royce . . . are you still angry about the child?"

"No, Lynette, I was never angry at you. I find it

hard to admit I am afraid of something. Can you not understand that I can only see myself losing you?"

"I have faith," she said simply. "And I love you more every day."

"Do you think that makes it easier?"

"Does it not?"

"No. Love is so precious . . . you are so precious. When you claim your love for me, it only makes the thought of what is to come harder to bear."

"We will be fine parents," she said, smiling up at him. "We will love so much the child will be smothered."

He laughed and turned to look into her eyes. "How is it, Lynette, that you have a way of easing troubles?"

Cerise rode up beside them again, and her sparkling eyes told of her pleasure in the smiles she saw on their faces. For that one precious moment the three of them were complete . . . like three separate pieces formed into a whole. It was at that moment that they were struck. Struck by a force that three men, one woman, and a child could never hope to fight. Royce drew his sword at the first sound, as did Giles and Ferragus, but none of them expected a force as large as this.

Royce glared at the armed knights that surrounded them. He knew their colors . . . Tearlach. A moment later Tearlach rode from the forest.

"What treachery is this, Tearlach?" Royce growled.

"You will find the answer to that soon enough, my friend," Tearlach answered. His gaze moved to Lynette and Cerise, and Royce forced his horse between them and Tearlach. But Tearlach only laughed.

"I am afraid the odds do not seem to be on your side, Royce."

"Lay one hand on them and to hell with the odds."

"Oh, I do not want to harm them, nor do I want to harm you."

"You lie as usual."

"Nay, no lie. You are going to return to Creganwald with your two men."

"And leave Lynette and Cerise with you? You must be mad to think I would do that."

"Oh, you will leave her with me," Tearlach said softly, "or you will see her dead here and now, before your eyes. Do as I say, or pay with her life."

"How could you expect me to trust you?"

"You have no choice." Tearlach smiled, for he knew quite well he had a force Royce could never hope to vanquish.

"What do you want?"

"William draws near."

Royce began to deny this, but Tearlach only smiled.

"There is no need to lie. I have been watching and planning for a long time. There are those who would give much to see him . . . gone."

"Robert was right," Royce said softly. "You do plan murder. You will not succeed."

"I? I plan murder? Nay, Royce. *You* plan murder."

"No one would believe that, and you can never make it happen."

"Can I not?" Tearlach chuckled, and it was a sound that made Lynette shiver. Cerise drew closer to her. "Take them." The order was given coldly, and Tearlach's men hastened to obey. Although all three men fought with every bit of their strength, they were overcome and held while Lynette and Cerise were dragged away.

Royce had known fury in his life and his share of hatred, but at this moment he would have slaughtered Tearlach like a pig if he had had the opportunity.

Tearlach knew this and he smiled, for it was just what he wanted. "Now, do you intend to listen to me . . . or must we go on to other means? There is only one way you will ever see your daughter or your wife again."

"What do you want?" Royce's voice was deadly.

"I will tell you my plan . . . and you will do exactly what I say."

"Where are you taking Lynette and Cerise?"

"To a place where you will never find them if you search a million years, and believe me it is a place that will be a nightmare for them. Your daughter promises to grow into a lovely thing. She will make an excellent . . . toy for a man I know, and as for Lynette . . . Beltane has his own plans for her."

"Don't harm them, Tearlach, or there won't be a place in this realm you can hide."

The men surrounding Tearlach shifted uncomfortably. They had heard of Royce's reputation and weren't happy at the thought of facing his anger.

"Listen to me well, Royce, for I will say this only once. You will return to the manor. There you will go on as usual until William arrives. When he does, you will have a celebration. While that celebration is in progress, you will open the lower gates and the hall to the men waiting outside. They will do the rest."

"And when Robert or one of the others asks for Lynette and Cerise?"

"You may tell them the truth, but if they take action, your wife and daughter will die."

Giles and Ferragus held their rage in control. Both knew the result of hasty action . . . but both knew that Royce would not allow his loved ones to die. Giles had to ask one question that burned within him.

"My sister, Oriel . . . has she something to do with this?"

"Ah, sweet Oriel. How easily persuaded she is. Beltane has had his way with her. It seems the wench is hungry for love. Promises of position and a rich husband have served us well."

Giles's face became mottled with rage, and if Royce had not put out a restraining hand, he would have attacked . . . and he would have been cut down.

"Hold, Giles, don't play into his hand. In time we will see what courage Tearlach has. William is no fool, Tearlach."

"Nay, he is not. But it is up to you to convince him to enter . . . and disarm. After that, it will be a simple matter to get your ladies back."

"I want you to know this, Tearlach." Royce's voice was stone cold. "If one bit of harm comes to mine, if you touch the slightest hair on their heads, you will wish to die long before you do. On that you have my oath as a knight."

Tearlach said nothing, but a ripple of fear went through the company. The cold eyes of Royce, his reputation, the display of his ability in the duel with Beltane were enough to give them second thoughts . . . and Tearlach knew it.

"I have given mine as well. Do as you are told and no harm will come to them. It is William we want."

After he spoke, there was dead silence. Then Royce spoke again.

"I want to talk to Lynette alone for a minute."

"I see no reason for that. Do you hope to stall for time?"

"No, I just want to tell her not to worry, that she will be free within a short time."

"Aye, console her." Tearlach's smile was deadly. "But the fulfillment of the promise depends on you."

"I know."

"Let them share a moment alone," Tearlach commanded his men, and they parted to let Royce by, closing ranks so that Giles and Ferragus could not follow.

Chapter Thirty-four

The three men who guarded Lynette and Cerise moved away as Royce approached. When they were out of earshot, Royce drew Lynette close to him and held her.

"Lynette, I'm sorry. I thought Beltane was the danger. He was just a distraction, and we were taken in completely."

"I don't really think he means to harm us," Lynette said cautiously. She looked at Royce almost warningly. She didn't want Cerise more frightened than she already was. "I think we'll be all right if we don't anger him and remain brave."

"I had forgotten just how courageous you are," Royce said quietly. "You are right. You know I will not allow him to hurt you, don't you?"

"Of course we know." Lynette smiled, and both were aware that Cerise was watching them. "Just as we know that William will not tolerate any harm to you or yours. It is only Tearlach who needs to learn that lesson." Lynette knew they could keep Cerise from panicking only if they remained calm themselves.

"Cerise, don't be frightened," Royce said as he knelt beside her. "Papa will take care of everything and you'll be home safe soon. Until then, you must do everything Lynette tells you to do, and be a good girl. Can you do that for me?"

"Yes, Papa." Her confidence in him shone in her eyes, and Royce tasted a fear such as he had never known before. He had only recently found his daughter, and by God, he wasn't going to lose her now. And the idea of spending the rest of his life without Lynette was unthinkable.

They depended upon him, and he had to use his wits. Trying to fight Tearlach now was impossible, and it would cost Lynette's and Cerise's life. He had to play Tearlach's game . . . for the moment.

Royce hugged Cerise to him, feeling her thin, small arms encircle his neck and cling. He inhaled a deep breath and held her away from him to smile down at her. "I love you, Cerise. Don't forget that."

"I love you too, Papa." She returned his smile.

Royce stood, and Lynette came into his arms again. He held her without speaking. There was nothing left to say. When he turned away, Lynette watched him go and struggled to contain the urge to cry out and run after him. It was only knowing how Tearlach would enjoy her fear that kept her from doing so.

When Royce, Giles, and Ferragus rode some distance from Tearlach's men, they slowed their horses. Royce was the first to smile grimly. He turned his gaze to Giles.

"Everyone has been instructed?"

"Aye." Giles nodded. "There will be a lot of surprises, but no harm will come to them. I would be near Tearlach when the time comes."

"I'm afraid that is going to be my pleasure," Royce replied.

"I will at least be able to see his face," Giles said with a chuckle. "That will satisfy me . . . except . . . "

"Except what?"

"I would like to know why. He claims to seek revenge for Perrin's death, but . . . "

"But?"

"I cannot help but feel the same," Ferragus said. "There is something he knows, or thinks he knows; some secret that he feels he has to act upon."

"Now you two are guessing," Royce replied.

"What if he has someone he thinks to put in William's place? Someone who would be in his control?" Giles offered.

"Who? Who would be able to hold William's followers?" Ferragus questioned thoughtfully.

"Someone of royal blood . . . someone who is loved, or who commands enough loyalty that he could draw all the knights to his cause."

"Well, I know no one, so let us assume that Tearlach wants power for himself."

"It matters naught. He will not succeed."

"Nay," said the usually silent and introspective Ferragus. "He will wish he had never placed a hand on Lady Lynette, or the child, Cerise. My sword hungers already."

"We must play out the game and we must be very careful. We know by now there are few to be trusted. We also have William to protect. Are you certain word has reached him?"

"Aye, I sent the message as soon as you discussed the plans with us."

"And the men you sent to find the hidden forces?"

"There was no trouble there either. They were found and infiltrated, and never knew the difference."

"I had not thought . . . " Royce's voice shook for a minute before he regained control. Lynette and Cerise needed his strength now.

"I know, we had not thought Tearlach would strike through Lynette and Cerise when they were with us. But they are still safer than he knows, and our plan will be completed before he understands what has happened, or how deadly William's revenge is going to be."

"And ours."

"Aye . . . and ours."

Lynette kept Cerise close to her, but she saw no threat from the men. They watched her but made no move to come near. The day grew long, and Lynette and Cerise were offered food. Lynette instructed Cerise to eat, for she had no idea how long they would be prisoners and she didn't want Cerise to become ill.

By mid-afternoon, they were mounted on horses and taken a greater distance from the original camp. Obviously Tearlach felt that Royce was clever enough to remember where they were and send men to take them by surprise.

It was only when they had been in the abductors' hands for most of the day that Lynette became aware of a subtle undercurrent. Both she and Cerise were treated with great gentleness, and she began to wonder if these men had their hearts in the matter.

Fires were built and a meal of sorts was provided. By the time full night was upon them, Lynette's suspicions were nagging her. She made a comfortable place for Cerise and covered her with her cloak. Soon the little girl was asleep.

Lynette couldn't sleep, and she sat in the shadows of a tree with her cloak wrapped around her and listened to the hushed voices of the men in the camp. Tearlach had not come near her again. Finally the sounds of the night were all that could be heard. Lynette closed her eyes and rested her head against the tree. She was startled when a soft sound came to her. She sat very still and listened.

"Do not fear, lady, there are those here who belong to Creganwald."

She listened again, but no sound came. Still, she felt a sense of relief and she realized that Royce had been better prepared than she had thought. It was clear to her that he had never trusted Beltane or Oriel from the beginning. Now she had to keep calm, and wait for any opportunity that might present itself. After a while she found a comfortable place near Cerise and slept.

Beltane kept a close eye on Royce when he returned. He knew when Royce went directly to Robert that Tearlach had taken his hostages just as he had said he would. Beltane wished he could hear what Royce said.

"That bastard!" Robert almost shouted. "I wish we could go after him now."

"Nay, it would spoil his plans . . . and ours," Royce said.

"It will be hard to be patient."

"But we will be," Royce replied. "William will be here tomorrow night. He knows all. When the celebration is started, I will go down and open the lower gate and let the traitors in."

"Let the lambs in with the lions," Giles said, "and let them learn how traitors are punished."

"Aye, it will be amusing to read Tearlach's face . . . and Beltane's."

"Giles, go cautiously and see that all is in readiness."

Robert stood silently and watched as Royce gave his trusted men some last-minute orders. He sensed there was something that Royce wanted to say to him in private.

When they were alone, Royce turned to the friend he'd often thought of as a father. There were answers he needed, and he meant to have them.

"Robert, Giles said something to me that has made me curious."

"Giles is full of inconsequential things," Robert said. "What did he say that has you so deep in thought?"

"He believes Tearlach hopes to put a puppet on William's throne, someone with the power to draw the knights together and hold this realm for Tearlach. Know you of such a man, Robert?"

"I think Giles has been tipping his horn of ale too often."

"You have never lied to me, and I have never asked you such questions before. But there is too much at stake, and if William has a mortal enemy with the power to claim the throne, then I must know of it."

"William has no such enemy with that power."

Royce looked closely at Robert. He wasn't lying, but he was certainly not telling the complete truth either. "Has he any friends with that power? Friends can turn to enemies quickly, if there is enough reason."

"The friends he has will not betray him."

"Robert . . . "

"Royce, you should not ask me what I should not answer." Robert laid a hand on Royce's arm and lowered his voice to a whisper, lest even the walls had ears. "One who is illegitimate took over the ruling of England. He is an honorable man and will rule well. But if there was another . . . perhaps one bred by someone close to the throne, he would be of blood royal too. With the knights behind him, he could take over William's throne . . . if William was gone."

Royce sucked in his breath, and for a moment wasn't sure where the next was coming from. "A half-brother to William." He breathed. "Am I . . . ?"

"Nay, not a half-brother to William . . . but the son of a man as close to him as a man can get."

"His name?"

"Will never be spoken between us or by me to any other. I have made a vow."

"Then how would Tearlach consider me?"

"I fear he has somehow found the truth, and he will split this land asunder to reach for power."

"Then . . . Tearlach must take that secret to his grave."

"Aye." Robert was silent for a minute. "Royce, it

is the truth you know. You could have more than you have ever dreamed of. All you have to do . . . "

"Is betray my king, destroy whatever love Lynette may hold for me, and surrender the friendship of you, my knights, William, and maybe even my daughter when she is old enough to discover that her father would give up all for a throne." Royce smiled. "Nay, Robert, the reward is not nearly enough to balance the cost. But . . . I would have his name if just to know . . . "

"Only for your peace of mind will I speak the name, but once . . . and only once. Earl Godwin," Robert said quietly.

Royce's face never changed at the sound of that name. He knew that he *could* have reached out and taken the crown, if he was willing to go along with Tearlach's plan . . . and to sacrifice Lynette.

"We hold the secret together for the rest of our lives."

"Aye, forever. This must never pass our lips again."

"Royce . . . I would have you know that I would have been proud to call you son."

"And I will have you know, Robert, that I always thought I was, and I have always been proud. I would keep you as my father and forget all else."

Robert was silent before an immense emotion that could never be put to words. "Then let us continue to protect our king."

Royce found little sleep, for even though he knew Lynette and Cerise were reasonably safe, he could not rest until they were back within his care.

He paced the battlements of the castle until the

moon was setting and a gray light heralded the coming day. All his plans were laid, and there was little to do but wait.

The next morning he broke his fast alone, and was eating thoughtfully when Beltane appeared.

"And so . . . you have done well, Royce. Tearlach will be pleased."

"Perhaps"—Royce smiled and rose slowly from his seat, his eyes holding Beltane's and filled with taunting amusement—"*you* are the one who will not be so pleased when this is done." He walked away. He knew Beltane's twisted mind. Those last words of Royce's would worry Beltane; he would soon begin to wonder if he himself had in some way been betrayed.

Chapter Thirty-five

William arrived with great fanfare. Royce welcomed his king with the same enthusiasm. He pronounced to all that there would be great feasting that night, and when William inquired about Lynette and Cerise, he was told that Cerise was not feeling well and Lynette would not leave her side.

The castle was surveyed carefully by William, who was free with complimentary comments about its construction and location.

"Were this castle in the hands of any but my loyal knight, it would make my crown sit uneasily upon my head."

"There is only one way this castle is vulnerable," Royce replied, "and that is by treachery within. Since all here are loyal to you, there should be no fear of that."

"Then let us enjoy tonight's celebration, and I will return to London much relieved."

William caught Beltane's eye for a moment and

smiled. It relieved Beltane's mind that no one in the castle was aware of his bargain with Tearlach.

The hall was full of both William's men and Royce's. They sat at table conversing freely. The evening told a bit on Beltane's nerves, and to make it worse, Oriel seemed to suddenly remember that she was supposed to be married the next day, and made Beltane uncomfortable with her attentions.

Giles watched his sister and was filled with sympathy. She was unhappy, and that, together with her ambition, was proving a dangerous combination. He did mean to save her as much grief as he could, but he could count on nothing if William discovered her connection to the plot. He had tried to get Royce alone to discuss it with him, and beg his mercy, but he had had little success.

Now as the celebration went on, he wished she would not look at Beltane the way she did for this would be remembered, and it might bode ill for Oriel.

Royce grew ever more tense as the time drew near to spring the trap and catch the traitors.

It seemed forever before the time came for him to carry out Tearlach's plan. He could feel the perspiration on his body and his hands.

Beltane had not seemed to be watching him, and Royce wondered, with annoyance, if Beltane was so confident that he felt it unnecessary. He rose from his seat and made an excuse to William and those nearby.

He left the noisy hall, finding himself momentarily alone as he started for the little-used back gate to let Tearlach's men in.

They were there, dark shadows against the night sky, as they moved inside, one by one.

Lynette had watched as the majority of the men surrounding them mounted their horses and rode from the camp. Now there were only five men left to guard them.

Cerise had watched Lynette for signs of how she was to act and behaved accordingly. If . . . if they were saved, Lynette meant to tell Royce that his daughter had inherited all his courage.

The firelight left them sitting in the deeper shadows at its periphery, and Lynette could not see the faces of the men about her. When one man rose and disappeared into the shadows, she was alarmed. Were they planning the prisoners' demise, here in this dark wood? They could bury them here and no one would ever find them. She had never been so frightened in her life.

A second man rose and moved into the darkness too, followed by a third. Only two were left, and Lynette did not like the way they were regarding her. One had a suggestive smile on his face, and the other a cold and vicious look that made her tremble. She wished she could find a way out of this, if not for her, at least for Cerise.

"What do you plan for us?" she finally asked.

"For you, as pretty as you are, a little celebration of our own," one man answered and the other laughed.

"How can you treat a child like this? Keep me if you must, but let her go. She is innocent, and she can cause you no harm."

"She will fetch a good prize when she is delivered."

"Royce is doing what you want. You cannot mean to harm his child."

"Be silent! We have our orders, and what's another child?"

Lynette understood their cruelty, and vowed that Cerise would not suffer at their hands, no matter what she had to do. But the matter was taken out of her control so abruptly that she was shocked.

The three men who had left the camp had come up from behind the other two. They appeared suddenly, like specters, and struck. In seconds the two men lay unconscious at their feet, and they were binding them.

She was sure that the men were about to attack her, and wanted to shriek as one of them came toward her. The look on her face must have revealed her fear.

"Nay, lady. Don't be afraid. We are Royce's men and we have been waiting for the right moment." He knelt beside her and looked worriedly at her as if he were afraid she would not believe him. "I am sorry you have had to go through this, but we had to wait until Tearlach was gone to move."

"Royce's men?" she repeated in disbelief.

"Aye, lady. It seems Royce was aware that Tearlach would come sometime, especially since William was so close. He sent us to locate Tearlach's force, and melt into his group so that we could notify him of Tearlach's plans. He did not expect him to strike at you or the child. We all thought the victim was to be William."

"But if William is in the manor and the plan is in force, what can we do to save Royce and the king?"

"We can do no more than follow Royce's orders,

and that is to hold you safe until he can come for you."

"It is not enough! Royce could be killed. Tearlach's force is larger than those in the castle."

"Aye, lady, but not as large as Royce's and William's combined."

"Then Tearlach has walked into his own trap."

"Aye, and it will close on him. It will be the last time Tearlach conspires to harm William or those around him. Can I get you some food or drink, lady?"

"Nay, I do not hunger." She turned to Cerise, whose eyes were shining. "Are you hungry, Cerise?"

Cerise shook her head and smiled. "I knew Papa would save us, Lynette. He told us he would."

"Remind me never to doubt him again," Lynette laughed. The three men stirred the fire to greater warmth, and sat waiting quietly.

Royce closed the gate behind the intruders and motioned them to follow him, which they did without questions.

They followed him silently through the dark corridors, and when they reached the assigned place they found themselves effectively surrounded. They had expected victims, taken by surprise. What they found was their own imprisonment.

Royce led a smaller group of his men up to the main hall, but not before they had changed into the armor and colors worn by Tearlach's men.

Within the hall, Tearlach was watching for his men, and when Royce returned, he smiled a smile of intense satisfaction. His men were in control. This was the time he had waited for. He had been right; Royce would do anything for the wench he loved, and the child he had just discovered.

Tearlach's heart throbbed with the fierce excitement that filled him. Learning Robert's and Royce's secret was going to give him a crown and all the power he had hoped for.

William had been watching Tearlach with growing rage. He waited. He knew there was something about Tearlach's plans that he did not understand and perhaps never would. He also had a feeling that Royce could have gained a great deal if he had not revealed Tearlach's plan. . . .

Beltane had been looking at Tearlach's men for several minutes before a feeling of alarm crept through him. Something was wrong . . . very wrong. The faces were familiar, and he had seen these faces among Royce's men. One he knew well had been in Royce's service for a number of years. He had to warn Tearlach.

But he was a minute too late. Tearlach had risen, and faced William. "It seems, sire, you have made a mistake in trusting your Sword of William. You do not know of his betrayal."

"Betrayal?" William asked mildly. "What know you of betrayal, Royce?"

"I know a great deal, sire." Royce's voice was just as mild. Beltane knew in his heart that all was lost, that somehow the plan had been discovered. There would be no mercy in William now. The full attention of the entire company was on William and Royce. Beltane slipped from the group so stealthily that none missed him. "I know that the man who would see you dead and this realm in confusion has just made his last and very fatal mistake."

Tearlach's face froze, and he gaped at Royce in shock. Would he truly sacrifice his wife for his king? He saw Royce's smile . . . turned to face William, and saw a matching smile.

"Royce, order your men to draw their swords and kill him!" Tearlach shouted, but he received no reply, and no action. "You fool, do you know you are giving up a kingdom?" This drew William's attention, but still he said nothing.

"Do you think I would want a kingdom gained by murder?" Royce said. "Even if I wanted one, I have no right to it and I would not take what was not mine by birth or right of arms."

"Right? Shall I tell you where your rights lie?"

"No! I will hear none of your traitorous words. The truth of this night is known by William. Your men are safely below . . . in irons. Will you surrender, Tearlach?"

"Never!" Tearlach drew his sword and faced Royce. But another voice came from behind him.

"This honor is not for a young man, with whom you might cry foul. Turn and face me, Tearlach, and meet your justice." Robert enjoyed the look on Tearlach's face as he turned to face him.

The two men looked at each other across years of hatred, and there was death in their eyes.

"I know the truth," Tearlach whispered raggedly.

"Aye, I do not doubt that you do," Robert replied, low enough that his voice didn't carry. "And you shall die with it."

"You are a fool as well. What man would give up a kingdom for this place and a woman?"

"You would never understand that man, so there is little use in explaining."

Tearlach was many things, but he was not a coward. He was a powerful man, seasoned in battle, and he could wield a mighty sword. Still, Robert faced him with the greatest of pleasure. Robert, too, was a seasoned warrior, and the men were evenly matched.

Royce watched, knowing Robert's expertise, and sure that his anger at this attempted regicide was a driving force that would bring him victory. Tearlach would die here before the man he'd intended to murder.

Swords met with a mighty clang, and everyone in the hall moved back to give the combatants room. William was watching both the fighters, and Royce. A kingdom, Tearlach had said. There was only one way for that to be possible. He began to wonder what blood flowed in Royce's veins . . . and if it was in some way mixed with his own.

Chapter Thirty-six

Robert swung his sword with a mighty blow, and Tearlach returned it with the same force. Again and again they struck at each other. William watched with what looked like detachment, but his agile mind was working and he missed little that was going on about him.

Royce was captivated by the force of Robert's attack. He had seen Robert fight before, but not quite like this. Robert had a goal, and it was to close Tearlach's mouth forever, to see that he took what secrets he knew to the silence of the grave.

Within minutes of their confrontation, Tearlach knew that he was facing a formidable foe, one who intended to give no quarter. But Tearlach was asking no quarter, for he did not mean for Robert to live either.

They circled each other like two predators, looking for an opening . . . a moment unguarded when one would strike home.

"You thought to keep a secret, did you not?" Tearlach laughed tauntingly. "It will be known to the world when I have done with you."

"You would cause bloodshed, and take innocent lives, just to see William dead?"

"Aye, and you as well. I will have my vengeance, and Royce will dance when I command him to dance."

"Because you think you have him in your power?" Now it was Robert who laughed and struck. "Do you not think we knew you were near?" He struck again. "Do you not think we considered all plans? And do you really think Lynette and Cerise are still in your power? You are wrong, Tearlach . . . wrong." He struck again and again with each word.

Tearlach battered at Robert, but Robert continued to evade the force of the blows, and to respond with a fierce attack that drove Tearlach back . . . and back.

All watched in admiration and wonder that Tearlach was still standing. He fought like a demon, but it was obvious to everyone that the battle was nearing its conclusion.

Suddenly, in one quick and deadly blow, it was. Tearlach lay dead, and Robert breathed a sigh of relief, for the secret had died with him.

Oriel had tried to escape the room, but Giles had reached to grasp her arm and hold her firmly. She would, for once, face the consequences of her deviousness. She had gazed at him hoping for pity, but when she saw none in his eyes, she remained still.

It was only then, when silence filled the room and William rose from his seat, that Beltane's absence was noted. Royce looked about the room with rising alarm. He and Robert exchanged glances, and without a word raced out of the hall, with many of Royce's loyal men behind them.

Their worst fears were confirmed when they learned that Beltane had ridden from the castle with ten of his men. Royce ordered his men to mount, and led them toward the location where Lynette and Cerise were supposed to be held in safety. His heart was thudding against his ribs, and he refused to entertain visions of what could happen to them if Beltane reached them first.

They rode as if the furies of hell were on their heels, but the sight that greeted them when they reached the meeting point brought a groan of agony from Royce. The three who were to see to Lynette's and Cerise's safety lay dead and both prisoners were gone. There were signs of a violent struggle.

Royce sent men in all directions to find traces of their passage, but it was some time before the trail was found, and then they had to search carefully for each sign. Royce followed slowly and methodically, his mind seething with thoughts of what he would do if . . . no, when, he got his hands on Beltane.

Lynette had engaged the three men in conversation, hearing the careful and very clever plan Royce had laid to prove, once and for all, that Tearlach and Beltane were traitors.

"He knew that Beltane had something brewing," one man said.

"Aye, just as he knew that Tearlach had to be somewhere close."

The third added, "With William coming, it was not hard to guess who their target was. The three of us weren't known to Tearlach's men, so we were sent to find their force and to work our way within. Tearlach is not a lord who worries about his men, or their welfare. Rape and living off the land by stealing is his way. That kind of leader is not one men confide in, so we were welcomed among them. From then on it was just waiting to see to your safety."

"But Royce did not know that Cerise and I would be taken."

"He did not know that." The first man smiled. "But he managed to get word to us after you were captured. He knows we will not let anything happen to those who are his."

"You are very courageous, and I am grateful. I am sure Royce will reward you well."

"Your safety is reward enough, lady. There is not a one of us to whom the Lord of Creganwald has not done some kindness. We look forward to living on Creganwald land for the rest of our lives and serving you."

"The Lord of Creganwald," Lynette said quietly. "Aye, that is what he is, no matter what his birth."

"Aye," the third man replied. "It takes more than noble birth to make a knight. He will serve Creganwald well."

Lynette was about to reply when the night seemed to explode around them. The three men were set upon so quickly that they had no chance, and within minutes they lay dead before Lynette's eyes.

Cerise screamed and clung to Lynette, who was gazing at the attackers in shock. Then, from the darkness, Beltane strode toward her with a vicious smile of satisfaction on his face.

"So, we are together again, little flower. Let us see what Royce will do now. This is one trick he did not count on, and the one that will cost him all he holds dear." He reached out and grasped Lynette's arm, and dragged her toward him until she rested full against him. Cerise threw herself at Beltane, small fists flying. But with one swipe of his hand he knocked her down. Then he ordered one of his men to take her.

"Let her be! Don't hurt her!" Lynette cried.

"Do as you're told and no harm will come to her," Beltane snarled. "Cause me trouble and she'll pay for it. Just remember, she is excess baggage."

"Royce will kill you for this."

"He will never find us. I have a safe place to hide until a ship can take us from here. Then he will never find you."

Beltane took Lynette before him on his horse, and ordered one of his men to take Cerise. They rode into the night, and Lynette was too disoriented to see where they were going.

It seemed to her they rode for hours, and when they did stop, Lynette could hear the sound of the sea in the distance. They were dragged from the horses, and their hands were tied before them. When Lynette could see where they were being led, she felt a shiver of disbelief. Cerise's dream came to her full force, for they were surrounded by huge rocks, and on the other side of them lay the sea.

They were taken to the shelter of the rocks and forced to sit in the sand, side by side. Cerise cuddled against Lynette, who could feel her body trembling.

"Don't be frightened, Cerise."

"Do . . . do you think Papa will find us in time?"

"He will not rest until he does."

"Will . . . will Beltane kill us?" In the darkness Cerise's eyes seemed large and terrified.

"If he meant to kill us, he would have done it when he first came. No, he has other plans, but the longer they take, the more dangerous they become to him, for your papa is not far behind."

"I saw him and this place in my dream, remember? I saw Papa too, and he was sad. Maybe he won't get here in time."

"That was a dream, Cerise, just a dream. We'll be all right." Lynette spoke with confidence, but her confidence was badly shaken when she realized that it was boats they were waiting for, and from the sounds on the other side of the rocks, the boats were landing. If they were taken aboard a ship, it might be impossible to trace them. They would truly be lost to Royce.

The moon was high, and she could see Beltane's face clearly as he walked toward her. He was accompanied by one man. "Take the child to the beach. I'll bring the woman."

Both Lynette and Cerise struggled, but they were torn apart, and the man carried a crying, thrashing Cerise away. Lynette stood, facing Beltane.

"Stop dreaming that he will come in time to save

you, Lynette. It is too late for that. It is quite possible that he does not know that we are gone from the castle yet. His attention was elsewhere when I left, and I was smart enough to see through his plans before he could stop me. Come peacefully, and it could be pleasant for you."

"With you? I would rather die here."

"And the child? You wish her to die here too?"

Lynette swallowed heavily. She had to buy as much time for Cerise as she could, for she would never give up hope that Royce would find them. "Where are you taking us?"

"That bastard spoiled all my plans, so I must find other goals. You will be my . . . companion until then . . . perhaps after, if you prove satisfactory. It would be well for you to try to please me."

He moved closer to her, and with her hands bound together, there was little she could do. She fought as hard as she could, but he took her into his arms and kissed her roughly. Lynette writhed in his arms, fighting the hard, seeking mouth that ravaged hers.

"Beltane, turn and face me you traitorous thief." The voice was cold and hard as a steel sword. Lynette thought she had never heard anything so wonderful in her life.

With a curse, Beltane thrust her from him, and she stumbled back against the rocks. Washed in white moonlight, the two men faced each other.

Beltane felt the blood grow chilled within him. He had faced Royce before . . . but not with this look in his eyes. Without another word Royce attacked, and Beltane had little chance to do more than raise his sword before Royce was upon him.

Within minutes Beltane was panting and beads of sweat were blinding his eyes. He had called once for help, but when none came, he knew the finality of this struggle. Royce's men were all around. It seemed as if his strength was being drained as he continued to back away from Royce.

Royce knew nothing of where he was. He did not see the moonlight or feel the sea breeze. He knew only one thing: Beltane had to die. Lynette watched and knew the reason for the rumors that Royce was mad when he fought, for now he looked mad. In truth he was.

Like two black-shadowed goliaths they fought, but any onlooker could have told the outcome. Beltane was trembling before the onslaught, and his eyes were darting about for any chance to escape. There was none.

"How did you come here?" he gasped.

"Does it matter to you?" Royce growled.

Beltane felt his arm grow heavy. His breath was labored. He could have wept in frustration, for Royce seemed like a ghostly shadow he could not touch. His last sight was Royce's grim face as he drove his sword home, and Beltane fell to the sand.

Lynette could only gasp Royce's name once as he came to her and took her face between his hands. He kissed her feverishly, over and over again.

"Lynette . . . Lynette, I thought . . . oh, God." He kissed her eyes, her cheeks where salty tears coursed, then her mouth. Lynette could not hold him with her hands bound, and she could not free her mouth long enough to beg him to untie her.

"Royce." She finally got his name out in a smothered sob. But it sounded pained to him.

"Are you hurt?" He groaned. "Did he touch you?"

Lynette did not know at this moment if he was capable of mutilating Beltane's body, but she would take no chances.

"Nay, I'm not hurt. Royce, untie me."

It was as if he had just noticed. He quickly unbound her hands, and in seconds found his arms full of woman. A woman who was kissing him and embracing him as fiercely as he had held her. It was several minutes before she could find the breath to ask, "Cerise?"

"She is well, and with Giles and Ferragus. The rest of my men are cleaning the beach of scum."

"How did you find us? How did you know?"

"We were on quite a chase, and I had almost lost hope of finding you. It was only when we remembered that Beltane had ships of his own that we considered how he meant to escape, and where he was likely to do it."

"Neither Cerise nor I had any doubts that you would come for us."

"My life, my heart, I could not have lived if I had lost you."

"Tearlach?"

"Dead, at Robert's hand."

"I do not understand their scheme. They meant to kill William, but that would have caused chaos."

"What they planned to do about that is a secret that has died with them. I only know that you, Cerise, and Creganwald are enough to fill my life to capacity. You are all I will ever need. Let William rule England. We will rule here."

"Aye," she breathed. "Take me home, Royce. It is time to fill our lives with peace."

He took her in his arms and kissed her again, a kiss of promise and of joy.

Epilogue

William and Robert sat alone, sharing a horn or two of ale and considering all that had passed.

"It seems this is where it all began." William smiled.

"Aye, we were discussing the safety of Creganwald."

"And you were discussing the well-being of Royce. It seems that all worked out to everyone's satisfaction." William paused. "With the exceptions of Tearlach and Beltane."

"Aye."

"Robert . . . something has been left in the shadows, and I had thought you might have an answer."

"I will answer what I can."

"There was something between Tearlach and you that escapes me."

"You think it wrong the way I dealt with traitors?"

"Do not be a fool, Robert."

"There is nothing else that matters now, and I have told you before, I am sworn. I—"

"Robert." William's voice stopped his words. "I know of both your loyalty and your ability to hold a trust. I ask . . . does it have to do with my crown?"

"You can trust me in this . . . No one is a threat to you now."

"Then that is well and enough. We will not speak of it again."

"Then let us speak of Royce's heir," Robert laughed.

"Do you bargain for the lad already?"

"While you are in your cups, and mayhap of a good frame of mind."

"All right, you brigand, let's speak of Royce's heir."

Royce gazed down on Lynette's peaceful face as she slept. He could not resist a touch, and bent to kiss her lightly, filling himself with the warmth of the love she shared with him. He wanted to give her all that it was possible to give, to cradle her, and breathe his love into her. He wanted her to know how deep the love he had for her went, but if he told her for all their lives, it would only scratch the surface.

Even now his heart ached when he thought of the agony they had both gone through just two days before. Their child had come into the world, and Lynette had suffered. He had been at her side every second, to the distress of doctors and all who attended her. Royce would not leave her. He had held her hand, feeling the force of her grip and hiding his terror.

With every moan, every cry, a little of him had

died. Then the small bundle was laid in his arms, and he wept with the joy of it. They lived, both mother and son, and he had begun to live again.

He walked to the cradle that held his son and bent over it. He had never felt such pride and wonder in his life. He reached out to take the tiny hand in his, and felt the perfectly formed fingers close about his.

"Royce?"

Royce turned to meet the warmth of Lynette's smile. She reached up a hand to him, and he crossed the room and took her hand in his. He kissed her fingers as he sat down on the bed beside her.

"He is beautiful, isn't he?"

"Aye, he is perfect. You are beautiful."

"Have you seen how black his hair is, and how strong he is?"

"He is big, and strong, and healthy . . . and last night I received an example of how lustily he can make his wants known."

"Yes," Lynette giggled. "He is much like his father. Cerise?"

"She has taken to him like a duck to water, and you will be hard put not to let her be second mother."

"She will be the most perfect of sisters."

"Which he will not appreciate until he is older." Royce's eyes grew serious. "Lynette, I love you, and I thank you for our son. I do not think I have ever been so afraid in my life."

"I was afraid too. But, oh Royce, look at what we have made together. I love you so much, and now we will be a family."

"You have not named him."

"I thought you would name our sons and I would name the daughters."

"Sons! Daughters!" His face registered shock. "You would not put me through that too often?"

"Oh, my courageous knight. Do not worry. They are God's gift, and will come when He pleases."

"I must attend Mass more often, and convince him to go slowly here."

"What name would you choose?"

"If you agree . . . Robert William."

"How wonderful. Robert will be so pleased. And if there is another boy we will name him for my father." She laughed at his groan, then grew serious. "It is as if the babe is Robert's grandson. . . . Is he, Royce?"

"Nay, Lynette. Only in honor, not in blood. But he will be in all ways . . . in every way I can make it so. Lynette, I would keep no secrets from you, but . . . "

"I would not have you say it, Royce. Robert is the grandfather, you are the father, Cerise is his sister . . . that is enough to give us a complete life. That is enough. I love you."

"Then we will make Creganwald a place of happiness."

"Aye," Lynette whispered as his lips met hers in a soft and promising kiss.

NIGHT WALKER

Sylvie SOMMERFIELD

He calls her Morning Sun, for she first came to him in a vision . . . misty and golden. But does her appearance at his village signal good fortune or disaster? Harsh experience has taught him there can be no union between his people and hers, yet her sweet kisses heat his blood until it flows like honey, until he knows that like two halves of one whole, she will always be the morning sun of his midnight desire.

___4359-9 $5.99 US/$6.99CAN

Dorchester Publishing Co., Inc.
P.O. Box 6640
Wayne, PA 19087-8640

Sylvie SOMMERFIELD

FOREVER

After serving two years at Yuma Prison for a crime he didn't commit, Steven McKean is released on a mission in Montana Territory. Experience has taught him women can never be trusted—and he is not about to let another close to his heart. Rachel knows Steve is trouble by the way his steely gaze catches and holds her like a panther stalking its prey. Against her better judgment, she finds herself hiring him to work on her father's ranch. But as dangerous as he seems, as much as his kisses make her forget all reason, she knows there is more to this man than meets the eye. And she senses that she has found a love to last forever.

___4491-9 $5.99 US/$6.99 CAN

BELIEVE

Victoria Alexander

Tessa thinks as little of love as she does of the Arthurian legend—it is just a myth. But when an enchanted tome falls into the lovely teacher's hands, she learns that the legend is nothing like she remembers. Galahad the Chaste is everything but—the powerful knight is an expert lover—and not only wizards can weave powerful spells. Still, even in Galahad's muscled embrace, she feels unsure of this man who seemed a myth. But soon the beautiful skeptic is on a quest as real as her heart, and the grail—and Galahad's love—is within reach. All she has to do is believe.

___52267-5 $5.99 US/$6.99 CAN

Lady of the Night

Cordia Byers

Manacled to a stone wall is not the way Katharina Fergersen planned to spend her vacation. But a wrong turn in the right place and the haunted English castle she is touring is suddenly full of life—and so is the man who is bathing before her. As the frosty winter days melt into hot passionate nights, she realizes that there is more to Kane than just a well-filled pair of breeches. Katharina is determined not to let this man who has touched her soul escape her, even if it means giving up all to remain Sedgewick's lady of the night.

___4404-8 $5.99 US/$6.99 CAN

PRETENDER'S GAMES — LOUISE CLARK

James MacLonan is in desperate need of a wife. Recently pardoned, the charming Scotsman has to prove his loyalty to the king by marrying a woman with proper ties to the English throne. Thea is the perfect wife: beautiful, witty, and the daughter of an English general. And while she can be as prickly as a thistle when it comes to her undying loyalty to King George, James finds himself longing for her passionate kisses and sweet embrace. Thea never thinks she will marry a Scot, let alone a Jacobite renegade who has just returned from his years of exile on the Continent. Convinced she can't lose her heart to a traitor of the crown, Thea nevertheless finds herself swept into his strong arms, wondering if indeed her rogue husband has truly abandoned his rebellious ways for a life filled with love.

___4514-1 $4.99 US/$5.99 CAN

JAGUAR EYES

Casey Claybourne

Daniel Heywood ventures into the wilds of the Amazon, determined to leave his mark on science. Wounded by Indians shortly into his journey, he is rescued by a beautiful woman with the longest legs he's ever seen. As she nurses him back to health, Daniel realizes he has stumbled upon an undiscovered civilization. But he cannot explain the way his heart skips a beat when he looks into the captivating beauty's gold-green eyes. When she returns with him to England, she wonders if she is really the object of his affections—or a subject in his experiment. The answer lies in Daniel's willingness to leave convention behind for a love as lush as the Amazon jungle.

___52284-5 $5.50 US/$6.50 CAN

Dorchester Publishing Co., Inc.
P.O. Box 6640
Wayne, PA 19087-8640

Please add $1.75 for shipping and handling for the first book and $.50 for each book thereafter. NY, NYC, and PA residents, please add appropriate sales tax. No cash, stamps, or C.O.D.s. All orders shipped within 6 weeks via postal service book rate. Canadian orders require $2.00 extra postage and must be paid in U.S. dollars through a U.S. banking facility.

Name_____
Address_____
City_____State_____Zip_____
I have enclosed $_____ in payment for the checked book(s).
Payment <u>must</u> accompany all orders. ❏ Please send a free catalog.

Prince Of Thieves

Saranne Dawson

Lord Roderic Hode, the former Earl of Varley, is Maryana's king's sworn enemy and now leads a rogue band of thieves who steals from the rich and gives to the poor. But when she looks into Roderic's blazing eyes, she sees his passion for life, for his people, for her. Deep in the forest, he takes her to the peak of ecstasy and joins their souls with a desire sanctioned only by love. Torn between her heritage and a love that knows no bounds, Maryana will gladly renounce her people if only she can forever remain in the strong arms of her prince of thieves.

___52288-8 $5.50 US/$6.50 CAN

Dorchester Publishing Co., Inc.
P.O. Box 6640
Wayne, PA 19087-8640

Please add $1.75 for shipping and handling for the first book and $.50 for each book thereafter. NY, NYC, and PA residents, please add appropriate sales tax. No cash, stamps, or C.O.D.s. All orders shipped within 6 weeks via postal service book rate. Canadian orders require $2.00 extra postage and must be paid in U.S. dollars through a U.S. banking facility.

Name_____

Address_____

City_____ State_____ Zip_____

I have enclosed $_____ in payment for the checked book(s). Payment <u>must</u> accompany all orders. ☐ Please send a free catalog.

ENRAPTURED

KATHERINE DEAUXVILLE

The twelfth duke of Westermere is simply out for a peaceful drive, until the Amazonian beauty tosses herself into his coach demanding he do something about the dreadful condition of his estate. This alone would not have flummoxed Sacheverel de Vries, but when the strange woman in the threadbare cloak babbles something about equal rights and social justice, rips open her dress, and claims he has attempted to ravish her, there is only one thing he can do. Skillfully maneuvered into a betrothal with the handsome aristocrat, Marigold Fenwick begins to regret her impulsive actions. And when Marigold decides to seduce the esteemed duke into an enlightened social consciousness, she hardly knows what she is getting into, for the aftermath will leave her thoroughly enraptured.

___4540-0 $5.99 US/$6.99 CAN

Dorchester Publishing Co., Inc.
P.O. Box 6640
Wayne, PA 19087-8640

Please add $1.75 for shipping and handling for the first book and $.50 for each book thereafter. NY, NYC, and PA residents, please add appropriate sales tax. No cash, stamps, or C.O.D.s. All orders shipped within 6 weeks via postal service book rate. Canadian orders require $2.00 extra postage and must be paid in U.S. dollars through a U.S. banking facility.

Name_____
Address_____
City_____ State_____ Zip_____
I have enclosed $_____ in payment for the checked book(s).
Payment <u>must</u> accompany all orders. ❏ Please send a free catalog.
CHECK OUT OUR WEBSITE! www.dorchesterpub.com